THE WANDERERS

Mphuthumi Ntabeni

CATALYST PRESS
EL PASO, TEXAS

For further information, write info@catalystpress.org

In North America, this book is distributed by
Consortium Book Sales & Distribution, a division of Ingram.
Phone: 612/746-2600
cbsdinfo@ingramcontent.com
www.cbsd.com

FIRST EDITION
1 3 5 7 9 8 6 4 2

ISBN 9781960803146

Library of Congress Control Number: 2024942203

For my mother, Nomathamsanqa Cynthia Ntabeni
(1942–2020)
And to all the parents who stay.

CONTENTS

Cessi, et sublato montem genitore petivi.
I gave way to fate and,
bearing my father on my shoulders,
made for the mountain.
—Virgil, the *Aeneid*, Book 2

FOREWORD

Mphuthumi Ntabeni's *The Wanderers* feels no need to trade-off between local depth and global connection, a trait that should earn it a place on African literature curricula and reading lists worldwide. It is equal parts Xhosa, South African, and pan-African, assembling an expansive continental geography from broken pieces of human relationships. Moving, as far as its plot goes, between South Africa and Tanzania, the novel is routed through minds also formed in Rwanda, Botswana, Zambia, Zimbabwe, and the Soviet Union. As *The Wanderers* re-constructs a father's life through his daughter's posthumous encounter with his journals, it strips such frameworks as "local" and "global" of abstract meaning. It deals only with people who love other people—some near, and some far—and who must make choices about how to set this love alongside other moral commitments.

In Ntabeni's version of anti-apartheid history, South Africa's freedom fighters are hearts rent in two rather than single-minded soldiers for a cause. While all fiction serves some purpose in its time, Ntabeni represents the distance that South African struggle writing has traveled since the "Soweto novels" of the 1980s. Njabulo Ndebele, referenced early in *The Wanderers*, once worried that the nation's writers looked to "the exteriority of everything;" Ntabeni, in contrast, is drawn to the internal monologue. For Phaks, his book's one-time African National Congress operative who then dies of AIDS, choosing to fight for a just cause means accepting a life without his wife and daughter, and writing through the loss. This is the stuff of novels, not pamphlets, though Ntabeni would doubtless acknowledge the world's need for both.

To say that *The Wanderers* is a literary novel is therefore far from as obvious as it seems. Literature, for Ntabeni, means openness to wandering, and that openness for Black South Africans has been historically hard-won. His first novel, *The Broken River Tent*, reconstituted the perspective of a real-life nineteenth-century chief named Maqoma, of the amaRharhabe branch of the amaXhosa people, who were among the first Africans to encounter white settlers when they arrived on the Cape's Eastern shores. That book used retrospective narration framed by present-day dialogue to offer a Xhosa point of view on this violent incursion which gave rise to the century-long period of the Xhosa or Cape Frontier Wars against the British and Boers. The text, nonetheless, is marked not by the anxious force of endless self-reflection, but by the exuberance of a mind eager to unfurl its abundant stores. A single paragraph moves rapidly from the twentieth-century Black Consciousness philosopher Steve Biko, to the nineteenth-century Danish theologian Søren Kierkegaard, to land finally on the biblical Job, lubricating its dialogue with cheap whisky and droll humor. *The Wanderers* likewise refracts political struggle through intersecting strains of erudition and human warmth. It takes its epigraph from Book Two of the *Aeneid*—"Cessi, et sublato montem genitore petivi"—and freely intermingles references to Shakespeare and Chekhov with idiomatic isiXhosa speech. There is no ultimate source, and no clear destination. In place of a strict cultural or textual tradition, Ntabeni offers a web.

This does not mean that some of its threads aren't thicker than others. St. Augustine, the foundational Christian philosopher and Bishop of Hippo from 396 to 430, has a special hold on Ntabeni's interest. As readers of this edition will soon learn, Augustine's *Confessions* is a touchstone text for both Phaks and his orphaned daughter Ruru. Ruru, at first, relates to it as an object more than as a set of ideas, meaningful mainly because it once belonged to her mother. Slowly, however, Augustine teaches Ruru to read, both in a literal sense, as her vocabulary grows, and then in search of life's defining questions. Self-exploration, the nature of God's love, and Augustine's views on art become the grounds on which *The Wanderers'* characters and time frames converge. In using the *Confessions* to close the gap between mother, father, and daughter, as well as between two African settings, Ntabeni presents his ideal mode of reading and writing. Augustine is a real figure, accompanied in *The Wanderers* by ample histori-cal detail. But his ideas also comprise a transcendent gathering place, host to whole lifetimes of tangled reckoning with words.

In a forceful way, Augustine's place in this book channels that of Africa itself. The ancient and cosmopolitan city of Hippo was located in what is now Algeria, adding another continental co-ordinate to an intensely South African story. "Why did you never tell me St. Augustine was African?" Ruru writes to the mother she has lost. Later, Phaks notes wryly of Augustine, "You meet the bastard on every forked road you encounter on matters of religious thought; whichever way you turn you cannot hide from the African saint and the scrutinizing eye of God he lived under..." Augustine's spiritual and intellectual power pervades the novel's physical geography—*all* geographies, in fact— which happens to be African. Meanings come first, labels later. And so, as Augustine's words in *The Wanderers* link pages to souls, Ntabeni helps South African history call out to the uni-verse. May the universe respond in kind.

Jeanne-Marie Jackson, Ph.D.
Professor of English,
Johns Hopkins University

THE
WANDERERS
Mphuthumi Ntabeni

THE GRAVEYARD

You grew up not knowing much about your father, a common enough thing in the black townships of South Africa. His absence left a vague mental torment, lacking the closure associated with death. All your mother would say was that he had been a political activist, studying at Fort Hare, the university renowned for producing freedom fighters the likes of Mandela and Tambo; that he "left the country under persecution, not without first planting his seed, mind you! The devil cannot be outdone in adventure."

Your mother said this in contrived jokiness, the attitude she often assumed when talking about things that provoked her discomfort. They were harassed by the apartheid security forces, compelling them to go "underground." When you were younger, you pictured men digging tunnels in the earth to hide from the security forces. It was only later that you realized that "going underground" meant going into exile to join the military wing of the Organization. Your mother always put an emphasis of...not disgust, but certainly disenchantment upon the word "underground."

As far as she knew, your father ended up in Tanzania via Botswana, the USSR, where he got his military training, and Zambia. There were sporadic letters from him, stamped from different cities, which she never answered. Instead she annotated them, writing notes on their edges with red or blue pen as if she were marking an assignment. The notes were written in a terse, dry tone in her beautiful penmanship, something she took pride in, taught to her along with cleanliness and godliness by that remnant of Christian missionaries, a Roman Catholic school run by Irish nuns. On one letter with a Parisian stamp, she wrote in answer to herself more than him: *I am no longer the young girl you hopped out of a taxi with to sweep off her feet, Phakamile Maseti, the seasons multiplied and shadows lengthened.*

You felt in your own gut the kick of that brusque rebuke, the blunt use of formality in addressing him by his full name, and the melancholic undertones in the end:...*the seasons multiplied and shadows lengthened.* Then again, there was always a measured poise in how she expressed herself. You recognized something of her tone when you read Njabulo Ndebele's book *The Cry of Winnie Mandela*. It is the tone associated with the Penelope Syndrome, and with what Ndebele calls "abafazi bomlindo"—women who wait: *I want to reclaim my right to be wounded without my pain having to turn me into an example of woman as victim.*

What interests you more now is how, in childhood selfishness, you monopolized the ache of those years, the loss felt at his absence, without consideration to what it cost her, what the whole thing did to her who had a living history with him. It is only now that you're thirty-seven, about the same age as she was when she died, that things are creaking awake within you, the tragic depths in the taproots of their story. You're beginning to learn how sometimes our old loves trail us, shadow-like, to the grave.

When you did your own research, you discovered that your father settled in a small town called Morogoro, about a hundred and ninety kilometers west of Dar es Salaam, working as a teacher at Solomon Mahlangu Freedom College.

"Why didn't you follow him into exile?" you once asked your mother without thinking.

"Don't be silly. Can you imagine me in foreign countries,

living like a vagabond?" She dismissed your question without taking her eyes off the apples she was paring for a pie. Foolishly you pressed for an explanation. Again she dismissed you, this time with a gentle wave of her hand to mark her weariness about the topic. "After all these years, I think I've earned my silence on that matter. The struggle has my contribution in the life I couldn't have." Her frankness embarrassed you into silence.

The first seed your father inadvertently planted, which would germinate in your desire to know him, was by leaving your mother in a hurry, leaving behind an aura of his intellectual life in the form of books and vinyl records. You grew up around his books of classical literature. Even before you began reading them you used to sniff the tomes to see if you could discern the scent of his life. The stories of ancient Greek and Roman mythology became your companions at a very early stage. Like Pluto to your Proserpine, this way he made you eat a pomegranate seed so you may not be able to stay away from him forever. With that, your fate as the goddess of wanderers was sealed.

Then there were his jazz records of The Blue Note and such that you later realized leaned on the kwela and marabi rhythm your mother made you dance a fowl-run dance to. And Makeba's poignant reinterpretation of your folk songs that always put your mother in a contemplative mood.

By the time the apartheid regime came to a fall and the first democratic elections were held in 1994, you were in your last year of primary school. You entered the new era of your teenage years in high school together with a new political dispensation in your country. Exiles had been returning home since 1990, as the ban on struggle organizations was lifted. But nothing was heard of, or from, your father. In later years, you made enquiries at the Organization's headquarters in Joburg, got very few answers, never anything concrete or enough to give clear direction. It all seemed so unnecessarily complicated to you. You chose to let it go.

It was when you were working as a doctor at Bhayi Public Hospital in Port Elizabeth that you experienced a betrayal and a derailment of your life which left you searching, once more, for your roots, a sense of belonging. The restless grip to know more about your father tightened. And so now you are here, settled in Tanzania, at Morogoro, working at Mazimbu Hospital through Doctors Without Borders, while hoping to find the answers you seek.

On the third Sunday following your arrival in Tanzania, having received enough information from different government sources, you steel yourself to visit your father's grave in Dakawa. Most of the South African exiles who died here are buried in this cemetery. The town of Morogoro has various remnants of South African culture and languages, especially in the village townships of Dakawa and Kihonda.

It is a moody day with the stifling humidity the summers here are prone to. The graveyard lies under a venerable cluster of trees that are wearily clawing the sky. You smile as you think there is everything around this graveyard except the silence of the grave. Not far away, young boys play soccer with bravado. Further still are stands, packed tight together, of costermongers selling different kinds of fruit and vegetables; a few scrawny chickens scrabble around on the ground where young girls play hop-skip-and-jump. Down the crowded lane are small dhabbas in corrugated-iron huts, buzzing with flies, selling fresh and dried fish, garnished boiled eggs, bruised bananas, shriveled oranges, sweets, cigarettes, plastic combs, traditional shrubs, and roots used as medicine. Most are managed by women, fanning themselves with cardboards, while their babies lie under shades wrapped in dirty towels, flies probing the concavities of their nostrils. A vendor selling roasted peanuts shouts to potential customers, "Chinniabadaam! Chinniabadaam!" Jalopies stand on alert for those who need public transport.

You walk out to the graves. They are either unmarked or have sandstone markings that have mostly faded. Looking closely, you discover familiar surnames as you search—Dlamini, Sikota, Vabaza—and you wonder about the lives of these young cadres who died so far from home. Sizwe Jikwa died at the age of twenty-three in 1979; Nomonde Kota died in 1981, only twenty-five years old. You stand wondering for a while what memories of beloved places, their lost worlds, these exiles recalled as they lay dying.

Third on the westerly corner, choking on running weeds, with a humble, undressed headstone, lies the grave you're looking for. The engraved name has been familiar to you since you were able to write your own. Sometimes you would practice writing that surname next to your first name, to see if they paired well: *Fikiswa Maseti.* You thought it had a good ring to it, better than Fikiswa Biko, with its association with Steve Bantu Biko, which always made you feel like a political fame usurper. When you were about eleven, your mother saw some of your scribblings of the stories you liked to write, inserting yourself into ancient myths and changing the endings and geography when they didn't please you, which as an African child was often. You had signed the story *Fikiswa Ruru Maseti*, instead of Biko. Your mother said, softly, handing the notebook back to you: "This doesn't surprise me. Young girls' loyalties are always with their fathers. Of course, the absent parent is always a saint."

It hurt you to discover you had such powers to hurt your mom, yet it also exhilarated you.

The inscription on the grave faintly reads: *Phakamile Maseti, Born 16 June 1959, Died 31 December 1999. May you find your peace in God.*

That is your father. You keep telling yourself this over and over again. Somehow, you keep waiting for the solemn moment to come, or at least a poetic one to camouflage the growing sadness you feel approaching from the recesses of your heart. You had thought that to stand here would be a moment of glory and triumph. You found him. United at last. But things simply go on: the pillow-like clouds keep rolling across the blue sky and a bird careers in aggressive normalcy, uttering hawkish shrill shouts now and then. Somehow, you feel the pull of your life, as you come back to the business of living.

So, he died on New Year's Eve before the start of the new millennium: an eleventh-hour man, always running out of time at crucial moments (this thought comes to you in your mother's rather judgmental voice).

"He liked to float with circumstances," she'd have said.

All your life, you have lived with this battle, fighting the urge to internalize your mother's impotent anger against your absent father, wishing not to be implicated, or at least to rise above her Chekhovian loss of making a home out of emptiness, even as you understood its merit.

You become fixated with the wrong birth date on the grave until you recall that the cadres of the Organization had to carry false identification to hide their true identity from the security forces of the apartheid regime. Phaks's true birth date must have got mixed up with this one. He was born on 16 October, you remind yourself as some form of consolation.

He died some years after South Africa attained the freedom he dedicated his life to, yet he never returned to the country of his birth to enjoy it. He never returned to see you, his daughter. Why?

A grave cannot give you the answer, so you prepare to leave, humming one of the songs your mother liked to softly sing when doing her chores. It always struck you as a song she must have heard from Phaks, because it is a solemn song of remembrance for amaMfengu, his tribe. You once attended a ceremony in Ngqushwa (Peddie) where people sang this song in a haunting growl. It is about how the Hlubi nation was almost destroyed during the chaotic era now known as iMfecane. The story is told poignantly in J.J.R. Jolobe's historical novel, *Elundini loThukela*:

Wemna! uLundi lunombizane	O my! The Tugela is vast
Wema! uLundi lundithimbile	O mother! The Tugela exiled me (×2)
Wemna uLundi loThukela	O my, the great-deep-vast Tugela
Wema! uLundi luyathukela	O mother! The Tugela waters haunt me

A homeless cripple, creaking crutches and all, approaches you as you stand with your thoughts. His face is tinted gray from alcohol abuse. He's wearing mismatched worn-out trainers, darned with copper wire where the soles have cracked.

You sling your bag to your shoulder and immediately unzip it to discreetly rummage for your Okapi, as you have a feeling things might soon go awry. He must have seen a lot of grieving relatives here and learned to take advantage of them, but you tell yourself you're not gonna take that shit lying down. Just about the time your mother taught you to carry pads in your bag, she also gave you what in the township is called a three-star knife, an Okapi, "for when the shit hits the fan, and it'll always hit the fan here ekasi." If he thinks you're easy pickings he has another thing coming, you tell yourself.

He extends his hand. Seeing your confusion, he shouts: "Mwiitu mani!" Because kiKamba, the language he's speaking, has lexical similarities with isiXhosa, you understand that he is demanding money from you. When you shake your head, he threatens violence by raising his voice: "Umunthi is the day you lose your uswi!"

Ayilo lizwe lenkene-nkene eli! This is not a poor country! Your mother's rallying call comes to your mind, her leitmotif warning that you'll need to stand up for yourself. You try to move away, preparing to clear a path with a stab of your knife, if necessary. He bounces toward you, blocking your way with an elbowing confidence, keeping his balance with one crutch while stretching out the other. Then, crutch propped under his armpit, he uses his hand to rub his crotch, gyrating his pelvis while saying something in kiKamba you do not understand. Momentarily he takes out his penis—erect as Moses' staff at the Sea of Reeds—and begins jerking himself, yelling, "Ndio! Ndio!"

His eyes, blank-staring and menacing as a demon's, speak seemingly of being under powers beyond his own volition. Seeing you're not interested, he emits what you assume is a catalog of cusses in multiple languages, because between the utterances you do not understand, you soon recognize isiXhosa swear words in his kiKamba dialect: "Mqundu wakho!"

What is this, you ask yourself. Ghost lives of those left behind to fend for themselves in exile? You fear the violence of vandalized minds. Realizing he is going to be a hard row to hoe, you toss him a panicked look before skedaddling.

SANDI

You're at a glamorous catered party hosted by one of your doctor colleagues who has a thing for you. He's a second-generation white Tanzanian of Jewish ancestry who means well but tends to be overly enthusiastic about wishing to be seen as fully integrated into the Bongo black life. He comes from old German money and doesn't really know how to relate to people without using his riches as show of his affection. Other than that, he's a brilliant surgeon and a right laugh.

To mitigate the feeling of dislocation among too many strangers you invited Sandi along to this party also. Sandi is the only person among your colleagues with whom you've really started to become friendly. Nurses and doctors don't always get along, but you two just clicked from day one. This is, however, your first time socializing together outside of work.

Sandi doesn't like your host of the evening, she says he has a "fakery about him." Having a fakery or false "wokeness" is a cardinal sin, the lowest personality trait in Sandi's eyes. She might be right about him because he has taken you out once or twice but something has always felt off between you.

Besides, your thoughts and feelings are somewhere else, with a guy you knew years ago who now lives in Germany.

Waiters waft around the grand room presenting platters with such delicacies as wasabi roe dip and squid liver crostini. Sandi pops an hors d'oeuvre into her mouth, chews and pulls a face. You suppress a laugh and continue your conversation, a discussion of a topic regarding which you discover you have much in common: absent fathers. Hers, a colored man from Cape Town, promised to send for Sandi and her Tanzanian mother when he left in 1993, as soon as he had settled back home in South Africa. They never heard from him again.

"Why should we go looking for him?" Sandi says when you ask, tapping her long, beautiful fingers that taper at the fingernails against the side of her glass. "He is the one who knows where we are." You recognize a kindred spirit in her. Absent fathers is the silent South African pandemic. As she talks, Sandi gesticulates, pointing and waving animatedly, as if she's rehearsed a speech. She has long dreadlocks, which tonight are pulled back and tied. They smell of fresh lavender and avocado. At work she tucks them under a gele wrap.

She soon moves on to one of her other favorite topics: music, especially what she calls African Soul. By this she means an eclectic mix of black folk music fused with the contemporary beats of global music. She's pan-Africanist and also thinks "...rap music is da bomb, girl! Da beat, maan! Da energy! Da pulse of those who live in the digs!"

It seems to you that "living in the digs" is Sandi's favorite expression. You're not sure what it means but you get the drift. You tell her you get the same feeling when listening to old-school rap, like that of Tupac, who to you is not only a modern poet but a prophet of your urban black oppressed lives.

So far, barring Sandi's companionship, this evening is a slow torture for you, because it's the kind of vibe where egos are on steroids, where only the narcissistic types thrive. The general talk is about stock options, fashion shows and holidays in Europe. The atmosphere is more perfumed than a Paris boulevard, with undertones of fluttering pheromones everywhere. Sandi and you are bored and out of place in all of this.

Sandi cocks her head when Zucchero's "She's My Baby" plays over the speakers strategically placed throughout the room.

"Come on," she says, strutting over to the big screen of the entertainment system. Brave as an arrow, she takes the music remote control, stops Zucchero's choking misery and scrolls the YouTube channel to Tupac's "Changes." She then drags you onto the dance floor. You are reluctant, and it shows a little in your rather unenthusiastic moves.

Sandi all but reprimands you. "Dance with your soul, sister, not your body. That's how you connect with your roots, let their energy move in your veins." She moves her hips to the beat. "The music is either in your blood or is not. Let your soul take over. Don't kill the spontaneity of it. We're black people, my sister, we know everything by feeling, deep feeling, maan, not by head. We use feeling to take part in realms beyond time. That is why we have use of diviners and spiritual guides. But you don't get that because you are too invested in the Western obsession with the intellectual."

You click your tongue at her and she laughs. You can't help but laugh too. Closing your eyes, you try to give yourself over to the music.

It is rather cheeky of the two of you to take over the playlist like this, but what better way to remind the guests about the elephant in the room: the American police brutality against yet another young black person, Atatiana Jefferson, shot dead through the window of her apartment in the presence of her eight-year-old nephew, that has been on the news all week, but which no one at this party is talking about. As the song ends, you open your eyes and notice disapproving looks and a stunned quiet. You and Sandi burst out laughing and leave the room to smoke a zol outside.

"We're being painted as problematic darkies," you say to her, when you've sat down on the stoep.

"What else is new?" she shrugs, lighting the zol fished from her handbag. "Hip-hop is the way we finally learned how to shout for attention to the world that ignores our pain. It opened an outlet for black youth to rant back at the world that's strangling them, especially in the US, that assault against black life by whiteness." She thinks for a while. "It's like jazz was for older folks, you know? But where blues and jazz consoled us about the oppression on plantation fields, hip-hop is a weapon—sticks and stones, bricks and molotovs—against the system designed to suppress us. The fact that white kids took up the genre is just another example of them appropriating what is exotic to them for their own greed."

She drags deeply and passes the zol to you. The weed is making her chatty. "Don't get me wrong, there are those whites who use hip-hop to criticize late capitalism, which is a good thing. Those ones we can use as they use us; after all, the real enemy is capitalism, the real roots of slavery and racism. It is only when we defeat capitalism that our true humanity will emerge, but I'm not holding my breath that this will happen in my lifetime."

The higher the two of you get, the funnier your little stunt on the dance floor seems.

"I think you might have blown your chances of getting laid tonight there, sister Ruru," Sandi giggles.

"Those destined to hang will not drown," you quote the Russian proverb, thinking about your guy in Germany. You take another drag. "Damn, girl, where did you get this stuff? It's heady as Transkeian weed." Your head starts buzzing. Starting to be high as a kite, you feel nauseous as usual. Weed does that to you.

Sandi throws her arm around your shoulder. There's a perceptible pause, a narrowing of eyes before Sandi takes up her discussion of music as if no time has passed.

"Only KenSoul is mature enough yet to compete at the level Tupac was at, lyrical wise. Do you listen to Liz Ogumbo, ehee?"

You have never heard of her.

"She's da bomb of KenSoul, girl, hee!' Sandi likes decorating her sentences with throaty laughs, filial grunts—hee!—that bring out the shimmer of her personality. Her smoky eyes turn gray when she gets animated like this. She takes out her phone from her bag, plugs earphones into the phone and hands one side to you. You both listen, head to head, to Liz. You're blown away by the pleasing eclectic style, the fusion of four languages: Kiswahili, French, Luo (Kenyan), and English.

Afterwards Sandi feigns seriousness and says, "What you mean you haven't heard of African Soul, girl? What you think Fela Kuti, Miriam Makeba, and Freshlyground sing?"

And then your music lesson on African Soul intensifies. By the time it ends you're wishing you were proficient in playing nyatiti and orutu.

In the weeks following the swanky party you spend most of your off weekends with Sandi. With her long pan-African swishing skirts, made from "only natural material, ehee!" like hemp and cotton, she gives an aura of ancient Numidian wisdom. She talks of visits to Shashemene, the Ethiopian Rastafarian town, is obsessed with coffee, and wants to open "a good coffee shop that sells authentic African beans from Ethiopia and Kenya" one day. She talks sadly about how Ethiopian coffee planters, "the originators of the craft," are exploited in the so-called free markets of the world. "The system sucks for us in the digs, ehee," she says. You spend those afternoons drinking slowly—usually Laziza, a Lebanese beer Sandi likes—listening to Soukous music, which you're learning to appreciate, or folk music from the American cotton slave days, which is more to your taste. You both love folk music. Sandi says it "brings the drowsy wisdom from the ancient fatigue of black lives." You don't really know what drowsy wisdom is but you dig the digs anyways.

When you tell her that you grabbed the opportunity to come work in Tanzania because you saw it as a chance to find out more about your absent father, Sandi is intrigued. You relate the disappointing and abrupt end to your investigations which had simply led you to his grave. But upon hearing Phaks's name and former occupation, she lets out a particularly forceful "ehee," and says, "I know who that is. And I know his widow. I'll take you to your father's wife."

MAMAN

The day Sandi takes you to see your father's wife, Efuoa, you find her, alert as a fawn, plonked under her favorite baobab tree. Her house is situated at the far south end of one of the many Julius Nyerere streets in Kihonda township. The township, like most black townships, is strangled by a tight, clawing poverty that is concealed by the exuberant energy of its people. The houses are poky and old, mostly built of brick walls, stacked without mortar in some places, and roofed by rusting corrugated iron.

Maman, as Efuoa is affectionately called here, gets up and comes to the gate to meet you. Apprehension grows inside you as you wonder how to broach the reason for your visit. The bile rises into your mouth as your stomach drops. You have chosen not to think too much about the fact that she might be the reason why your father never came home. Why he abandoned you. Had he not found love in her, or solace, or companionship, he perhaps would have been compelled to return home with the other exiles so as to find it in your mother and you. Settling with her could only mean one thing: that he was out of love with you, a too shattering thought for you to contemplate.

But is it fair to blame Maman? After all, you reason, his neglect of you began way before he settled in Tanzania, before he met her.

Sandi gently pats you on the shoulder for reassurance when she notices your faltering steps.

"You chose a windy day to visit. How did you wake?" Maman

asks politely, wearing an invincible smile and letting you and Sandi through the gate. You had not even noticed the wind was blowing hard.

The first thing that impresses you about Maman is her towering height. Her face, though bereft of glossy glamor, gives a suggestion of a lithe Winnie Mandela with her high apple cheeks and beautiful oriental-sculptured eyes. She must be in her early fifties, you think to yourself as you greet her, yet the only signs of aging are black pouchy patches beneath her glazed almond eyes.

"Well, we come in trumpet blast, like the Lord," Sandi teases. She has told you that Maman is religious. "Remember I told you I'd bring you a visitor from Mzanzi today, Maman? This is Fikiswa Biko, aka Ruru. She's a doctor at our hospital. I work with her."

Sandi's formal introduction makes you more nervous; it seems as though she's trying to steer away from your actual identity. But Maman goes straight to the point.

"Welcome, my child. I hear the blood of my husband is in you. This is your home too. Your father told me a lot about you. He would have loved to see you." She hugs you. Her clothes have a smoky-soapy smell.

Your bladder goes on the loose, as it always does when you're anxious or excited. "It's an honor to finally meet you, Maman," you reply earnestly.

"The honor is mine, my child. Come inside." Her dark eyes twinkle moistly.

You all move into the house. As your eyes adjust you see that it has a pleasing simplicity and neatness. It smells of damp plaster. Though open plan, the house is sub-sectioned into a kitchenette and sitting area, where an old wooden divider, stacked with books, stands. On top of it are painted glass ornaments and pictures in small frames you're not able to identify from a distance, a gramophone, and an old TV, the kind with a wooden cowl. Maman directs you to sit on two old sagging brown sofas that face each other while she takes a seat on the single one that faces the front door. What you assume to be the bedroom is partitioned by a dark curtain. A single unit of cupboards with a metal sink and two-burner electric stove on the countertop furnishes the kitchenette, with a kerosene stove next to it. The floor is sealed with cow dung, as they do in rural South Africa.

Maman gets up and fires the kerosene stove to boil water, apologizing to you for the fumes, telling you that the electricity supply is sporadic in the township and will probably come on after six in the evening. The African amulets she wears clink on her arms when she moves them. She is soft-spoken, gentle in gesture, with an intuitive smile and assuring earnestness. You cannot resent this woman.

You ask for a toilet to relieve your bladder. You're directed to an isolated concrete-block outhouse in the backyard. The toilet has a hanging cistern that flushes through a long, noisy pipe. Upon your return you find Maman and Sandi waiting for a pot of tea to prove Sandi is trying to convince Maman of the qualities of coffee. You want to support Sandi by adding the claim that coffee wards off Alzheimer's disease but feel obliged to ingratiate yourself with Maman, who thinks coffee is an overrated, slow poison, though this is not really your sentiment. As you express your support for Maman's argument, Sandi is jokingly horrified by your "ignorance."

Sandi tells you on your way home that when Phaks died Maman was left with little beyond the dirt beneath her fingernails. That the meager pension the Organization paid them was discontinued after his death and she could not renew it because they were not legally married.

A dull anger rises within you as you listen, triggering old losses with renewed intensity. Before you left, Maman handed you a box of exercise books, saying, "These were the jottings of your father in his last days—always with his nose in a book, that one." She gave an affable smile that teased out your affection as she handed the box to you. "Perhaps you find something useful there?"

You must have looked startled because she imperturbably reassured you. "Fine it is to have. Go on. I give more when you're done with those, if there's still interest. He called them Pillow Books. They lent the strength of the hills to his hope during his last days."

A tightness from joy and anticipation came to your throat and prevented you giving an adequate reply. The silent grave might speak to you after all.

In your room you start reading from the Pillow Books. You begin with the one with the earliest date. As you read, it becomes apparent this is not the first notebook. It is impossible to tell which one is, because some are not dated. It is impossible to arrange them chronologically, so you begin packing them thematically. It becomes obvious also that, although some were begun much earlier, the bulk of them were consistently written in 1999, his last year. That devastating year.

You remember you also began keeping a strict journal in 1999 when your mother died. Her death came only a couple of months before Phaks's. And what fate killed them almost at the same time? Does fate join our life experiences on its hip?

The Pillow Books are exercise books yellowing from age with tattered edges from mice bites. They're in cursive writing, not always easy to read, sometimes nothing more than lines and dots, but once you get used to the style you find it easy to decipher the meaning. His penmanship isn't as beautiful as your mother's but the prose is more graceful, giving you the feeling of listening to a Cicerone speech, which is emphasized by the soft yellowing exercise books whose dust induces your sinuses.

You take out your laptop and begin to type them up to better preserve the writing. This is something you did some time ago with your own handwritten letters to your deceased mother —they are now preserved in a folder on your laptop where you decide to insert the Pillow Books also. In reproducing the Pillow Books, you follow a thematic narrative order that is not always chronological. You allow yourself only the privilege of lending proper medical terms to what he refers to concerning his sickness and the medicines he took.

The writing limns the workings of an active mind, a reserved character who lived a bold life of courageous defiance of injustice. Somehow profound but detached, and sometimes melancholic almost to a fault without being dour. A man who coped with life by living his passions through literature, etymology, history and philosophy. Obviously his head was often in the clouds, with an elevated nose sometimes, but he had poetic insights and mystical longings. Because he studied classical literature, and went to a traditional Roman Catholic school, there's an aura of Latinate and spiritual order in his diction and gestalt, pleasingly non-sermonizing. The self-imposed isolation in Kihonda, after his global experiences, gives an impression of a monkish and scholarly control upon his passions, an impression of a stoical and eventually resigned man.

THE WINDOW
19/03/99

I'm sitting at my desk at the window, looking outside. Thick mist mizzles on deepening twilight. In truth, it is not even a window, just an open slit in the wattle-and-mud wall, "enough to let the light in while keeping the evil spirits out," according to Efuoa, my common law wife. Perhaps not even that. I've never really asked her opinion about our living arrangements. One thing I know is that, if there are angels among us, she's one of them.

I feel downcast.

Mist is spreading, filtering through the cracks of the walls of my head. The sinking sun leaves behind the gloaming, a growing mantle of darkness, ghostly effusions, as it draws the curtain over the earth.

"The mist brings us tidings from the other world," says Efuoa as she drops a plate of cooked fish and mashed potatoes on the desk for me.

Watermelon is just about the only thing my system stomachs these days, but I eat mashed fish for protein. She cooks the fish into pulp, to make it easier for me to swallow.

I have esophageal thrush, complications of cryptococcal meningitis which no longer responds to any kind of treatment. Being fully blown with AIDS will do that to you. I started my ARV treatment late. Is that not just how it is with us African men? One is not really sick until one is dying. The government can't afford to hand out ARVs at public hospitals here, so you hold out as long as you can before you have to dig deep from your own pocket for them in private hospitals. There are a myriad ways for you to die from poverty in Africa. When I started my treatment, I fell victim to what the doctors call "lactic acidosis," a dangerous build-up of acids in the blood which sometimes comes as a side effect of stavudine (d4T) and didanosine, my ARV treatment.

I don't mean to write about my health condition in this diary, but I suppose it is unavoidable since writing has an inevitable tendency toward morbid introspection.

Efuoa comes close behind me, so close I can smell her on-ion-and-garlic breath. She rubs my head—her way of taming the mist. My mother used to rub my head like that when I was young and feeling agitated. I get these excruciating headaches that make me scream like a pig at slaughter. They scare her. So she massages my head to prevent my screams. The doctors told me the fungal yeast—the cause of the headaches—began in my lungs and quickly spread to my brain. "Soon," they said, "you shall lose the use of your mental faculties." That scares me. Anything but that. Please! When you are left with nothing much to show for your life it feels like a cruel fate to be robbed of your mind also, your memory, your last refuge, the solace for your ebbing vitality. Memory is our last bank when all else fails. Now the mist is threatening to rob me of that in spreading the darkness that is in the offing.

Efuoa has moved to the kitchenette. "Abide with us, for the day is far gone," I hear her sing. I find myself joining softly in her song, like some confused disciple of Christ on his way to Emmaus. At least their eyes were opened by the breaking of bread. Who will break the bread for me?

It'd be a lie to say I'm not afraid of dying. Actually it is not dying I'm afraid of, but death, the event of being dead, of being no more...

My writing got interrupted earlier on by Efuoa sweeping our bedroom. I cannot stand dust, it chokes me. Her sprinkling the mud floor with water no longer helps either. I had to go to the kitchen window to watch the darkness descend. The watched darkness encircled the house and watched me back. Nietzsche was of the opinion that when we stare at the abyss long enough it stares back at us. The mad old fool was right as usual.

The day is far gone.

This disease has strangely honed my senses, especially that of smell, which has become intolerably acute. I cannot stand strong odors. But my virility, strangely, is at its peak, in between the attacks of downbeat vomiting, that is. The virus is decaying everything but my élan. What cruelty, to be robbed of ability while honed by desire. Better the blessed fatigue of saints which raises them above carnal pleasures. Despite the coming mist, I see more clearly in my mind, for now at least. I guess the meteorite spreads its brilliance as it falls.

I'm back after supper and a walk. I managed to nibble at my food. Efuoa asked whether I wanted to go for a short walk before bed. I didn't want to. It feels doglike to be walked after supper, to be so dependent. But I didn't want to disappoint her. It is in the nature of a dog to be grateful and loyal. My clan name is Ndlovu, the elephant. The bull elephant secludes itself when it senses death on its body. It prepares when it detects that it's time to surrender its body back to the earth by moving as far away as possible to avoid death contaminating the herd.

Ndidleni maxhalanga ndidumbile! That's the rallying cry of the brave dying men in our culture: Take your pick of me, vultures, I'm bloated!

"Sure! Perhaps we'll get a chance to read the tidings brought by the mist," I'd said to Efuoa, making an effort to sound flippant and strong as I psyched myself up for the walk. She fetched my walking stick and we were on the gad.

Outside, the darkness was almost complete except for a few dotted flickers of orange light coming from house windows.

Everybody knows us around here. We know everybody around here. It is not a big township. We're foreigners, strangers in the land. The German word "Fremd" and the isiXhosa one "ukumfenguza" signify both foreign and strange. I like that. They capture our state best.

Both Efuoa and I came as strangers to this land, fleeing the political demons of our respective countries. I left my country, fleeing, or rather looking for strength to face the Leviathan of the apartheid system. Efuoa fled from Rwanda after her family was butchered by "evil spirit men," as she calls them, "carrying machetes." That would be the Hutu militia in popular language. She was eighteen when an attack on her village happened, one of the early attacks, some years before the fullblown genocide of 1994. She survived only because she had been to the bush to relieve herself when militia men came sowing death in her village. When she came back she was met by the wailings of her people dying. First she thought it was some kind of celebration, "because everyone had gathered inside a community church." Only to discover soon enough it was not celebration, but lamentations. Hiding, she saw through the window decapitated, twitching bodies, like slaughtered chickens, and was stung to the hilt. Up to this day Efuoa does not know why her people were murdered. She has resigned to explaining the whole thing by identifying the militia as "evil spirits." At those rare moments when she talks about the incident, her sentences always begin with: "Before evil spirits came to our village…" I guess this is her way of maintaining her trust in humanity. She reached Tanzania when she was about twenty-two. I met her a year after that.

I have nothing to take comfort in but my own despair. I guess, if one is Christian, that sounds satanic? So be it. If we're gods in our ideal state, we're devils in our fallen one. And if my life has taught me anything, it is that the curse of Cain is heavy upon my shoulders.

It is, to me, inconceivable that the world will just go on after

I'm dead. Not because I'm too conceited to imagine a world without me. That I can easily imagine. After all, the world existed before I was born. What I cannot imagine is myself without this world. It seems unforgivably cruel to just disappear as though one never existed. And I don't want to just exist in the diluted biological data I've transmitted through my only child, who, if my tally is right, should be finishing matric this year—no one gives us much news anymore since the government of our Organization took over.

Isn't it ironic that when our Organization was banned in SA we were better informed than now that it is in government? We got left behind in every sense of the word. Phone calls to comrades are too expensive. Efuoa and I have been drained of every penny we had by this disease. I wonder if I'll ever see my daughter. She must be a very beautiful girl. Her mother was a stunner. There are many things a man can forgive himself for, but abandoning his family is not one of them. He can make excuses about being called to do greater things, but deep down inside himself he knows those excuses ring hollow. I hope I shall not be the last person to tell the story of my life so that even the faults that are too glaring for me to look at may be exposed. The ones left to tell family stories are the ones with the greater burden, because they are doubly pained. First comes the knife in their side which is the absence, then there's the act of lancing the wound by storytelling.

The only thing I can say on my behalf is that a soldier's mind never comes back from the battlefield. So the kindest thing to do for your loved ones, if you're irretrievably damaged, is to stay away so they may preserve their innocence. Odysseus coming back home wreaked too much chaos in Ithaca. It would have been better for all concerned had he been lost at sea. Sometimes we cannot mend what we've broken, or reclaim the paths we left behind. Our only recourse then is to accept the mark of Cain, of wandering the world.

But no, this is not all I can say on my behalf, if truth be told. Need I say more now? What good would it do?

These Pillow Books are my version of a whimper to the Creator whose face is now hid from me, "...a fugitive and a vagabond on the earth..." I am the one who has kept my prayers and curses under my tongue all my life, and now that my tongue is about to be cut at the stem, I might as well release them.

When I was twenty-two, in full obedience to my heart's command, I stepped out of a taxi before reaching my destination, to ruin the life of someone I would love with the madness of my soul. Since then I've known very little beyond the loneliness of my prodigal soul. And now, like all humans who died before me, I'm discovering how irredeemably alone we are before death. Fate was too strong for me. In my heart of hearts I know I could've remained behind, plowing my fields with salt, when others went to battle. I chose exile over my domestic bliss.

As I was saying, I want to exist as I am, not through my daughter, or at least as I've been, with my memories and consciousness. Christians say the soul—the vessel that bears our personality, intelligence, and memory—survives physical death. I want to... no, no...I need to believe this. I've lived my life in an unshakeable belief in facts and exploration. Now that death is creeping in, the first thing I'm losing confidence in is facts. Somebody somewhere said there is nothing more uncertain, more contradictory, more unsatisfactory than the evidence of facts. Anyone who sits for an hour in a court of law, listening to arguments from both sides, would concur. Facts can always be used to bolster one opinion over the other, but they're not necessarily the truth. There is hardly anything that cannot be manipulated to inform or bolster preconceived ideas. Worse still, the politicians have now learned the art of making facts serve their lies by disconnecting them from justice, thus making them mean nothing in saying everything.

Make what you like of historical facts, but for Christ's sake, don't swear on them. They've been manipulated, or at least arranged, to fit the narrative of the storyteller, mostly the point of view of the victors. Venerable as he was, Thucydides, whom most academic historians regard as the first real historian, also had his blind spots, like his predecessor Herodotus, who took for fact too many ancient myths. Those who followed, up until the present age, have themselves at times not been free from the maladies that plague the so-called objectivity of historians. "The most reckless theorists are those who allow facts to speak for themselves." I recall reading something along those lines from some English historian who wrote it while compiling history to fit the gestalt of his country's Empire pretensions. Unfortunately, that irony was totally lost on him.

I say all this not to be showy, but because certain areas of my life experiences have fused with the fiction of my imagination, or the other way around. Let no one accuse me of insincerity. Do I believe, with Borges, that everything that passes through memory is fiction? I wouldn't go that far, but I know that memory, the means by which we claim back our experiences from the past, decays; because, as the American poet Christian Wiman says, *time is a robe stitched with dust.* The recollections of memory are an act of language, which is subjective reality.

I write what I remember, the way I remember it, to fit what I understand, in trying to explain why I understand it so. I'm sure other people, especially those whom I've wronged, have a different take on events. But writers and victors have the advantage of setting the tone of argument. Obey, or go and invent your own version of history. Is that not why victors used to decapitate their enemies? To annihilate all versions of history contesting their own?

I'm trying to discover why Efuoa's worldview suddenly makes more sense to me. There's no doubt that she has more courage against death than I do. In fact, I'm starting to believe that death is afraid of her. First she was the sole survivor of her family's brutal killing. And now, how do you explain the fact that there's not a trace of HIV in her body, although we slept together without protection before I discovered I had HIV in my system? The doctors talk about HIV discordance, but Efuoa attributes it to the magic of her necklace. "My grandma gave me this necklace to ward off bad karma."

A few weeks ago, in her indefatigable kindness, she took the necklace off and put it around my neck. "To ward off bad karma," she said. It's a hyena's tooth strung on a strip of black leather. Unfortunately, the luck has not rubbed off yet. The mist is spreading, spreading fast. It'll be night soon.

As a philosophical tramp I had always believed the convincing lies of philosophers that when death comes for me I'll naturally enter into a certain disdain for life that will make death tolerable, even desirable to me. Nothing of that sort has happened. Instead, as it turns out, in an Aesopic sense, in coming to Delphi I lost all the sense I had. From the day the doctors told me I had the virus I was assailed by incontrollable regret and a growing appetite for life—an appetite as keen as death itself. The thought of my death in the offing brings a searing pain in my heart. Fear, too, sometimes.

What is there on the other side, if anything?

THE DEATH OF ME

Dear Mama

Since we buried you I spend a lot of time trying to think myself out of my sadness. I lie awake missing you all the time, or thinking about how much I am missing you. Aunt Zenzile says she needs to go back to her own house over the weekend. Shem! The poor woman has been here for over two weeks already. She says she will come back at the end of the month to check up on me, and to see if I'm still sure about staying in this house on my own.

I sometimes hear her talking with the neighbors, begging them to keep an eye on me. Their talk makes me sad because they're making me into a community burden. I cry sometimes, but wipe my eyes before she comes into the room. I don't want her pitying me again.

Aunt Zenzile thinks I'm still twelve, since this was the last time she saw me before you died. I try to make her understand that I'm seventeen now, and have been looking after myself since I was fifteen. You used to leave me in the house, I tell her, for days, even weeks sometimes, when you had training or something. I managed just fine. I've told her this but she still worries. I worry, too, that when she is gone my missing you will make me cry a lot.

When she is not here I go through your things, wondering what to do with them. Today I was looking through your kist and I found the copy of St. Augustine's Confessions you were so frantically looking for the other day. You must have put it in the kist and then forgot about it. I've started reading it. But the actual reason I was looking in there is that I knew it was where you kept your important stuff: certificates, vinyl records and all. The vinyl records have all gone wobbly from the heat, by the way.

I even saw a photo of you and Phaks—saying out loud the name of my father I never knew sounds funny—that you never showed to me, the one in which he is wearing a beret, Che Guevara style. He looks handsome as the devil. And Lee jeans? Is that what you guys wore then? Lee jeans are totally so uncool now! He looks like he was a dish, the bridged brows, marbled-humbug brown eyes and all. He has a fresh complexion. I can see why you fell for him—can we talk about these things now? Girlfriend, you were the bomb, hot like stove samalahle with your curly perm, floral skirt, and pink top. And his hand on your waist. Is he really wearing an off-pink flannel shirt to match yours? Off-pink, mother? You made the poor man wear a pink shirt? I can't tell properly, the colors are faded. But if it is, it is so cute you guys are wearing matching clothes. Did you plan the photoshoot together? Was it still early stages of your courtship? Only your big square glasses I don't like. You did well in switching to contact lenses.

I have this lump in my throat since the day I heard you died. It won't go away.

I guess I will have to go to school on Monday. It's been three weeks already and I'm sure I will have a lot of catching up to do. But I worry because I can't pay attention to anything with this sadness always on my mind. I have a permanent dry taste of sick in my mouth.

Veli spent the whole day with me yesterday, updating me ngomgosi wase ngingqini, so we gossiped all day. Although it was great having my BFF here and we laughed until our ribs hurt, things are not the same. She is always looking up to see if I'm okay, and I keep trying not to make her see I'm sad inside. Sometimes my laugh sounds hollow to my own ears, as if I am laughing in a cave.

Besides, Veli should not be laughing either. She has big problems. I don't know if you remember Soli, the boy whose parents own the shop yakwa Johnson? The one you said is quite full of himself. Well, they have been snogging and all, now Veli says there's something growing in her stomach. It's a baby, she's fuckin' pregnant, and I had warned her about that. The worst part is Soli is behaving like a jerk, talking about paternity tests and all–acting as if Veli has been sleeping around when he knows he is the only person she has been with. It looks like he was just getting his rocks off and is not at all serious about Veli. I've never liked him. I wanna moer him with bhakstina even now but Veli won't let me. I'm glad at least they're breaking up. But the damage has been done. I'm afraid I couldn't help saying to Veli how I was glad they're breaking up–me and my foot always in my mouth, something I inherited from you. I think that boy is a tad OTT, but Veli likes people who are popular. Try as I do to feel for Veli, I am unable to understand when it comes to that boy.

I think my sadness also makes me mean to other people, uncaring about what other people feel. It makes me selfish and unable to look at other people's pain. I think when Veli comes next I must show more feeling for her. I wonder what she is going to do. How will she support the baby? Her daddy is gonna kill her, that's for sure.

Final exams start in four weeks, and I don't know whether I'm going or coming. Man, am I glad now you brought me those past exam papers! I think my approach will be to try and answer them and look over whatever I don't understand from the textbook. It's the only way I might be able to survive. I certainly am not planning to be in high school again next year. I'm sick of it!

When I went in your room I saw your purse on top of the dressing table waiting to be picked up on your way out to work. I burst out in tears. It's the little things that get me and make me see the hole left by your departure. Death! Death! Death! I need to say this word over and over again to make myself understand that you won't be coming back. It catches me all the time when I'm out of the house and I come back and you are not in the kitchen cooking or something. It is very, very strange to discover you are not here. The other day I caught myself going around the house looking for you in the backyard. Your death is going to be the death of me, Mother.

THE SEA, THE SEA...

Dear Mama

Aunt Zenzile left this afternoon. When I walked her to the taxi rank she nearly ran out of breath giving me instructions about what to do—minute by minute details for every day until she comes back in three weeks' time. She says if it were not for the need to plant her fields before the rains come she would stay longer. I never really did understand your relation to her. I know she is your cousin, but in what sense? You liked keeping things from me. Now I don't know how to ask about it without appearing rude to her. I like her.

Many of our neighbors come to visit me after school, bringing me food to eat or cook. I'm now the proverbial child that's raised by the village. I'm not complaining. Things could be worse. Still, I feel isolated from them, alone. The feeling makes me sad. I don't know how to make myself interested in their talk. I want to talk to them, thank them, laugh with them, but I don't know how. When I manage to laugh with them I feel sad because I'm laughing while you are dead. Sometimes I feel like I'm suffocating because they all swarm around me like bees. Sometimes I feel I'm an embarrassment to everyone, like I'm disturbing their lives. Now they must come and cheer me up.

All these things make me feel tired and sad. But when I try to sleep I'm too tired to fall asleep and all I do is think how much I miss you, and how tired I feel in my head. Then, to make my head feel better, I think about the time you took me to East London's

< 31 >

Bonza Bay beach in Beacon Bay on New Year's Eve. Do you remember? It was raining that day and the sea was gray. You said, "It's a pity that the first time you see the sea, it is sad." I didn't care. I was surprised at how quickly the sea had appeared before us when we went past the forest. And how vast a thing it is. I read something in a magazine I memorized: Besides the sky I don't know anything else with the courage to test the resolve of infinity like the sea. *I really liked that very much. I wanna be writing like that when my writing style matures.*

I remember on our way to East London I had thought we would see the sea from a distance, that it would be green, like it is on the holiday brochures or TV commercials. I thought it would announce itself from a distance, but it didn't. First there was salt in the air, the smell of life, like when I'm on my period. Then the swishing sounds of the wind. I remember you told me that's the reason amaXhosa called the area eKhwikhwini, which whites simplified to Quigney when they couldn't pronounce the name. And then the green river of Nxarhuni snaking into the sea. White people called it Nahoon. Then suddenly, beyond the forested sand hills, the sea in her vastness as only the ocean can be, ebbing and flowing, panting with ancient effort. It stunned me into silence. The expanse of the sea dwarfs the land, I thought to myself.

Remember, you said the sea is God's heart in the world; that it draws out all dirt to purify the world; that in the end all things go to the sea. Remember, remember, I ran along the ebbing and flowing of the water screaming: "The sea, the sea, the sea!" And you asked me not to rush. Please remember. You said I must first just dip my feet in the sea and feel its temperature. I hesitated. Then you went before me. How is the temperature of the sea, Mummy?

CONNECTING

Your days run like a rosary string, a daily bead prayer till after seven days you repeat it all. By the time you get home from work in the evening you're drained. In your staff cottage, you take a shower, change into your night shirt, quickly pan-roast a zucchini to serve with fried onion, green pepper, tomatoes, chilli, bay, fennel and other herbs. You throw in the supermarket saffron-spiked orzo when everything is reduced to a sauce. Then you're good to go for a solo supper in front of the TV. You keep the leftovers in the fridge. You can eat this every day of the week. You miss having the option of umpokoqo namasi, but it is not easy to find maize-meal around here.

There's nothing good on the TV, so you scroll on your cell phone. Your friends on Facebook share links to newspaper articles on the Zondo Commission into state capture. Journalists speculate about when Jacob Zuma will appear before the commission and whether this means he'll soon be in court to face corruption charges. There's a universal glee from the reporters who think this finally means Zuma will be going to prison soon. You're not holding your breath.

You scroll past a photo from your guy in Germany. You have been avoiding replying to his latest email. There is something you need to get off your chest and it might mean the end of the two of you before you've even really begun. In the end, you go back to his profile and press the "like" button beneath the photo after all.

You get a whatsapp from your friend Ami in Johannesburg. She tells you about the hot new instructor of her yoga class and how she wishes her husband would also do something to destress—politics is not good for his health. You experienced at first hand the luxuries of Ami's lifestyle shortly before you came to Tanzania and marveled at where your old university roommate has ended up. Although you don't envy her life in the slightest. She works for a big international accounting firm and she married a Tswana guy she was in class with at varsity who's high up in the Premier's office in Gauteng Province now, or some gubernatorial office you can't remember well.

So what have you found out from your father's journals so far? Any dirt? she asks. You do not want to share too much; it feels too personal, even to tell a friend you've known for so many years.

It is strange reading his regrets about abandoning me and Mama, is all you say. *But I'm still not sure I can understand why. I'm grateful to Maman for the books, though. He's really writing from the depths of his soul. I feel I can get to know him, somehow, if I keep reading.*

Somehow you also feel you'll get to understand yourself better if you get to know your father better. You don't admit this to Ami, nor do you tell her you've also started to reread your old letters to your mother. It has occurred to you that both your journals can be seen as a means of reaching out to each other within the triumvirate of your love: you calling out to your mother and he to you, almost at the same time. The binding force of your blood making you inseparable though apart.

It might sound crazy if you were to tell this to Ami. So, you change the subject to the Zondo Commission. Ami soon seems to get bored of this and bids you goodnight.

Then you whatsapp Sandi.

See you on duty tomorrow. Nites.

She ghosts you, as is her habit. You forgive her because you know she hates cell phones. In bed you read more from your father's Pillow Book. You think you'll prepare a fish dish to take to Maman on your next visit, having learned she's pescatarian by preference, if not deliberation. You need to thank her for your father's books.

SURPRISED BY JOY
21/03/99

The fields are full of damp silence today, dripping trees and fences under moody skies. Efuoa pops in with her unobtrusive deftness. Her careworn face gives me an uninhibited smile before disappearing back to her chores. That's the burden of living with someone needing palliative care. Their silences worry you. She wants to hear the signs of life coming from the room, otherwise she gets worried.

Sometimes when I sit at this desk, knowing she's about to bring me lunch, I notice myself trying to leave an indelible image of my writing life to her; to give an artificial artistic impression so she may look back and think she lived with an important writer in this hovel. This embarrasses me to no end about myself, that after all is said and done I am just as vain as the next person, but I am unable to check myself. So I try to think about my life before I lost my innocence.

What was my life like before this? Alas, I remember too well; I was young, arrogant as a knife, still believing in meritocracy. At Fort Hare University I studied a Bachelor of Arts degree, majoring in Classics as a sniff of my hero, bra Chris Hani, who was born just outside my hometown in Cofimvaba. I thought if the brooding feelings grew stronger I'd do Philosophy and Theology, perhaps even try the priesthood if the voice of God also grew within me. Fort Hare then was the most political university in the country, with alumni the likes of Mandela and Hani when it was one of the only institutions that catered for the tertiary education of black youth. I was looking for ways to influence my life with wisdom; literature and philosophy seemed like a good place to start. Politics, naturally, came into the mixture. You cannot, as

Nadine Gordimer said, depict a single life without plunging it into the situation of its society. And our situation was that of apartheid South Africa. You must begin *with a stain in the ocean*, Gordimer declared. In the end, literature, in fact all art, became more and more a weapon to respond fully to the circumstances of my/our lives.

How did I meet my paper wife? My paper wife—that's Efuoa's way of referring to the mother of my child. Asking me to tell the story is Efuoa's way of keeping me hopeful by making me think of the good days in my past. She does not know I answer to please her more than anything else. This is how it goes: It was a rainy day. We were on a taxi from East London to King William's Town. She was seated next to me, smelling of pleasing womanly smells—Efuoa always smiles when I mention this—a much-needed dilution to the wet-dog stench of the taxi. I wanted to talk to her but was afraid of eavesdropping passengers. To my horror she got off at Berlin junction—here Efuoa frowns, no matter how many times she's heard the tale—about twenty kilometers before my stop in King William's Town. I made up my mind, in a split second, to follow her—Efuoa smiles again—although I was meant to proceed to Alice from King to Fort Hare. It was already getting late. I put the sling of my small bag across my neck and jumped off. ("Phakamile, you daring devil," Efuoa routinely exclaims at this point before assuming a listening posture again.)

"May I help you with these?" I asked the young woman, picking up the two plastic bags of groceries she was carrying.

My paper wife was grateful, saying she had thought there would still be touters at the bus stop she could pay to help her with the parcels. I was glad she was pleased with my chivalrous offer, opening a door to further possibilities.

"You're kind. My home is in that second valley, which is quite far with this entire load. Where do you live? I've not seen you around here before?" she asked matter-of-factly.

"Oh," I tried to act casual, "actually my home is in Queenstown. I'm currently studying at Fort Hare."

"So you are visiting here in our village?" she asked further.

"I guess you could say that, if you're taking any visitors," I ventured boldly. There was a momentary silence, which I took to mean she was digesting what I had just said. I forestalled her anticipated reply by adding, "Look, I saw you in the taxi and liked you, that's all. I knew I'd regret it for the rest of my life if I didn't at least get off to ask you your name."

"Just like that?" she asked, her quiet-as-a-lake eyes not giving any suggestions about her thoughts. It was always difficult to read her moods because of the resigned manner in which she carried herself. That day I just hoped she would at least be pleased with my courage and not take exception to my presumption.

"Ja, just like that," I said. "I'm tired of sabotaging myself with my tendency to overthink things." Frankness was my only recourse at that moment. "My name is Phakamile Maseti, by the way. I'm hoping when I return from walking you home it'll not be too dark, so I may still be able to catch a taxi to King. From there I'm certain I'll definitely be stranded because there'll no longer be taxis or buses to Alice. But I'll cross that bridge when I get to it."

"I see. My name is Nosipho, Nosipho Biko; no relation to the late Steve Biko from down the road here in Ginsberg." She paused, then added nonchalantly, "You do know there are no taxis from our village after dark also?"

I didn't know that. A melancholy dusk was drawing a curtain upon the land, making the mountains of her village appear like stranded giant shades on the darkening purple sky. To the east the open fields were starting to be covered by a diaphanous mist, spreading from the hills like an amorphous army.

So her name is Nosipho, *Gift*, was the thought I had, my mind galloping to the fields of my youth where lay buried a memory of another Nosipho, my first love and the reason behind my damaged heart.

"I guess I'm stranded then," I shrugged.

"I'd say you certainly are." There was another silence between us, broken only by our footfalls and a rising cacophony of crickets and croaking frogs that suggested a lake nearby. "Unfortunately, my father does not take kindly to strangers," she broke the silence after a while.

"Not even those who have plans of marrying his daughter?"

"Especially not those," she bloomed with amusement.

"That's very unXhosa-like of him. I thought stranded strangers were honored guests in our custom?"

"Gone are the days when a wanderer's stomach was a small thing. These days they've stomachs at their backs too."

I remembered just then that I had left my dry-cleaned university blazer in my hurry to get off the taxi. A very costly mistake. "I'm not only stranded then but a fool also. I left my parcel in the taxi."

"Oh, shem! Left in a hurry, did you?"

This is going to be a simpatico relationship, I thought to myself, presumptuously.

"I guess you can say that." I started wondering what to do with the situation. The funny thing is I didn't even feel stranded or anxious. We walked in silence for a while before I felt compelled to break it but she beat me to it almost as I was about to utter my words.

"There's a hut that no one uses at my home. We might be able to hide you there until morning if you promise to behave. But we'd first need to know your full identity, so as to know where to trace your mischief should necessity arise."

"Ndingu Mdluli ngoku mfenguzana."

"I'll be very disappointed if you're just making that up," she replied with a slight laugh. "Otherwise you seem to have landed yourself in a situation that's very apt for your clan name."

I was very pleased she understood that as the Hlubi section of amaMfengu we refer to ourselves as wanderers, hence abeDluli, the wandering passerby. As such we don't call up to any chief when we're thankful, like amaXhosa would say "eNkosi"—to the chief/lord. We say "eMdluli"—to the wanderers, the passersby—because our chiefs were killed during the mayhem of iMfecane.

"I'm from a little village called Zingquthu, thirty kilometers outside Queenstown, or should I say that's my father's home, since I was born in the township of Mlungisi in Queenstown, eKomani. Ndiyi ndlovu edl' igoduka ngokuswel' umalusi, an elephant that grazes homebound because it lacks a shepherd?" In my wish to impress, I rather gabbled and overreached, ndaloqa.

"Looks like the elephant has lost its memory and missed its way home today," she quipped.

"Or it has found its way home by wandering. Depends on how you look at it, or on what is nesting in this night."

"Kutheni tana, ingathi ubusuku bufukame nto?" Funny she should sarcastically ask if I was hoping if the night was nursing my luck because I was feeling exactly that.

"I didn't mean to be too forward. It's your kindness that's making me bold," I answered sheepishly.

"UyiMfengu then? All the more reason not to let my father see you. He does not like amaMfengu; he calls them the sell-outs who made it possible for whites to steal our land. My father is an old-timer."

"Are people still hung up on that around here? It happened two centuries ago. Can't we let bygones be bygones? It's a wrong opinion of history anyway."

"It's the opinion of most Xhosas around here. I personally don't have any problems with amaMfengu. But for my people the scar still itches, the wound ran deep."

"That *you* don't have a problem is all that matters to me. Besides, it seems too convenient for amaXhosa to blame amaMfengu for their woes, when they were the ones fighting left and right with each other, which is the major reason that weakened them against the British colonial invasions."

We reached a river, foaming dark, floundering with fluvial debris. Seeing my clumsy way of fording, she was so concerned she almost came to rescue me. We climbed a steep sward where I kept losing my balance also. She was close to carrying me on her back, which would have been beyond embarrassing for me. It was the first time I felt sorry for myself for not being a bumpkin.

"Careful there!" She kept getting alarmed for my sake with every misstep I made. In that river ford is where I first saw her svelte and nubile legs, and fell in love with her instantly. She had an apricot complexion, thanks to the Khoisan blood running through her Gqunukhwebe clan blood.

"You must wait here for me. I can see my father is still out in the kraal tending to the sheep. Do you see the glowing ember there?"

"Yes!" I lied. I saw fokkol. Rural people have keener eyesight than city slickers.

"That's his pipe. I'll go inside. When he sees me he'll come to greet me. I'll make tea for him and we'll talk a little, then he'll retire to his hut and wait for supper. That's when I'll come and get you. Don't go anywhere!"

I lay supine in the furrow listening to frogs sing the woes for Pharaoh. I watched the deep darkening skies, the polverine stars, the purple shadows hovering in the valley with my mind racing to the sleeping arrangements for later on. The hushed words *Don't go anywhere* harvested my hopes and made me feel happy as a full moon. After a while the scotch mist turned into a drizzle. By the time she got back I was thoroughly drenched from the salacharail.

"Are we wet? Poor thing. You shall catch your death. I'm sorry I took long. I had to prepare supper for my father. He says my aunt has gone to a funeral in another village." Her commanding tone was replaced by a touch of geniality as she used a towel to dry my head and draped it around my shoulders. I was by then beside myself with joy. I reminded myself that one day, when I write this episode of our meeting, I must title it: *SURPRISED BY JOY!*

"I brought you a flask of tea. We must wait a bit until he settles inside and lights the oil lamp in his hut because the dogs will make a racket when they see a stranger. Then he'll be obliged to come and investigate what they're barking at. If he's not suspicious, he won't come out of his hut until the morning."

Nozi (in my mind I was already calling her by this pet name) went before me when we eventually left for the hut. A mongrel dog came out to challenge me though I followed at a close distance. She tried to shoo it away, but the stubborn bitch went into a frenzy. Nozi eventually got it under control, but not before it had torn the turn-up of my heavyweight Brentwood wool trousers. The door of her father's hut creaked open, pouring a slit of light in the courtyard darkness. Luckily I had already passed the illuminated zone. I was certain the old man's eyes were not adjusted to the dark to properly see what was going on outside.

"What are the dogs barking at, Nozi?" he shouted.

"Nothing, Tata, they're just quarreling among themselves."

"They don't make that kind of noise when they quarrel among themselves; it must be somebody…"

Rural people and their exactitudes, I inwardly cursed, disappearing into the hut. He came out holding a jerrycan, passing the kraal to get to a pigsty. I couldn't see him very well but heard him call out to the pigs. "Xha! Xha! Xha! Yeee piggy piggy! Xha! Xha! Yeee piggy piggy!" She went to meet him, to make sure he didn't decide to come investigate the hut. Coming back after a while, with my happiness on her face, she inquired if I was hungry. I was famished after all the excitement of the day. It turned out, to my eternal joy, that she had decided to let me sleep in her own room. A huge portrait of her stood on the sideboard against the wall with her face screwed into a mask of high seriousness. She had beautiful, lively eyes, calm and alert at the same time. I couldn't wait to hear what those eyes had seen. The room smelled of mustiness and straw, and had the cellar coldness of an underground place. There was a small wooden wardrobe not far from the bed and a dilapidated dressing table under which lay an upside-down washing basin. The floor was of pressed soil, screeded neat and clean with cow dung. She told me that she was going to dish up dinner, and would soon return. I looked at her face until she became shy. Averting her eyes, she coyly smiled in disbelief about her own chutzpah in trusting and letting a stranger into her life so swiftly.

She came back after a quarter of an hour or so with a plate of umphokoqo namasi. "I'm sorry, I know it's cold, but my father refuses to eat anything else. I'll warm a pot of yesterday's meat if you'd like."

"I'm not here for the food," I fawned.

We talked through the greater part of the night. I learned that she was a trainee nurse at Frere Hospital in East London who didn't like the sight of blood. She told me about her friends, most of whom stayed in Mdantsane township. She told me many things about her life, including her fear of the "one-eyed snake," which she had never really managed to tame. Then came time to sleep.

"Since it is too cold to sleep on the floor, I won't be so cruel as to make you do that. We'll both sleep on the bed but in different directions. You'll sleep with your head at my feet. Is that okay?"

"Ndingu mhambi, as a wanderer you won't hear me complain."

"Turn to the wall then, I need to wear my nightie."

There's nothing I would not have given just to have a peek at her body, but I kept my back turned. In any case, I was preoccupied with other concerns about our sleeping arrangement—the smell of my feet. My All Stars had not seen water in seasons.

"Okay, you can turn back now. If I've invited a killer into my home, then tonight is the end of my life, but please spare my poor old father. Tomorrow I must spring-clean the house. You can leave in the morning, if you're able to beat my father in waking; he gets up at four-thirty."

I blew out the lamp before taking off my clothes, hoping darkness would soften the smell of my shoes. I took off my jersey and shirt, leaving the elma before taking off my slightly torn Brentwood, leaving only my bvd to sleep in. Her blankets smelled of soapy freshness and womanly things: perfumes, skin-care lotions and hairsprays. There was a background note of Cutex nail polish coming from her feet. I left mine outside the blankets to mitigate the impact of the odor. Alas, the dreaded comment came regardless.

"Your feet smell." We both burst out laughing. I fell more in love with her candor. Because we didn't want to talk too loudly so as not to attract the attention of her father in the next hut, she eventually said, "You'd better just come up this side, and let your feet be as far from my face as possible." My smelly feet did something positive for once, I thought, as I changed direction. Her breath smelled of cooked pumpkin. The chorus of frogs continued unabated outside.

"My grandpa used to say frogs sang Pharaoh's doom when they croaked like that," I told her.

"Well, your grandpa was wrong. Those frogs are calling their mating partners."

I usually censor this part from Efuoa and say we slept after that, not willing to tempt her kind heart too far. But the whole story is that our feet, Nozi's and mine, touched. She ignored my hand when I tentatively threw it around her waist. I extended my reach to brush her stomach. She allowed me still. After a few minutes I turned her to face me, which she did by easily rolling over my other arm. Soon this arm was cramped, but I would have been damned if I was going to take it out from under her body. I caressed her breast with my other hand. She sighed. Her nipples became taut. She rolled easily when I turned her face to kiss her lips. Then she raised her head slightly to allow me free access to extend the kiss to her neck, her breasts, her stomach, and her crotch. I lost my breath in trying to pull off her panties. She lifted her bum for my ease. Her bush smelled of smoked oysters. She gave a deep sigh and took a shaky breath when my tongue touched her clit. I sucked the oyster. Then I knew her.

There was a wild jerking force in her legs as I entered. I could feel her letting go, yielding to my energy, her body shuddering as she received me with a long sigh, a strain, and a wince. I became concerned lest I hurt her, but she urged me on. She quivered more with my thrusts, her sighs growing louder with my rhythm. She came quickly, with a suppressed scream. I wanted her again. I knew then that I would want her forever. We began again after a while, this time slower, and measured. I wanted to prolong everything, but when the time came, hurry overwhelmed me. I came in muted groans, writhing like a roped bull as my penis throbbed inside her. She got her greatest pleasure on the third try, forcing me to hush her with a hand on her mouth. Then we drifted to after-coital sleep.

When, around three, I recovered my hard-on, my hand searched for her body and we were at it again. We were insatiable. Thereafter, I searched for my underwear around her bed, and finally found it by her left foot. I dragged it up, balled and stuffed it into the pocket of my pants lying next to the bed. Rule number one: when in a strange room, know the nearest exit point, and keep your pants and shoes close by. That's the only thing my older brother ever advised me on concerning the issue of sex. We must have drifted into sleep again soon after.

In the early morning, still half asleep, I stood and walked to the door, gradually feeling my mood opening up to the day. I could see that the village was small and bounded on the west by the bluish melancholy mountain air where the alpenglow didn't reach. Close by, foothills made a border. I feel safe when surrounded by mountains.

A sagging windmill beyond the pigsty made occasional creaking sounds, punctuated by distant dog barks. Broadcasting down the river were faint, boisterous shouts of boys herding lowing cattle. The sun, already starting to shoot hosts, shone with slanting shafts in a manner that told me the time must be after six, toward seven. When my eyes completely opened, I took a slight fright because we had overslept. I glimpsed Nozi's father leaving his hut, wearing a white sieved cotton vest and gray trousers with suspenders and carrying a pickaxe. I immediately closed the door before he could see me. The sound of the pickaxe against the stiffness of the soil rang out; he was burrowing like a mole. I could hear him break wind almost with every blow he struck.

Although aching to introduce myself and help him with his chores, I restrained myself. I sat on the bed, smelling the faint smoke from his pipe as his daughter slept in mesmerizing stillness. I felt giddy with unnatural happiness.

When she woke she took panic. I shushed her with a finger on my mouth, pointing at the courtyard where her father was. She slowly fell back on the bed. I began kissing her and we resumed making love with the intensity of a stolen moment. When she came, a teardrop popped out of her left eye. I've made journeys to the edges of the world but it was the only time I received a teardrop as a gift for coming that far.

CONFESSIONS

Dear Mama

I woke to the sound of a spade against the soil this morning. Peeking through the curtain I saw Hlathi, who tends your garden, working on a flowerbed. I went out to explain to him that now that you have died I can no longer afford to pay him. He told me this was his garden and he didn't come only because he was paid.

He asked me how I felt since you were gone. I said, "I am underneath the broom tree…"

I was wonderfully surprised when he finished the sentence with me: "…asking to die?"

We laughed until we pissed ourselves, tears streaming down our cheeks, remembering in fondness your saying.

He's probably the only person I have a clear recollection of during your funeral: how he kept collecting the rubbish people left behind, and cleaning not only the yard but doing some house chores also. I felt so grateful but mute to express it.

We talked more about you, things you liked to say. In the end, Hlathi shook his head, wriggling a finger at me in amusement, saying I was starting to sound like you. Then he went back to his work.

Twenty minutes later I brought him tea and his sandwich. He asked if I had R5 for him. "No! No!" I refused. "Thyini!" I reprimanded him slightly for I knew he wanted to go buy ivarantyontyo with the money. I refuse to sponsor his early death with cheap alcohol.

Laughing and shaking his head again, he muttered something I could not hear before repeating that I was turning out to be exactly like you. "I hope you grow to be as kind as her," he said in the end.

That brought a lump to my throat. I could no longer refuse him the R5, even though I knew it was wrong of me to give it to him.

I told you I found a copy of St. Augustine's book in the kist when I was going through your things—by the way, I do not know what to do with your clothes. I think Aunt Zenzile would love to have them. She wants me to come and stay with her eDikeni this summer. I've not yet made up my mind, but if that's what it takes to forget about you a little, so be it.

You always told me St. Augustine is pivotal for anyone who wants to travel the journey of self-exploration, although personally you preferred his mother, St. Monica. Since starting to read the book in the past week I'm beginning to understand what you meant. That's not to say I understand St. Augustine. He uses words I'm not familiar with. I spend more time looking them up in the dictionary —some words are not even there—than reading the book. Besides, I'm still taking him in small chunks until I finish my school exams. Then I'll read him for real.

I feel I've got all the time in the world to learn. The feeling is rather strange since I would have thought your passing away would have caused me to think more about the passing of my own life, a sense of contingency (another word I learned through St. Augustine) on my own.

I like this book of St. Augustine's, not necessarily for what is written in it, but because I can smell you on it. I keep it under my pillow.

You used to say, if you're going to be reading any book it is better you read the Bible because it's got everything you need: history, geography, biography, poetry, and fiction, with an added advantage of cultivating good manners and the ultimate relationship with God. I'm not in the right frame of mind to deal with God at the moment.

St. Augustine is more appropriate because he deals with God for me. I find him interesting in a strange way. His putting himself in the dock, accusing himself of all sorts of things, is a little showy,

CONFESSIONS

but is refreshing at the same time. I'm more used to books that prefer to put others in the dock.

I got confused this evening. I was feeling claustrophobic inside the house so I went outside and sat on the stoep. As I watched a crack in the stoep where the ants pass into their nest, something spoke in the thrum of silence—did I steal that from St. Augustine? I don't know, and frankly don't care. It was not your voice, but I felt known, if you know what I mean. I felt someone, something, gazing upon me with warm eyes. Do you think I'm losing my mind?

You know my deep distrust of silence. You said even as a baby I hummed to myself, just to break the burden of silence. You liked to say I have a "free-floating anxiety," which is why I'm not good at things for which one needs to be alone. How do you suppose then I will manage without you? Yhuu! Hayi olady ndiyakukhumbula! I miss you like crazy!

I miss how we used to read together after supper—St. Augustine is nice and all, but sometimes I prefer my chick-lit books. They make me forget things I don't want to think about. Marian Keyes's humor is therapeutic to me. Remember you tolerated her better than Danielle Steel? You said if she is Irish then she can't be that bad. Even now I run to her when I want a break from all this talk with and about God of St. Augustine, which sometimes cloys at me (hahaaa! I'm using a word St. Augustine taught me against him).

I think God does not want to talk to us. I don't see why we bother trying to talk to Him. I don't even mean that in a bad way. I don't see the point of talking to ants, although I like watching them go about their own business, as long as they don't pinch my skin. I think God adopts that attitude with us. He likes watching us going about our business, dragging stuff to our holes–wait a minute, St. Augustine would say our "lares." Well, I'll watch my lare; if God wants to talk, He knows where to find me. I don't know where He stays.

I'm looking at the sky, the twinkling stars. The gum tree in our yard you liked sitting under is withering, and I wonder if it is protesting your death when it swishes and sways. A pair of hadedas have adopted it as their home. They make a racket in the mornings but are strangely silent in the evenings.

I had an urge to smash everything and burn the house down. I thought if we're to do this honesty thing, I might as well tell you that also. I don't understand what's come over me.

AS I RUN

About two decades ago I traveled on my nerves out of South Africa, with the devil at my heels, leaving behind a woman I loved on her first trimester of pregnancy. I didn't get a chance to say goodbye. I believed then I would be back soonish, mañana as the Mexicans would say. A year, or five at the most. I lived with quixotic hope of returning to my motherland as a conqueror, coming to liberate my people. I even had Vusi Mahlasela's song as the theme to that day ringing incessantly in my mind: *We'll beat the drums when you come back home...*

But life is not that neat. Things change, often change utterly! The conquering mood disappeared into regret when months in Botswana translated into years in the former USSR, and then more years here in Tanzania. Regret slowly transformed into sadness. Now I find I have no clear recollection of my life in South Africa. That's the major crime I place against the apartheid system, that of robbing us of our memories. As if that wasn't enough, the engulfing mist is skulking to complete the process of taking memories, my last refuge.

I feel old enough to see the end of my days.

I sometimes hear Efuoa describe me to other women of the village as "an important man of the liberation movement." I get confused about who she's referring to. I'd accuse her of staging a harlequinade out of my life if I didn't know she meant well. Yes, I've been around the world. Once I stood on Trafalgar Square and felt nauseated, with winter settling in more ways than one—I had just met O.R. Tambo in North London. In that meeting he briefed me about Amsterdam, instructed me to take a holiday after I concluded the Organization's business there, see his physician because it was becoming clear there was something wrong with my health. Ever since, Dam remains, in my mind, a city of open kindness and strange foreboding. The height of my political career was in winning the Scandinavian hearts to support our cause, financially and morally. Afterwards I took my working holiday in Prague, whose canals and bridges, surreal in my mind even then, are something no living person should die before walking. We had good times drinking pilsner and exchanging wisdom with a sublime poet, one of the best human beings I've ever met, who later became the president of that wonderful country. The Eiffel Tower in Paris, if it is to be seen, must be seen with someone you love, as it gets very beautiful in early evening, and lonely when everyone around is holding hands. The Notre Dame cathedral holds my respect as an example of the wondrous possibilities of human creativity when mystically inspired. French people won't give you their money, but they will open their homes to you to feed you good food. New York has a contrived beauty and magnificence, showcasing the ingenuity of the capitalist system; the wonders that human enterprise is capable of. Fall is the best time to be there, to walk in the crumble of fallen leaves that gives Central Park a haunting quality. You'll get the sense of something breathing about us in vacant air, that the poetess Mary Oliver speaks about. American black and Jewish people, I found, know how to put their money where their mouths are. The crown city of my experiences is Leningrad, now St. Petersburg again. I don't suppose one has lived until they've sat with a book, by Pushkin or Gorky, before the calm coldness of the Neva River. Say nothing of the decaying background of imperial splendor, built by Peter the Great in the eighteenth century. And then go back to the warm embrace of a woman you love, who keeps the samovar burning to boil you black tea. And watch her sip the kvass while skinning a fillet of sole, boiling potatoes to prepare okróshka with the background music of Thandi Klaasen igniting the moans of your heart: I had no chance to say goodbye to romance, "Sophiatown."

To watch from a mist-frozen window the boulevards, most of which were stripped bare by the Bolshevik Revolution of 1917–18. To watch, from a hotel window, the gilded breadth of Nevsky Prospect—St. Petersburg's main street—under falling snow is a wonder none should die without experiencing. Lucky is the traveler who arrives in time for the April thaws when the mujiks chisel channels, gradually discharging the pent-up river before it vents its fury in a great flood with the sudden collapse of frozen barriers. Standing at Lomonosov Bridge, watching all of it coming down in dream-like mesmerization.

I spent precious years in the USSR learning to hate capitalism, only to discover in the end that we're all capitalists at heart. And a few years in Lusaka, playing cowboys and crooks with apartheid agents—talk about saddling tigers—while working for Radio Freedom, only to discover we were being edited by an apartheid regime spy. The incident cast a dark shadow over all of us who worked in that office, which was why the Organization posted those of us it couldn't prove treason against to different dead posts, as ghost operatives. This is how I ended up here in Tanzania, a teacher and born-again hermit, trying to medicine my manners and enlarge my soul. My God! What has my life amounted to, besides this combat of fatigue? Perhaps Efuoa is right in calling me "an important man of the struggle," although the struggle is of another kind.

In my mind I'm better than my life.

There is a mortuary coldness inside our house tonight. My table is set under a small opening where I look toward the forest ocean. Even in the dark, or when thick mist is rolling, I know the trees are there, keeping guard on Macbeth's moves. Like the forest that doomed him, I know they're closing in.

If paleontologists are to be believed, the cradle of humankind is in this country, the Ngorongoro Crater. So it is fitting for me to return my dust to where life of man's dust first sprang.

"Tell us about your life in Sawusafrica?" Efuoa often asks as she helps me to lay down on our lumpy bed. Us Africans know the stories we tell to ourselves to trigger our memories, remind us who we are and what we have survived. She does not want me to concentrate on my dependency upon her. She knows I'm not humble enough to be improved by this humiliation. I'm part of secular Pelagians in this regard. I don't want forgiveness, nor gifts from the gods. I just want to be left alone to strive and be alive. I don't even want false hopes, security, or comforts. I want my little portion under the sun, and to have an understanding of *why* when I'm suffering.

I've no time for false religious comforts, delusions about the coming world, that hypocritical begging need for God as your Santa who dishes out only the goodies. If you believe God created the world, then honesty demands you admit that, however good God may be, there's evil manifest in the world that God allows. God has never asked us to excuse Him on this, just to believe there's a higher purpose to it. And there's no use speculating on the higher purpose when it is clear that its mystery has not been revealed to us.

It takes a while to understand when Efuoa talks about South Africa because of the way she pronounces the word, as one lisping. She wants me to talk about fond memories of my motherland. I want to talk about hers.

Efuoa was born in the Rwandan province of Kibungo. The area is mostly swamps and pasture land, with intolerable humidity during summer. She does not like to talk about it because it reminds her of Kalashnikov-toting men with nail-studded clubs, masus, and machetes that "smash baby skulls."

I remember vividly the few times she did tell me the story of what happened to her village. "Why you want me to talk about bad things? Why must I go through that horrible time?" she demanded at my asking.

"Because I want to leak it out of your subconscious mind." I tried to sound learned, as if this was just a doctor—patient thing that had nothing to do with us.

"No one can know what go through there and here"—she pointed at her head and heart—"not even those who there; better let it go," she said, when I tried this with her. Her French is better than her English, but mine is rubbish. I had a sinking feeling in my stomach as she narrated how they first heard rumors of Tutsis being killed, but did not worry much about it, thinking, at worst, it must be something happening far away in cities like Kigali.

"When we asked why Tutsis were being killed no one knew for sure, so we thought it a lie. But rumors of killing men became thick, people thought they'd be safe in numbers at the church so they collect there. Not my father, he tells our family we remain home. Then I have to go to the bush to relieve myself, you know. My shit saved me, I guess." We both smiled. "The killing men come when I'm shitting. And now after that we are enemies—Tutsi and Hutu."

She stopped to survey my reaction before she continued. "The evil spirit men come. I see other people—Hutus of our village—try to find out what evil men want. The priest go talk to them. I never see him again. I see a man I know who has pretensions of being a mwami walk with them, so I think they're good men then. I want to ask where my father is but I'm afraid and confused when I see they have masus and machetes. I hide and follow them behind, very far, wanting to go to my parents, but the militia are in my way so I must hide more. Then they reach the church. I hear people shouting and screaming. I think maybe they're glad, but their screams are strange, like squealing pigs. When it is very dark, I come closer to see. The militia men are already tired of killing people and are sitting around the fire drinking beer and roasting meat. The pretentious mwami is sitting and laughing with them. He helped them kill; the mwami helped them kill us, even though he was one of us..."

She fell silent for a while.

"The screams I hear inside the church now are in my head, following me all over the village as I run. There are screams following me through the mountains as I run. As I run the church looks like the slaughterhouse in my head so I run, and as I run I feel I might never see my family again but I must run until I don't hear the screams anymore as my blood is throbbing in my neck and head, but when I stop the screams come again in my head, so I run some more, until my breath burns and I'm unable to breathe, but I must run some more because I can hear more voices of militia men. I want to run faster, to get away from there and the screams and the slaughterhouse, as far as I can, but I can't swallow my own saliva as I run because it is heavy as metal and tastes of bitterness."

Last night Efuoa was screaming in her sleep. It happens sometimes, though less frequently these days. The first time I heard this I didn't understand. She was shouting "Akuzu! Akuzu, wind of destruction!" in Kinyarwanda, her mother tongue and the language of her dreams. I first thought she was saying "kanguka, kanguka"—"wake up, wake up" in Kinyarwanda. I wondered who she was waking before listening closer. In the morning I asked her what "akuzu" meant; she was so frightened I regretted my faux pas. I later gathered that the Akuzu were the core of the concentric webs of political, economic, and military muscle and patronage that came to be known as Hutu Power. They're the ones who controled and incited the Hutu militias, the Interahamwe and Impuzamugambi.

Efuoa says sometimes she dreams of Nyabarongo River—the meandering line of water that connects Rwanda with Ethiopia— floating with dead bodies. Nyabarongo River did float with dead bodies in the height of the 1994 genocide. She'd shield herself away from Rwandan radio news with my body, demanding that we make love to "keep away the evil spirits." But the mist always finds ways to sift through, so she began to have these dreams. It was a problem in those days when I had to go somewhere. I had to cancel many an appointment in the city if I couldn't take her with me. I wonder how she will cope after I'm gone? Fuck this pusillanimous nonsense—after I'm dead.

AS I JOG

Dear Mom

In my book of life, according to St. Augustine, I've only read a page. He says the world is a book, and those who do not travel read only a page. Why did you never tell me St. Augustine was African? Is the animal hippopotamus named after the city he came from, Hippo? And where in Africa is Hippo? I'll check it up in the library.

I'm tired of this lack of willpower to do anything about my life. Feeling out of the loop with always being inside the house, I thought I would go jogging to clear my mind. It was in the early evening air, like we used to do sometimes. If I can't travel the world, I will run my streets.

The clouds, from the direction of East London, were heavy with rain, threatening to fall as I was jogging. Peach trees budding, sparrows returning, finches singing: "Tshi-tshi-tshi!" But their song was not for me.

A tent was attached to the house four houses up our street, meaning someone had died there. Neighbors from the shacks across the road were walking about our streets looking for a house to draw water from. They still have no tap water despite the government's promises. Last week construction vehicles came. Green flies say they'll soon be building RDP houses. If I recall, that is what everyone said last year when it turned out they were only building a community hall, which stands as a white elephant now while people have no decent houses to live in. I invited them to help themselves to our water. *I know you don't like that because it hikes up our water bill. "Once you invite one, they all come, not even bothering to ask—in for a penny in for a pound," you used to say.*

I jogged down Mvezo Street, where it bisects the main street. At the corner yakwa Sirayeli I turned left and saw the black Israelites, in crow suits, choreographing the David dance for worship. They sounded the horn as I passed esiBaneni, the Big Lamp, where I was chased by a big dog to the disinterest of a malnourished one with a shaved pelt that sits on the street counting its last breath. I started thinking about Enoch Mgijima, who led those black Israelites into political defiance that resulted in the Bulhoek Massacre. I bookmarked the event in my mind to research in the library. I tried to think how you survived when the white people didn't allow you to use libraries, because your knowledge of African literature is greater than that of anyone I know. I went through the dirty streamlet where scavenging rats as big as puppies were seeking something to devour. I passed the blue Jeep carcass—where Veli's child was probably conceived—with its exhausted look. I gave the bored municipal workers in blue overalls along the road something to be excited about as they began catcalling me. I passed the graves behind the stadium that look like anthills in a neglected field of weeds. Are black people the weeds of the world, I wondered. The late autumn chill became severe when I was exposed in an open field near the military barracks. I came back through Kwanca High School and met up with children playing games in the street, stretching across the entire road. I remember you telling me that is where Phaks went to high school, and that they say he was a great tenor in the choir.

I remember how sometimes on your way home from work you joined us in skipping rope. And Mother, you were good at it! I couldn't believe the first time you did it. I apologize for feeling a little jealous because my friends gave you all the attention. It was always hard for me to stand in your shadow—beautiful and kind and calm as a weasel in everything you did.

I remember when they lowered you into your grave, all I could think was: what a waste of beauty. I'm too old for childhood games now but seeing children play brings to mind something lost along the road. I miss netball and athletics.

People poured out of buses and taxis as I passed the terminus. They looked like termites going on a forage. Smoke rose from houses to meet the drizzling rain. Dogs barked their excitement to add to the confusion as boys wheeled their car tires. Lovers under bus stop shades secretly kissed, making me wonder how it feels to be kissed. There were dwindling fires on street corners, drunks tottering.

Make something of yourself! Make something of your life! *The words kept ringing in my head as I reentered the gate of our house with the rainwater sweeping our street.*

How? How do I make something of my life? Thoughts of anger rise to my head because of your dying, and because someone has stolen our hosepipe after drawing water from our tap. I've no clue how to make something of myself, like everyone keeps telling me. And because St. Augustine is always speaking in a begging language to a God with whom I am angry, I've no interest in opening his thick book again. And I know I'm going to hell because of my swelling pride but I'm shocked that I don't care because hell no longer scares me now that I've had a taste of it. I'm tired of all this talk about ecstasy, drawing God into our wishes. And of being terrorized by God away from saying how we really feel, and what we think.

I'm sick of it! School! Oh, God, school! I can't stand it!

Everyone keeps talking about this Y2K thing, afraid of the havoc the computers will cause not working properly when we reach the year 2000. I don't care! I'm sick of it! Nothing interests me.

And I'm tired of this township, of ungrateful bastards who stole our hosepipe even though I gave them our water for free. Of this place where someone is dying every week. Tired of walking among the dying breed.

I don't have the will to do anything about my life. Sometimes I can't even read novels.

I'm sick of the pounding shebeen music. I can't sleep with all the drunks making drunken noises outside, sharing Black Labels and hitting each other, leaving blood on the sidewalk. Tired of the screaming women who swear at you when you try to help them against their abusive boyfriends who sit smoking, looking at you like you're nothing but an irritating fly. I'm sick of it! God! I'm sick of it! I'm sick of it all!

LEAD, KINDLY LIGHT

One late Saturday morning, you and Sandi walk through the open field of crackly dry bush, and pass SOMAFCO with a hint of hesitancy. She told you you were going to see some sights.

"That's the school your father taught at." She points it out.

It catches you unawares that you're walking on the road he walked on. You go into some kind of pretense, as if you've always walked this path. For some reason you had expected a sprawling, luxurious college, but the school is mostly just a cluster of low cross-hipped buildings, some prefabricated, with a dingy fence and bushy with wild grass all around. But when you think this is where he went every weekday of his life, you feel faintly overwhelmed. You stop to look closer at the portrait drawing of Solomon Mahlangu on the entrance wall of the school. With it is a caption: *Tell my people my blood will water the seeds of their freedom.* This was what the young revolutionary is purported to have said just before the apartheid regime executed him.

Barking dogs protest the injustice of things at a distance, bringing confusion to your head that makes you feel light and inadequate, guilty even for being alive when so many fell along the road.

Sandi says, "I'm sure Maman wouldn't mind if we drop in at her place since we're already close by. We can chow by her, the woman is old school, there's always a pot on her stove."

The idea of getting and reading more of Phaks's Pillow Books makes your heart pound in anticipation. You follow Sandi's lead with a watering mouth because your stomach is telling you it is lunch time.

You find Maman sewing on her machine. She asks Sandi to warm a dish of food for you, chicken tikka masala and urwagwa, which you learn she makes on special occasions because it is made from a Rwandan potato that is very hard to find in Tanzania. You discover with a spark of pleasure that the two of them had planned the visit all along without telling you and this is the special occasion for which Maman has prepared the dish.

As your belly is warmed by the food, so is your heart by Maman's kindness. She has opened her home and her life to you.

After eating, you and Sandi wash the dishes while Maman listens to the radio, a habit she says she learned from your father. Twenty people have died in the flash floods, and a commission of inquiry has been established to investigate another twenty who died following a stampede at an evangelical Christian church in Moshi. Because Moshi is Sandi's hometown you ask, "What actually happened there?"

She tells you that a man who called himself an Apostle poured so-called holy oil on the ground, provoking the gathered crowd to surge forward in an attempt to touch the oil and be cured of their sicknesses and misery.

"The funny thing, sister Ruru, is that the police exonerated the so-called Apostle based on the report he submitted. Was the man gonna go pen a report that implicated himself? Obviously the hands of the police have been greased, eheee? So there's been demonstrations and riots in Moshi of supporters and accusers clashing. The president gave in by finally establishing this commission of inquiry. But it's gonna go nowhere because they all go bongo together, them pastor and the president. He go just fool them people."

Something about it feels like déjà vu to you, reminiscent of the workings of the so-called prophets in South Africa who don't only plunder people's money but rape their daughters in the name of God also, and make them eat grass and drink gasoline as acts of faith. You talk about the need for an official structure to regulate religion, an institution.

"But powerful men of institutions protect each other also. Look at the scandals of the Catholic Church?" You bridle, only to slightly regret it when you recall that Maman is Catholic.

But she supports your statement by replying. "Many *un prêtre* Catholic are evil men."

Sandi asks whether Maman is talking from experience and pushes her to tell you about her life in Rwanda before she came to Tanzania.

Remembering what Phaks wrote about Maman's horrific past, you cringe at Sandi's tactlessness, but Maman's response comes almost instantly, as if she has been dying to tell, or is weighed down by her memories. "O! We lived what you call *ordinaire*, ordinary, lives, like anyone everywhere else before the evil come; so it cannot be that the genocide is the only thing we talk about when we talk our lived lives. The remains of death are there for the world to see in Rwanda, but very little of our ordinary lives in *mémoire*, which is very sad. Nobody ever ask about that, as if we were born killing each other with hundreds of corpses lying there, piling on each other for TV cameras to see. Those days on TV I try to follow the camera when I see *une* hill or *un* building I recognized still standing, but quickly it would disappear. They did not linger on *vivant* ordinary things, *un* life in Rwanda, everyone was always looking to unearth a grave story, as if all people see about us *le décès* and destruction. Our leaders also, how you say it, go for what you call *la pornographie du génocide*, unhealthy genocide voyeurism, milking, milking the world's guilt for foreign grant monies and loans. It just brings more oppressive *régime*, government, you say? That kill people like *facistes africains*. Anyhow, what do I know? Your father is responsible for these thoughts in my head. I liked listening to him after he listens to his radio news."

"Would you still want to go back to Rwanda some day?" you ask, praying you have not overstepped your mark.

"My place is with my husband now. Where he rests I must be. This now is my home. In my end I lie next to him. But I like to see places I remember from my youth again someday, even if for the last time. Places that exist in my head now. My husband said he, too, grew up around sharp knives, with difficult choices, 'badgering perplexities of township life,' he called them. I liked memorizing the clever terms he used to express things by; he had such a way with words. Circumstances forced homelessness on us. But we find home in each other. I can't imagine things were any better for you?"

"I had my mother. That made all the difference."

"Yes," Efuoa nods. "She must be a strong woman?"

"She was. She died. Months apart from..." You can't bring yourself to call him Efuao's husband because to you he is your mother's. Although, from what you read in the Pillow Books, Efuoa has no jealous feelings toward the "paper wife," your mother. "Months apart from, eh, Phaks, actually."

"I'm sorry to hear," is what Efuoa says.

"Anyway," you say. "You sort of get used to township life when you don't know anything better. I know I did, but the up-ending of your world overnight, like in war, that I cannot begin to comprehend."

"None of us can until it happens. Then we try to survive best we can. If you do, you then have to live with your escape from it. That is all. No one of us is born with special capabilities for *traumatisme*." She stands, brushing your forehead as she walks to the kitchenette, where you can faintly hear her gurgle water.

Coming back, she tells you more about her life since the death of Phaks.

"In the end, what we're all left with is finding kind ways to live. And not so uncomfortable ones to die. It is very easy to miss our chances of happiness, because they come to us undeservedly."

She giggles softly. "Never make the mistake of dwelling too long on your pain; you'll miss a chance to live."

She cocks her head sideways toward you like a courting pigeon and asks with kind eyes. "Sandi tells me you're Catholic?"

"When I'm not lapsing, yes I am!"

"So am I, but laziness to travel far makes me attend the charismatic congregation not far from here. Perhaps if I had someone to go with I would go to Mass tomorrow. One's getting tired of money gospel that prospers only these happy-clappy pastors while the rest of the congregation get poorer. A Catholic church exists in Nyarowa Street; your father accompanied me there sometimes, though his heart was not in it. He did to please me, bless his soul. They also have a French Mass, which you can use to learn the language."

"Sure, we can go," you reply. "I've not been to Mass since I came to the country."

"It's settled then. It would, how do you say, gain us time if tonight you spend the night here; after all, it is practically your home too."

"But I have no change of clothes," you protest slightly.

"I'm sure between Sandi and I we find you something." She looks at Sandi as if requesting approval. Sandi nods.

"When done with Mass," Maman continues, "we can go visit a few places around here."

Later on Sandi goes home, leaving you with Maman, who calls you to the bedroom, where she takes out one of your father's boxes.

"Your father looked too much under the stones, his problem was, always scribbling something," she says as she pushes the box toward you with her foot. Opening it, you find more Pillow Books and papers.

"I have no use for those, but am sure they can be of use to you. It is always a concern to find what your husband really thought of you in black and white. Dying people have an un-lying tongue. I'm choosing to remember him as he is in my head and my heart." She gestures to both as she speaks. "I do not want to know if he thought differently of me than what I believe in my heart, so don't feel you need to tell me anything that's written there if different to my love for him."

She walks back to the kitchenette to boil water for tea. You remain standing next to your father's desk, trying to…what? Catch his aura?

"Do you think tomorrow we could visit his grave also?" you ask Maman hesitantly as you join her in the kitchenette.

"Sure, child! Where are my manners? Anytime, anytime. Is why I say we visit more places after Mass."

You're not sure why you're acting as though you have not been to the graveyard. You want to be there with someone who knew him intimately. You feel something warm running down your cheeks. Maman notices and catches a tear before it falls. You didn't anticipate your stay here would be this emotional after all the years. It feels as though the dust of the years is blowing away, being wiped as Maman wipes your tears with her apron.

"*Quel est ton tourment?* What are you going through, child?"

You don't know how to answer as you continue sniveling. It suddenly occurs to you that you never cried when your mom died. When the people from her choir came to inform you about the accident, and that your mother was among the live people who died, you just stood there in disbelief and in mounting…not sadness, but anger. Then they sang, keeping the wake, making themselves tea in your house. You just looked on and allowed them to do whatever they liked, but you never cried. You didn't cry even though they encouraged you to. They felt pity for you. Their singing grated your nerves. But you said nothing and shed not a tear. Sometimes it can feel as though you invented that day, were it not for the fact that your mother was no more thereafter. You have to think hard to really remember the events of that day, to try to distinguish it from the things you've, through the years, reimagined about it. You get confused about what really happened and what didn't. When you tell Maman about this, she reveals that she has similar sensations. "The doctors who were sent by the UN to help us with trauma explained it in some way, but I can't remember the terms."

After tea at the kitchenette table, you help Maman make a bed for you on the sofa in the lounge area. When you're done, the two of you sit, talk, and feel connected to each other by some sort of unannounced grief.

A silence falls between you in which only the buzzing of a greenbottle fly is heard. Then Efuoa speaks up. "Sometimes, when your father and I lay together, after he reminded me of being a woman"—she winks as she says this—"he would talk about his wish to meet you one day. He really yearned for that, but he ran out of time. I think he would have gladly believed in miracles had that happened, had what he called his winged words reached you."

He had plenty of time after 1990 but chose to stay, you think. You manage not to say it out loud, even as you feel anger aching back into you again. Instead you admire her dedication to him, or his memory. You're strangely reminded of a Homeric line by this talk: *Dead bodies are their lineage.* But you don't say this to Maman. The memory of Phaks, his dead body, certainly found its lineage in Maman and you.

"Phaks was so preoccupied with the search for what he called an authentic life that he almost missed out on living at times," she says. "The minute I saw you I sensed the same energy in you. You both have searching minds, I think it is part of the reason you're here."

Shifting leaves rustle in the silence outside the window.

She tells you at length how your father went from the Tikkun olam of Judaism to the Sufi sense of ecstatic love in Islam to the Catholic mysticism of *The Cloud of Unknowing*. She tells you of the evenings around the fire when he talked about these things. How she wished for someone to explain it to her, to explain her husband to her. "Perhaps, in you, my answers are also answered," she says. "Sometimes I was embarrassed for not knowing, for always stopping him to explain things." She talks about how he knew a lot of things and places, how he liked to read his books, which was what mostly kept him out of trouble and made a good person out of him. How he was a good husband also, "never sleeping in taverns and chasing after dirty women. I never ever had to worry about that like other women who envied me, saying: You're lucky because the professor is a gentleman who never pokes his stick where it doesn't belong, bringing you diseases. I was indeed lucky."

She was lucky, yes, you think, but not because he was disease free. Is she choosing to forget that he died of AIDS? Or she does not know that you have read about the true cause of your father's death in his Pillow Books? Maman was lucky not to have contracted HIV from him. But where did he get infected, if he was so faithful as she claims? Before they were together? There is no way that you can ask Maman this. Perhaps it will be revealed in his journals.

"He called himself 'a virtual religious missionary' with no faith," Maman continues. "He'd say, 'I lack the gift of faith! That's my problem.' He don't like pastors very much…"

You remember from his Pillow Books his strong feelings against them, what he termed "vituperations," something to do with St. Jerome in the fifth century, calling them lazy men who eat like elephants and belch over altars things they've not experienced or understood, more concerned with going around in huge cloaks to cover their fat bodies while sleeping with widows, choir girls and altar boys…

"I tell him priests were some of the kind men I knew in Rwanda who saved my life. He don't care, and say there must have been something in it for them." She turns her head to look out the window and smiles. "I guess you can say we loved each other, but sometimes I don't know what that means in people who meet in our situation, when the shadows were already drawn in our lives." She looks back at you. "You young people think love is everything. But sometimes love is not enough. What is important is being kind to one another even if we don't like each other, especially when we don't like each other. I was lucky because not only did I like my husband, I loved him also with my life.

"The Lord knows, I loved that man, your father; the only person I ever felt complete around. He had strengths I lacked, like to hate God when he felt God deserved it. I've no ability to hate God, because I understand God's ways with my heart rather than my mind, the way your father did. Sometimes I'm tempted to hate God, but I don't have strength to do it. There's so much more I like about the nature of God than the ugly things I see in the world. God is good, and nothing we do can ever change that, no matter how much we try.

"You asked me earlier if I didn't want to go back to Rwanda. Part of me wanted to say yes, but I now know I don't have strength to face the people who killed my family. I fear they'll make me into someone I don't want to be, so I don't go—*if your eye causes you to sin, pluck it out, better to enter heaven with one eye* etcetera. Even if they are in prison, they'll come back, say after a few years, when their prison terms finish, or even before that if their lies convince the officials. What then? They'll come back with shining complexions and clean nails, perhaps start talk to us about the forgiveness they received from accepting Christ as their personal savior and all. That'll put my soul in jeopardy, because I'd hate Christ for forgiving them, although I want Christ to forgive them. I know I would! I'm not saying Christ should not forgive them; on the contrary I pray for their souls and forgiveness. But I don't want them to be forgiven close to me, so I stay away. I don't have that strength, perhaps I'm a hypocrite, I don't know. All I know is that I don't have the strength to watch them freely live their lives without feeling the anger of my dead family for them. It is better to know how you limit so we may cease from tempting ourselves beyond our strength. I ask God, every day, to have mercy on my soul, that I'll never be tempted beyond measure, especially by them who caused us so much grief, who auctioned their souls to the devil by running our lives into the ground. I pray that our souls, too, don't grow weak because of the hate that's killing us inside. And for God to give me strength to expand the powers of my soul, and to give me insight into my own wrongdoing so I may seek true repentance. But I cannot be close to those who are the source of my family's grief, not yet. Perhaps in the next life."

You're both quiet for a moment before she changes the subject.

"Your father would have given anything to see you. He talked about you all the time. Wondering how beautiful you look. And my Lord, was he right. You're a stunning little thing. You must have broken a lot of hearts growing up. But he had no emotional strength to travel to South Africa. Too many things he didn't agree with had happened and were happening, he even said some were still to happen, so he chose to stay away."

As you lie in the darkness in the early morning, around 2am, the guardian angel hour, your naked thoughts demand to address your soul. You can hear the curtain breathing up and down from the wind like some kind of lung. You think about how you have always craved a more capacious idea of a family but seemingly you're always ending up with the capricious two. You have been charmed by Maman's gentle personality, her indestructible optimism and lack of hostility, her self-reserve, discipline, self-effacing kindness. You can now easily see how a man like Phaks would be besotted with her.

Maman spoke about the hearts you must have broken. Yes,

you have broken a few, including your own. And you know you'll soon have to break the heart of the only man you truly love. It will be for his own good, but that doesn't make it any less painful. It doesn't mean you don't sometimes wish for things that can never be.

Sometimes the burdens we carry carry us. With this thought, you softly sing yourself to sleep, toying with your mother's rosary beads in your hand.

UNSOUND MIND AND BODY

Dear Mummy!

I woke up feeling spacey. I've these terrible headaches that make my head feel as though it's being pounded by a huge rubber hammer. Funnily enough, it gets better after drinking coffee. I dropped the mug this morning. It shattered at my feet like shards of my life. The other day I dropped the casserole dish when I was washing it. I don't know why I'm so clumsy lately.

I think sometimes I make my sadness feel like an accusation against you. I've never known any life without you. Now that you are gone I do not know what to do with my life, what to make of it when you are not here to tell me what to do. I feel I'm coming apart from the inside.

Sometimes even the soft tick of the arms of the clock in the lounge sound like a harrowing hammer inside my head. I don't know why that clock must keep ticking when you're not here—when you're dead dead dead! So I smashed it against the wall just so I may hear it shudder. I felt so ashamed of myself as I swept its pieces into the dustpan that I began crying. Why am I becoming this angry person? This hurt I feel is inside, I can't examine and bandage it. I sometimes have this excruciating pain in my abdomen, as if my insides are twisting, okanye amathumbu ayashwabana. Yhoo! Hayi sana, kubuhlungu!

Hlumelo, the boy from down the road at Mvezo Street, came around to invite me to church the other day. You used to say he's cute as a button? And that he has the manners of a gentleman. I sometimes think the only reason I like him is because you liked him so much, but then I recall that I liked him before you died, so it can't be that. He thinks I should go see someone—a shrink. I'm like: What da hell, dude! You trying to say I'm losing it? I nearly bit his head off. But I don't know, perhaps I should because I am always angry all the time.

I've seen the adverts for a "healthy mind" at the clinic. There are rooms where you can make an appointment to see a psychologist or something. But then people are just gonna think I've gone loco. Yhooo!

I learned a new phrase from St. Augustine today. Well, it's in Latin but I looked it up: mens sana in corpore sano, which means "a sound mind in a sound body." Mummy, my body is not sound, not at all. I'm not all right but I don't know what to do. I slept almost all day on Sunday to wake, still tired, on Monday morning into a situation. Hlumelo had come to my house to insist I go to school with him. I suspect his father put him up to it. I had no argument against it. Problem is, Veli came also, almost immediately after him, with other ideas. She's not been feeling like going to school so she comes here early in the mornings to spend the whole day talking and watching soapies, and I'm too tired to protest. Most of the time I appreciate her company because, if not for her, I think I'd soon start talking to mice. She was taken aback by my decision to go to school with Hlumelo, and went on bitching about how I no longer have time for her and all, shoulders shaking, almost sobbing and all that boring drama. Conflicted and annoyed, I wanted to punch both of them. She's my BFF, and he's my PBFF, and somehow I agree with both of them, sort of.

I told Veli she could spend the day in my house since she was feeling drowsy all the time at school and unable to take in what was being taught. Promised to rush back from school first chance I got. Still she felt let down, but there was nothing to be done about it. After all, I cannot avoid school forever, not if I want to make something of my life. Actually it was rather creepy how she almost went crazy with the whole thing, the glint of desperation in her eyes and all. On the other hand, I could see Hlumelo himself was making a mountain of this hill, ready to go mental if I didn't agree to go to school with him.

I felt rather self-conscious walking to school with lines of dirt in the creases of my black shoes, with their almost worn-out heels, not to mention the shine on my school blazer sleeves. School, as I expected, was a nag. Teachers who normally are bog-down-standard boring were stupefyingly nice to me today. They kept trying to cheer and reassure me, getting embarrassed by my pain when I didn't respond. Like, they've become really, really irritating. I was so not feeling like being there. Classmates treated me like a psycho or something, as if I am some kind of egg whose shell has broken. My gosh! It was like, so, so embarrassing. You don't know how embarrassing it is when everyone is trying to be nice to you just because your mother has died, buzzing about you like bees all the time, offering to do stuff for you. Shit! I wish everyone would leave me alone. They make me feel like a wounded bird, ready to be sacrificed to the gods or something. So, so not cool!

Our Natural Science teacher, Mr. May, says crows (a murder of crows—did you know this is their collective name?) mob one of their own when it shows signs of sickness. Mr. May says this is their way of protecting the rest of the group from whatever disease the sick one could be carrying. Oh, the unkindness of these birds. It sounds cruel to me, but nature almost always seems like that. I must say as people we behave more like elephants. Siyamkhunga umntu ohlelwe lilishwa—we pray for someone who has suffered misfortune—is what makes us human.

I know it seems like I'm bitching and all, but this is why I prefer to be on my own, to close the door and bomb out in bed reading novels. It is the only thing I can stomach at the moment. Even when Principal Ratsibe offered me a lift home in his car that smells of a moldy lunch box, I wanted to scream. He talked long about how *the whole school is looking to our class to put the school on the map. My heart was just not in it. When I said I was cool with walk-ing, he insisted, and gave me the Study Aids for all my subjects and told me to bring them back only after exams. He said I must look over notes of other students for the period I was not at school and told me to put emphasis on doing the exercises at the end of every study book. Yhoo! Hayi sana ndisentweni; everyone is clawing at me like jackdaws. Phofu ke, ndizaba strongo, I'll be strong, I guess. If I can survive this dog year that's been the pits for me, I can survive anything. I am starting to look at things with a returning soldier's eye, like* The Best Years of Our Lives *the b&w you liked to make us watch though it bored me. I see now its whole point, the feeling of resigned indifference after you've been torn apart. I'm afraid this is making me inconsiderate to other people's needs.*

RAVENS AND PROPHECIES
25/03/99

The mist has hidden its face for a while. But I can still see its lingering whiskers on the river surface as the rising sun bakes the earth. Soon the sun will rise not for me. But, for now, I'm alive. Being alive is a constant act of finding value in atelic activities, a trick of staying ahead of the emptiness within. I think it was Camus who said the literal meaning of life is whatever you do that stops you from killing yourself. And I am saying the patience of the oyster is the only available way forward for a dying man, to coil within oneself, weaving one's pearl.

Death is the end of desire.

I've lost my desires. Even obtaining what I want now fails to make me happy. Perhaps, because I still want to be alive in my consciousness, even if not in this world, my desires then are not strictly lost but superseded. I notice the prosaic desires I used to have—for food, wealth, sex, and other corporeal needs—sitting flaccid on the floor of my soul. They no longer stir my blood or quicken my soul. Could this be what Schopenhauer notoriously referred to as the "futility of desire?" When not having something is just as good as having it?

Saul of Tarsus, when he started calling himself Paul, said being alive or dead is all the same to him, as long as he obtains the power that was in Yehoshua, his Christ. So the philosophers did not mislead after all. It does happen that when you resign yourself to the demands of death you lose desires, that is the will to live in your body.

Knowing must be accompanied by the transcendental know-ledge of not knowing for philosophy to be born.

There's a pleasing commotion of birds outside my window, the scar through the thick tenurial fabric that gives me a tunnel view of the world. The roof is screeching. Sounds like monkey eagles. No, no! It's those thieves that fed the prophet in his time of need in the wilderness: ravens. I've just spotted one. The unkindness of ravens. The klaxons, screeching hard against the corrugated-iron roof, sound like a harrowing rake. One caws, its plumage shiny and black as Italian hair. God, I didn't know they can get this big. They're huge, almost like vultures, and hooded as nuns. They make me think of what Homer said about winged words, the messages sent in ancient times through ravens. Ravens were telegraphs of the ancient epoch.

Winged?

Birds are winged. But can words, on their own, fly across the mountains and sea to impinge upon, or penetrate, the consciousness of those we love? Strange talk this talking about winged words.

Ravens—I read in the Bible, when I still cared about such pleasing fables—stole from the granaries of King Ahab to feed prophet Elijah when he fled from Jezebel. Maybe they'll spare a morsel for this sinner, even if my vision is not sharp enough for prophecy.

I once won a collection of Shakespeare's plays at school because I knew, from reading the encyclopedia our mother bought for our house, the difference between crows and ravens. Ravens travel in pairs, while crows often flock. A crow's tail is shaped like a fan, while the raven's is wedged. Crows give a cawing sound, but ravens produce a lower, croaking one. By this understanding it is a murder of crows that has flocked to my roof then. I wonder if whoever wrote the pleasing fables about the prophet knew this difference, because I suspect it to have been crows that fed Elijah, instead of ravens. Or does it strictly say a pair of ravens fed him or a flock? It doesn't matter, I'm too lazy to look it up in Efuoa's Bible. Besides, the story loses nothing by confusing the two. I'm just being my old, pedantic self.

My paternal grandma, preparing to go under the knife for a minor colon operation, woke up on the day of the operation to the sight of a pair of ravens—or was it a flock of crows? (I can't recall the details of this family fable.) She claimed that seeing a raven, first thing in the morning at that, was a bad omen. So she refused to go to the hospital. No one was able to convince her otherwise. She died eight years later, her colon problem having turned into a malignant cancer. I was nine then, given to reading into things signs for my satisfaction and entertainment. Ever since, death, in my mind, has been associated with ravens. We cannot escape our upbringing. We can only tame it with education a little.

Have the raven-crows come to sing a dirge for my life? By the way, Romans used to read signs and omens from bird entrails, and identified seeing a soaring eagle as a sign of victory. We still have countries with pretenses of being empires using the eagle insignia as its coat of arms. So, leave my grandma and me alone with our fear of ravens, even if we're no prophets.

Ravens are a dominant feature where I grew up. People are often woken in the morning by the sound of raven klaxons scraping like metal saws on the roof sheets of their house. Their shrill cawing in the evenings; God, they've terrible voices: "Kwarrr! Kwarrrrr!" It used to drive me crazy. They and hadedas are master irritants in the mornings in our area. Hadedas even have clan songs, so their *wawaaah-wawaaah* is not meaningless gibberish, it's them planning and organizing their day according to their clans.

With age, and death in the offing, things change. You become more tolerant of other life forms around you. You even find yourself longing for them. You realize how much richer, more eventful life is with them. Things you took for granted suddenly acquire grandeur, like ravens on your roof. You get seduced into seeing the hand of providence in them, like Elijah.

I'm no prophet, and Efuoa is no widow whose *barrel of meal shall not waste, neither shall the curse of oil fail, until the day that the Lord sendeth rain upon the earth*. But the question now occurs to me too: When shall the Lord send rain our way? I'm getting pretty tired of the dry patch that has been my lot in this sojourn. I'm losing my moorings in this dust storm. Our hearts are not strong enough to mend what we've broken, or to reclaim the life we left behind, when the mark of Cain overwhelms us. No one can ever come home again after spilling his own brother's blood.

UNDER THE HARROW

Dear Mama

Hlumelo says his father, who is the reverend at the Baptist church, insists we try and make something of our lives now that we will soon finish matric, because they as parents are not going to be around all the time. Hlumelo wants to study journalism at Rhodes University. But it seems his father's church is only prepared to give him a scholarship for ministry. So things are beginning to get on the fritz. He really, really does not want to be a Baptist minister and says he is prepared to flee from home if his father forces him to it.

Girlfriend, this is where it gets interesting—I think he has ideas of fleeing with me, if it comes to that. He wants us to elope or something. Apparently I don't have much of a say in all of this. I'm just expected to live a vagabond's life to help him study journalism, and flee his religion. Mind you, before I know it, I'll be washing his underwear and hanging baby nappies, doek on my head and all, apron over my skirt with pegs on the pocket and resentment growing in my heart like sisi Mandisa who fed rat poison to her taxi-driving philandering husband. Yhuu! Hayi sana andicingi mna! I wanna go to medical school mna. Besides, we are not even an item. I don't know where he gets these silly ideas. He thinks because I'm now an orphan I'm desperate for whatever. As if!

He says his father is inviting me to attend their congregation. And I'm like: Ndi ngum Roma mana sana. I don't want to be rude to him or his father, but I'm like, dude, I really don't wanna go to the church you anyway also don't wanna attend, and be happy-clapping all the time. It's too noisy for me, and OTT in a big way, with all that foot-stamping and speaking loudly in tongues like drunk demons. Yhoo! Hayi, hayi sana! My head is not ready for that. I'm not in the mood for their born-again drivel about the loving God who is supposed to take away our sorrows from the cross. We're already on the cross here, is that not enough? Must we invent more ways to torture our lives with superstitious religion?

I told Hlumelo I've never seen God take away anybody's sorrows. He felt embarrassed for me and said: "You could go to hell with that sort of talk." Apparently he still thinks I care.

"So what if I do?" I ask. Such things lost their power to frighten me the moment I heard you were dead and hell came to dwell within me here and now. And then he feels more embarrassed for me because I speak like a devil: I WILL NOT SERVE! We then both keep quiet because we don't wanna hurt each other's feelings by talking about God from different perspectives.

I don't know why people don't want to admit that we're already under the harrow here; there's no need to invent stupid things like hell. God's love does not spare us the pain, so what do we gain by these happy-clappy empty tricks?

I like it, though, when Hlumelo comes, even if just to have someone I can be irritated by instead of this constant loop of sadness. I just wish sometimes he'd stop talking and just be here. To me the need to talk gets less and less with every passing day. I find what we have to say is drivel most of the time and I wish we would all just keep quiet.

This afternoon Hlumelo left his pocket money, R20, on the coffee table without telling me. He must think I don't have enough money for food or something. Aunt Zenzile stocked the fridge to last me at least a year. It's full. I can't even find the water bottle in the midst of all the things she put in there. I don't have an appetite for food in any case. Something is even starting to smell in that fridge but I could not be bothered to look for what it might be and throw it out.

Sometimes Hlumelo admits that he does not really like the God of his father, but what he does not understand is the fact that I think God is bad. "What would be the point of being bad if you were God?" he asks. "I mean, you have all that power to do whatever you like, and you decide to do bad? It doesn't make sense."

"What if you were a bad God?" I ask him.

"How can you be a bad God? If you are bad, you can't be God. That's the whole point. Being bad means being against the nature of good, which is God. Why would you create the nature of good and then decide to be against it? It does not make sense!"

Fair enough, he has silenced me, for now at least. But he has not silenced my soul ache. I feel death is going to come again, like it has forgotten something I need. It wants to take away everything. I feel it's not gonna come for me but for something I need, to keep gnawing away all the things I like, piece by piece, until I evaporate from pain. I looked at myself in the mirror this morning. I think I am disappearing piece by piece, and the biggest chunk went away with you. I feel damaged. And I don't know how to live with the damage that is myself.

JUST IMAGINE

You close your laptop. Reading your old letters to your mother again brings back painful memories. You were so lost back then; darkness was closing in on you. Time is slowly thawing the memory of the events surrounding her death but you're still reluctant to visit that compartment of your soul. You just steal a peek now and then. On this quiet evening in your staff cottage, you allow the memories to come.

You and your mother lived a typical township life. She worked at the Mlungisi Community Health Center. One day she went to Port Elizabeth for a choir competition. A few days later you received a late phone call telling you their bus tipped over a craggy cliff on the Winterberg Pass, iNtaba ze Nkonkobe. Soon after, you learned that she was among the five dead. Then your life was turned upside down.

The only thing you could think of initially was how she used to remind you when the two of you drove through the pass toward the Katberg Valley that these were the mountains that amaNgqika, under the leadership of Maqoma, used to launch their guerrilla wars against the British. Sometimes during this account, she would add that your father, Phaks, was doing similar things against the Afrikaner government by going into exile, staging guerrilla wars in Mozambique, Namibia, Angola and other places. It all seemed like something that had happened very far away, like intsomi, a fairy tale that has no end. All you took from it was that your father's life, like that of your forefathers before, was swallowed up in those craggy mountains. And then the mountains swallowed your mother also.

You remember the day she left, looking pretty as always with her high plum cheeks, broad dark lips, zentshongo, of soot, as she used to call them, and doe eyes, calm as shiny stars flickering with a sense of impermanence. Your mother waye yinzwakazi elubhelu. Whenever she was going somewhere, she sat at her dressing table and allowed you to doll her up in traditional Xhosa ways. And when you'd finished, she'd ask for the darkest lipstick, saying, "Ndiphe apho entshongweni." Give me a little of the soot, the sticky tobacco juice from the smoke pipe that Xhosa women have, for ages, used as lipstick. Hence, among skin colors, the jersey-cow skin color, amanz' andonga, beige, was regarded as the most beautiful. That is why KhoiSan wives were the choice of Xhosa aristocracy and royalty, for their apricot skin color. The Xhosa call the jersey-cow color "bhelu" and a beautiful woman is referred to as "inzwakazi elubhelu"—the jersey-colored beauty. You wonder if the more recent obsession with "yellow bones" has its roots in this.

That morning when the choir came to pick her up, just before she left, she tried to say something but her friends and colleagues were waving her onto the bus, joking that she'd never leave you alone were it up to her. As you came out of the bathroom, toothbrush and -paste all over your mouth, she kissed you goodbye on the cheek and forehead—the handle kiss. Then she turned to say something but all you could hear was the last part: "Just imagine…"

Today you still don't like the taste of toothpaste in your mouth, nor the phrase "Just imagine…"

At the mortuary, her cheeks were sunken, her cheekbones prominent, forehead slightly deformed. Her face showed no expression of pain or horror. They said her skull was fractured, that's why her facial features looked distorted. Her hue was darker than normal, grayish, with a blue tint on the lips. A tightness in your throat choked you when they pushed her back into the fridge. You could've cried, you should've cried, but, as Phaks says, some pain is beyond the expression of grief. You were numb.

Poets have the ability to express the inexpressible, which, you guess, is why, according to Shelley, they're our "unacknowledged legislators." If poetry, as Phaks says, is the art of being present at the frisson points of life, then it is no wonder poets are also called emotional historians.

You're no poet. The frisson points of your life stun you. You do your best to shun away from them. But sometimes you feel the weight of emotion, the brick and mortar by which poets build their shrines, take uncontrollable possession of you. During those moments—Phaks called them "Emergent Moments"—you feel your experiences, in an existentialist manner, matter also. That the pain wants to move you past the ubiquitous, fucked-up fakery of your imagined life into a more authentic one. To trust in your own feelings and thoughts about how you see the world, though choked, especially because you're choked by the experience of your mother's death and the particulars of the day of her funeral.

You remember the black hearse rolling slowly, the crushing sound of crunching pebbles under its tires. Sometimes that sound haunts you in your sleep. You remember the metal clunk against the cobblestones in the churchyard; the way the sun slanted hesitantly, as if about to heed your command to hurtle down to earth in fiery speed, because everything was spoiled now. Cracked. Leonard Cohen, taught by Buddhists, says that is how the light gets in. *Just imagine*, you heard her last words reverberate. With the hallucinatory intensity that makes stones bleed you surveyed that day; with the blood sweat of a Gethsemane: the sun, our gilded guillotine; the silencing, if not comforting, charity and the grammar of love from relatives and friends; the rustling of leaves on that autumnal day in the winter of your life; the mountains spangling with lion's mane grass, upright against the vindictive glee of death. *Just imagine*. The limits of words when the soul is involved with eternal silence.

That day is permanently stored in your heart as an icon of how, in a second, things can change, utterly. You'll forever be imagining it. For ever imagine how every soul that has loved must keep the door ajar for pain. How, like Noah, in sunshine we must also prepare for rain. How when we hope, we fear—for death, like a rat, is the only permanent tenant in this house of dust.

THE BOY
24/05/99

"Tell me about your life in Sawusafrica, Beast; you have not done that in ages," Efuoa said this morning as she put down a tray with two cups of tea and scones she'd baked on the small bed-side table. The bed sank and moaned to welcome her weight. This is her trick when she sees I'm exhausted, or agitated. She wants to take my mind off things. The virus feeds and thrives on my exhaustion. It has gotten to a stage where I can't sit up on my own without support. I like my tea black and smoky, from Russia or China preferably, but these days she forces me to take a little milk with it, to introduce dairy in my diet.

"Tell us about your paper wife and your young daughter." I like the "us" in that, as if she knows I need to hear it too, to re-mind myself that I have a daughter. Efuoa is very intelligent. The "paper wife," as she calls her, is my supposed wife back in South Africa. She calls her that because I said I married her in a white man's court of law, where they give you a paper to say you're married. I was lying of course, though I wished I had married her before leaving South Africa.

What I remember most about her, my paper wife—although I did not express this to Efuoa this morning—are her calves. I know this sounds shallow and lusty, but the psyche gets fixed on its own fixes and overwhelming impressions. Her nubile legs are what I first fell in love with—before I was charmed by the gifts of her mind when she opened her mouth—how the hem of her skirt fell just below her knees to reveal the perfection of her legs and the petit tenderness of her sandaled feet. She had a beautiful structure overall, boyish but voluptuous where her breasts cupped. Her complexion amaXhosa would term "manz'andonga," which describes the water that gushes on the donga when it rains, coffee-with-milk color. She could easily have become a model.

When I hesitated in responding, Efuoa searched my wallet for the photograph of my daughter, leaving me to think of something to say. She calls her "our daughter," which is the true African way of course, but coming from Efuoa you get the sense that she means it most sincerely. My paper wife managed to smuggle the photo through a comrade who gave it to me in Leningrad as we walked along Moyka Canal. This comrade eventually became high up in the post-94 South African government. She phoned me once, trying to convince me to come and serve "in our government." She, too, is now dead, from cirrhosis due to alcohol abuse—we die piecemeal from bad habits we acquired along the way. What were we to do to ward off the cold but drink vodka? Then again, vodka is useless against the inner cold. My daughter's photograph, taken on her sixth birthday, brought me inner warmth that lasted the whole of those years in the Soviet fridge.

It is told that when my mother heard I had skipped the country, she was concerned at how I was going to travel. "He gets motion sickness when he travels long distance, you know!" she kept admonishing people. She died of renal complications when I was in Lusaka. I couldn't attend her funeral, nor have I ever seen her grave.

This morning, as Efuoa fiddled with my wallet, it was a different photo that caught my attention—that of my younger brother mending his bike. I took it and recalled the circumstances in which it was taken. I could see the boy I was at thirteen, waking up on the top bunk of the double-decker metal bed we shared in our boys' room.

As I watch with the eye of my mind, the boy is waking up with excitement.

It is Saturday; the new movie of Bruce Lee, *Enter the Dragon*, is playing for the first time at the communal hall bioscope this afternoon. The boy's heart is beating faster than usual in anticipation of going to watch it. He goes outside to meet the newly minted sun, connects the hosepipe to water his mother's garden: *Watering of the garden must be done in the evening or early morning to avoid the water evaporating from the heat of the sun*— it's written in his Agricultural Science textbook. The boy sprays water over the seedbeds of carrots his mother planted the previous weekend. He had to go to the bush to collect thorn shrubs to put on top of the bed, to prevent stray dogs from urinating and stepping there, or birds from eating the seeds. As they were planting, the boy had to admonish his mother *not to plant the same plant in the same soil again and again*, as stated in his textbook.

Now he's mulling over the parable of the sower and four soils he heard at church. *A sower went out to sow his seed: and as he sowed, some fell by the wayside; and it was trodden down, and the fowls of the air devoured it. And some fell upon a rock; and as soon as it was sprung up, it withered away, because it lacked moisture. And some fell among thorns; and the thorns sprang up with it, and choked it. And other fell on good ground, and sprang up, and bore fruit an hundredfold. And when he had said these things, he cried, He that hath ears to hear, let him hear.* The boy had taken literally the part about Jesus crying and added it to his mind's collection of the other instances he did. He noticed that Jesus cried almost always when people refused to take notice or understand what he was saying, like when he looked over Jerusalem and lamented his intentions of wanting to gather the people like a hen its chicks under its wings, but the chicks kept running off and falling victim to birds of prey. He knew from experience what happens when chicks wander too far from their mother.

The morning is glorious, but of course the boy has no conceptual grasp of that, to him it's just one of those mornings that smell of "freshness" of the earth, of life. The boy goes inside to check if his baby sister is still asleep. He finds her awake, sitting on top of the bed. The baby is seven months old, sweet as a baby can be. The boy thinks he has finally found a way out of his boarding school dilemma. "Who'll look after the children when I'm at boarding school?" he'll ask his mother when she comes back from her night duties at the local hospital. The baby never gives any troubles anyway, except when she's hungry. He always keeps a ready-made warm milk bottle next to the bed—not drinking cold milk is the only fuss the baby has. The boy can live with that.

He takes the baby to the kitchen where he starts firing the primus stove to boil water for her bottle. When the water cools down, he'll pour it in the baby's bottle with two spoons of glucose and three drops of gripe water. His brother, five years younger than him, comes in rubbing his eyes, stretching his body as he walks from the bedroom to the kitchen. He goes out to the stoep where he jumps over the tricycle of their still-sleeping younger sister, almost two years older than the baby. The boy is annoyed that they left the tricycle outside the whole night; he feels lucky his mother didn't see that.

His brother comes in again, passing through the kitchen to the toilet, where he discharges jet-like urine that's accompanied by an uproarious fart. He pulls the chain to flush and drives through the kitchen on his bike, which he has just taken out of the bathroom. They've recently moved into this newly built township which, though less than fourteen kilometers from the town of Queenstown, falls under the Bantustan of Transkei. The apartheid law of separate development requires black people only for their labor, the Bantustans must take care of their settlement needs. It is the first time they see houses with plumbing for black people so living here is more salubrious and hygienic than their previous township of Mlungisi, which had no reticulation.

"Don't drive that thing inside the house. And I know you're not thinking about going to the street at this early hour." The boy's firm voice has limited effect, since he is hardly thirteen and his eight-year-old brother is in a rebellious stage.

"I just want to oil the chain. I'm not going anywhere," his brother cheekily answers. The boy takes the boiling water from the primus stove and puts on a pot of milk to warm for their cereal. They use the UTH processed milk because they have no electricity, thus no fridge to store fresh milk. The township streets are electrified but not the houses. Soon his house is going to be the first to have domestic electricity because his nurse mother, when she went to Cecilia Makiwane Hospital for Public Health training, had seen it done in the bigger township of Mdantsane in East London, about two hundred kilometers from their town. Her friend in Mdantsane introduced her to the black electrician who cubed her house. The electrician will come the following month and has promised the boy's mother a broker fee of R50 for every new client she brings in. So, the electricians will camp at their township and the boy's mother will make back the R300 she paid the electrician to cube her house.

With the baby still on his arm, the boy goes out to move the hosepipe. They get a little shower from the sprinkle. The baby loves it, chuckling at the spray. The boy is annoyed with himself for muddying his newly washed white All Stars. He'll have to steal more chalk at school now to keep his footwear white as snow. He'll wash the All Stars and rub them with the chalk while they're still wet, then scrub the chalk with a brush until they're spick and span. By the time he comes back, the milk is overflowing, spilling all over the stove.

"Shit, shit!" The boy tries to maneuver the pot off the primus stove with the hand that is not holding the baby, taking care not to burn himself and her in the process. His other sister, nearly two, giggles because the boy is swearing. Half the milk is spilt over the stove. The sulphuric smell of burned milk is intolerable. He opens the windows so the smell will be gone by the time his mother returns from night duty. He pours three bowls of cornflakes, adds warm and cold milk, calls his brother, and makes him say grace before giving him his bowl. He goes out to move the hose again. He discovers that the hose has drenched the carrot beds and gets worried the water will drown the germinating seeds. Taking care this time to take off his All Stars and put on his old North Stars he keeps in the garden shed, he wades in, ntambanana style. This sends the baby on his arm rollocking with laughter as though she is not sure why they are now tap-dancing like a secretary bird on its wade into the garden. "Don't laugh, little girl, when you gonna be the first one to fall when my ntambanana walk fails and I trip," he teases her, rubbing together their noses for her to understand he is addressing her. She seems disappointed when there are no more invigorating showers from the hose.

The boy's brother, back to fixing his bicycle, is winding its pedals while slowly dripping in the oil on the chain. He asks without lifting his head: "What's intambanana?"

The boy is slightly irritated with him but his teacher instincts kick in. "Is a secretary bird, and the traditional bird of amaXhosa. It wades the swamps, fishing for frogs and prawns. It tap-dances like that when it kills snakes for food."

The morning grinds on with the sun starting to shoot more of its hosts. He knows his mother will give him hell for allowing his brother to sit on the red polished stoep in his clean pajamas. She'll be annoyed with him, but the boy does not have the heart to tell the cheeky bastard off.

Inside the house he takes the Polaroid camera off the shelf and the new film his mother brought with it. He sits down on the kitchen stool to feed the baby, but first he loads the film. When the baby finishes her bottle the boy raises her to his shoulder, rubs her back to help her burp. His mother told him it prevents the baby from being gassy, thus cranky, telling him that "eructation" was the medical term for it. The boy filed the term in his memory.

After she burps, he takes her outside and aims the camera at his brother, who is still testing the chain strength of his bicycle. He clicks. Within no time the picture comes out. Fascinating! This is the boy's first experience of a same-time camera. The camera's manual says one must wait for about three minutes before peeling off the print to reveal the picture. Three minutes proves intolerably long for the boy, so after about two and a half, his conscience pricking him, he peels the picture to see the first image of his brother slowly developing before his eyes. Fantastic! His brother is fascinated with the image but unable to appreciate the miracle of same-time photos, since he is not even aware that pictures usually take more time to develop in the darkroom. This lack of appreciation frustrates the boy. He decides to look for someone more mature who can understand the concept. The rather dull neighbor coeval is the only person in immediate range, but he decides, after some deliberation, that he will do, recalling something about desperate times requiring desperate measures. He wonders if Shakespeare said it.

He has just discovered Shakespeare because he won his *Complete Works* on a debate question about ravens and so was digging deep into the plays. He found the Old English frustrating until he learned the trick of reading it with intuitive logic. He recently read *Julius Caesar* because when his older brother came home for the holidays from boarding school he had gone on and on about *cowards dying many times before their deaths*, and pretentiously reciting from the bedstand: "Friends, Romans, countrymen," which the boy, who was made into a reluctant audience, found showy and tiring. Worse still, he refused to let the boy touch his setwork books with the lousy excuse that he was gonna ruin their covers. Meanwhile, everyone knows how much the boy likes books, treating them better than toys. If anything, his brother was the one who shouldn't be allowed to own a book because of his barbaric tendency of leaving them strewn everywhere. Once the boy thought it opportune to quickly read one of the books when his brother was out playing tennis, but he couldn't bring himself to do it because he had given his word that he wouldn't touch the stupid books.

Now that he had not just one but all the plays of Shakespeare, he couldn't wait to rub his brother's nose in it. Although initially he felt the language of the plays to be rubbish, he quickly discovered that if he didn't overthink it, and allowed the reading to enter his mind almost subconsciously, he understood well the meaning of the quaint English. He felt inspired to finish the plays before his brother came back at the end of the year. The obvious complexity of the stories challenged his comprehension, which was still on the level of *Treasure Island*.

"Mzuki!" he calls out to his neighbor across the fence. "Come and see this. You'll not believe it. See this picture? I've just taken it."

"What do you mean you've just taken it?"

Try as he might to explain, the asinine Mzuki, although a year older than the boy, just does not get it. The only way to make him understand would be to take another picture in front of his dull eyes, the boy decides. But he was given strict orders by his mother not to waste the expensive film. And the boy does not want a picture of Mzuki in his family album anyway. It would be silly to take another picture of his brother with his bike. Mzuki could take one of him and the baby, but the boy does not want Mzuki's dirty hands touching his family's new camera either. The boy solves his dilemma by deciding to take a picture of the family dog, Lion. He aims, and click!

"Where's the picture?" Mzuki asks anxiously, almost immediately, irritating the hell out of the boy.

"We have to wait a few minutes before retrieving it." They wait a moment, then Mzuki presses again. No wonder they call him Lui Letta, from an Afrikaans poem none of them like but were made to learn in class: he's just as lazy and crazy, the boy thinks.

"Where're the pictures? You're a liar! You said they'd come immediately."

"Oh fuck it!" The boy, in extreme irritation, no longer feels the whole demonstration is worth this flaying of his nerves. This time he wanted to wait the whole three minutes, but what can one do when surrounded by doubting Thomases? So he peels the picture, this time before even two minutes have passed.

"Let me see, let me see. You're a liar!" Mzuki continues shouting, and the boy has a good mind not to let him see the picture at all. If it were only about impressing Mzuki, he'd leave without a second thought. But the boy has a reputation to maintain with the township coevals. He knows if he leaves before showing the photo the fool will scatter all sorts of stories around the township that the boy lies about making same-time pictures.

Lion's image slowly emerges into view on the photograph. It blows Mzuki's mind. Somehow seeing Mzuki's stupid, flabbergasted face doesn't give the boy the satisfaction he hoped for. Mzuki wants to take another picture, himself, to brag about on the street. Fat chance! The boy collects the picture, the camera, and his baby sister and walks back home. Mzuki follows him, begging, but the boy is not moved: *I'm constant as the northern star*, the boy thinks, recalling *Julius Caesar*. Mzuki gives him a confused look. The boy cusses in disdain as he walks away, feeling a little guilty with every step but he recalls Cassius' warnings to Brutus: *The problem, dear Brutus, is not in our stars, but in us that we're underlining*...or something like that. He turns back to face Mzuki and says: "I refuse to be an underlining!" When he notices this confounds Mzuki even more, the boy waves his hand and leaves.

The boy is not even sure what an "underlining" is and so later on asks his mother, who tells him to bring his Shakespeare book to look up the quote properly. She then admonishes him to never use quotes carelessly. "Either you give a proper quote or you don't quote someone. That causes confusion." As it turns out, the proper quote says: *The fault, dear Brutus, is not in our stars / But in ourselves, that we are underlings.* And he learned that "underlings" were lackeys. At least he used the meaning in the right way since he somehow meant to say he was no lackey.

His brother liked to make the boy join in acting out school-book plays, only to be annoyed when the boy asked legitimate questions, like whether Julius Caesar wore North Stars like his or not. And if that was the reason he was "constant as the northern star" because the bloody shoe is very strong.

An unforeseen consequence of his brother's acting classes was that by the time the boy got to reading the books in his own class, he knew them well, which got him into all sorts of complications with teachers with low self-esteem. People in his class started calling him Shakespeare. But some teachers didn't like smart alecs, so they were easily offended by the boy's showy erudition and anticipation of scenes. They avoided calling his name during question time. And the boy learned quickly to keep his mouth shut unless spoken to.

His brother always assigned the juicy characters, like Julius Caesar and Mark Antony, to himself when they were acting the plays, which also took the fun out of memorizing sayings of the plays. His brother assigned the boy the silly roles, like that of a soothsayer standing on the side of the road, shouting stupid things in a strange voice and dressed in strange attire: "Yea! Caesar but not gone!" when his brother, the Caesar shouted, "The eyes (ides) of March have come." Nyea Caesar! Nyea Caesar! But not gone, my foot, the boy thought. He'd disrupt the play-acting when fed up, which earned him a ban from being a soothsayer, gravedigger, and the rest of the menial roles assigned to him.

To rub salt in the wound, his brother would give the role to Mzuki, knowing very well how this would piss off the boy. All of a sudden, when they were playing marbles, Mzuki would be murmuring: "Lomans! Country men? Lend me your ears..." with a lisping tongue. The boy never forgave his brother for this treason, allocating the role of Mark Antony to Mzuki when he had refused it to him. Blood out! The boy decided to boycott his brother's acting sessions and all that shit talk about months having eyes and walking forests. He started playing house with the girls, where he was treated with the respect he deserved by being made the head of the house.

The boy's mother arrived late morning, tired from work and from having to wait for the Natal Building Society bank to open to withdraw some money because it was month-end. Although tiring, she didn't mind the night duty because it paid more and meant she could also look after her kids in between her naps during the day. She listened patiently to the boy's rendering of the happenings of the previous night and that morning after taking off her white uniform and navy cape, which the boy had to carefully hang so it didn't crease. The white nurse's cap gave his mother the most trouble until the boy let her in on his secret of washing his All Stars with chalk. The boy became a hero in his mother's eyes, and those of other nurses at the hospital, because everybody adopted the trick.

The boy, the mother, and the baby go outside to see how the garden is coming along. Having satisfied herself on that score, his mother warms more water to wash the baby and makes a list of groceries for the boy to go buy in town.

Taking a look at my brother's photo in Efuoa's hand was very difficult. He looks distracted, almost withdrawn. There's a certain struggle in his eyes I never noticed before. In the recesses of my soul I can still smell the engine oil he used to lubricate his bike. There was a time when thinking about him made me very angry. The apartheid security forces detained him without trial for over six months after I skipped the country. I'm told that when

they released him he was never himself again, always murmuring unintelligible things. I'm told he liked the sound of buses,
and knew them by the revs of their engines. They say he always
wanted to hug them, to go somewhere. (He had been detained
in a deserted area with only the occasional rumblings of passing
buses, transporting township denizens to town; it was the only
connection the detainees had with the outside world.) When,
later, he liked riding in buses, they say he would ask the passengers if they were going to see me in Lusaka. And he was eventually hit by a bus and died while trying to hug it. I don't even
know where he's buried; I have never visited his grave.

I cannot go home.

What is there for me? Everyone I know is either dead or scattered around the world with their own lives; my sisters and other
brother are also in the diaspora. Coming home means having to
face up to the ruins of our family. Who cares for that? The reality
of our lives, growing up, wounded us enough.

I also don't want to be part of what is happening in my country—a glorification of empty freedom. Perhaps there never were
any real solutions, but I'll not collaborate in the perpetual serf-
dom of my people by holding empty political crowns. I've now
lived long enough to realize that it is possible for a man to be out
of step with his era and the collective psyche of his own country.
At this stage even death comes almost as a relief, as though I
willed it on myself. The face of the oppressor in my country is
also gradually becoming our own, the men I stood in the trench-
es with. This is what hurts me the most, the pigs growing human
faces, in Orwellian language. The greatest illusion that has been
pulled over the eyes of our people has been the Mandela myth of
reconciliation without justice. It is a grand illusion that relegates
all demands of justice to the periphery to serve the greed of our
born-again oppressors to perpetuate the monster of apartheid
under new guises. The pseudo masters are now mostly black
and parasites of white capital. They exchanged the strife of our

humanitarian struggle to achieve justice and an egalitarian society for dining on the crumbs of individual greed. Is this what they meant about the revolution devouring its young? Fire next time. *How I wish it were already blazing.* Perhaps Jerusalem cannot be redeemed?

Let me go to the peace of my grave with my integrity, in chilly remoteness and stunned resignation, perhaps. But it is what is mine, what I know, sitting in a corner in a state of stasis, courting imperviousness, and surprised by the kind love of a simple woman who entered my life as a maid and ended up its queen.

GONE NOW

Hi Mom

So my plan with Hlumelo—unfortunately, Veli has decided not to sit for exams—is to finish two Study Aids per subject, and answer three past question papers (timing ourselves) every week. We will go according to the exam timetable, starting with the subject we are writing first and so forth. That's how we think we shall be able to cope with these exams.

Last Friday was our matric dance. A group of us went wearing jeans with pajama tops or painted T-shirts with slogans like: 1. Fashion Is a Creature of Mediocrity. 2. Black Man Mandate. 3. Define Your Own Freedom. 4. Be Free Enough to Question Everything. 5. Biko Didn't Die for This T-shit. 6. Black Like Biko. 7. Absurdity Reigns OK. 8. Stop Glamorizing Mediocrity. 9. Black by White Imitation Is Powerless. 10. Lift up the Spear of Maqoma. Naturally, we took away all the unhealthy attention from the boring, expensive gowns designed to bankrupt our poor parents, to the extreme irritation of the fashionistas, I must add. It nearly caused a riot between us and them. They had the teachers' backing, which we didn't care about. Most of the T-shirt slogans were written by Hlumelo, but the ones about glamorizing mediocrity and Maqoma's spear were mine. I felt proud of them. Hlumelo and my friend Phanye wore them. I wore his about Biko not dying for this shit. I'm afraid we made a nuisance of ourselves, and some of our teachers thought we were rather too big for our boots.

We call ourselves the Magnificent Black Ten now, and have meetings in the house, where we talk about all sorts of things but mostly BC (Black Consciousness), with Biko's I Write What I Like *as our Bible. (Hlumelo stole it from his brother's shelf.) We quote and discuss books we're reading. We take pride in planning to have the top ten best marks in our school in the matric results of this year. What we have in common, besides the love of books, is believing in ourselves as the instruments of our own development, as Biko teaches...*

But the days are now on the run since we started exams. I don't have time for anything except my schoolbooks. Sometimes I go to bed so late that I fall asleep within thirty seconds of lying down. And then, though tired, I can feel myself thinking in my sleep, looking for solutions and answers to problems I encountered earlier. I thought your brain was supposed to rest when you sleep...

I saw Veli today at the bus stop, she looks totally oxidated. She has the tired face of a middle-aged woman and a look of sorrow in her eye. I could not help exclaiming, "Girlfriend, you look like lamb dressed as mutton!" This might have been a little cruel, but I was shocked at how much she had aged. I felt so bad for not seeing her in more than two months. I didn't know how to leave her and ended up accompanying her to the clinic.

She has ballooned and told me that the previous night she peed herself. "The baby has taken over my body, and I've no control over my bladder." She looked totally, totally not cool at all. Looking closer at her I saw again that glint of desperation in her eyes, darkened by disappointment; but this time it had something behind it. I think she has given up on her life. This makes me angry. I don't know why she acts as if falling pregnant is the end of her life. She's young, and can still pick herself up next year if she gets proper support. Somehow, as I looked at her, I knew she'd never go back to school again. Don't ask me how, I just know. She has a sense of a darkening sky all over her. I felt she was going into the storm while I was moving away from it.

The sad part is I don't know how to be her best friend anymore, what to say and how to help her. I feel she's embarrassed hanging around me, and is pushing me away every opportunity she gets. Her life now, after she delivers that baby, will be about going to work in the factories: waking up at 4.30am every day to get to a seven-to-five job that pays R7 an hour. And then we will lose our friendship forever, because she will no longer be interested in being friends with anyone who doesn't work, or walk those wintry mornings to the factories with her, someone who does not know what it means to leave your house at dawn and come back at dusk. She's gonna be one of those people you told me about who do not know what their township looks like at noon during weekdays until she is told she's no longer of use to anyone for work in the factories.

There'll never again be those careless afternoons when we laughed until our ribs hurt; when we rolled on the lawn until our bodies itched; when we ran from stealing peaches at Madlomo's house while she in turn aimed curses at us as we disappeared around the corner; when we walked so close together we breathed each other's breath; when we carried the wax candles and brown bread you sent us to buy kwaJohnson, chewing imixangxatho we bought with the change. All that is gone now! Gone with this year you died in that bus accident, this year she allowed that boy to get his rocks off inside her because she wanted to be popular with him.

As for me, shem, even if it kills me, I am gonna make something of my life. I am shooting for the moon. The devil can take the hindmost.

AMAMFENGU
01/06/99

According to the Xhosa calendar the first day of the year is in June, the month yesiLimela, the Pleiades, the seven daughters of Atlas according to the ancient Greeks, and the constellation of the south according to Job. Ever since I told Efuoa this, whenever she now goes to the vegetable garden she says she is going to lima. The word "lima," where Limela comes from, means to dig or plow. The Pleiades were known to amaXhosa as the Digging Stars. Their appearance signaled the need to start digging and hoeing the ground. By tradition Xhosa men also count their manhood from the ceremony of circumcision by isiLimela, by the number of June months that have passed ever since. So, this is the season of digging.

I was sixteen when I went to the mountain, fresh from writing my matric exams. I saw from afar, down the street, that smoke was coming out of my house's hearth. It signified the proverbial hive house where the bees enter, meaning there was a ceremony. I just assumed my mother had forgotten to write to me about it. Imagine my surprise when the women started ululating as I entered the yard: "Heeli, heeli, lililiiiii! Halala! Halala!" It turned out, as they say: Into ingam. The celebrations were for me.

How the years have galloped on the steed ever since.

These days people tend to confuse issues by forgetting that circumcision is but a minor part of this rite of passage. It is also the time when you are supposed to learn about your roots and traditions, ukuba uzalwa ngobani, what has given birth to you, as they say in isiXhosa. I started learning there that I come from a line of resilient people, the breed that fled Mfecane wars from the banks of the Thukela in the late parts of the eighteenth and early parts of the nineteenth century, to reach Xhosaland, the eastern parts of the Cape, broken and emaciated. That we were referred to as amaMfengu, the blighted wanderers. That our family was part of the group that settled on the mountain belts and green valleys the British colonial government called Glen Gray, the land given to them by the queen of abaThembu, Nonesi. That abaThembu, Mandela's tribe, knew the area as Komani, after the river that bisects the land. That in their usual effrontery the British established a farming town there when they realized it was alluvial land with a successive chain of dams and springs from the surrounding mountains. That they called the town Queenstown, after the royal Thembu queen, Nonesi, whose people, the so-called Emigrant Tambookies and mine, the Fingoes, were to act as buffers for white people against the irascible Gcalekas, under Sarhili, who were still resentful due to the loss of their land in the War of Ngcayecibi. That my people lived rustic self-sufficient lives after the ruse that saw them co-operating with white people to rob amaGcaleka of their cattle and land. That as blighted wanderers they subjected themselves to be indentured slaves of the Brits, which was a life better in degrees to the so-called dog-like existence they led as servants of amaGcaleka. That they were sensible enough not to participate in the Xhosa national suicide during the later part of the nineteenth century that was fostered by Nonqqawuse's mystical visions of delusion. That they emerged from that tragedy to be the first black land owners and sometimes employers of now emaciated Gcalekas. That they became the new black aristocrats of the region. That they were also the first to acquire Western education. That they exchanged roles with amaGcaleka and amaRharhabe who by then were a spent force from losing their cattle and land to the white settlers in a series of wars, termed

Frontier Wars, that took over a hundred years to end. That this earned amaMfengu the ire of the black nations. That in the end the colonial masters took the land from amaMfengu too by introducing laws that prohibited land ownership by black people, laws which eventually formed the foundations of the apartheid system. That this reduced amaMfengu also to overnight vassals and landless beggars, again, sending them, as their forefathers before, to seek work on white farms and as general menial workers in the established towns of Cape Town, Port Elizabeth, East London, Kimberley, and Johannesburg. That because they had begun concentrating on the might of the pen over the sword they also took up the political fight through writing, and were at the forefront of organizing the native congresses for the betterment of socioeconomic conditions for all black people, which eventually became known as the African National Congress.

My great-grandfathers and grandfathers worked at the docks of Cape Town harbor, offloading cargo from ships; they drove wagons in the streets of Wynberg and Rondebosch, and lived in the dock slums of what is now the Foreshore before they were moved to Ndabeni during the breakout of the bubonic plague. And then the apartheid regime forcefully removed and dumped them on the outskirts of the city to form the current Langa township. This cycle of internal migration in our family was broken by my father, a formally trained agriculturalist and medical nurse, who was among the first people to get any real education in our village. His work meant he had to spend most of his time living a township life, where he met my mother. I spent the first decade of my life in my father's rural home but didn't visit it much after they split up, except for mandatory traditional ceremonies. The last time we visited, after a long absence, I must have been fourteen or fifteen. Grandpa greeted us with his usual animated emotions.

"Awu, children of my child," he said, his eyes straining with tenderness, "is it time for me to join my ancestors that you should visit after all these years?" Grandpa had a clean style of speech, and a keen sense of phrase I admired. He could turn and lift his words in rhythmic ways appropriated to imibongo. "Abantwana bomtwana wam! Abedluli. Ndlovu ezidla ekhaya ngokuswela umalusi; abamfenguzi. Children of my child! Sojourners. Elephants that graze around the house because they've no shepherd. My children the wanderers." There was always a living force in his words that now acts as inspiration in my own storytelling attempts. He taught me how to identify the transcendental in the ordinary; to live with a variety of experiences and adventures in a multiplicity of situations. He was a well-read bus driver, chef, and hotel porter in Cape Town, before moving back to his rural home to farm in his old age. I'm told that my looks and most of my character traits I take from him, including a melancholic disposition. His moral seriousness fostered a religious and artistic temperament. He liked telling stories against the kraal stone wall as an oral poet of lyrical majesty in close touch with the past. He reveled in history and the telling thereof. In other words, a typical Mfengu. Nations who've undergone deep atrocities, like my people, the Jews also, tend to do that; in the telling they invoke their tragic past to edify the present. They have an Aesopian, aphoristic storytelling quality.

On another day, we were met at the front door by Grandpa's mudcaked shoes laid against the wall to dry. There was a caked hoe next to them, leaning on the wall. After perfunctory greetings, our mother explained to Grandpa that we were not there for a social visit. She needed to leave us with him for a few days as she was going for training in Port Elizabeth. When my mother left I joined Grandpa, who was seated under the towering gum tree in deep discussion with his cousin, while my younger siblings made a nuisance of themselves inside the shop where our grandma, his third wife, having outlived two, spoiled them with sweets. Sitting on piled rocks we listened to his cousin, who suspected Grandpa of becoming soft toward something I had not understood yet. The cousin was squatting on his haunches, one hand on his mouth, choking with stranded thoughts as he listened to my grandpa explain his point of view. In his other hand was a worn lime-green chamois hat which he used to occasionally flog flies away. Grandpa's cousin had a habit of coming to confirm political news or rumors with him because "You've seen the blinding lights of big cities, Mnyamezeli..." The cousin coughed like a sangoma's bag as he sat listening patiently, splattering expectorated dark phlegm with blood tints. Around him, dry phlegm shone like snail trails. He used his handkerchief to wipe the brow of his crevassed face because he had a tendency of sweating profusely when he spoke. Compared to him, Grandpa looked like a young man, although he was eight years older.

"Even during my prime, in Cape Town, I didn't eat everything. I was particular. Cousin here, like a swine, mixes everything. Look at him now. Only last week I had to take him to hospital; the doctors warned him to stop smoking, but still..."

"True, mnyamezeli," his cousin interjected, grunting and mopping his pate. "When you worked in Cape Town you were a gentleman. But that does not give you the right to laugh at another man's wounds. Besides, you're evading my question. Nothing betrays weakness such as an attempt to deceive. You always tell us that you know the minds of learned people. Do not cut me off at my knees and call me Shorty. The government of white people has done many bad things to us, but this making us pay taxes for our dogs is the last straw that'll break this camel's back. The last time I asked you about taxes you said I shouldn't worry, because only working people are supposed to pay taxes. You tell me then, where does my dog work?" He proceeded to take out his tobacco pouch from his shepherd purse of A1 Horseshoe, dirty as a dog's liver, and began sorting it before continuing. "I'm now as old as these mountains, I've seen what white people are capable of, but I must say they've stooped too low this time. If I was still in the spring of my youth, I would take to the mountains and organize amabutho. Things are going too far with this learned bullshit of yours, now we must pay taxes for dogs."

As I now recall this I'm still amused by his show of passion on that issue. Of all the dreadful things the apartheid government was doing at the time, this was what infuriated him the most, because, perhaps, it touched him directly as a sign of ultimate insolence.

"Do not mind cousin here," said Grandpa, looking at me. "He's more headstrong than a billy goat."

His cousin lit his pipe, dragged on it with relish, coughed, and proceeded to take a swig from a huge draft of amarhewu that Grandpa had placed before him. Slurping through his thick lips, he regarded the hills with a vacant look before saying, "That's what you'd say." He burped with great enthusiasm to show his approval for the brew, and tried to take another pull from his pipe, but it had gone out, so he settled for dragging and swallowing his own spittle.

At length Grandpa stood up and said: "Come inside, cousin, and hear the kettle whistle. I have condensed milk for your sweet tooth." The elderly men took their sticks with them, and Grandpa made as if to challenge his cousin to a stick fight.

The cousin jumped up saying, "Rha! Myamezeli ngeze undifeze. You know you would not make the time."

"But I used to floor you every time when we were growing up."

"There were many things you floored me on, mnyamezeli, school being one of them. But never in stick fighting, you all drank under me when it came to that. Speak the truth and shame the devil."

Grandpa bent to whisper in my ear as we all walked to the house. "He's correct, he was the best in stick fighting and had no competition among us."

"I hope you're not feeding children lies," murmured his cousin as he followed us.

After tea we changed the venue by sitting on the west side, against the kraal, so as to get maximum heat from the sinking sun. I very much liked sitting with Grandpa against the stone kraal, listening to the stories he told, especially those about our land. He knew every field, every rock and every mountain in our region by its name. With him you felt the future would only blossom out of the past. This is how he recited praises for the princely Mt. Lukhanji on whose foot our village stands. It is a traditional recitation that goes back to the era of the War of Gcayichibi (1877–79), when the princes of abaThembu, Gungubele, and Mfanta defied their queen Nonesi by joining amaGceleka and amaRharhabe against the British colonial forces in that war. You'll find it in different praise-singing arrangements by imbongi, like DLP Yali-Manisi's poem, "Idabi Lasegwatyu." This is how my grandpa rendered it:

Ah! Mt. Lukhanji.
Tower of Ndaba's mountains.
How glad am I
to be standing
where your lengthening shade can reach.
Did you think
I'd forget you in my gallivanting?
Let the she-goat forget her kid,
a matriarch elephant forget the water spot,
before I do.
What is this I hear?
News is
you were unconcerned
the day the British usurped Phalo's land.
Are you so remote to human squabbles?
The fog of their passions touches not your feet

when Gungubele was at loggerheads
with those thugs
you warned Mfanta
not to leap into action.
You told him
there's no use resisting those thieves;
they fight with magic sticks,
they produce thunderbolts like wizards.
Mfanta ignored your advice,
weapons clashed at Gwatyu;
weapons fell at Mthentu.
The rod of Victoria
crushed the shoot of Phalo.
The Brits took Gungubele and Mfanta
to follow Maqoma who followed many
to be incarcerated
at the Leper Colony
And to catch its breath,
the nation of Phalo
curtseyed to Victoria's tears.
A double curse
the sons Albion brought to our land.

DOLLED UP

Dear Mom

Hlumelo and I went to town today to submit our CVs, if you can call them that, for summer holiday work. Regretfully, I snapped at him. He was not happy with me spending a little time at your dress-ing table, dolling myself up. I was just applying base, thin eyeliner, some gloss on the lips and all, because I didn't want to look be-reaved. I wanted to look good so I could feel confident when asking for work. It's not like I was going for the red-carpet look. But it got Hlumelo a little OTT. He went on about me not being comfortable in my own skin—throwing BC shit and Biko's quotes here and there like confetti. I got fed up and snapped. I think I scared him. Who is he anyway to tell me he likes me better with a natural look? He is not my BF. Even if he was, I don't want someone telling me how to look, especially not someone who can't put back a toilet seat after peeing. As you used to say, a man's entire inner landscape can be determined by how they behave in the bathroom. If he's selfish in the bathroom, and goes all over like a fire hose, it probably extends to the rest of his life.

He has this thing of thinking he is paying me a compliment by calling me a tomboy. Okay, he uses more sophisticated magazine terms like "handsomely understated," or "seductively restrained." Still, I am like, da fuck, broer? You calling me a tomboy? I'll preppy up whenever I want to. I don't need no permission from you to do whatever the fuck I wanna do with my looks and my hair. We're not an item! And even then it would be messed up...I think I went on and on.

Now I feel bad, because he is giving me the silent treatment. I mean, he was like that all the way to town and back, and is still on it. It's driving me crazy, so I told him it was better he went home if he wasn't gonna be talking to me. The bastard called my bluff by leaving. Now I feel like shit. I was just throwing a red herring, but the kaffir grabbed it. Fuck! I mean if you try to strike up a conversation with someone who's mad with you and they dismiss you you're in double jeopardy. Me being me it has just put me in an even nastier mood. Now I'm like: Whatever, broer! At least we accomplished what we needed to do, even if we hardly uttered a word to each other, except his saying goodbye with a tell-tale wounded-puppy look.

PERIOD PAINS

Mama

As you know, I've always had problems with period pains and pro-longed bleeding when I'm menstruating. Well, it's been getting worse. It now feels as though somebody is stabbing me inside there when I'm on my period. I think it might be the knife of your death. And I keep gushing blood. I have to change my pads every two hours.

When I don't feel so tired I'm gonna have to go to the clinic. I hate going there, meeting your friends and all who are gonna ask how I am, while feeling sad and embarrassed for me.

I think after writing my exams I'm going to go to the banks and look for work as a teller or something. I can work as a bank teller until I save enough money to go to medical school.

Hlumelo says his sister worked at a restaurant in Cape Town until she went to university, now she has a house in Observatory. Yesterday he said he's going to stay with her if he gets admitted to UCT.

"I thought you were going to Rhodes," I interrupted him.

"Not if I don't have money to pay for my studies."

He thinks she would agree for me to stay there with her also, and attend UCT Medical School.

"But I've not applied at UCT," I said to him, hating to be the one pointing out the flaw in his master plan.

"They can still take you if we tell them your mother died," Hlumelo reckons.

I don't understand his logic. Also his sister can chuck us out, then he'll have to work at white people's mansions as a gardener or something, walking their dogs every morning and evening. And I'll have to clean their windows, iron their clothes, while thinking about the sea all the time, as you said your sister used to do in Durban. Or work as a check-out person at Checkers or something, catching diseases from the tills like Aunty Zenzile's elder daughter who died of a mysterious cough.

Hlumelo says I'm a pessimist when I mention all of this. I like to think of myself as someone who plans for all scenarios. I excused myself to collect myself in your room because I didn't want to quarrel with him again, but I still came back angry at this remark about me. So what if I'm a pessimist? It's not like life has proved me wrong.

I think I don't want to study next year. I want to work, look after myself. Then study when I have money for it. But Hlumelo says his mother says people who start working never go back to school; the money becomes too good.

When he asked me if I still wanted to be a doctor I said I was not sure anymore. I don't think it is a good idea if I'm going to be sad all the time. He said his father says if he does not pass his matric he will have to go and stay with his aunt at Humansdorp, work on the white people's farms picking apples. He thinks we can go there together if he fails.

"What if I pass and you fail?"

He had no answer to that.

Besides, all the girls I know who went there came back with children or pregnant. I remember you said your cousin went to work at pineapple farms in Peddie and Grahamstown and got pregnant within six months; that is why she never went to train as a nurse after school. Then she spent all her time at the banks of Xesi River uttering strange sayings until everybody agreed that the ancestors were calling her. So she ended up being igqirha instead of going into nursing. She wanted to cure people the traditional way, looking after their spiritual needs also. Yhuu! Hayi sana! I don't want to be pregnant within six months and have to chase after Hlumelo because he thinks I must have a paternity test done before he admits he knocked me up.

It would seem as if my refusal to attend his father's church has earned me an invitation to spend the summer holidays and Christmas with them. If I do that, there won't be any getting away from all that preaching and happy-clappy singing. And what if Hlumelo sneaks into my bed at night, even though we are not an item, and before I know it, I'm pregnant and he is denying it's his.

He says he does not understand why we are not an item, and why I always think the worst of people.

"We're not an item, what is there that needs to be understood?" I pull back when I notice him sulking. I don't want us to quarrel again. I remind him that we've known each other since we were four, how can we be an item?

"Why not?" he asks and I am unable to answer, but it feels wrong somehow, like being an item with your relative. Yhoo! Hayi sana! I need to think this thing through very carefully.

FREEDOM DAY
27/04/99

Freedom Day in South Africa. Freedom from political and social condescension into more economic and financial deprav-
ity? Freedom that leaves the majority of its people unfree is not
freedom.

I can't see well in this cloud of angry thoughts. I need to find a
way of thinking away the violent arguments in the laboratory of
my mind. It is the only way I'll finally be able to walk away from
the landscape of my scars. I need to hone my heart, concentrate
on what is important, what must remain when this dust blows
away. Whatever it is, it must include the welfare of Efuoa. With
my pen I must, like Keats, *glean my teeming brain* before the mist
brings it darkness. Let me not waste time investing in grievances.
For what? The anger will just eat away the little time I have left.

There was a time when the hours, the minutes, and the seconds of my life were a burden to me, a heavy span in the field of
my depression. Then Efuoa came, gave me a new understanding of the fundamentals of life that bring me joy in being alive.
When I am dead, I want someone to read my words and say: A
man was fully alive here.

To fear death is to think we know what we do not know. Who
said that? Does it matter? I am saying it now. I am not afraid yet
I'm not not afraid. The philosophers and poets say the special
way of being afraid is to recognize how ignorant you are, and to
realize the risk that you might die that way and never achieve
the beatific consciousness. I share that fear.

When the wrong kind of fear gets hold of me, I see myself as I ought to have been, not as I really am. This brings the humiliation of failures to my mind. For I know what is written in my dust far falls behind what I feel about myself in spirit. Perhaps this is what is meant with the notion of Judgment Day. It is where we see ourselves stripped of all our illusions, wishes, lies and pretenses. When we will see ourselves as we've Become, and we no longer have the power of illusion to tame the disparities. As the philosopher-poet TS Eliot saw, humankind *cannot bear very much reality*. It reminds me of Paul Valéry, who claimed that only the poems he failed to compose remained perfectly beautiful to him, *in perfect keeping with the impossibility of being done*. He called only that which couldn't be expressed in words, though it remains real in the spirit, poetry. These past few months, at least, have made me understand that you need to be living on the edge of death to fully appreciate how glorious a thing it is to Be.

Another thing I'm afraid of is to not have a link to Love. That would be the definition of hell for me, of having lived a futile life. I've always been interested by the inner lives of spiritual people. I used to think it meant some kind of psychological programming. Just more ways men hide from reality. I've changed my mind. I've never really been interested in soteriology as an intellectual discipline. I thought my mind too skeptical to be taken up by such cannulas. But I've always been curious about mystics. I now think mystics are soteriological geniuses. Though not caring much about being delivered or not from life's vicissitudes, I'm very committed to all verisimilitudes. Which is why I love art, literature, and poetry in particular. Though I try my best sometimes to gain what Beckett called a *self-immersed indifference to the contingencies of the contingent world* I am unable to do it. I am too involved with life to develop an attitude of extricating myself from it. My only salvation would come from being involved with the life of this world, else I'm doomed.

Christians say when we die we are judged by Love? A double-edged sword, if ever there was one. Judged by how much we've loved, and Love—Yehoshua the Christ, the Word made flesh who is God's Love—is the judge. That is basically the Christian story? The rest is elaboration, necessary and unnecessary, into unfounded lies sometimes. Most religions, including Christianity, are powerful speculation through mythology that has been skillfully infused into history, invented and otherwise, and superimposed by either superstitions or revelations into the spiritual realm.

I reckon I could have found a way of slotting myself into the structure of the Christian faith. But for me, something still remains, voiceless, propelling me further into the stillness of the Still, sometimes even against these convenient fables of the Christian religion. In that stillness of the Still is where I want to be, like the American poetess Emily Dickinson, to *dwell in possibility*. Because I'm merely a man, a wretched creature that is Becoming. This realization of my limits, as a mere human creature, somehow pleases me by displeasing my contentment. It explains the incomprehensibility of God to my mind. For I know, in my heart of hearts, I could never be able to worship a deity I can comprehend.

I never planned to turn out this way, to be pleased by things that displease me, even those that disappoint me. Even things that pain me secretly please me, not in a masochistic sense, but in the sense of relief that the anticipated pain has not vanquished me. It seems to me as if I am standing within a vortex that pulsates with possibilities. I want to be open to all of them. I guess I am more a Maundy Thursday character than a Friday-in-Golgotha type. The night of anticipation in the Garden of Olives brings more shudders within my soul than the death on the hill of skulls, Golgotha. By the time the crucifixion takes place, my spirit has already transcended, leaving only its echo, for that is what physical sensation is: an echo of what the spirit has already gone through. With this, my physical death, I am now entering the echo realm. Bold in unsparing realism, my spirit is transcending. I am starting to feel the peace of that transition as the howling tempest within my mind subsides.

THE HUNGER

Mummy!

I had a big hunger today so I cooked pap and curried chicken. I was glad to have the freedom to add more cumin and curry leaves without worrying about you complaining that I've made it too spicy. And I could throw away the chicken insides–because I can't stand them– without you lecturing me about waste while there are "children starving on the street."

I don't even know why stores sell the innards with the chicken in the first place: it's not like we're in Peru where they serve guinea pigs–their delicacy–with feet, head, eyes and all still on the carcass, to prove it's not a cat. (I read that in a magazine.)

My stomach is now not happy with all the food I put inside it. It's grumbling and turning, soon the runs will start. My farts are toxic.

I told myself I don't want to think about you all the time because it makes me sad, but then I discovered it also makes me sad not to be thinking about you. I feel this sadness is taking me away from you. Everything now seems to make me sad.

If I had better faith, I would pray to God to quench the sadness and to give me understanding, like you used to pray. But the words don't seem to come as easily to me as they did to you. I wonder if proud waters have come over my soul, or if I've acquired Lucifer's disease because of your death.

St. Augustine says one cannot be a Christian without humility. When I think about that saying, tears blur my eyes, because I discover I don't care about being religious anymore, and so it must mean I have no humility.

I have this strange feeling that something is coming my way at high speed, in this dark tunnel I find myself in. I know it is better to duck and dive, pretend I love God and accept His wisdom, but I'm not in the mood for games. So whatever is coming I shall meet it head on. If the collision leaves me in pieces, so be it. The pieces will still be God's anyway, according to St. Teresa of Calcutta—yes, yes, I know the Church has yet to pronounce on her sainthood, but she is my saint of choice for our times. That said, God and I need to deal with things before my heart finds a curse in His ways.

I can't shake the feeling that St. Teresa called Lady Diana away from the abusive kak she had to endure at Buckingham Palace. That she wants to talk things over with St. Peter at the Pearly Gates on her behalf. I know, I know it's superstitious but it is how I console myself at her leaving her young boys with the wolves at such a young age.

MOTHER DEAREST

You like the atmosphere of emotional intimacy you get around Maman. You visit her often, with every excuse you can find. You also pick up more of your father's Pillow Books when you visit. Reading about your father's life is like standing next to a field that has been left to weed. It is amazing and harrowing at the same time.

On the visits you make sure to steal a moment to stand at your father's window, silently watching the fog rise from the bottom of the wood, and listen to the crooning cooing of pigeons, in amazement at the thought that these are the sights and sounds he saw and heard while committing his thoughts to paper, sending out winged words. You neaten his desk to fend off the bruising thoughts in the discerning silence. You now understand better the urge to write your letters to your mother during those years both your father and you were drowning in pain. You wish you could've come sooner, to at least have had the opportunity to nurse him as he went gently into the last night. But you were really still a child then and had much to learn about the world, about selflessness. You still do.

You understand that writing, for him, was a battle against loss; replaying the details of his life in memory. When you stand here, wondering about his life, your own anxieties and resentments seem to dissolve. They dissipate when you're in this house with Maman. You understand how words can bridge divides as you feel him reach out to you out of time; showing you his world, his life, and the reality of those he met along the way. You're amazed at how, in this short moment, he has managed to compel you to think both your lives into literature, which he calls the shiver of consciousness. You're learning something you first suspected during your own first bout of depression: that literature makes you more open-minded and alert to what is going on around you, saving you also from the disease of narcissism by awakening you from the sleepwalk of your living days.

When you notice how skeptical of absolutes your father was you can't reconcile his Weltanschauung to your mother's religiosity. You read in his Pillow Books how vivacious your mother used to be before the bug of religion robbed her of her vitality. You remember her record collection, the soul of The Temptations, Brook Benton, Aretha Franklin and all she used to listen to before the born-again thing. And you wonder to yourself if Phaks, mild-mannered as he was, would still have been in love with her evolved character, and how much of your mother's late personality was in response to his absence.

You recall how a member of their choir, a debonair and sober-minded man, spoiled his chances with your mother by revealing his atheistic tendencies. In those days your mother and you would quarrel about watching TV on a Sunday evening, the time when she wanted to listen to the obituaries and choral music on the radio, some gospel show. Truth be told, you were just being childish because that's about the only time she ever demanded that you turn off the TV. "You can never know when someone very close to you has died," she'd say, turning on the radio. You wonder now if she was listening for possible news of Phaks.

This particular day the member of their community choir was visiting. He became bold enough to turn on the TV, with a secret nod to your thirteen-year-old self, when Mother went to the kitchen after disallowing you from watching it, telling you to go finish your school homework instead. Naturally, he wanted to bribe his way toward your affection.

"I know you didn't just turn that demonic box on at this sacred hour!" Ma shouted at you from the kitchen. When she began her sentence with "I know you..." you knew the shit was about to hit the fan; same as when she called you by your full name of Fikiswa, instead of the pet one, Ruru.

"It's not me," you protested with the exaggerated bravura of a rebellious teenager.

"Nothing wrong with a little TV now and then?" the visitor intervened.

"All you ever get from that demonic box is perverse mediocrity and suggestive ways to sin; that's what is wrong with it. I don't want my child growing up like that," Mother snapped as she came into the living room and put a tray with tea and biscuits on the coffee table before him. He knew better than to pursue the topic any further. When Mother had made up her mind, not even the Pope could dissuade her.

For some reason, they ended up talking about what the visitor called the "irrelevance of religion in our modern times," which spoiled the party even more. Mother was always of the opinion that "religion is the manner by which one resolves one's spiritual tensions." That's how she tried to convince you to go to Mass.

By high school, when you were starting to learn strange things from Hlumelo's elder brother, who was studying Psychology at university, you argued incessantly with your mother about the relevance of religion. Hlumelo later told you that his brother dropped out of varsity due to drink, but pretended to his parents he was expelled for his political opinions. His father sent him to work on the pineapple farms in Peddie, where he was fired because the farmers said he was causing other workers to foment with his political talk, and that he refused to go to work because he tippled. You remember checking in your dictionary the meaning of this strange word "foment" everyone mentioned in hushed voices, which to you meant there was some mischief associated with it that the white government was not supposed to hear, or, worse still, that it had some communist associations. So, when Hlumelo's father said, "That communist is not allowed in my house," you all knew his brother was done for, and there was no more hope for him except to become a hawk. But he came back anyway, and you were warned to stay away from his "communist laziness." This only succeeded in making him a god to your youthful eyes, so you listened intently to everything he said on any topic, from sports to fashion to booze, admiring his intellectual, political acumen. Anything the boring parents were wary of meant fun and independence to you.

Eventually Hlumelo's brother left, supposedly to become a hawk, but rumor had it that he didn't even make it beyond Swaziland because he was always driving the lambs, as the Xhosas would say of a drunk. It turned out he was drinking his liver dry in the Cape Flats with a colored girlfriend who was five years older than him. He married her when she got pregnant for the third time. She was the breadwinner, while he paid his dues in life with big lies in the shebeens, like tales of his supposed sojourn in exile, which gained him false prestige.

When his brother left, Hlumelo assumed his aura, hence he was always talking about Steve Biko, psychology, and Darwin, which, admittedly, was not as fashionable as communism, but it meant defying the Bible so it was good enough for you lot.

So, when your mother came to sit on the side of your bed and asked why you refused to go to Mass, you replied by saying, with airs, that you preferred Carl Jung to religion.

"Because these things are better explained through psychology. Its logic is more penetrative to the human condition," you answered as you turned back to sleep.

Your mother, who knew psychology better than you because she had a black psychiatric nursing stripe, asked, "And what happens to the rest of us who have no psychology?"

Slightly irritated that you had to explain these things to what you took to be her ignorant self, you answered without turning around in your bed, "Everybody is born with some kind of psychological insight."

"I suppose you are soon gonna tell us you don't believe in God?" She tried unsuccessfully to hide her amusement.

You wanted to talk about Darwin but just could not come up with something relevant to blow her mind. Try as you might, you could not tie it together like Hlumelo's brother could, the fact that if we evolved from animals it meant there was no God. More than anything you wanted to see the shock on her face when she realized you were an atheist, or agnostic, or even a communist, or whatever was in fashion then. But you had no talent for blasting forth about things you hardly understood or believed. So all you could manage was, "All I'm saying is that I'm no longer interested in religion as a set of beliefs, ideas, rituals or customs. Conscience is more interesting to me now. Although I'm interested in the search for beliefs, ideas, rituals or customs that make up religion and the rejection thereof, I no longer have any personal beliefs on the matter." Although you had borrowed most of this from things you had heard, it sounded closest to what you felt inside.

Your mother was not impressed. "You're getting too big for your boots," she said as she stood up from your bed to leave, giving the impression that psychology defeated her.

On the Sunday of the TV row, your mother came to pray with you at bedtime. When you asked what had happened to her visitor she answered in her typical cryptic way: "The higher the monkey climbs the more it exposes." You somehow knew you wouldn't be getting more visits from that man, which was a pity because he was kind. Your mother sat on the edge of the bed, kissed you on the cheek, and sang, as was her habit before praying. Although you believed religion to be a scam, you still drank from the spiritual fountain that came with black traditional gospel song, so you joined in with her singing:

Yesu uyinqaba yam.	Jesus you're my fort.
Andinawo mandla.	I've no other power.
Yiyo sendisithi uyinqaba yam.	That's why I say you're my fort.

Oh, how you miss your mother, even now.

THE ARID SOIL
06/04/99

I could not wake up today. My body felt too tired from the previous three days' lack of sleep. Exhaustion, combined with sleeplessness, is a rare torture the devil visits on his chosen, the depressive. Having subsequently finally slept, almost the whole day after dawn, it is now close to midnight and I'm awake with pouncing anxieties, the Baudelairean dread of feeling *the wind of the wing of madness*. There's a disturbing spirit of ominousness in the air, which gets stirred up in the fog of sleep.

When my spirit manages to contain the conniption I sit in wonder about the night. What has the night been doing while I'm engaged in the greatest battle of my life, the urgent confrontation with my mortality. I get spooked by the aggressive peace of the night. It seems to be avoiding my stare. It's funny how I thought, like everyone else, I guess, that death would only become an imminent reality for me after I was seventy years old or so—something to do with three scores plus ten—but things have not worked out that neatly for me. Why must people always learn their fate retrospectively? I'm forty years old, well, almost, and dying of an incurable disease.

I feel a stupid surprise within my soul at how little I had considered death before. I've seen the face of stupidity in death before, on cadavers of young township boys who died too early from stupid things like a knife or bullet wound at a shebeen. Too late they realized they were not invincible, which is what leaves that print of stupefaction on their cadavers. I now see death everywhere, glaringly unavoidable, sitting and mocking our pretensions of being in control; knowing that when it comes we are as helpless as lambs before a ravenous wolf.

Be merry, but remember death: *Memento mori!*

Sitting at my desk, looking at the inky darkness outside, the mist brings no tidings from the distant land, but I wait. The trick is waiting without panic or fear, to see things as they are. That's not easy. There are too many illusions and nothing is exactly clear. In the whirling the wind orchestrates outside I hear the strength of my loss gain momentum. I feel emotionally vacant. I worry for Efuoa. I'm tired.

My marasmic hands can hardly hold the pen; still I must push on. Let come what is in the offing. I do not want to be surprised by death sneaking upon me like a thief in the night. What must come will find me with my eyes wide open. The Freudians say the aim of life is death. If so, why prolong the torture? I've nothing in common with those pretentious fucks and their dire psychology. I prefer the existentialists like Camus who see death as the only real philosophical question. Just as I prefer the philosophy of freedom from men who know how it feels to be slaves.

Let's sum up: I dislike psychology. I wish to see my daughter, even if only once—I've left it too late. I've no ability to judge God. And I am in love with my wife. Death simplifies.

Dawn is struggling to be born outside. The light is still feckless on the horizon, that *Slant of light* the American poetess of necromantic intensity, Emily Dickinson, says spoke to her of the chill of extinction, death. Have I stayed at this window too long? I sometimes think daylight gets tempted to abandon the effort against the tormenting darkness. Just for once, it thinks, let me abandon the effort and feed things to the devil. But the light eventually gains strength, then the fog begins to send notes from the river. The notes tell me: If you let go now, that'll be the death of us also. As the hours pass they reveal wan skies, the mist droops down the mountain slopes and the forest trees troop down for Macbeth. The shiny eyes of the wolves are on the lead. I must prepare my way. Trees sway and dance before the coming storm even if it'll leave them uprooted.

I'm tired of spying for dawn through this fractious hole. I'm drained and forlorn.

It's been two hours since my last sentence. My hands froze. I had to sit and stare at the nature of things. Efuoa is up now. She massaged the muscles of my hands. The sun, steadily burning through the thinning gauze, warms her face when she opens the door. There's a steamy fetor in the air, the hissing and crackling of winds. I'm trying to memorize the atmosphere of this day in case I will need to account for it in the next…next what?

Things are going to their own. The wilderness, says the poet-singer Leonard Cohen, is gathering its own. "To die would be an awfully big adventure"—that was Peter Pan. I suspect one needs to be dead to see the true wonder of being alive, and to properly test that statement. Still I wish I could drink the kumi kumi that'll turn me into a cabbage that renders me invisible to the death demon according to West African mythology.

"How's the mist doing?" Efuoa asked just now, disturbing the draught of silence I was drinking. The drawn curtain of my mind pulled open.

"No tidings yet," I replied, bemused by my incapacity and defeated by exhaustion.

The fact that I never saw death coming amuses me, really; it's fucking amusing—to live all those years without an inkling of associating death with your own life. Fucking amusing masterpiece, I tell you. Even though we see dying people every day, it never registers that it might be us soon.

Efuoa brings me tea and the wonder of love in a dancing cup. Her lips cleave a smile. She has a silvery film on her eyes, the way she does when overcome by the extreme emotion of love. It reminds me of the first time I saw her, skinny, hurried-looking, and profoundly alone. It was during a timorous time when I needed to be a hero to someone who would look up to me; someone I had not deserted who had not yet seen through my lies and omissions. Her need validated my life. She came telling me of things like mist bringing good tidings from the other world. It gave me hope. My God, no one should have seen the things she has seen.

I'd like to sleep but am too fatigued. Sleep evades me in this state—precious sleep; poor Lady Macbeth. The perennial use of Shakespeare is because of the way he gives us a vocabulary for what is going on in our lives. What's my guilt? What is left behind and cannot be retrieved? Efuoa has no guilt, her strength is in leading a life that is tethered to innocence. She does not sleep when I'm awake, or away. So she has been aware all the time that I was awake but decided to provide me with the space to brood. She has made runnels run in the arid soil of my soul.

The first time I saw her she was sitting outside this hut, looking vulnerable and bedraggled as a hen. When I asked what she was doing in my yard, she answered, "They told me to go to the teacher's house and ask to work there." The first thing in my mind was to try and identify her accent. I had been in Tanzania for only a year. I had heard a lot of different accents and learned to match them to their countries or regions of origin, but hers baffled me as she was speaking English in almost a Belgian-French accent. We understood each other by and by, switching to Swahili now and then. She was looking for work, I was not looking to hire, but something in her, a deep-seated need coming close to desperation, made me want to please her. That has never left me.

"What can you do?" I asked, to buy time, trying to figure out a way for us to come to an understanding. When I agreed to let her work for me she gave me a well-pressed hug, her face blossoming with pleasure.

My understanding was that she would just do laundry for me

two days a week, but she immediately started doing the dishes, and from there took over the household. I was too grateful to protest.

When evening came, I went to the veranda expecting her to leave for her home before I settled in for my siesta. I must have fallen asleep because she woke me by serving me a full supper: rice with cured venison and vegetables I didn't even know I had. Being a bachelor teacher, women of the village-township took it upon themselves to supply me with such things, sometimes without my knowledge. Eating from Efuoa's table meant learning to battle with spicy hot food.

As the evening wore on I was surprised to learn I had not only acquired a domestic worker but a lodger also. I wasn't particularly thrilled with the idea of someone doing my domestic work —I still had strident socialist ideas then, and she made it worse on our first night by refusing to sit at the table with me, preferring the permanent mud seat behind the door. I resolved this by joining her there and we ended up sitting down on the floor. This seemed to please and puzzle her.

I later laid a makeshift bed for her on the floor and left for my own, waking up at nearly midnight to find her still squatting on the mud chair. When I asked why she was not asleep, she told me she was not tired. There was a struggling tension in her pinched eyes but I left it at that.

Within a few months we were already speaking like old friends who grew up together. By and by, when we'd finish washing and drying the dishes, she would sit on my bed telling me stories from her youth, and we would fall asleep next to each other. This happened so often that it eventually seemed futile to have the extra bed, so she joined me in mine.

We talked, sometimes all night, about our pasts in different lands, under the pale shavings of the pumice moon. She has this domineering laugh when she's pleased that illuminates her noble features. Eventually we discovered we were cohabitating as a common-law couple. People were already talking anyway. Not that we cared. I found colors seeping back into my life.

But just as I could start to see us leading a quiet, happy and fruitful life in this corner of the world if I should revive my writing career, I discovered I was already out of time, the virus was ravaging my insides. Then again, if anybody should have known that the wind never tires of blowing ghosts to the ground, it is me. And now we're here, trying to bloom even though our flower has already been cut at the stem. These Pillow Books are the vase that holds the bunches of my life's flowering; perchance to give it a decorative look, perhaps even a pleasing scent to the world for a moment before they wilt and wither, decay and die as all life must. *As for man, his days are like grass; he flourishes like a flower of the field; for the wind passes over it, and it is gone, and its place knows it no more.* That wisdom of the psalmist is undeniable, as long as we still breathe we must listen to our motji.

The first time I was admitted to the hospital, she told me she couldn't sleep without me. It is a selfish comfort to learn that there is someone in the world who can't sleep when you are not next to them. Even now she's only able to sleep when she tucks and spoons herself against my body. I wonder how she will sleep when I'm gone? When I'm DEAD!

Looking back on my life I see that different women I've loved affected me in different ways, placating and nurturing different emotions. Efuoa aroused a deep sense of compassion I didn't even know I possessed. I don't even know when our association turned into romantic love. What I know is that I find people I can be vulnerable with attractive. I remember my growing fondness for the strength of her character, finding myself gravitating toward her with the hesitancy and alertness of a fawn.

My father, when he taught me how to ride a horse, told me it is important to establish a relationship of trust with it first. That I must allow it to get used to and trust my scent by feeding it directly on the mouth, and running my hand over its nostrils and up its head onto the back of its neck, which I must gently stroke until the horse drops its head. That is the sign of its trusting me. To Efuoa, I think I was a wild colt that needed to be tamed by establishing a bond of trust first. She likes to say, "Your mind flutters too much, Beast. It's because of all these places and things you've seen." Then I start wondering if she's talking about me or herself. Anyway, she established a relationship of trust with me by brushing my head, banishing the mist and gradually taming my fear of love, and now death. She's the only person I've ever consciously allowed full access to the nape of my neck, my ultimate vulnerable spot.

THE GOOD OLD ROT
OF PATRIARCHY

Dear Mama

Yhuu! Hayi sana, Hlumelo has verbal diarrhea these days. The dude just won't stop talking. I feel like shouting to him: "Zip it already, dude, for crying out loud! I know you're trying to be nice and all to me but for crying out loud zip it already." I can't stand his ongoing nonsense about whether we should be an item or not. I mean, really; I said to him, "My mom is hardly cold in her grave and you're already trying to get into my knickers?" Of course I felt a little bad after that because I know he's just trying to be closer to me. But gosh, he can be insufferable these days. I like him more when he's his good old silent, sulky self, it makes him cute.

I miss the days when we could be uncomplicatedly bored togeth-er without thinking something is wrong, when the only thing I wor-ried about was the gossip and stuff about who kissed behind whose back. Now everything gets on my nerves or scares me. And this, this trying to butter me up and court me is not on, it's very boring and so unlike him.

And St. Augustine is boring me also with all this talk of "impecu-nious idleness" and "sexual temptations and adventures in widening circumlocutions." The irony is that I'm grateful to him for providing me with the vocabulary with which to also stab him. But I'm a little sick and tired of hearing his Confessions: all that pious mom (Monica) and philandering dad (Patricius) nonsense is tiring. I wan-na be like: "Dude, you lived with two women you loved, in Carthage and Milan, one of whom bore you a son. Yet you don't even see it fit to mention their names, let alone that you dumped them to fend for themselves when your so-called pious mother and holy vocation demanded it. If you'd lived now, you'd be like Soli, demanding DNA tests to establish paternity before you dump them. Fuck off already! And when you were in Carthage, you went to church only for hook-ups at first, using it as your dating site. And now you go on and on about this adolescent behavior. Your behavior is typically male. You were just cunning enough to make yourself more modest than most men of your era. So what? Aarghh! It's so boring. Your fellow patriarchs gave you sainthood for it. So what? Let's get on with it already. Jeez!!!

THE BALM OF GILEAD
12/03/99

Two mornings ago I woke from a partial coma with faces staring at me in extreme concern. The doctors had warned me that my neuralgic headaches would induce such comas at some stage. People from Efuoa's church were singing and shouting prayers over me. I almost wished I was dead when I woke up to it.

The previous day we had traveled to the hospital in Dar es Salaam for my check-up and viral count. I won't lie, I was secretly hoping for a miracle, or news that my HIV was quiescent at least. Well, there are no miracles here. It's almost certain now that I shall die from AIDS. Knowing the worst is not consoling at all, it's worse than hoping for the futile best.

My head itch became worse on our way back—it's partly psychosomatic and easily induced by stress, the doctors say. I had such an attack of itching, but we managed without any major incident on the bus. The first thing Efuoa did when we got home was to trim my nails, because I had torn some skin off my bald head trying to scratch the itch away. She tried distracting me by rubbing my head gently, using a soft toothbrush and rolled-up terry cloth, things she has learned to give me relief in such states —talk about chiseling the mujik's channel on a pent-up frozen river. But it was of no use this time, the flood burst through and flooded the plains. I was overwhelmed.

I'm told I fell into an epileptic fit. These uncontrollable convulsions are what terrifies Efuoa most, so I am not surprised she went for help, returning with her pastor, who does not like nor trust me. He thinks I'm a bad influence on Efuoa, and "a constant danger to her soul." He's probably right, but these are no times for that. I woke to his braying in tongues on top of me. I resented most his wet hands on my head so I was extremely irritated when I woke up, something he interpreted as my lack of gratitude for him bringing me back from the dead, and a further sign that I was "demon possessed."

According to him, Efuoa's escape from HIV is because "the Lord delivers his servant from the lion's den and the venom of poisonous snakes." It's a pity his Lord is so finicky, because I myself can do with some deliverance, but I'll settle for Efuoa's healthy presence in my life, which brings me peace in the Lord's absence. She is the only miracle I've been given, *my balm of Gilead*, in Jeremiah's language. I'm grateful also that I have eyes to see, as the Jews say: *Lefum tsa'ara agra*—as is the suffering so is the recompense.

NYARUBUYE

About a year ago, I was still capable of helping and protecting Efuoa, instead of it being the other way around, not that she ever needed much help or protection from me. But I do take pride in one incident when greffiers (court officials) kept coming to see Efuoa, wanting her to collaborate with their investigations about the Rwandan genocide and I was able to act as a deflecting force, seeing her distress at their incessant questions. How many times did she have to indicate that she didn't want to get involved? It tried my patience seeing them traipse in here; it pissed me off, to say the least.

One day a UN man in a swishing black suit, who spoke in the plaintive tones of the injured, as if he had taken it upon himself to transform his life into a victim of Rwandan genocide, showed his face here. When I walked him out of the house after the meeting, the man kept pestering me. "You see, it is imperative that you somehow convince her to speak. Without people like her we can't bring to justice those who did horrible things in Rwanda." He continued, "You don't know how difficult it is to actually understand in certain terms what happened there. The survivors are few, and most of them are still in shock, or denial."

"Don't you think, though," I interjected, "it is understandable that they should not wish to talk about it? Don't you think there's some form of emotional intelligence to that? And that, perhaps, instead of helping, you're in a way persecuting them again? I doubt in any case whether you'd learn anything new from them; they themselves are as baffled as you are about the whole thing." Initially my tone pleaded empathetic understanding with the UN official before I lost patience with him.

"I have gone through the reasons for the Rwandan genocide several times in my mind for many years now," the man said, after thinking for a moment, "but I still have not found an answer that satisfies me. One thing is certain. There were always incidences of clashes between Hutus and Tutsis, as early as the beginning of the 60s up to the 70s, and then the worst came in 1994. My studies tell me this was instigated by a missile that hit Habyarimana's plane over his palace in Kigali. Before then, the clashes were isolated incidences, but the assassination of Habyarimana that early April morning meant the beginning of the Rwandan genocide. Is that so?"

"How should I know?" I bridled at the man's question. "What I know is that the attack she survived happened before the famous ones in 1994. She knows next to nothing about those, so you're just wasting your time. That shit has been happening in that country for a long time and no one took any notice. In fact, I bet you it's simmering as we speak. Perhaps now you should be concentrating on putting a check on your benign autocrat Kagame since he's taken all your NGO and UN monies and decided he's the messiah of Rwanda? And refuses to give up power? Rumor is he has started assassinating dissenting voices against his government. That he, too, has started jailing and killing his political opponents. Are you then going to admit to your complicity in arming him with resources to oppress the people who disagree with him? I'm sure that'll also take you by surprise when it happens. If you want to make any semblance of sense about the whole thing, I recommend the writings of Fr. André Sibomana. He was a Rwandan Catholic priest, journalist, and leading human rights activist who researched and spoke of the whole thing without a secret agenda. He'll make you understand even the complicity of his own church in the matter."

The man nodded incessantly yet pressed on with his inquiry.

"Was she part of the group that fled to Goma or Kitchanga in Zaire? We have better leads and an obvious culprit there."

"No!" I was now getting extremely irritated. "She was already in Tanzania by then. But I know someone who said something about meeting survivors from Mokoto monastery who had crossed to Goma, and were crossing back to Rwanda because Zairian Hutus, armed by Mobutu men, were killing them. I remember because he emphasized how the blue berets, your people, watched as they were being butchered, which might explain the survivor's suspicions against the UN at large. She said the UN gave them blankets and food to die on after they had been butchered. This is why most of them fled to the DRC and Tanzania, crossing at border points like Rusumo."

"Excellent! Can you give me the contact details of that person? And perhaps you'll be prepared to stand on oath for that?"

"Fuck you and your oaths! Are you not listening to me?" I was livid. "In the DRC they fell on another time bomb that soon went off. There might have been a Tutsi minority ready to welcome them, but the rest of the population in the country's hinterland are Hutu and Hutu sympathizers. That shit, complicated by the emerging warlords, who were beginning their violent scramble for the natural resources of the area, made the kak hit the fan soon enough. Many, especially young boys, were taken as child soldiers or slaves to mine cobalt, to satisfy the growing demand as the industry of home electronics and cell phones was taking off. If you had any sense, that is where you should now be concentrating your prevention strategies. But no, you people are always reactive, coming after the damage has been done. There's too much at stake now, I guess, with occidental countries and big electronics firms finding it much easier and profitable to deal with warlords than with real democratic governments for cobalt and all."

"How do you suggest we address that? The task is too vast,

and symptoms too vague!" The man was back to his plaintive bleating.

"Leave well enough alone then, if you can't," I responded. "But if you come to bother my wife again, there shall be hell to pay. The people who know anything about the hilltop church massacre at Nyarubuye are the ones who were at the camps in Goma, but you'll never hear them speak, because in that mess you mixed together victims and perpetrators, all seeking asylum as refugees. That fine mess was what actually created this tragic game of cat and mouse, where the victims cannot speak because their killers are closer to them than your international protection." I took a deep breath before continuing in a calmer tone. "I'm not blaming the UN, but it could have handled the issue better if only it had learned to invest more in local intelligence and common knowledge instead of foreign know-it-all solutions. As for people like my wife who survived a massacre— allow sleeping dogs to lie unless they bark of their own accord."

"Impressive. If we could just get her to talk…"

"What's impressive about surviving a massacre?"

"I mean, it's exactly what we need."

"What about what she needs? What they need? Have you ever stopped to consider that?" My anger was returning. "Have you ever for a moment thought that perhaps a massacre survivor might not feel like reliving the whole thing again in front of strangers. Or are you so lost in your research that you've lost all sense of empathy?"

"But it is good for her to talk about it. It's cathartic!"

"Have you been to Nyarubuye, sir?"

"What? No."

"Well, I have. Perhaps you should pay a visit there and see if you might not come back with a changed mind about what is 'cathartic' and what is not."

On a visit to Nyarubuye I had heard the haunting story straight from villagers, whose trust I had gained. The massacre took place soon after the genocide started. Many Tutsis, some 4,000 in total, living in the region, sought sanctuary in the church at Nyarubuye. It was then the only safe haven in the vicinity because news of marauding killers was spreading in the prefectures. But it was not long before the Interahamwe surrounded that church. At first the priests negotiated with them, and the militants seemed willing to allow a safe exit for the masses. But the Interahamwe were just playing for time, calling out for the Presidential Guard and other armed militia from the provincial capital. Once their reinforcements arrived, negotiations were stopped and the priests were given half an hour to save their skins or suffer the same fate as the beleaguered Tutsis. At five in the morning the priests abandoned the church; the killers moved in, hacking with machetes, axes, and hoes. They spared neither women nor children, and cut the tendons around the ankles of their victims to stop the able-bodied from running away, before retiring outside for an orgy around the fire. The slaughter continued for two days, and when the killers got tired of killing with axes, they resorted to blowing up the women and children with grenades.

In the end most communities in Rwanda chased away the all-knowing UN experts from their villages, preferring their own prescription to combat depression: that of sun, drum, and dance, as most Africans have done from the ancient times to get the blood flowing. It seems to be working. Africans know that dance is also therapeutic for releasing negative energy and loosening up muscles, taking you into the spiritual.

I think about the time I visited Nyarubuye in Rwanda. It's a village on a hill, with quaint buildings of the colonial era, boorish, projecting church spires, dust lanes, and dongas. A swift, peat-frothed river snakes at the bottom of those lush green hills. Village women, with children strapped on their backs, sing as they walk. Birds, dressed in the plumage of summer glory, test their wings by scissoring the vellum-blue sky. Nothing about the village looked tempting to the Reaper's scythe; all you see is Rwandan women wearing thatch crowns on their heads to balance their loads. As you climb the hill you remember another man, who climbed Calvary wearing a crown of thorns, another victim of fallen nature. Nothing tells you you're about to encounter sites where gruesome scenes were enacted, where numerous people died hugging the betrayal of the church doors. I've never been to Auschwitz, but I'm sure those dreary factories of death communicate, somehow, from afar, the nefarious deeds that were committed there. Nothing does that in Nyarubuye. All you find is a haunting ordinariness, a downpour of humdrum without a trace of the hanging pall of depression you'd expect from a place with such a gruesome history. When you reach the crown of the hill, where the church of death still stands, you become overwhelmed by incomprehension: not sadness, not anger, not revulsion or something like that, just mere incomprehension, an inability to penetrate the reality of it all. Disbelief, if you like! You try to comprehend how people with machetes and masus killed about one thousand of their fellow countrymen who were more or less known to them all their lives, without feeling remorse and guilt, just because they were of a different ethnic group.

Inside the church the essence of horror is stripped naked.

I didn't believe it initially, but there's high wisdom in not celebrating the place in sculpted memorials and all that rubbish. The church must remain stripped of all lies and denials to be a true memorial to those gruesome events. Let it testify to what we are, what has happened since Calvary; walls riddled with bullets, bodies left to decompose where they fell; pews draped in black mummified human remains, everything melting down to the floor, to dust. Dust to dust! Decapitated children's skulls, like mere monkeys or baboons, confronting your curiosity with menaced accusation. Ashes to ashes! Let it remain, no matter how overwhelmingly stabbing the sight is. It's time we faced up to what we are. If we're blinded by the sight into despair, so be it. It's time we are done with these trimmings to fit our denials, prejudices, and ignorance.

I once read *Elegy for Iris* by the guy Iris Murdoch was married to, John Bayley. Somewhere in the book Bayley says: *Rubbish becomes relaxing if there is no will to disturb it.* He links that with Keats's epic poem "Hyperion:" *But where the dead leaf fell, there did it rest...*I suspect there is wisdom in that. Before I came to Nyarubuye I tried to convince Efuoa to accompany me so as to confront her demons. I came out of the church having understood her wisdom in refusing to come, and the wisdom of enchanted detachment of those who go about their business as if nothing happened there. To hell with psychological mumbo-jumbo. Some pain is beyond the attention of grief. The best you can do is to let your innate wisdom deal with it in its own way, at a subconscious level, while you dance to the rhythms of what remains of life. *Ring the bells that still can ring*, according to Leonard Cohen. Only the soul's dance can wipe away that much blood.

What am I? Who am I? I'm a son of wanderers; of numerous people scattered among the hills of Southern Africa to be vassals of other tribes and nations. Is that enough? Who are these people that burden my memory with humiliation commingled with pride? *Who are my people?* Even if their blood runs in my veins, are they really still my people? I'm a son of wanderers; my genes transmit wondering. Does that mean my daughter is condemned to becoming a wanderer also? No! In us, always, is the ability to rise above our genetic codes and circumstances. That's the nobility of being human.

It's not uncommon in Africa to see the sun setting in fiery light like a wreath of blood, leaving shades of death and gloomy grief behind. Yet, as we all know, darkness, too, helps in isolating the essence of things.

Will my death bring light to my daughter's life? If my father's death taught me anything, it is that to know something well is to understand its tragedy, to hear its voice calling out to you from the silence of the grave.

The sun's bleeding away, causing the darkness to come in tidal waves of blankness. I'm writing under the grip of necessity because every particle of my body says I must die.

CHEESE AND MICE

It's Sunday evening and you feel emotional from reading the diaries. You prepare yourself a quick meal of seafood pasta. The fresh prawns and calamari, fresh squid rather, you bought this morning will make a delicious dish. The secret is to add a tin of smoked mussels to the stew just before mixing it with the pasta; the smokiness and garlic olive oil they preserve them in is "da bomb" according to Sandi, who taught you the recipe.

Before you sit on the sofa to eat, you search on YouTube on your phone for a historical documentary about the Rwandan genocide tribunal in Arusha. After meeting Maman, hearing her story and reading about it in Phaks's Pillow Books, you want to know more. The documentary is replaying old recordings from the Gacaca court proceedings. Unlike the South African TRC, the whole community was involved in providing evidence against the perpetrators. In theory it seemed like a noble idea, but it turned out not to be practical. For one, the perpetrators were, most of the time, powerful people still living in their respective communities.

The journalist speaking in the documentary claims they still had influence and money to secure positive testimony on their behalf. They were able to bribe officials and community members, or to threaten them with the mercenaries they kept to do their bidding. "You can see this in the way the accused spoke: in angry, arrogant tones. They were not repentant. The plaintiffs, when put on the stand, cowered from being intimidated by these powerful men." A chaotic situation was created where community activists were in conflict with tribal activists who were on the side of perpetrators, because their hands had been greased. This reminds you of Maman's voice of disappointment as captured in Phaks's Pillow Books: *The mwami helped them kill us though he was one of us.* Often the hearings descended into chaos and had to be abandoned. You feel the fallen human nature acutely.

An expert commentator on the program, some psychology professor, goes on and on trying to explain how the Rwandan genocide was a psychological disorder that could've been avoided if communities had access to anxiety-controling drugs. You listen with mounting anger, thinking he probably read of the genocide from academic books, and now he was postulating these theories as scientific data. He says he thinks that the genocide was caused by a confluence of several factors: over-population, resulting in the so-called "Cheese and Mice" theory, where Western institutions throw cheese (money) at caged mice (Africans), which initially makes them healthy and happy, but increases their population in an unmanageable manner. Once the population reaches a given "density" the quantity of cheese being thrown into the cage is not enough for all the mice, so they start killing each other. He claims the intrinsic tensions between ethnic groups promotes rivalry, and in Rwanda the tensions between Hutus and Tutsis were fanned by other forces, such as the influence of colonial power and the imposition of Western standards of democracy and norms of governance. This, according to him, destabilized the established traditional social and political structure, leading to "anarchy and chaos, in which the influence of an evil, vengeful elite provided the match that ignited the volatile mix." All this was not helped by the Rwandans' "hypnotic compliance with the commands of their leadership." He even postulates that a similar thing nearly happened in South Africa, especially in provinces like KwaZulu and Gauteng where people were permanently ready to resolve tribal issues with violence ahead of the first democratic elections in '94. When you can't take it anymore, you close the YouTube channel to check your WhatsApp messages.

You wonder why people cannot just say that they don't understand what happened there; that ancient animosities spiraled out of control; that we could have done something to prevent, or at least mitigate the massacre had we paid more attention to earlier warnings since the Sixties, instead of calling them tribal skirmishes. Everyone failed, because no one thought what was building in Rwanda was important enough, since there was no vested interest in the country, not like in the DRC where there is mineral wealth. The powers that be can lie and say from now on we are sure as hell determined never to let it happen again anywhere in the world. And the rest of us can pretend to believe them. And what of the African old boys' club of leaders in the AU who are starting to outdo the imperialists in political mischief? What has become of Kagame, the hope of Rwanda then, now turned a little Putin? Your Mugabes? Your Magufulis? African politics is a Sisyphean affair.

You know your thoughts are starting to sound like Phaks's Pillow Books. And Rwanda's history is feeling closer to home because of Maman. You are being shaped by what you've found out here about your father and his life.

THE DOCTOR

Moeder

I finally went to the clinic today. I got the feeling they do not know what is wrong with me, but next week I'm going to East London for more tests. I'm a little scared. I told you something is waiting to take more pieces from me. I am disappearing piece by piece.

Hlumelo is such a sweet thing; he left a cool note at my door that he was here. He says he is going to hire some movies and come to watch them with me later on. I'll make hot dogs and popcorn.

I learned another Latin phrase: Ficus ut vivus: *Get a life. (I wonder if there's somewhere one can study Latin without needing to study theology or something like that? I'm starting to like it, it's so precise!) I'm gonna try and hack away all the melodramatic bullshit, stop being such an asshole (excuse my French), especially around people who care for me and are trying to support me. Chat later...*

I'm back! Among the videos Hlumelo brought was a doccie about the spread of English as the dominant language. I wasn't much interested in it at first, figuring it is something only he would find intriguing since he wants to study journalism and all. When he made a comment about me not seeming interested, I asked him how he would feel if I were to ask him to watch a video on anatomy. He said, with a naughty smile, it would depend on which parts of the body were being diagnosed–dirty sot.

I went to your room and fetched one of your old anatomy books from the top of the wardrobe where you thought you were hiding them from me. After looking at them he got my point, but he lingered a beat on the part with pictures of genitals.

I like hanging out with Hlumelo, I don't mind his hand falling on my knees now and then, or our hands touching when crossing a busy road; but kissing, groping, and the rest of the hanky-panky is out of the question. He knows it is a slappable offense. I don't want to fall pregnant before I make something of my life. He accepts the rules. Of course to please him I laugh at his jokes, and don't mind when he introduces me as his girl to his friends, though he knows we're not really an item. I'm not ready to be kowtowing to a guy. Next thing I know I'm wearing iJarimani and going like, with curtsey: "Ewe tata ka zipeqengeshe..." Nooooo! Not me, girlfriend. I've things to do and places to go before that shit happens for real.

THE QUIET REVOLUTION
22/03/99

I find myself looking back more and more because looking forward does not provide a pleasing vista. Try as I may to appear calm, I'm raked raw by thoughts of my impending death. Better then to look back, to remember the boy I was in the township of Ezibeleni, Queenstown, on my thirteenth summer holiday:

The boy's mother sent him to town for the usual Saturday morning shopping. It was the time when white rulers policed every habit of black people; had it in their hearts to put their boot heels on their necks. The boy learned from the mouths of the adults about such things like "racism" and "apartheid," but they didn't really mean much to his mind. To him the fact that black and white people lived one superior to the other was just the nature of things. Rumors were rife of courageous black men forging plans to overthrow the white masters, but that was inconceivable to the boy. White people knew everything; they had stuff: money, new cars, big, clean houses, and shops that smelled of new things. Why would anyone not like them, the boy secretly thought to himself.

This Saturday morning, the boy was beside himself with excitement, thinking about the pocket money he would have after buying and bringing home the groceries. As he walked to the bus stop he tried to imitate the karate strokes of Bruce Lee he would be watching at the bioscope in the afternoon.

A troop of older boys who like pouncing upon him for sport were congregated at the street corner, smoking cigarettes and dagga. They taunted him as usual.

"Hey, sissy! Finished with babysitting and changing nappies? Will you be bringing groceries to cook for us later on?" Buying groceries and babysitting were girly things in the township, but the boy didn't have an elder sister, so he had to do these things himself. He cooked and washed dishes on top of looking after his younger siblings. He really didn't mind it and even preferred it to spending time with these morons, who didn't even know where Macbeth's Scotland was when asked by the teacher in class. One of them, the loudmouth then shouting at him, said it was in Johannesburg.

The boy was the first to cuss out loud: "Mfxim!"

This prompted the mistress to say, "Tell him where Scotland is, Phakamile." The boy recited the information he memorized from his encyclopedia about a small, beautiful country with an intense native culture that had been destroyed by the Roman and English invasions, and went on to romanticize its Highland culture as something akin to the Xhosa one. But such things made his classmates resent him as a teacher's pet. He waited over an hour at the bus stop. The buses had no definite schedule. They left town when they were full, and returned after rounding all the stops in the township. The boy was lucky this day: his favorite bus, Jujuju, appeared first. Jujuju, an Oshkosh horse and trailer, "drove like mad," according to his mother. It was indeed the quickest way of getting to town by public transport. His mother hated Jujuju, never getting on it except when she was really desperately in a hurry. An Indian fellow called Mathumbu ("intestines," because of his huge stomach), the son of the bus owner, steered Jujuju. The boy heard, from the green flies, that Mathumbu liked black girls, bought them sweets and such if they agreed to brush his stomach. Some said it was not only the stomach the girls brushed. It baffled the boy what else there was that needed brushing.

Upon reaching town, the boy ran his errands, making sure not to buy from boycotted shops like Checkers. There was a lot of confusion about which shops "comrades" allowed black people to shop at since, according to the grownups, they often changed "depending on which shop owner bribed the comrades that week." Then there was the natural censure of white owners who did not sell anything to blacks, calling the police the minute a black person dared to step inside their shops. As a shopper one had to find out, either through hard experience or word of mouth, where one could shop, and make sure to check every second week or so whether the information was still accurate, to be on the safe side. The boy was prudent, cunning as a snake, and harmless as a dove. He knew all the right places to shop; even his mother deferred to him for such knowledge.

This Saturday the boy went to the popular Indian shop—the flavor of the week—called Pillay's. It was ridiculously expensive, of course, taking advantage of the white man's shops boycott. This always got the boy into fights with his mother until he learned the trick of keeping the till slips.

That morning, as was always the case during weekends, the "comrades" furtively patrolled the streets for the "liberation struggle." The boy distrusted the "liberation struggle" thing because most of those involved with it were known criminals, or rowdy miscreants of the township. His uncle, who knew about these things, said the "tsotsis pretend to be freedom fighters, but are just bringing the political banner they organize under into disrepute."

All the same, being a comrade came with social powers and fearful respectability. Sometimes the boy thought he would have liked to be a comrade but he was forbidden to even consider this by his mother. Besides, he didn't really know how to go about joining them.

Shoppers were extremely afraid of offending comrades as very bad things happened to those who did. The comrades had self-appointed rights to scrutinize everyone's plastic grocery bags. If they found you had bought boycotted products, or shopped in boycotted shops, you were made to devour all your groceries, soap and all, before their eyes—and that's if you were lucky. If you were not, you were taken to a secluded area and beaten up, perhaps even killed.

On his way to the bus that day comrades found a Bar One chocolate bar in the boy's shopping parcels. The boy was not aware that chocolate bars were prohibited, and because of that ignorance he incurred his first political offense against the comrades. But the searching comrade was merciful to him. Instead of making the boy swallow the bar, or beating him up, he confiscated the chocolate and put it in his pocket—to dispose of it properly later in a comradely manner, no doubt. Despite regret for his sin, the boy was a little miffed about his chocolate bar, which he had planned on enjoying during the bus ride home.

After getting off with a slight reprimand from the comrades the boy walked, relieved, for a few blocks but was soon stopped by a police van as he crossed at a stop sign. One had to be extremely lucky to come back from town without encountering either the comrades or police in those days, but to encounter both within minutes of each other was the devil's work, as his dead grandma would say. The police liked to pick on black people on one pretext or the other. They were supposedly employed in this thing they termed "Protecting the State," which mostly meant being a nuisance and a menace to black people whenever they wished to be. Carrying parcels meant one had passed the comrades' scrutiny, which made one a viper's brood in the police language. And those who passed the police without being molested were automatically informants, impimpis in the language of the comrades. And so, somehow, as a shopper, you were always caught between a rock and a hard place; the devil was always at your heels no matter what.

After the police stopped the boy, they asked for his permit to be in town. Since the township of Ezibeleni fell under the bantustan homeland, Transkei territory, black people had to carry traveling documents to town because Queenstown fell under the Republic of South Africa. So whoever came from the township, though it was hardly fifteen kilometers outside Queenstown, was from another republic and another world, and needed a passport. This included his parents, who worked in town almost every weekday. Apartheid geography was *that* complicated.

The policemen became very mad after learning that the boy had no traveling papers, and one of them threw the boy in the back of the police van after making a thorough search of him, verging on tousa dance. The boy's parcels burst and scattered as the policeman shoved him into the back of the van. There were other people inside, all black, who casually picked up, ate or pocketed the comestibles from the boy's plastic bags, without any malice, it must be said. Some put things like tinned pilchards in their pockets with such benign casualness that the boy was confused whether he, too, was expected to join in the booty. Another person, with threatening bloodshot eyes, pilfered the change from the boy's pocket. The boy felt his hand as it went into his pocket but was too afraid to protest. He just sat there, helplessly letting the man rob him in broad daylight.

The van took them in rounds around town, picking up more people until there was hardly any room to breathe. The air inside was a mixture of human filth: stale alcohol, cheap tobacco, sweaty armpits, dirty socks, and grease. When they finally reached the police station the "criminals" were booked by a police officer for traveling without passes. When the black booking officer reached the boy, he asked why he hadn't told the police that he didn't need to have a permit because he was still under age. "I did!" protested the boy, happy that someone at last saw his point of view.

"And what did they say?" asked the policeman with bored disinterest.

"That I had no business traveling on my own if I was under age."

"Is coming to town traveling?" the officer asked rhetorically, then told the boy to get out and never put his foot in town again.

The boy left the police station with relief and with his heart, like Job's, full of speech and grievance. He stepped briskly onto the sidewalk, seriously thinking about becoming a hawk. In township lingo, anyone who joined the Organization's underground army in Lusaka or wherever was said to have turned from a dove into a hawk. The boy didn't like hawks much though. He had seen the damage hawks could do to their neighbors' chickens, ripping open their stomachs and leaving their guts hanging out. But desperate times called for desperate measures. He had to become a hawk, to show he was a man. How could he continue letting people walk all over him, arresting him for permits he couldn't have, taking his groceries and money for the bioscope, and robbing him point blank while he watched helplessly? Yes, the only way to redeem himself was to become a hawk, right there and then if possible, since he was not relishing the idea of explaining himself to his mother about the groceries.

There was also the complication of bus fare since he no longer had a cent—robbed on the highways and byways, according to the church lingo he heard every Sunday. Always, the boy, when things went on the fritz, thought through Bible scriptures or literature, his last refuges against the meaninglessness of things.

Near the bus terminal the boy noticed fierce curls of smoke rising to the sky. He hesitated, because one of the township survival rules is never go where you cannot see clearly what's going on, for this is like entering with closed eyes the valley of death the reverend frequently spoke about. And yet he took the chance.

When he got closer he saw people were chanting around a burning bus—the bus that was supposed to take him home. Momentarily, he found himself in the midst of a toyi-toying crowd. The boy was obliged to chant with the crowd, raising his legs and arms in guerrilla-like fighting gestures. He usually

liked the excitement of toyi-toyi but this day his heart was somewhere else—he needed to get home soon if he were to salvage
any hope of catching the bioscope. But he did not want to be
suspected of being impimpi, so he tried harder, putting more
enthusiasm into his chanting and his steps. This day he was
wishing those useless police would come soon and disperse the
gathering, even if it would surely rake the fury of the protesters.
He didn't care, as long as they dispersed so everyone could go
about their business.

The longer it took for the police to arrive the more concerned
the boy became about his bioscope, but what could he do, he
was now liberating the country. He tried to forget the "frivolous
bourgeois pretenses," as his sullen uncle called the bioscope.
Disconsolate and unhappy, he plunged his energies into the
toyi-toying:

Dolo phezulu!
Hayi!
Guerrilla!
Hayi! Hayi!
Eita!
Hayi!
Thaaa!
Hayi! Hayi!
Nyamazana!
Hayi!...

The police vans eventually arrived with screaming sirens and
barking dogs. The crowd dispersed in hurried scampers, crouch-
ing away from discharging guns and the intense smoke of
teargas.

Something was different this day, but the boy didn't quite
catch it until he heard a voice shout: "They're shooting real bullets!" And then he saw that people were falling for real, not just

in his imagination. He caught his breath and ran for dear life. His heart started stabbing his chest with fear as metallic spiders shot above his head. There was confusion, the noise of invasion, panic, and chaos everywhere. Shops pulled down their steel shutters. The wind accused those who delayed as it passed at satanic speeds. Terrifying sounds everywhere: dogs yelping, sirens screaming, engines revving, tires screeching, guns stammering, and a lost child crying in a daze. Teargas plumed from the streets to the sky.

Someone fell in front of the boy, forcing him to sidestep. The boy tried to jump the razor-wire fence, missed a step and the wire tore his back. He fell with his face in the soil and when he stood up his mouth felt like it did when he went to the dentist. Women were wailing like Rachel did for her children in Ramah and like she was still wailing ever since, according to his uncle, who said, "the Israelis' boot is now on the necks of the Palestinians." Someone shoved him down. He started running on all fours in an ape-like crouch. When he could go no further, he found himself lying supine, breathing dust with a pounding headache.

The boy lay like that for some time, until things quieted down. When he believed it safe to do so, he struggled to stand and started making his way to his cousin's home in Mlungisi township, not too far from town. His back was burning and streaks of blood were running down his body, telling him something was wrong.

When he reached his cousin's place, his aunt almost collapsed with shock before she could examine him. When she started to dress his wounds, the boy noticed that the thumb on his left hand was stiff, and so was his jaw. People were telling him he had been hit by a rubber bullet on his hand and his back. There was also a nasty cut where the razor wire had gone into his back, and from what he could see in his aunt's eyes its bleeding was what concerned her. In hushed tones they praised God that nothing had reached the boy's spine.

The boy was confused by the gathered crowd on the veranda who he couldn't remember seeing in the toyi-toying but who were narrating, in strange detail, what had happened, making the boy doubt the testimony of his own memory. And he kept thinking this is how history is told, by people who were not there but were first on the scene to examine the situation of the dead and the injured, and who then inserted their opinions of how the situation came to be. They told the history to fit their own fancies. They told it with unearned authority, as if they had been there, because the only people who could dispute them were either dead, injured, or beyond speech with shock.

The thumb subsequently swelled like a Russian sausage.

Real news finally came of the day's carnage: a fellow schoolboy was among the fatally wounded. He had been shot with two bullets, one in his back coming out through his chest and another in his head. People everywhere in the township were angry; grown men wept.

It was then that the boy started feeling a debilitating loneliness, like the physical pain of a broken arm. Something was screaming in the boy's silent depths, something intense and deeply felt that the boy had no vocabulary for. He later understood it to be the beginnings of his quiet revolution.

He wanted to go home, but a state of emergency had been declared by the white masters, so no one could be seen on the streets after curfew, except essential workers with permits. His aunt said they had no way of informing his mom. Black townships had no telephones at that time.

Then his cousin thought of something clever. Because the nurses, as essential workers, were allowed to go to work even after the curfew, he sneaked to the street behind theirs to tell Lizo's mother to tell the boy's mother that he was safe when she went for her shift at the hospital. (The boy later learned that his mother broke down in tears when she heard the good news at the hospital.)

From then on people started treating the boy with diffidence and awe because he had survived that damned murk storm.

THE GLEAMING,
BALEFUL EYE OF DOOM
23/03/99

The dead schoolmate was called Rondo. The boy silently tried to think fond memories of him. Rondo was not even his real name, come to think of it, but a pet name he earned, rather invidiously, when he was caught stealing margarine trading by that name from the school tuckshop. Brother Macarious, as punishment, made him parade with a block of Rondo margarine on his head on a rather sultry day that made it drip down his face. That's how he ended up with a silly name like Rondo. The memory of Rondo's comical face dripping with melted margarine brought a faint, involuntary smile to the boy's lips. He remembered how Rondo's stiff tongue could not even pronounce the "r." He used to refer to himself as Londo.

The boy felt bad that he had been jealous of Rondo for having fallen off a tractor the year before. Authorities had started treating Rondo with courteous circumspection after the accident. It had seemed, to the boy, that people gave Rondo too much undue respect for surviving the tractor accident. Rondo had already been the best in making wire cars, and he then used the extra leisure time, after the accident, to hone and perfect his craft. No one could catch up with him again after that, all the scales had tipped in Rondo's favor, it seemed. That was why the boy had become jealous, veering close to hating Rondo. But now that Rondo was dead, the boy wanted to take his jealousy back. He wanted to tell Rondo, "It's okay, you can fall off the tractor all you want, I won't be jealous. Even if you get hit by a car on your way to Umtata, like Sr. Gertrude's boyfriend, it's fine, as long as you don't die. Just come back, Rondo; it's okay. I'm not jealous anymore."

These things had always made the boy feel left out, when other boys would sometimes come to school with knife wounds and such. Nothing as dramatic had ever happened in his dull life, which was surely what made him a suspected sissy, he thought. He was proud he now had a scar of his own, earned doing something heroic, like burning a bus. In his mind he'd conflated the whole issue into himself starting the riot, because the police had detained him without trial for political reasons. It was how he resolved to tell the story when parading the scar on his back, making sure to leave out the groceries part that made him appear a sissy. He also skirted away from the details of his humiliation by people who pilfered his money right in front of his eyes in the back of the police van. In his new version of things he was the one who handed over some food and groceries to his hungry fellow detainees. He saw no harm done in censoring useless pieces of information; it sounded better when he was the hero. After all, every story needs a hero to be interesting, according to Sr. Bernadette, who taught them English literature. In the conflated and embellished version of the story he defied the arrest and the comrades came toyi-toying, burning buses, to his assistance. He even had a new version of a struggle song for it:

Ngomso ekuseni ngo four o'clock,   Very early at four o'clock,
sikhulul' uMandela uPhaks!   we're freeing Mandela Phaks!
UPhaks, uPhaks, sikhulul' uPhaks... Phaks, Phaks, we're freeing Phaks...

Surely, he thought to himself, when they're old men, their faces puckered with lines, sitting around the fireside, the township people would mention his heroism and how he freed them all from the bondage of this apartheid thing. The history books would tell of his deeds. But first, when he got back to school in a few days, his scars would earn him the respect he deserved. He wished also that his finger, no, hand, would stay swollen and get infected so they might put a new hand on him, like *Die Man van Staal*, with all that mechanical strength and those powers. He could almost imagine people looking at his back saying: "Hoo! Wow! Did you see that? It must have been a huge blade." And all the talk about him being a sissy because he cooked for his siblings and was knowledgeable would end there and then.

DIKENI

Mommy

I'm writing from eDikeni today, at Aunt Zenzile's rural place where I'm spending my holidays—I bolted out of town to avoid being detained in happy-clappy tents the whole December.

I woke up with a scratchy throat and runny nose. Aunt Zenzi went into the woods and came back with a sprig of umhlonyane to make tea for me. Luckily, there was some wild honey to mix with it; it is unsavory to drink on its own. Full marks for its curing effects, though. I am almost feeling myself again this evening. It is a good thing the commercial world is not yet savvy to its effects, otherwise we would long since have heard someone patenting the African wormwood bush as something they discovered, like they're currently doing with rooibos tea.

I feel I did well with the exam, though History floored me, because you cannot fake what you haven't read. I'm not worried too much though because it was my extra subject.

I can't see very well to write in the light of the wick-lamp we use here, the smoke is giving me runny eyes. The pitch darkness of the night outside scares me. All I can think of when going to the make-shift toilet is that a snake will slither up and bite my bits. I can't even take a relaxed dump.

I go around in circles like a dog in the kitchen because I cannot bring myself to sit down on the cow-dung floor. I fear the dirt is crawling with insects, but Aunt Zenzile says the dung repels insects.

When we were milking the goats I spilled my bucket because the goat went, well, goat-like. It went all loco on me. That made me the laughing stock among my cousins, but Aunt Zenzile was quick to reprimand them. Then we sat around the fire, waiting for the pots to cook, singing songs I didn't know. So I just went inside and tried to read from St. Augustine, but I was defeated by his talk about "wounds of ecstasy" and all, I just wasn't in the mood for it. I understand that he collected everything that wounded him in his life, exaggerated it in his imagination and gave it to God to judge and redeem as he saw fit, but geez, does he go on and on about it.

Our priest, when I talked to him about it–which pleased him a lot–said this is what saints do, transforming pain into "a beatitude" as opposed to merely an art form. Ecstasy, St. Augustine says, comes when art meets sanctity in a person. But the meaning of this word "sanctity" defeats me, even though I looked it up in the dictionary. It does not seem to say the same thing St. Augustine is referring to.

So, a little frustrated, I picked up one of your isiXhosa books, Imfene ka Debeza, which I had also brought along to read. It reminded me of when you said one of your classmates, "the long-fingered Maqanqa with garlic-smelling hair," tried to bribe your teacher. I still laugh when I recall the story of him about to be flogged for not doing his homework, how he wet his pants and all, begging the teacher not to flog him, promising to bring twenty rand the following day for her. "And how is a porridge-brained fool like you supposed to come up with twenty bucks?" the teacher asked, amused, you said. He replied that there was a baboon in his house's attic that brought them money at night. Poor Maqanqa, shivering like a leaf, got his comeuppance regardless. I was surprised to read a similar account in this book. You had told me one of your setwork stories and pretended that it was a tale from your own life. You're funny, Mommy.

The priest also gave me a volume of Aesop's Fables, which I am enjoying very much. I'm finding in it a lot of stories I've already been told as iintsomi of Xhosa lore. How did they end up in Aesop's

Fables? Or were they translated by someone from Aesop into oral Xhosa stories? Is that how they became our iintsomi? Or did our people carry them from the north on their journey south? I find it all too confusing and confounding. I might after all decide to study BA for a chance to look deeper into all of this. I've made it my second choice to MBBCh at Wits. I find reading African literature brings me closer to you somehow because you loved it. Well, I could always read it on my own when studying medicine, whereas medicine is a little piratical, I need training in it. My first choice is still medicine—after all, that is what you wanted for me. I know you preferred me to go to Durban, University of Natal. But I'm actually fancying Johannesburg, Wits. I want a chance to see and know the golden streets of Jozi. I've decided to dream big, Mommy. You get the medical student daughter; I get the big city lights—fair compromise, don't you think?

There's a line written at the back of the book in your handwriting that says: Wishing to go where you don't belong is the condition of most people in the world. *I wonder what you meant by that? Was it a longing for things that were never really explored in your life? Did I tie you down, Mommy? Or were you directing those words to Phaks with a lump in your throat?*

I think Aunt Zenzile is worried I will get bored here in the rural village. She told me there's a guy studying at Fort Hare, Alice, who is going to come fetch me tomorrow to show me around town. "He is a good boy that won't give you any troubles, his mother was your mother's friend," she said. I'm kind of excited because this is your home area, and where you met my father. I wonder if I may be able to convince him to take me to your homestead? I know Grandpa died and all but I'm curious to see who lives at your home now, whether they'll remember me, I was young last we came here to bury your father. I feel like a bloodhound on the trail of your secret life.

KWARHARHABE

Dear Moza

I had a lovely tour around eDikeni, eXesi, KuQoboqobo naseQonce namhlanje. I saw the house of Jabavus, Ngqika's Great Place, Sandile's Dam and Burnshill Memorial, where Maqoma and Sandile's warriors ambushed and killed British soldiers on a wagon trail. We went also to your village. What I think was your homestead is now a lair for jackals. When I stood in its dilapidated courtyard and empty kraals I understood the saying "Kungafa Intaka endala amaqanda ayabola." When an old bird dies, its eggs rot. It broke my heart. I tried to imagine your life here, the day you naughtily brought a stranger home to take your virginity–a stranger I am born of. What mixed feelings I had. I silently wept.

I didn't know this area had such historical sites, albeit mostly colonial, about the wars of the Xhosas and the British. I could not absorb everything but we went around driving in Sidima's father's car. He showed me the land Maqoma fought for so fiercely against the British. It extends all the way to eBhofolo, where the British established citric farms after confiscating the land from amaJingqi, Maqoma's people. We saw the forests Maqoma used to launch the guerrilla warfare against them, and the Tyhumi village that was Ngqika's headquarters when the missionary, in the person of Van der Kemp, first came.

Oh, the shame of it, Mother, King Ngqika's grave is a roofless, dilapidated rondavel, a little short of being the jackal's lair like your

< 169 >

home. *The grave of the king of amaRharhabe, what a disgrace this is to our country.*

Why don't we respect and take care of our history and cultural heritage, Mommy?

It was a lot to take in from Sidima, who speaks fast in a weird isiXhosa. He's twenty-three years old, majoring in History at Fort Hare. He gave me a book that is a collection of Mqhayi's writings. I've already read a few pages, it's fascinating. He also gave me Notsizi Mgqetho's poetry collection, the first by a black female in our country, Sidima said. She was mostly published by Mqhayi's paper. I never knew such wonderful isiXhosa literature existed.

Sidima's father is a chief of amaJingqi and has been collecting the family history from which Sidima is trying to write an isiXhosa play he hopes will debut at the Grahamstown Arts Festival next season. He made a copy of it for me on strict terms that I don't distribute it. I've read the first act, it is hilarious, about the first arrival of British missionaries to the house of Ngqika, Maqoma's father. The play is titled Maqoma: Isitshingishane, The Hurricane.

THE HEAVENS ARE RUMBLING

When the boy reached his home the day after the protest, he recalled how he and Rondo, the boy who was killed, once snuck out of school, dodging the manual work period, to go to the delicatessen. The memory of that day came rushing back the moment he lay on his bed.

It was a long walk to the delicatessen, about forty minutes there and back. They had to cross private fields with golden ears of corn, ready to be harvested. On their way back they decided to rest under an apricot tree. The boy remembered thinking then if the sun had a smell it would be of ripe apricots. They talked and laughed, dreaming about how, when they were older, their wives would be best friends, while they watched a bird build a nest—"nidify" he later learned from his encyclopedia was the correct term—on one of the branches, amazed at the precision and efficiency of the work it left behind.

Then Rondo climbed the tree and destroyed the bird's nest.

The boy, as he lay in his bed, started wondering if Rondo's death was not a delayed punishment, karma, for that mischief. In their culture, destroying the nest of a lightning bird, intsikizi, brought serious misfortune to you, like being struck by lightning. He relaxed when he remembered that their bird was certainly no intsikizi. He started humming the folk song about it:

Ingakhal'intsikizi madoda   If the lightning bird screams
Izulu liya zongoma...   The heavens are rumbling...

After destroying the nest Rondo hung from the limb of the tree narrating a story about a white Christian reverend who had to pass through similar fields. The reverend was on his way to a weekly assembly with his congregation in some godforsaken village. A rather disheveled man tried to stop the reverend. This man was employed by the owner of the farm to prevent people from passing through the farm because it was not safe. The reverend dismissed the man as a crank, telling him that he had been passing through the farm for many years and had permit papers from the owner to prove it. The poor man tried to explain to the reverend why things had slightly changed, but the reverend would have none of his explanations. The man eventually gave up, leaving the reverend to his own prerogative. It wasn't long before the white reverend came back, running like mad, shouting for help, with a lion hot on his heels.

"My friend, my friend! Please help me. There's a lion chasing me," the reverend gabbled frantically.

The poor man, seeing the danger and the chance for his revenge, called out to the reverend: "Show it your permit papers, oh dear reverend!" Then he himself took to his heels.

The boys laughed their pants wet before realizing the time had far gone. Rondo rushed down from the tree and they were on their way. Upon entering the school grounds the boys found they were in trouble for "flushing"—going out of school premises without permission. They were given the punishment of emptying twenty slop-pails each from the toilet reservoirs. Rondo filled the sixty minutes of stinking punishment with the rest of the reverend's story, summoning all the gusto and skill of a protean storyteller.

The lion panted on the heels of the reverend until he took advantage of a nearby tree, climbing it in groping moves. Reaching a high limb, the poor reverend reclined in desperate silence, his heart knocking against his chest, while the lion crouched underneath. The reverend's desperation doubled when at that moment he heard a hissing sound above his head. He turned to look and saw a snake coming toward him, constantly darting its Y-shaped tongue. The reverend's hopes of surviving the double ordeal became almost extinct at that moment.

That's when the man of God decided to cash in some of his faith fund. He sent his last arrow of hope to the Person he spent the greater part of his life witnessing to. His prayer was terse and direct. "God, see how many dangers move against me; how baleful the eye of my doom gleams. Soon my tomb shall be the belly of this beast if you don't come to my aid. If my work means anything to you, come expeditiously to my aid and deliver me from these dangers. And, please, with due respect, don't send small boys like Jesus or Gabriel; they'll take too long getting here, you know how boys are, they like playing. Come in person or there shall be an end to me soon."

As soon as the reverend finished his prayer, the branch he was balancing on broke, dashing him onto the lion's back. The lion took such fright it jump-started and ran as far and as fast as it could. The reverend, not wanting to tempt the Lord, did likewise—in the opposite direction.

"Never underestimate the power of prayer," Rondo ended his story.

The boy wondered if Rondo had the chance for a last prayer. The boy wanted to say something honest and real to Rondo; some form of valediction that could grasp the significance of their lives, define their relationship without mawkishness. But his unformulated feelings stood in the way and left him with nothing but private dissatisfactions. He felt a strange alienation to everything around him. "I already miss that lisping fool," sighed the boy as he turned his head on his wet pillow. Hedged in that sigh was Job's declarative complaint: *Why died I not from the womb?*

Too many decades have now passed since the disrupted innocence of our youth. Although the years have not been without
their own misadventures, the first cuts always hurt more. I now
feel as if rising from the dream of time, looking from a cold,
lonely window into a world I no longer recognize. When I try to
categorize things, a flood of feeling overwhelms me. I'm growing more attuned to and familiar with the silences of the night.
The frozen grief within, the primitive loss of innocence all of us
are born into by our maturing years, will have to form part of
the grave burden. Is the day too far gone to seek redemption
this side of heaven? Although nothing can be restored, everything that has happened can be improved upon, so that the past
that is always with us can be redeemed. The past, the only created thing that fails to die, is eternal, even if the mist makes the
future feeble.

THE BLOOD ISSUE

Mom

I've hidden some things from you but I think it is time to come clean. It's been quite some time since I last wrote to you. The truth is I was ashamed to tell you everything that happened. I know this is nonsense because if you are truly watching over me, you already know it all. But putting it on paper makes it so much more real.

A while ago, when I was still studying for the matric exams, I met Litha, the light against the darkness you left me in. I was having those pelvic pains I told you about that come with my excessive menstrual bleeding. I went to the public hospital where the doctors wrongly diagnosed the problem as fibrosis. I don't know if it was the medicine they gave me but after those visits I started having excruciating headaches. Some suspected a tumor. They even sent me to a psychologist when the internist in East London found nothing wrong with me. I looked for a second, third, and fourth opinion. By then I was beginning to feel my only cure would be to touch the garment hem of Jesus, like the woman in the biblical times.

That's how I met Litha, when I went to his surgery for a different opinion. I had heard of the new young black doctor everyone was praising, who had what was termed a holistic approach to medicine. It was said that he had fresh ideas compared to the old, mostly Afrikaner practitioners of our small town. He was also a public health specialist, fresh from Groote Schuur and all. I told myself that even if he could not help me, it would be great to meet someone who had successfully dodged the small-town dead-end jobs, dangerous streets, and suffocating clutches of poverty that come with our black township or rural lives. I wanted to see how a black doctor carries and conducts himself.

Initially, he, too, suspected fibrosis but by my third visit, when I told him I was still suffering the same problem, he diagnosed endometriosis. He explained how sometimes the tissue from the membrane lining the womb grows out of the womb into the pelvic area, where it interferes with the natural feminine biological process. "The cause of this is still a mystery in the medical field, but the condition is becoming more common, which might point to something to do with our diet," he said. "A hysterectomy is the easiest option after childbearing years, but since you're still a young woman, I'm afraid you'll have to learn to live with the condition until they find a cure for it. The best we can do is to suppress your menstrual periods a little with medication."

We were immediately into each other, though we both played it safe. He started visiting me at home, supposedly to check on my progress. I think he also genuinely felt sorry for me.

"I don't know how you can manage to stay alone and be responsible for yourself at your age," he said, after learning about my home situation.

He asked what I planned to do after matric. When I told him I was actually thinking of going into medicine, he told me to be realistic. "You do know it is a demanding field that requires a good pass rate? You won't be admitted based on your good isiXhosa marks there." I felt mocked. This was because he saw me reading the isiXhosa setbooks you used to read. I felt intimidated by Litha, and couldn't find the words to tell him what I thought of his condescending attitude. I wanted to take him down a peg or two, but I kept quiet. At least it made me more determined to get into the best medical school in the country, if only just to show him.

I felt myself transforming after finishing my exams. I was still reading a lot but was now more interested in classical literature and *isiXhosa fiction above all else. The people my age began to seem im-mature to me. I felt apart from them.*

Hlumelo came less and less to my house. He must have seen the change in me and perhaps he didn't like it. People kept telling me he was carrying on with another chick from Zone 3 called Nomonde. I told them it is his right because we were never an item anyway. I was surprised how little my feelings were hurt by it.

THE HANDLE KISS

Eve's curse today. You're struggling as always because it comes with excruciating cramps. You managed them much better when you were a young woman, but when they got worse with age, something needed to be done. In the end, during your Jesus year, you had a hysterectomy because the endometriosis had gone to stage four. You had initially decided, with your doctor, on a myomectomy, but after discovering four fibroids, your doctor got concerned and strongly suspected some cancer cells. The doctor knew if she did only the keyhole surgery to remove the fibroids by a transverse lower abdominal incision she would just be postponing the inevitable. Worse still, if things were delayed any further, the endometriosis might have become cancerous. So you decided to go ahead with the hysterectomy, which meant you would never bear children of your own.

After the excessive bleeding stopped and the pain subsided, it got dulled from physical to emotional pain. But the headaches remained, as the itch of the scar where your womb used to be, a side show of your low hemoglobin levels, the same way the stump itches for its missing limb for life.

The idea of not having kids used to depress you when you were still afraid of ending up alone, of never having a family of your own. You lost those flocks you were tending and made peace with everything. The question now is whether it is fair to expect someone to tie his life to yours and give up their hope for children also? You know you have an email to write, to sever the ties that will bind the one you love to this fate.

You change into comfortable sweatpants and a T-shirt and take out your laptop to write the email. But instead you click on the folder containing the typed-up letters to your mother. You revisit the one on Litha that you read the previous evening.

It is easy to say one thing led to another between Litha and you. But that takes the agency out of it, when, in truth, you wanted one thing to lead to another. At the beginning you were not aware that he was married. Later on, when you learned this fact, you were in too deep and felt trapped. Trapped in the sense that you didn't want to be the cause of his marriage breaking up but, at the same time, you didn't want to let go of him. It occurred to you that no married man could spend so much of his free time with you unless there was something wrong with his marriage. You consoled yourself with this thought: that his marital problems preceded your coming into the picture. When you learned that his wife stayed in East London, about two hundred kilometers away, it put a damper on your comforting logic but you didn't let that worry you too much.

You awaited his visits with the tingling anticipation of the jittery teenager you still were; applying lipstick and perfume, most of which he bought for you from Edgars. You spent hours scrutinizing yourself in the mirror, dolling yourself up for him, and creating the hairdo you knew he liked, a pixie bob. When you couldn't control the constant burning desire to see him, you invented an excuse to visit his surgery. He always greeted you with kindness, as if he, too, was dying to see you. He showed it through complicit smiles, the meaning of which only you could read. You hadn't had a real boyfriend before him, so you'd no yardstick against which to measure the proper procedures of dating.

You recall that when you returned from eDikeni, Litha took you out to dinner for the first time.

You panicked about the invitation to the restaurant because

you'd never been inside a restaurant before, let alone with a man. You were surprised by how dark it was inside, by the fragrance of cooking wafting in the air as you were shown to a table covered with a white cotton cloth in the corner. You now know that he must have been a regular customer because you were given what you judge to have been the best table, quite something for a black man to achieve in the late Nineties in a conservative white farm town.

The waitress, an Asian lady with beautiful slanting eyes and an apricot complexion, stood with attentive expectation next to the table. You found this slightly distracting when having to concentrate on what to order. You were not used to being waited on, but she was courteous in suggesting dishes and drinks. You ordered her suggestion of a white wine. It was your first glass of wine. It immediately gave you a warm rush to the head and later a slight headache, establishing your lifelong aversion to white wine. He ordered a beer, a pilsner with a foreign-sounding name.

You don't remember what you ate, your guess would be Thai Basil Minced Pork or something, since you seem to recall it had the fluoride taste of basil and green chilli. Whatever it was, it was certainly very hearty. He ordered something that baffled you because it was called Crying Tiger. When the dish came, and he fed you a taste from his plate, you found out it was a succulent rib-eye steak on a delicious dark soy sauce.

Beneath the table of the restaurant your feet kept touching. You ate and talked, occasionally throwing smiles at each other. He told you about his plans to specialize in epidemiology, perhaps through the University of Stellenbosch. You teased him about his obsession with white Afrikaner conservative towns. He said, in rather a stern tone, that it had nothing to do with that; he was more interested in excellence, which Stellenbosch happened to offer in that particular field at that time. He said that he didn't feel he could make the needed impact in private practice, which was why he was involved in politics. He would like to direct the national policy on public health one day, hence his interest in epidemiology.

He used to attend political branch meetings on Thursdays and when you went out with him, he wanted you to familiarize yourself with local politics also. You noticed that Doc, as everyone called him, was the cash cow they came to for their financial problems. He cherished the prestige money awarded him. You admired his determination, but noticed he never took any of your contributions seriously.

He also dismissed your dream of becoming a medical doctor, until your B aggregate pass symbols came. Even in congratulating you he made it seem as if it were some kind of a fluke that you passed well. He told you, grudgingly, that he had a C aggregate for his matric results way back in 1986.

Coming out of the restaurant that evening you were met by a summer twilight. You saw swallows diving now and then for mosquitoes, the setting sun leaving a rosy trail behind, and neon lights flickering to life. His hand landed on your waist with studied carelessness. His hands were soft, rather too impatient and clumsy for a doctor's. The evening had an ethereal air about it.

You suppose there were other people on the street but you don't remember. Your concentration was on his hand hanging on the waist of your jeans. He was courteous as you took a long walk, passing the library toward the railway station, climbing the flyover railway bridge in placid casualness. You stood a while at the apex of the bridge before a train sounded a whistle below at the station platform. A buck moon hung close to the mountain ridge, looking like a celestial eye, gazing down on retiring earthlings below. You giggled like children at his juvenile mischief of throwing sand stones on top of train carriages. Your laughter sent sounds of merriment to the sky. At that point, your greatest longing was for the two of you to be together like that forever.

The watchman alerted you that the bridge gate was being locked. Instead of moving back to the car, Litha urged you with a tug of his hand to continue toward the leafy suburb where he stayed. The air on the suburban streets was fresh with the scent of flowering daisies, tinged with decomposing windfall peaches as is the case during late summer in your region. The birds were retiring their chirrups.

It was your first time crossing the railway line to the other side, to the white area of the town. It felt wonderful and marvelous to escape the polluted streets and shabby dwellings of the township, even if for a while. To be surrounded by luxurious houses with pristine white walls and green and blue window shutters. He showed you where he lived, but you were not yet ready to go in even though you were curious to see how the house looked inside. You knew by instinct that he'd interpret it as your readiness to have sex with him. Though you wanted him, it would be your first time having sex and you were a little nervous. You wanted to delay it a while longer. "You live with white people," you commented with a teasing smile.

"Predominantly, yes, but more black people are slowly coming into the area also. Besides, white people don't bother me as long as I don't bother them," he replied as a meteor fell from the sky.

"Oh! Oh! Make a wish!" he said, pointing to its vanishing tail with boyish glee.

"What makes them do that?" you asked, as a test of his knowledge outside of medicine more than anything. "The falling stars, I mean?"

"Oh, when they come too close to the atmosphere they burn themselves to death with excitement, a price we all pay for curiosity," he quipped and the obvious innuendo made your heart beat like a drum.

"I don't make wishes on falling stars," you replied with a familiar feeling of melancholy returning, a feeling you couldn't even explain to yourself.

"That's fine. Make it anyway—for me. Those of us who have little faith live by everyday signs."

"By superstitions?" you asked, more stridently than you had intended. A moment of silence passed before you realized he was really expecting you to make a wish.

"What?" you asked in forced seriousness.

"Come on, tell us the wish?" he replied in a pretense of mawkishness.

"I thought the idea was not to tell anyone so if it comes true you'd know it really came from the gods?"

"That may be so, but I'm curious."

You hesitated, not wanting to spoil the evening, but he insisted.

"I wished my mother happiness wherever she is."

He did not know how to answer that, leaving you with a tremor of guilt.

"The dead are unvanquishable rivals," he said eventually, disappointing you that he should think he could ever rival your mother for your love. You walked back under the clasp of that disappointment in awkward silence to the car. He drove you to a recreational area called Bonkolo Dam, about eighteen kilometers outside town. He parked the car facing the glassy water. You recognized the purplish dark mold of the distant Mt. Lukhanji, standing majestic and proud against the sky. The quiet sharpened between the two of you inside the car. You felt the quiet, in vague contentment, hovering over the water surface like God's breath on the third day of creation. The vast cerulean African sky was patiently canopying the serrated mold of the mountains, cuddling the dam and suffusing the lush valleys. Perhaps it is possible to be happy, you thought.

At the foot of that mountain was your father's rural home, which you'd always wanted to visit. But you had been wary of bringing your baggage to people who might not even be aware of your existence. You thought if Litha was able to be this still, perhaps there was a future for the two of you.

After a while, still seated on the driver's side, Litha craned his neck to kiss you. You were surprised by your candor and greed in kissing him back. Where does this audacity come from, you thought. You knew yourself to be one of those people who meticulously plans everything in advance. His gentleness gave wings to your imagination. His skin smelled of what you learned was Old Spice. The skin of his arms, coarse with bristling hair, his minty mouth—you found all of it to be aphrodisiacal. He suggested again that you both go to his house. You again surprised yourself by agreeing, by contradicting your own resolution of less than an hour earlier.

You don't remember the ride to his house. Only his fumbles with the door keys as he was trying to kiss you at the same time as unlocking the house. Inside, it was silent as a church. You felt a draught on your thighs as he slipped off your jeans, worrying whether you wore appropriate panties, not the ones with moth holes. You stole a peek as he threw the jeans aside and were relieved to see the peach lace fabric of your new underwear.

You dropped your gaze as he kicked his trousers off and discovered he was already fully masted. He pushed you onto the sofa in the lounge. You inhaled sharply, and uttered a whimper when he entered you with a force you didn't anticipate. White sparks flashed under your eyelids. Your breath labored. Your vagina burned as he began thrusting. You couldn't breathe. But somehow you didn't want to breathe nor did you want him to stop. You were lost as to what response was expected from you, so you reacted to the pain and the pleasure by thrashing and thrusting. A drop of his sweat fell in your eye and it stung. It helped take your concentration off the burning sensation between your legs. The velocity of his body moving up and down on top of you gained momentum with every stroke.

Then you started observing the whole thing from outside yourself, as though it were happening in a distant past. You began seeing it as a memory, thinking about decent ways you'd be able to narrate it to your mother. You saw yourself spying on yourself, making up excuses and phrases to describe it later.

The acute pain, the tearing sensation in between your legs returned. You felt like a child caught in the middle of a thrilling mischief. You were aware of his weight like a heavy bag of meal-ies on top of you. And how beastly his desire seemed, contorting his face until he convulsed, like a snake shedding its skin.

For what seemed like forever he remained on top of you, pant-ing like a dog after a chase. You wanted to tell him you couldn't breathe but your lungs were not up to the task. Finally, he rolled to the side, giving you your breath back.

Then you got confused. You couldn't remember if you had had a say in this or not. Things were still tearing inside of you, both physically and emotionally. Your mother's voice came to the ear of your mind: "No woman surrenders herself with im-punity to bodily pleasures." Your pelvic bone felt bruised as you lay in meditative silence with your inside bits still burning. So that's sex, you thought to yourself. You were surprised to realize it must have lasted less than four minutes. It had felt like forever.

He was a hugger. You discovered the pleasure of your body being cupped by a man's for the first time. It brought the illusion of security. You fell asleep and woke up just after midnight with a racking thirst. You stumbled out of bed, confusing his bed-room with your own. You hit the stool where both your clothes hung and nearly fell into the glass of the window. The racket woke him.

"What's wrong?" He seemed startled, a sign you took to mean he was used to being alone in the house.

"Go back to sleep, I'm just getting a glass of water." You were surprised at how authoritative that came out, as if you were the owner of the house. You bent down to brush your burning shin. You grabbed a bottle of still water and went back to bed.

Soon he recaptured his desire and made love to you again, which you endured more as a chore than a pleasure. Afterward, you lay still, for the first time realizing the room's pleasant smell of soft lavender, a refreshing contrast to the kerosene smog township houses smell of. Your engulfing melancholy retreated a bit in the arms of his spooning embrace.

As he drifted back to sleep, you disentangled yourself from his arms and went out through the sliding door for air. It was threatening to rain, with a crumpled sky and all. You passed the porch to sit on the lawn where a mechanical water fountain was pumping water, its soft sound the only thing breaking the silence of the night. Raindrops, dense as blood, started to fall from the sky.

You lingered a while in the comforting darkness, almost expecting your mother's hands to clasp your face. You remembered how she liked to sneak up on you when you were playing on the lawn alone and clasp her hands over your eyes, asking: "Whose hands touch the pasted dust of the princess?"

You were meant to reply: "The slimy webs of the changing prince."

Then she would say, "Let me kiss the dust out of your eyes so you may see," as she pulled you by the ears, something she called "a handle kiss."

You looked through the glass of the sliding door and wondered if the man lying there was your prince. Somehow you knew it not to be so.

THE SEXUAL PREDATOR

You wake from a nightmare after three in the morning. The nightmare comes back to you in flashes. You're in a darkened flat in Johannesburg, crying and shivering. The darkness is smothering you. Litha is hammering on the door, and shouting for you to let him in. You shake and try to scream for help but the shadows in the room snake around your neck, squeezing the breath from you.

You wake up out of breath. Blood has leaked through your pajamas and has soaked into the sheets. You get up, clean yourself up and pull the sheet from the bed. You put a wash basin on the floor of the shower and fill it with warm water before dropping the sheet in. You'll give it a proper wash later. Now you need to get some sleep before your shift starts. Then the worry starts again. Maybe another fibroid has grown. You try to disperse the thought by thinking more about Johannesburg, the evening when you had to stand up and write a letter to Litha. You're scared again that your mind has started playing tricks on you, especially after you spent the previous evening replaying your relationship with him. You had resisted thinking about the way it had all ended, but your subconscious is forcing you to confront and examine it. So that is what you do.

What Litha hadn't told you was that he had a wife, that his wife had had a child at fifteen by another guy before she met him. That when she married him the child was about fourteen, living with them in East London. That he became close to the child, too close, as it turned out, and that some time after they began fucking. All this you only heard through the news when his wife charged him with statutory rape of her, by then, sixteen-year-old daughter. At the time you were nineteen, in your second year of medical school in Johannesburg.

Over the phone and via email he told you the girl and her mother were framing him because he had asked for a divorce so he could marry you when you finished your medical studies. You didn't believe him. You were starting to have an independent life away from him in Johannesburg. To this day you are convinced that he had an affair with the girl while he had one with you also.

His political enemies or someone leaked the police report to the press. It became a big deal in your small town, with newspapers reporting: *Young Doctor Arrested for Statutory Rape.* You had no choice but to end your affair with him, no matter how grateful you were that he had paid for your first year of medical studies before you got a scholarship. You don't know whether his wife lost the edge of her anger; or if she was asked by family members, parents from both sides, to give him another chance; or whether, as a housewife, she saw that she'd lose the golden-egg goose if he went to prison; or if his political connections pulled some strings; or perhaps a combination of all the above, but the case died as quickly as it flared up. He was lucky it was before the #MeToo movement, you think now.

What of you then? Do you count as an enabler for having never reported him? Would you show up to corroborate another woman's case against him? Sometimes you think about the source of your contradictions when it comes to him; if you were also under the Lolita-syndrome spell. Because if one thing is certain, it is that men like that never stop, unless they're caught and sentenced. Like a dog to its vomit they always go back to their predatory ways once their sexual hunger returns.

You've always prided yourself on taking responsibility for your own actions. Looking back on it all, you try to think where your culpability ends and his sexual predation begins. At the time it didn't feel—it never does when it's personal—like you were a victim, or part of what is now known as a Sugar Daddy situation; you felt a little coerced perhaps, but nothing more. You were concentrating on how he gave you hope for your life goals, how the excitement of anticipation kindled in you whenever you knew he was on his way to see you. The laughter in front of the TV as you ate bad pizza takeaways. His gaze on you and the sense of validation, of no longer being overlooked when you were around him. His playfulness like that of a cat playing with a stunned mouse. The way his nostrils flared when he was angry with you—it took very little to set him off, small things, like not wearing a dress he had bought you when you went out on an occasion. The overreactions when a guy, especially of your age group, talked to you. The childish tantrums when he'd storm out and leave everything, including you sometimes, at whatever place you were visiting.

There was always an element of emotional terrorism with a tinge of psychopathic tendency about him. You excused it as his misdirected ways of showing his love. You were too inexperienced to interpret and read the warning signs properly. You now know that they point to a disturbed personality, but then...then you were desperate for love and attention and someone to take care of you. Besides, things always appear clearer in retrospect.

TO THE RIVER
08/06/99

We're told that there were cultures whose women and servants killed themselves when their masters died, because they could not fathom their lives without them. This pathological generosity, beyond its real roots in oppressive patriarchy, disturbs me. I distrust such slavish loyalty. I no longer trust Efuoa's innocence. I'm flattered by her need of me, but I do not wish to be needed. She's beautiful, intelligent, and kind, especially kind. *He was kind!* What an epithet. I'd like my life to be defined by such things, but that would be a lie. I have at times had to be cruel to survive, wrestling with angels and devils: *taking the kingdom of God by storm!*

Mr. Stoner, in John Williams's novel *Stoner*, has this line: *The dying are selfish, he thought; they want their moments to themselves, like children.* Ain't that the essential truth?

In the ancient times of our culture a dying old man would seclude himself from the tribe, live his last moments in the wild, preparing to be food for wild animals and vultures. Tell me that's not perfect cyclical ecology. But the missionaries, in their usual sophisticated ignorance, were flabbergasted by this, calling it vulgar and heathenish. Ntsikana—the Xhosa mystic who was instrumental in converting the nation to Christianity—was the first to heed the body burial practice from the first missionaries. The missionaries taught our people to hide their decaying bodies in funeral boxes, six feet deep underground, so as to await the Resurrection Day, as if the demiurge who fashioned our body out of dust would fail to keep up with its whereabouts when it returns to that dust. Quantum physics is now starting to understand that the bonds atoms make to form physical entities are inviolable, they cannot be broken. This, naturally, is starting to give credence to the notion of resurrection within the scientific world.

I woke up to a raw autumnal morning, sharp with biting air. I went outside because I wanted to feel my old self again, to recall how it was before the daily doses of Versed, which deaden my nerves and reduce the clarity of my eyesight. The sun was climbing toward the crest of the hills with a burning intensity that enveloped the whole village in a rosy red hue. The trees shed their fiery leaves, covering the land with matted gold. This served to illuminate the dry season in my heart. Things were decaying, dying, decomposing in silent grandeur to fertilize the new life they'll give birth to.

Shepherds led their flocks. I tried speaking to them but my voice simply moaned in my ears, leaving behind a ringing sharpness—tinnitus? I had an unformulated grumble in my heart. All I could think was, I must go to the river. Israel must cross Jordan and be baptized. What's there for me? Who's at the foot of this cross with a jar of perfumed oils preparing for my burial? Efuoa? Nothing left of this body, the virus has left it emaciated—just skin and bones. I must go to the river. *I have no one to dip me when the angel of the Lord comes to stir up the waters.* I tasted sickness in my mouth like iron. I couldn't walk properly. My feet were leaden with death. Silence was commanding me to reach for something but did not tell me what. Ah, the dampness of river water around my ankles. Neva? Igqili? Ouse? Where am I? I'm a mustang. I must gallop down to the river. Something was calling, someone was calling. Another wounded voice. It was Virginia Woolf. She was saying something. I couldn't hear her very well; something about us having to *tolerate the spasmodic, the obscure, the fragmentary, the failure*...My God, I couldn't go where she was bidding me to come. I knew where she'd lead me. My life has been a dismal failure. I must climb back to my life. I must recite the Pietà scene for Efuoa's sake. I was losing my breath. I had no breath. I'd no strength. God, I don't want to die! Not yet! Not yet! My voice kept ringing in my inner ear.

The dampness of grass on my face. I remembered Grandpa telling me you can determine the character of a place by how it smells after the rain. Where I was, it smelled like dog shit, wet dog and pig shit. Ever noticed how the big cities smell after rain? Mostly of decay, something festering at their bowels. My head was spinning. There was a salty wetness on my face. There was a swirling gray mass of fog that stood before me. Then I saw it was a man, stringy as an underfed chicken, wearing a wounded expression. Primo Levi? Gaunt and ill-dressed as a scarecrow from the camps of death. He looked at me in astonishment.

"What are you doing here this early, teacher?" His voice came as if from a deep hole and disappeared like sound in a canyon. He called me teacher. They still call me teacher, though I've not taught their children in a while. What could I answer to satisfy my need for honesty and his ability to understand? That I was looking for ways to express my inadequacies? No, he wouldn't understand that. That I was hiding from my imminent death... shit no! There were no words to explain what I was doing in the woods that early. Something of the truth always escapes compre-hension. His face creased to suggest a smile. He coughed on his fist to conceal his shame for me, perhaps to suppress a giggle? Fuck him! His face was turning. My eyes were pricked by tears. I was seeing things in the prism of a rainbow. I was insulted by his need to help me. Then the darkness descended.

I woke with a taste of elixir, codeine base, in my mouth and the voice of Efuoa in my ear. "Where you go this morning, Beast? Where you go that early?" There was a dull serenity and silent patience in her tone I found irritating. I asked for a glass of water.

Efuoa is not preparing for my death. She seems to have convinced herself that my sickness is a passing phase. Nothing I say defeats her hope, her willed ignorance of the fact that my sickness is incurable. When I try to make her understand the reality of our situation she ignores me and insists on making me a cup of tea. The pain in my head was excruciating. The mist was engulfing, thickening into fog. I wanted to be alone in my dying.

"I make tea for you, Beast, sweet and hot as you like. Sweet and hot..." I heard her voice fading to the kitchenette. I detected the change of tone, the hiccups of tears. I felt sad, for her, for myself, for my daughter, for the world. She left behind a vague sense of shame hanging in the air. How is it possible that witnessing all those horrible deaths in Rwanda has not left her with a sense of life as ultimately tragic? How did she manage to escape with her innocence?

She came back with the tea, started praying for me, for us. She read from the Bible: "Lord, you've been our refuge from generation to generation/ Before the mountains were formed..." She started reciting it from her memory. Her eyes were now shut. I found no prayer in my mind, nor in my heart, so I said none. It's not about belief or non-belief, but about dealing with what is in one's heart without a need to invent or embellish.

Now, recovered somewhat, I am able to write about the events of the day but I cannot get over the feeling that I nearly died. I nearly reached my end today. This makes me think about an anecdote of a question that was asked to the English philosopher Bertrand Russell: "What if, as a lifelong atheist, you arrive in heaven and find you were wrong? What would you say to God?"

Russell is said to have promptly replied, "You didn't give us enough evidence."

Paul would disagree. He thought God left enough evidence in creation to convince all people of goodwill—"of goodwill" being the operative words here. This scares me, that my lack of faith is a result of my lack of goodwill. Only a fool, according to the psalmist, says in his heart: *There's no God.* Many fools also

< 193 >

worship the God of their imagination and superstition, which, if you read the Bible properly, is the perennial message of prophets.

Isn't the lack of evidence pretty much the whole point behind the requirement of faith? The demand of love, not intellectual capability? And I suppose there's something to this purity-of-heart thing also—men of goodwill—as the basis of faith.

"It is by faith you were to seek me, and by love find me," the Christian God would say to Russell.

"Love what I do not know? That's kind of absurd, isn't it?" Russell would retort.

"And how would you expect to know what you do not love?" the Christian God would ask. And, voilà, a stalemate is reached.

I'm with Jack (CS) Lewis here, who thought there are moral questions God can't answer because to Him they are nonsensical. Like: is yellow a square or round? Jack thought half of our clever questions are like that in the all-comprehending mind of God. Furthermore, the concept and nature of God does not pose any problems; it is just that our minds have not developed enough to accommodate all the solutions. This is why, according to Christians, God insists we have faith until things are clear to us too. We should just get on with observing the commandments, especially the two about loving God with all our heart and soul, and loving our neighbor as ourselves. That is sufficient for us to learn humility and wisdom. Augustine—you meet the bastard on every forked road you encounter on matters of religious thought; whichever way you turn you cannot hide from the African saint and the scrutinizing eye of God he lived under—was right in saying the core of this Christian thing is *humilitas*. It is impossible to believe the absurdities of Christian claims without humility.

Death, in essence, is running out of time. And life is a struggle against time always slipping away. It is therefore wise to prepare for death by making sure you get the fundamental things done while you still have time, like loving your loved ones. Running out of time may put an end to the making of your own history, but not necessarily to the full awakening of your consciousness, so say the Christians. In fact, they claim that death is the final, complete awakening of your consciousness. This is a last hope that remains in me.

Comte's subjective immortality is not sufficient to me. I don't want to achieve immortality through my works. I want to achieve it by not dying. Who cares about finding immortality through the continuing effects of one's work, or in the memory of loved ones, if you'll still be dead? Those things are fine, but our protest against death demands much more than that. Humans tremble before death because they are being separated from the essence of their nature. Humans were not created to die; there's nothing natural about death, hence the whole of our being is repulsed by it. The Christians got that right. Comte's doctrine is a mockery of our nature. What happens when all the works of men are swallowed up in the cold silence of the sky? When Levi's hydrogen no longer condensates. What then?

Giving up hope may seem like the intelligent thing to do when you are faced with an unsalvageable situation. But show me a single skeptic who has ever followed through on that at the hour of death. What clever men, as opposed to wise ones, don't understand is that human intelligence has already been defeated the moment we know we have to die. We're already in the realm of the absurd, of faith, of the foolishness of the Cross that defies all human intelligence.

Personally, the immortality I'm looking for is that of my unending conscious existence. I don't care about neural computation. I want to keep and develop further the history of my own consciousness. Not necessarily consciousness as physiological activity of the brain. What I want is to keep the consciousness of my existence, my mind, even without my biological brain, in whatever form it may take after my moment of death. The resurrection of this particular body is the promise of Christianity,

which to me is not even necessary—although it would be a bo-
nus, a cherry on top, so to speak, because it's a body I've grown
accustomed to during the years of my material living. But, hon-
estly speaking, I wouldn't care even if I were to be given a new
body, as long as I keep my consciousness, my accumulated
experiences that have made me who I am. The Judeo-Christian
religion promises this, hence I'm attracted to it in this hour of
my greatest need—the branch turns toward its roots in the hour
of thirst.

It probably would have been easier for me to kill myself if
it were not for Efuoa. Have I a right to do so if she is still here,
despite all she has endured? Let heroes fall on their rusty swords.
I've things to understand still from a peasant woman who is now
the love of my life, and probably my only shot at heaven, if that
exists.

THE HOSPITAL

It has been a hectic day at the hospital: two infant deaths from kidney failure caused by ecoli. You're trying to raise awareness among the community about the dangers of giving babies raw animal milk to drink, because it sometimes contains pathogens. Along with a few of your colleagues, you're even trying to establish an NGO, to be led by young local women, that'll educate people on some basic hygiene requirements, among them how crucial it is to heat goat's or cow's milk. But you have to grant the young ladies stipends and traveling money also, otherwise they get discouraged. You've written to several philanthrophic entities for assistance, to no avail. And your Doctors Without Borders salary does not stretch far enough to enable you to cover the costs.

Something about the day reminds you of your unpleasant experience of Bhayi Public Hospital in Port Elizabeth when you were a young doctor. After med school and your two years of mandatory service, you spent five years working as a doctor at Bhayi. In your fifth year there was a complication during one of the maternity deliveries, a premature baby, due to cervical incompetency—when the cervix dilates early and starts labor. You had already detected the problem of a urinary tract infection in the mother, and knew it would end up inducing early labor. Hence you had taken caution to admit the young mother so as to monitor her. Such premature cases were common in your patients there, who mostly came from poor backgrounds in the colored townships of Gelvandale, Korsten, Cleary Park and so forth.

The hospital, and the province at large, had a shortage of neonatologists, so it mostly relied on private practitioners who come two or three days a week to public hospitals. You knew that a quick delivery would give the infant the best chance of survival, so you delivered the baby yourself without waiting for a neonatologist when the patient showed symptoms of early labor. You had the help of a respiratory therapist and a neonatal specialist nurse.

After delivery, when you saw the infant was a little blue, you knew she probably had lung problems. She had fused eyelids and flattened ears also, which is normal on premature babies. You suctioned the amniotic fluid from her lungs, placing her on a heated mattress while fitting an endotracheal tube used for continuous air pressure to the lungs. You administered surfactant, a mixture of protein and fat that's mostly given to premature babies with lung problems. You asked the nurse to place the baby in an incubator. Naturally, as an experienced nurse, you assumed she knew how to insert the catheter into the infant's umbilical artery, as the means to monitor blood pressure, oxygen and carbon dioxide while in the incubator. You left, satisfied that the baby was stabilized, trusting the nurses to put her in an incubator when one became available.

Hence you were surprised and angry when on your rounds the following morning you discovered the baby had died during the night. Prematurity and hyaline membrane infection were stated as the cause of death. This didn't sound right to you. You had examined that child closely. You did admit there was a possibility you could have missed something, but what made you suspicious was the manner in which the management actively blocked you when you tried to find out if this was really the cause of death.

You had not had any X-rays done to determine if there was

any alarming mucus on the lungs, which would be the cause of hyaline. This was not a standard procedure. But common sense dictates that you do it when the infant is showing serious symptoms of low vitality, which had not been the case with this one.

After interrogating the specialist nurse your antennae stood up. She told you all incubators were occupied when she left, but she had given specific instructions to the night-duty nurse to make sure the infant was put in the incubator next, after the two patients due to be discharged that evening were released. It soon became apparent to you that your infant had spent the night outside the incubator, which led to the infection. When the nightshift staff realized this, they gave false information to the doctor in charge to certify.

Naturally you were angry. You wrote a formal complaint, requesting the matter to be taken further. The hospital administration, afraid of drawing a scandal to itself, tried to sweep the whole thing under the carpet. You suddenly became very unpopular for insisting the matter be investigated. To make matters worse, the young mother seemed more relieved than angry that her baby had died and was not willing to pursue the issue, so you got no co-operation from her either.

One day, you were called to the superintendent's office. The superintendent, a sixty-something-year-old Indian man with a handsome face crowned by a salt-and-pepper mop of hair, asked you to take a seat and said the hospital board had had a meeting where your case was discussed comprehensively. You were lost for a moment, not knowing what "case" he was referring to. He reminded you of the infant that had died two weeks ago, and spoke in a riddling manner.

"It has come to our attention that the incident has affected the morale of the nursing staff," he said wheedlingly.

"In what sense?" you inquired.

"Well, for one, none of the nurses want to work with you now, especially in theater, for fear of being used as scapegoats when things go wrong. And on occasion they will inevitably go wrong, as you know."

"Used as scapegoats? Are you serious? This was a clear case of professional neglect." You bridled your anger.

"Well, they feel you accused them of incompetence concerning things that are not their responsibility."

"Since when is putting a premature baby in an incubator not a nurse's responsibility?" you asked, getting extremely irritated.

"Well, since you failed to detect the hyaline case in a premature baby…"

"I failed to detect!" you interjected, incredulous. "There was no indication of a hyaline case until that baby was left outside the incubator for the whole night. The nurse who assisted with the delivery knows it, and you can ask the respiratory assistant also. In any case, if that is the case, why is the hospital not charging me with negligence so we may get to the bottom of the matter?"

There was a momentary silence before he said, "You don't have to be angry with me, Dr. Biko. My job here is to put out stray fires. And this is definitely a stray fire. No one wants to draw the hospital into this kind of a controversy, except perhaps you. So, you put me in an awkward position. We are doing this for your own good, I hope you realize. It is not the nurses' expertise to determine such things but the doctor's. And if I may ask, why did you not wait for an available neonatologist to handle the delivery?" he asked in an accusatory tone.

"Because the probability was that one would have been available only three days later, and the infant would have been still-born by then. I didn't have the luxury of waiting, so I made the call."

"And it was the wrong one?"

"How was it wrong if the infant was born alive?"

"The infant died the following day, but let's not concern ourselves too much about that. It is not the intention of the board to make your life difficult. You're young, and have a good future before you. No one wants to spoil all that for you. I will give you a good reference for whatever hospital you wish to be transferred to."

"Are you asking me to leave?"

"Well, we're asking you to explore your options for the greater good of the hospital. That would also help with the staff morale. I don't have the luxury of probing or firing the whole nursing staff, and since they do not seem to trust working with you…Besides, the whole experience must have also been traumatic for you—losing a patient in your care and one so young. I will be willing to give you a few weeks' paid leave for that, which will give you time to apply to another hospital, citing as your reason for leaving the wish to further your career."

That was your first real experience of how bureaucracy works when it cannot afford to draw negative publicity to the institution, and so a scapegoat must be found. You felt betrayed and disillusioned. But you swallowed your bitterness and left.

ON THE ROAD

When you get off your grueling shift where two babies died it is almost time for your planned trip to Dar with Sandi for the long weekend. Seeing her sitting on the stairs of the hospital, reading with intense concentration, brings relief from your horrible day. You resign yourself to the state of your own exhaustion as you fall into each other's embrace. You explain to her what had happened as you both walk to pick up your bags at the staff cottages. It feels like an opportune moment to open up to her about your unfortunate experience in Bhayi Public Hospital. You feel you cannot properly know each other until she knows this part of your life also. She's flabbergasted when you tell her about it.

You had asked one of the Indian doctors, who lives in Dar, to give you a lift. You check the time on your cell phone. "Shit, he must be waiting already." You and Sandi briskly walk to the hospital gate where he agreed to meet you. The doctor is already there, looking gangly and flushed. You notice that he looks drunk. He throws you his car keys with a casual boldness that is in contrast with his usual milquetoast character during duty hours.

"You girls are going dick diving this weekend?" he boorishly comments, obviously pumped up on the high glow of chauvinistic egotism. You've never seen him this cocky before. You keep quiet for the benefit of your working relationship if nothing else. You know that he has his eye on Sandi, who you only notice then is a little glammed up, penciled eyeliner and tweezed brows and all. You assume these to be clues that she's interested, since she seldom wears makeup. But surely his remark has spoiled his chances because Sandi's feelers are hypersensitive when it comes to patriarchal bullshit.

"Hands on the plow, lady and gentleman, we're late, let's mend our pace," you say, quoting from Phaks's Pillow Books, as you fire the German engine. You drive for an hour or so with the falling dusk curving around the horizon. You leave by the A2 national road toward Kingolwira. Your mind immediately falls to Phaks's writings the moment the open vastness of the land is before you. He has started to not only influence your worldview but the way you speak also; you've been seduced into his observational tendencies. Ordinary things that usually escaped you, now begin to intrigue you. For instance, somewhere he says the mountains are the spine of the land and rivers its veins. Now everywhere you look, as you snake around the foot of the mountains, race parallel to their river veins, you see what he meant about them containing history's messages from the past.

You've often heard that traveling is pleasant because it holds the promise of rescuing us from ourselves. That journeys are midwives of our thoughts and new beginnings. Nowhere is this clearer than in Africa's vast landscapes, but the promise is rarely fulfilled. Roads may be veins of hope, but perhaps hope in vain, as they can easily lead to more disappointments.

You drive through areas of thick mimosa growth covering the gulches of reddish earth, through the macchia forests, before it clears to empty plains. Then there are scenes of the moribund activity of the African day everywhere along the road: beasts of burden pulling the last plows; women with babies on their back; forbidding vertical rocks like ancient scars; glinting water on rice fields; alert thorn trees, embellished by the silky architectural wonders of spiders' webs; and vaguely stunned cattle chewing cud in bovine sturdiness.

The amber light of the setting sun burns red and urgent,

firing the tan grass fields as you reach Kingolwira. Road signs point to Mikese, where your young doctor wants a bathroom stop. You park at the filling station. After that the road rises and falls toward the Kiulangalo Forest Reserve. Sandi corrects your pronunciation to Kitulangh'alo. She shows you glinting shambas as cassava fields and banana groves alternate in steeps and valleys across the rutted ground.

The pleated green hills, with accordion grooves, draw their protective curtain in solid defiance of time over the lush valleys. At times, you can't see well but feel mountains so tall they totally block the last rays of the sun, making it seem as if the night has already come. Other times it feels as though you're sailing into the eye of the sunset that's drowning behind the mountains. Sometimes when you crack the window open it sounds like the wind is racing the lea. Then darkness draws over you, dented only by the car light shining ahead. You feel assailed by life. Sandi tells you to slow down and be careful because there's a lot of wildlife crossing the road in the thick of that forested area. You find yourself humming a popular Xhosa song:

Lakutshon' ilanga,	When the sun sets,
Zaku buy' inkomo,	When the cows come back,
Ndaku cinga ngawe,	I find myself thinking of you,
Sithandwa sam...	My dear love…

The wind picks up and lashes the car. Inside, as you admire the natural beauty all around, the quiet develops into an enveloping peace. You find yourself wondering if this means this is your home now. Phaks answers with a Delphic puzzle in your mind: Your home is where your attention is. The young doctor, in the back seat behind Sandi, who started the journey wound-up like a spring, touching Sandi's neck in mock massage, whispering sweet nothings into her ear, is now sleeping, crestfallen and deserted by his capricious courage. This is a good thing, you think, because his licking-dog manners were strangling her interest and ratcheting her nerves up a notch.

By the time you reach Dar, almost four hours later, the night has completed its leaking into the sky, creating the backdrop for a cluster of vivid stars. The young doctor leaves post-haste after dropping you at the hotel, his face ashen with the babalaza his body has obviously begun manufacturing. This prompts your giggles. You're pleased by the salt-licked ocean air as you check into the hotel. From the rooms you can hear the *whaaa-whaaa* sounds of expiring waves from the recommencing sea.

THE GLOAMING TIME
23/05/99

It is now Canzibe on the Xhosa calendar, the month of the bright star Canopus, one of the things I missed seeing during the epoch I was in Europe.

I was hospitalized, for the second time in two months now. I don't feel like writing about it. I want to think about beautiful things from the pieces of memory still left so I brought my Pillow Books to bed with me to write, because I no longer have strength to get out of bed except when necessary to relieve myself. I want to write as things happen—record this very moment.

I ask Efuoa to lie down a bit next to me. I want to listen to the thousand meaningless things she says to keep me company that mean a million more to me. I need to hear her voice, like a baby needs their mother's voice, to reassure themselves in a strange new world. She has seen my book and my furtively writing hand. "It's gloaming time, Beast!" she says as she sits on the bed.

Often she gets excited about this hour she calls gloaming time. I've never asked her what she means by that, but get the idea from her insistences: "Come on, Beast. We need to milk the udder of your memories." I've learned to understand that this is about as good as saying: Kwahlala, kwahlala kwanga ntsomi... what our Xhosa elders say to gather us beside the fireside to listen to folklore and the mythologized histories of our origins.

Today she is satisfied with me committing my stories to writing, I do not have to speak.

The gloaming time, for me, is an hour where, in falling darkness, I see the eye of God gape to reveal the news of my death. I feel deeply the sense of loss, for it is mostly at this hour of moribund light that the realization of my own death holds me with an asphyxiating grip.

In the past, when I thought of death, it was as a literary event, an opportunity to demonstrate the superiority of my moral courage and detachment from mortal things. Sometimes, when I pretended to be wise, I understood how it could be a slow, quiet attrition of time against the weakness of the flesh. But thoughts about death bring with it a quiver to my soul now. Not because I now fear death. No! It has always been the process of dying that's my concern. I had always wished that death would spare me the banalities of dying, the humiliations of slow decay by getting on quickly with the deed. That process personalizes death too much for my liking, making it breathe on your neck with a language I'm unable to comprehend, though I hear its whispers. This shakes me.

I can't help but I want to feel the beauty of my healthy blood coruscate through my veins instead of this poisonous fungus. I want to think about the time life was simple. To think about St. Petersburg, Red Square, and the bell ringing to change guards. I want to feel the melting cold of ice cream on my hand. I want to be drunk after pouring thirty-five kopeks worth of bera on the public tap, and sit on a sagging sofa before a slow-burning log next to a woman who loves me with her faults and mine, and her passions. I want to talk sweet nothings until the first gray creeps in as the snow dusts the window. I want that feeling of being permeated by life in that flat again. To talk that talk we had about poets being emotional historians and engineers of the soul. I want to come home with the telling of high tales and the snowstorm sweeping outside. I want to reach the point of reflective saturation that banishes the cold of accretive loneliness inside. And I want to take Efuao with me this time, so she may understand that it is sometimes possible to bankrupt evil even on this side of heaven, that we don't need to wait for death and the coming world for goodness and justice to reign. That if the Prince of Peace is long delayed in coming, we can be his vicars on every corner we stand. I want to smell dark wood in the library of the International Lenin School in Moscow, even if it means hearing the harsh voice of my instructor shouting at me because I forgot to call something by its proper Russian name: "Po Russki, tavsrishchi!" I want to feel the coldness of snow again on my skin as I kneel before the grave of J.B. Marks; to go back to the comforting loneliness of my flat on Pushkin Square; to listen to Comrade Gorbachev talk about perestroika and glasnost, opening up to the world. To feel the palpable hope I felt then; to think how "uskorenie" and the principles of scientific socialism would accelerate development in my southern Africa. I want to feel hope again; to buy from a black-market taxi driver Tovaritch vodka, spasiba; with the hand of a hooker buried in my crotch; to feel the exhilaration of freedom and the whiteness of snow blinding me; to try and understand what J.B. found in all the Russian talk about the literature of the human spirit which they termed "novaya poeziya," the new poetry; and how that connects to Goethe's old call for Weltliteratur, world literature. To understand the pain of J.B. and Bloke, taking their last breaths in foreign lands. To understand what drove these wanderers and sojourners to feed their souls on foreign diets. I want to feel love forever. To fall asleep in the arms of a woman I love against the background of soul music, reverend Al Green, if that is permissible under the skies.

I am here now. Here within my dying moment, and with a woman who loves me beyond comprehension. She is asking for something, trying to break the stronghold of the dying thoughts that are seducing me away from the living. She means well. But I'm not the type to take solace from false hope. The loop of my life's horizon has curved back. The snake is devouring its tail. I'm almost amused by the absurdity of it all—I mean my dying—

until I hear her voice pull me back to the present moment.

"What was that? I didn't hear you?" I ask.

"I said would you like me to turn on the BBC World News service; it's almost time for the news."

"Yes, please. I would like that very much." The BBC is now my last window onto the world—what strange relations we have with our former colonial masters.

Efuoa and I sit in comfortable silence listening to the news. But I've zoned out; I'm writing. Have I mentioned here yet why she calls me Beast? It comes from a story I once told her while we were listening to World News. The news reported that some American pharmaceutical companies were contesting the developing countries' right to develop affordable generic medicines for AIDS and such. The whole thing reminded me of Aesop's fable "The Dog in the Manger." To while away time, I told it to Efuoa as she brushed my head, because the itching had started. The doctors had wasted time suspecting my itching was some kind of a psychosis, a coetaneous delusion. They said severe stress and other emotional experiences can give rise to a physical symptom like that. The internist I went to in Stockholm, courtesy of O.R.'s wallet, even suspected trichotillomania, what she called an obsessive-compulsive disorder that makes you have irresistible urges to pull out your hair. I had made the mistake of telling her that this used to be my reaction to stress in class when I was still a young boy.

Anyway, as Efuoa brushed my head I narrated the story of the dog in the manger to her: "Once upon a time a dog lay in the manger that was full of hay." Her face relaxed into pleasure for the gloaming time. The only thing missing was the response to the start of a fable in Xhosa culture: Chosi ntsomi singaphumi impondo. Like most Africans, she loves fireside stories, iintsomi.

"Hungry, the ox approached the manger and was about to eat the hay when the dog started in an angry snarl. This happened twice, thrice, until the ox turned in anger, cursing the dog.

'Surely, beast, there's something seriously wrong with you. Since you cannot eat hay yourself, you'll have no one else enjoy it.'"

Efuoa laughed and I smiled. I like very much to make her laugh, to see her happy. Better still, I liked that I didn't need to explain to her how the story links to American pharmaceutical companies.

Henceforth she took to calling me Beast. I think in her mind the word correlates also with Brute, the deodorant I use. She says she loves the muskiness of that deodorant on me, and spends hours lying with her head on my arm to smell it. She calls it my smell: "Come here, Brute, I want your smell!" She says things like that sometimes. I think the smell offers her familiarity and a semblance of peace and safety.

Now, the news having ended, Efuoa gets up and walks to the kitchenette, asking over her shoulder: "Would you like a cup of tea?" A cup of tea, overflowing with love? *My cup runneth over.*

"Yes, please!" Shouting takes my breath away. What does the Bard say? That we must *not strain the quality of mercy*. To those who've experienced severe mercy, kindness is no strain. In the language of T.S. Eliot, *these fragments I have shored against my ruins.*

BEACHCOMBING

You wake with the sun igniting wet fire on the immense sea surface. You go outside to meet the morning. The ocean is foaming and shivering on the rocks, giving you the shivers also. You walked toward the soft colors of the alpenglow-tinged tugboats and the sea-kissed wrinkled faces of fishermen with their shacks checking the ocean's pride through the eloquence of their poverty. You make your way through their press as they go to sea on their dhows. The sea-crows travel between the sky and the sea. Dhows sail against the dazzling golden light of the sun watching over the unflagging ancient patience of seamen. People shout in languages you don't understand. This bars you from blending in and exposes your fake habitué attitude. Like a gadfly your mind refuses to rest, so you walk toward the rocky side of the beach where women are collecting clams in buckets.

The corrugated sand is still icy on your feet when you take off your flip-flops. The beach path you take carries you to a slightly deserted band where you encounter a rather stranded stream into a shallow estuary as the streamlet crouches to the sea. You do a little risk assessment in your head and feel no elementary danger, which is how you would, sadly, feel in South Africa as a female alone on a slightly deserted part of a beach. Another comfort of being in Tanzania has been letting your guard slowly slip in such situations. It gives you deep shame to admit that the culture of violence in your country, especially against women, is not necessarily from poverty, but from a patriarchal sense of male entitlement to female bodies. Perhaps there are also some hidden national traumas left to fester untreated from the apartheid era in the psyche of your men.

This morning, fate has beautiful things to show you. As you make the bend, the vastness of the sea and the library of silences it creates becomes visible and audible. You spy your first white rainbow above the horizon. You had read about fogbows but never seen one in real life before. You interpret this to be some kind of good sign for the coming years of your life.

You decide to investigate a little. There's a sandstone formation that creates a natural channel for the pounding waves to form runnels. You hike your skirt as you dip your feet. The sea-kissed wind dampens your face. You walk to the other side of the cliff where the wind sighs on the caves as the sea claps against the rock. You bend your ear to the sea as you trace the marks of history on the rocks. Only a pair of what looks like Andean geese is curious about your doings. You walk back to the beach path thinking about how you read somewhere that they mate for life, and one of them commits suicide when the partner dies, sometimes by violently throwing itself down a cliff.

You cast your mind to the meaning of your father's journals for you. You see how they have become memory residues left behind by the receding tide like an envoi of his life.

FLÂNEUSES OF DAR

Back at the hotel Sandi looks soignée in a blue polka-dot dress. After breakfast in the hotel dining room, Sandi's alma mater, the University of Dar es Salaam, is first on your itinerary. You walk around the main campus, mostly looking at the architecture. You then walk downtown along Samora Avenue, memorizing the ancient cultural city with your feet like flâneuses, aimless wanderers.

"What I love most about them ancient cities, my sister," Sandi says to you as you walk, "is they been built before the mania of motor mobile, hence they're friendly to pedestrians." Then she drops her eyes to row after row of cobblestones that crust the Dar streets as if she were studying their patterns.

"You can walk them for hours, even if the only place you aim to get to is within your head," Sandi continues.

You keep quiet, feeling honored to be feasting your eyes even on the wounds of Dar's poverty, feeling somehow you have slipped the bounds of your responsibility and gone back to the innocence of your own youth, but with mature, comprehending eyes.

Dar is crammed with trade: vegetables, spices, rice, fabric, building materials, smoking and cooking utensils. The streets bustle with traffic, surge with pedestrians in the narrow spaces between old buildings. Entrepreneurs, like in most African cities, sit at stalls made of ragged tarpaulins and sheets of plastic, some playing strange games, others attentively watching European football on a small television set up in the street. Somehow real business also manages to get done amid all of this. Men mostly wear tribal dress, turbans, white smocks, or Western crimplene suits or jeans with tweed jackets. Women, in heels, heavy makeup, cartoonish long eyelashes, talk and laugh loudly with each other. Some have kids strapped to their sides or tugging on their skirts. You decide to buy fiber for your braids, toiletries, and clothes. In the fitting room where you're trying on a kente-cloth dress you ask Sandi, "Do you think Maman would like it if we buy her a dress?"

Sandi thinks about it. "Perhaps cloth will better suit her, my sister. She's a seamstress and so likes making her own clothes. We can go buy her some kente cloth and she gonna go do magic with it. Let's go look for some stylish jina she can make a dress from."

So you buy Maman different cloths, and you later learn that jina is the material you know as khanga and it has different labels. Sandi chooses the Mungu ndiye tegemeo letu for Maman, which she says means "We depend on God."

"She gonna go wild, girl, when she see you go buy her this," Sandi declares with excitement. She choses the Nalidumu letu pendo for the two of you, explaining its meaning as something like "Let our love stand forever."

You feel content and excited and start planning the pattern you want Maman to make yours into, a knickerbocker. You also shop for toiletries and a perfume for her.

From there you move on and linger at the Square Gardens to look, among other things, at the Askari Monument: a black soldier with a bayoneted rifle in attack mode on top of a stone base. Apparently, the monument was donated by the British government in the Sixties. Sandi explains to you the fucked-up history of Tanzanians killing each other on the side of both the British and Germans during the European tribal wars called World War II.

"But why did the Tanzanian government accept it?" you ask, naively perhaps.

Sandi shrugs her shoulders. "One day I'll take you to meet my uncle. He was in that government of Julius Nyerere, who accepted the monument. You can ask him."

You think about how in your country these soldiers, with bayoneted rifles, are usually white. That it is a black man here upsets you in a way you didn't expect. You think of how your people also died in foreign lands as the Carrier Corps, coming back from WW I to sow the seeds of death from the Spanish Flu pandemic on the urban areas and rural villages. And then being insulted by gifts of bicycles when their white counterparts were given houses.

As you walk toward the beachfront you think about how statues are a way of freezing reverence, which makes you wonder what the objectives are of those who say the statues of your disgrace must be kept for history's sake. The history that we were once askaris who assisted the axe in cutting down our own nationhood? That our misery has colonial roots? What are these statues supposed to contribute to us? That you must be in awe of the process of your own enslavement? That you must adore and never forget it? That you must be wary and never repeat it?

When you mention all of this to Sandi she urges you not to upset yourself. "Don't give them power to violate you even from the graves of history. We're here for fun, and fun them will not be robbing us of."

You lunch on a diwani-biryani, which you eat cross-legged on grass mats at a beachfront restaurant. You down the meal with a potent garam masala chai and some drink made with fermented milk mixed with spices and sugar, the name of which you didn't catch. You contemplate visiting the Kunduchi Ruins, but by then you're too drowsy, wobbly-kneed and too full to go anywhere.

After digesting the food you go back to the hotel, sit in the lounge with sundowners and chew the fat. You graduate to copious amounts of the weak Kenyan beer they have on tap as Sandi narrates to you the history of The House of Peace, السلام دار Dār as-Salām—Dar or Bongo if you are local—the oldest city in Tanzania. She tells you that where you took your morning beach walk are remnants of the charms of the small coastal village called Mzizima that Dar used to be. In Kiswahili it means "healthy town." And from the breath of fresh air you inhaled there you know exactly what they mean.

Like most port cities, Dar quickly grew into a moral risk-zone because of unsavory influences, Sandi tells you. She gives a mischievous smile before making a tlofo-tlofo sign, putting her index finger in her other cupped hand. Then she bursts out laughing. "Liquor shops attracted prostitutes like flies to cow dung." This, she explains, is known thanks to the recorders of the city's early history: priests, imams, starchy colonial government officials, and district police superintendents, themselves not too averse to spending stolen moments with the demimonde of Bongo City. The city's nightly dance pleasures, and its population's lack of impulse control where sex or violence was concerned, struck fear into official conservative hearts. But exploiting venal appetites brought by the colonisers as they passed through the port on their way to Zanzibar for spices became the foundational business of the city. So Bongo City survived and thrived. Her anatomy, to date, carries with it the scars of colonial influence in the form of dull but effective German architecture.

Dar's character today has a dynamism that comes from its mixture of Middle-Eastern punctiliousness, Indo-Asian enterprise, and German fastidiousness, topped with African unruliness.

At some stage, as the purple sky welcomes winking stars, the barman who has been serving you all night starts to look handsome and charming. You take that to be a sure sign that you are getting too drunk and decide to go to sleep.

ECDYSIS

With a pounding headache from the excesses of the day before, you go to lunch at the harbor. Most of the buildings you pass are moldy, slightly crumbling, with exposed black timber ribs and broken windows, and look neglected with efflorescence, the dandruff of decaying buildings. This defines the character of not only the city, but the country as a whole sometimes. But through all this is still a certain propulsive rhythm of quotidian ordinariness you fall in love with.

You sit at the outside tables of the restaurant on a veranda built on stilts. You sit there drinking and eating peri-peri prawns and chips for the greater part of the day.

At dusk you're joined by Sandi's old chums at a different restaurant, which sells wholesome Ethiopian cuisine. Sandi orders something called Beg Alicha for the group, which you later discover to be a savory lemon leg of lamb, falling off the bone, poured into a communal bowl that's lined with injera. It comes with Ayeb Be Gomen, a wild spinach sautéed with onions, garlic, herbs, spices, and crumbled cottage cheese. Somebody added spiced prawns on the side, while someone else ordered chicken wot and azifa, a blend of lentil soup. When you finish eating, feeling light-headed from too much tej, the popular honey wine, you have coffee, served in pots called jebena—probably the best coffee you've ever tasted.

"What did I tell you, maan? See what I mean? Nothing, and nothing beats Bongo City," boasts Sandi when she notices how pleased and impressed you are with the situation, especially the coffee. The two of you stay seated while her friends go to freshen up in preparation for hitting the club scene.

She continues, a look of nostalgia in her eyes, "There was a time I didn't see myself go living anywhere but here in Dar."

"What happened that you had to leave?" you ask, curious but not wishing to intrude.

A young boy with a polystirene cooler-box tries to sell you some cool drinks and ice cream. You politely decline by shaking your head.

"Had to grow up, maan!" says Sandi. "Everyone wants to go work in big cities and town, and not rural areas. So the government had to be tough on us, it paid for university, compelling us to go serve rural towns and villages. It took over nine months for me to make peace with being dumped on what I thought to be the backside of civilization, like Morogoro."

A ferry arrives from Zanzibar, choking you with diesel fumes. Then there's a sudden change of music in the restaurant—from the slow rhythms of Khadja Nin to the psychedelics of Fela Kuti to accommodate white tourists—as the ferry passengers disembark. Sandi's friends return almost immediately after, with glistening eyes, which you gather is from the hashish pipes.

They drag you to the club around the corner, on Market Street. The moment you enter you're marked by a Rwandan guy with a hyena laugh wearing a brown open-neck African shirt and brass-rimmed spectacles. He shadows you everywhere you go, sponging off of your beer without really asking, just pouring himself a glass from the pitcher. Initially, you thought he was with Sandi's friends, while they thought he was with you. You try to dodge his flirtatious maneuvering politely, but to no avail. You make sure your Okapi is secure in your bra. He complains about how cruel Tanzanians are to them as refugees. He tells you, eyelids drooping, that alcohol makes him horny. He licks his lips, looking at you.

His presumption irritates you. "Look, man," you politely say at first, "go to South Africa. Zimbabweans and Nigerians feel unfairly picked on by the locals. The Namibians can't stand the Zimbabweans in Namibia, but love the Mozambicans and South Africans. The Nigerians loathe the Ghanaians in Nigeria, and the Ghanaians return the favor in Ghana. The Somalis think everybody picks on them because they regard themselves as Arabs. The Arabs, from Tripoli to Cairo, think sub-Saharan Africans are slaves fit for the yoke. It's the way of the continent, man. Get on with your life."

You realize you were a bit harsh in your reprimand because you were getting fed up. He claims he lost his family during the Hutu–Tutsi genocide. You don't believe him, and feel angry that he's trafficking on other people's tragedies and pain. You feel he uses his Rwandan status to sponge beer and bum cigarettes off of the patrons. The drunker he gets, the more obnoxious he becomes and suspicious of everyone who wants to talk to you, including Sandi.

On the dance floor he tries to dry-hump you. As you walk away, he pulls you into a corner and proposes marriage over the ghastly noise of the dance floor. You're fed up with him and tell him to bugger off. Then he tries to take your hand to feel his erect penis under his trousers. You pull away and let him see a glimpse of your knife and he reluctantly backs off.

It's around four in the morning when you leave the club. The Rwandan, still ogling you with concealed hostility, turns his head away as you walk past his table to the door. Outside there are already signs of the slow approach of the pink-fingered dawn. It inspires a deep sense of *the Lord maketh everything new* in your heart, a process of ecdysis, the shedding of an old skin. The smell of oil and stale galleys brings you to your reality. You start throwing up in the alley with Sandi holding your arm and pulling your braids back.

"That's it, girl! Better out than in!"

The rising sun stabs your eyes as you slowly walk, hand in hand, back to the hotel against the muezzin call for adhan.

THE HARBINGER BIRD
20/06/99

"Are you a god?"
"No," he replied.
"Are you a reincarnation of god?"
"No," he replied.
"Are you a wizard then?"
"No."
"Well, are you a man?"
"No."
"So what are you?" they asked in confusion.
"I am awake."

This is the answer given by the Buddha, Siddhartha Gautama, when questioned on the road after his enlightenment.

I am dying, but I feel fully awake.

The best that can be said about my sickness is that it brought about the healthy evolution of my thoughts. The idea of death initially scared me; then it upset me; now it does not really concern me much. I've become a stranger to my own dying body.

Yes, I live more in memory, in fellowship with the dead rather than the living. Their condition interests me more now. I know that's unfair to the living, but it is what it is. I'm living on borrowed time—God, I hate these clichés. I'm resigned to things taking their course. But, somehow, I feel I must find the means to reconcile my past with my death, my future that is not.

I'm not sure why this is coming to me now after so many

years, but when I was about nine years old—the age of conscious awakening—still living in my father's rural home, I once woke from an afternoon nap to discover my older brother, my only playing companion then, gone. I didn't know where. My mother made a mystery of it when I asked so I left well enough alone.

It was early evening, a leisurely dusk was setting, drawing the curtain behind the mountains. Nothing indicated the day would be any different from the others, although things were a little slower than usual. I was at the age when we're most unsympathetic toward others and selfish in our demands. Not sure how to dissolve my bothersome sulkiness, I walked to where my feet carried me. Evening was drawing a dark veil, hastening down the purple sky. I wanted to climb the hill behind our house, to the spot where there's a rock table on which my brother and I usually held our picnics, munching things we had pinched from home, but it was too late already, and bushes could be full of unexpected things at night, like tikoloshes and zombies, so I didn't want to tempt fate.

At that spot we'd once seen an insectivorous bird with black plumage and a brilliant chestnut underside hovering before swiftly dropping to the ground to catch a locust. It impaled the locust in a thorn tree before pecking at it with furious urgency. The bird picked the locust apart piece by piece until only a miserable skeleton was left. My brother had thought it was cool. I'd thought it revolting. It'd seemed too cruel in my eyes, but I had not wanted to be accused of being a sissy so I'd played along.

On my bored walk I decided to investigate the cattle kraal, sheep pen, pigsty, fowl-run, and pigeon aviary—chores I was loath to do under normal circumstances, but time was one thing I had plenty of that evening. Unfortunately, everything was in order—no platform for an adventure. I shouted: "KULUNGILE!" just to raise my voice above the low murmur of the brown river snaking against the cliff, acting as our natural promontory. The echo brought my voice back to me thrice over.

Above, the dassies kicked the stones in retreat to their holes in the cliffs, suspicious of my intent. I reminded myself of the Xhosa proverb for those who invite trouble: Udibene nembila zithutha—he met up with migrating dassies. This is because dassies shove and push everything before them out of the way, sometimes tragically down the side of a cliff, when they're migrating. I wanted to shove and push things, but there was nothing, really nothing to encounter. I remembered from Sunday School that the dassies, *though they cheweth the cud they divideth not the hoof, so they are treif.* Cursed may they be then, I thought.

Next, I walked grudgingly to the rock I once injured my forehead against while playing rugby with my brother. I raised my hand to feel the scar, the fruits of my hurried clumsiness. I had the urge to piss on the rock, to remind it of who was boss, if nothing else. I unzipped my trousers and pushed. Not even a drop to justify the effort. Everything felt impotent. I considered myself then the expert of pissing against the wind and letting my fart fly unbounded to the skies. Impotent anger—my perpetual nemesis—started to swirl nausea within me. I turned my back to the river and got ready to walk back home.

That's when I saw, perched on a barbed-wire fence, a pair of swallows. In the sky, other swallows dived for mosquitoes like jet planes. I picked up a stone and thought, if only I could aim well enough to hit one of them it would blow my brother's mind. A swallow was a supreme prize in the hierarchy of bird catching, because it flies high and is very deft. I threw the stone violently but with indifference to the outcome because in my heart of hearts I was sure there was no way my aim would find its target. My gaze didn't even follow the stone's flight until a sickening thud pulled my eyes back. A single swallow was frantically flying toward the sky. Where's its partner, I wondered. I dropped my gaze to the ground where a strange black mound lay. I went closer. A swallow was lying dead from my blow. My first reaction was to look for witnesses, someone who could corroborate my story when I bragged. There was no one but the wind. This seemed tragically unfair. I took my spoils and went to sit on the threshold of the house. I examined the bird. I had never seen a swallow that close before. Indeed it was a magnificent bird. Where was my brother? What was keeping him so long? Who would believe it was not some wayfaring hunter who had sold me the swallow? Maybe I could show it to my mother, her corroboration would be crucial when questions arose later. But maybe not, she had no hunter's instincts.

I examined my prize further, the glorious feeling gradually turning into a confused anti-climax and hollow triumph. Something was invading and rooting out my killer instincts. The triumph was slowly turning feeble, superficial and vapid. When eventually I could no longer muffle the brutality of my act I ran river-ward with no clear intentions. By the riverside, scalding tears running down my cheeks, I sat. I was not sure what was wrong with me, or what to do. Why was I so feminine and unlike my brother and other boys?

The river was peaceful. It did not accuse. Usually, nature's insouciance troubled me but not that day. The frogs sang the sorrows of Pharaoh. I crouched down to hide from the eye in the sky, putting my arms around my knees and my head between my legs, harboring unexplainable violent feelings against myself, and the croaking frogs by association. Slowly I drifted into an unguarded sleep.

When I woke up, the stars shone. I stood to walk home, thickets and thistles scratching for my attention. Open primrose lilies expanded the white light of the moon on the fields before me. I hesitated at the threshold of the door until the gentle wind pushed me inside. I knew there was going to be trouble for my returning at that hour. My brother was back, sitting nonchalantly at the table with our mother, as if he had not deserted me earlier. Mother gave me the sharp look she usually did when angry.

I took my food from the iron oven, opened the lid and sat with them at the table.

The questions started coming, first from the Judas that was my brother. "Where have you been? We were worried stiff, looking everywhere for you." It irritated me that my brother was commanding the interrogation, giving himself airs of self-importance, as if he were my father, especially when everything was his fault to begin with. I wished someone would just beat me and get it over with because I'd been a very bad boy. But all they did was talk and talk: *WORDS! WORDS!* as Hamlet would say.

I stared at my hands, the hands that had learned to kill that day. Like Lady Macbeth, I wanted to call attention to the invisible blood on them. Instead I withdrew to my usual, deathlike silence, my eternal defense.

That night I had a strange dream. Men in ugly costumes and strange, fluttering wings encircled and taunted me with questions, asking me to choose between a snake and a locust. I screamed that they should leave me alone but they wouldn't. Since I had a terrible fear of snakes, I eventually chose a locust. Apparently I shouted out the answer because I was woken by my mother, who gently put me back to sleep after she was satisfied I was okay.

I woke early the following day, dug a grave on the spot where the bird had fallen, and buried it with a short, avian prayer: *For only a penny you can buy two sparrows, yet not one sparrow falls to the ground without your father's consent. As for you, even the hairs of your head have been counted. So don't be afraid: you are worth much more than a sparrow.*

Later on in my life, when I discovered that locusts and swallows are symbols of wanderers, I found the judgment fair.

CHRISTMAS IN THE TOWNSHIP
16/06/99

Bloomsday, the day all the action takes place in *Ulysses*, is Youth Day on the South African calendar. There, when Leopold Bloom is done vagabonding, he gets confined to a room where he must quietly sit, thinking about how, where, and when things started going wrong. But because mine is an African story, there's no proper telling of it without revealing how the wolves came down the mountain—we need to go back in time a little.

The boy's mother moved them into a two-roomed house in the township of KwaMlungisi, in Queenstown. His father became a fleeting visitor who occasionally dropped off groceries. The two rooms the boy's family rented were attached to the house of the township councilor; this was a man of affluent means who, according to the comrades, the boy later learned, was a stooge of the apartheid regime. It was the biggest house in the township, among the red-brick boxes and mud possies that were the common abode for most people in the area. The house was on the busy main road, across from which ran a dirty, stinking streamlet referred to as Voyisana. Because of that the boy's street was notoriously known as Kaka (Shit) Street. In that house the boy lost his faith in Father Christmas and most of the delightful illusions of childhood.

Christmas Eve he stayed awake, expecting a dodderer with a long white beard in a red suit to ride up in a reindeer-drawn cart from the North Pole and deliver the Chopper bicycle he had requested. The boy was determined to beat sleep this time, unlike other Christmases, to see Father Christmas, who had an irritating habit of coming just after he had dozed off. To his regret, he was too successful. Around midnight he spied, through the split he'd made in his blankets, his parents pushing two bicycles, not even through the chimney, but the bloody mundane door. The boy was too embarrassed for them to jump up as he had planned to do when the dodderer appeared.

The following day they relayed how Father Christmas came "while you boys were asleep…" They boy felt shame for them, for their fake exuberance orchestrated to give the impression they were still a family; for the insight he got watching them lie about Santa and their family. He wanted to cry, not for himself, but for the shame he felt on their behalf, for their pretending that everything would be all right, though the pieces of their family unit were strewn on the floor.

Then the shame turned into fury when they tried to convince him to exchange his superb Chopper bicycle, gears and all, with his older brother's stupid brake-pedal Clipper. The boy had spent months and months on research before coming to his choice. Now he had to just hand it over to his older brother who had carelessly chosen his. The boy could not believe his mother, in particular, would betray him like that. When he confronted her, she said, "But the Chopper looks more mature, baby. Your brother, who is older, should have it." Of course it looked more mature, that's the whole reason why the boy chose it, figuring he might ride it until high school. To parents who don't understand the idiosyncrasies of a nearly-eleven-year-old boy, one bicycle is just as good as another. So the boy ended up with an idiotic red Clipper and a lump in his throat. To add insult to the injury, it had a childish brake-pedal he hated, because one couldn't unwind the chain by pedaling backward when on the free control downhill.

It irritated him that his mother refused to fuss over his anger, acting as if she hadn't noticed he was not riding the bike. His anger extended to Christmas as a whole—he refused to eat the stupid Christmas food, though he stole a piece of the roasted Cornish hen when no one was looking. He finally understood the anger of Esau when that greedy upstart Jacob stole his inheritance for a bowl of lentil soup. Normally his sympathies were with Jacob, because they were both second-borns. But the bike incident drove him into Esau's corner.

Nonetheless, a snipe might not be game but it is still a bird, so slowly, during the following days, the boy noticed some endearing qualities about the Clipper as his anger lost its edge. First to attract him was the flaming-red color of the frame. Even the stupid ballooned tires, the color of a lion's mane, that initially seemed like pork sausages, slowly acquired an alluring aura. Before he knew what hit him, the venom had leaked out of him and he was riding the bike.

On the third day, the day of resurrection, things lost their punitive edge. The boy, filled with the excitement and pomposity of being a proud owner of a bicycle, something rare and exotic in the township then, found himself riding the bike wildly in the streets, making himself a nuisance to the milkman with his bicycle cart by provoking him for a race.

Late that night in bed he thought he needed to find his way back to Jacob, his favorite, without upsetting Esau. He thought about it for a long time before finally deciding to climb up to his brother's bed to show there were no hard feelings between them. Normally, the boy hated sleeping with his brother, who snored and kicked like a colt and farted almost every half an hour. But the boy wanted to set an example for Jacob and Esau to let go of their anger.

GIFT

The boy loved staying home because of the councilor's daughter, Nosipho, who was nine months older than him—not a year, as she liked to claim. He was her playmate at the pain of being ostracized by his older brother and friends. Boys in the township played with boys, unless they were so-called sissies. The streets were macho, chauvinistic, and unforgiving. Sissies were the bullies' favorite targets. Luckily for the boy, he had the unsung protection of his older brother. So sometimes he played house with his neighbor's daughter, dolls and what have you, for countless hours, to his brother's hidden disgust.

During their game she was the wife who cooked, cleaned, and looked after the family; while he, the man of the house, went to work. The work thing had no clear definition, so he sometimes took the opportunity to go shit in the ditches, or check on his bird traps as asked to do by his brother. They had two imaginary children, a girl and a boy. The boy was a rascal, always getting into trouble; smoking, sniffing glue and all things. In his father's eyes, the boy was only good for military school; the girl was the apple of her father's eye, being groomed to become an architect one day. Because he thought designing buildings and wasting space was the coolest occupation on earth. He loved building architectural and train models, things he used to enjoy doing with his own father before he became scarce around the house.

Sometimes there was very little that was imaginary about the husband's work. He had to collect empty milk or cold-drink bottles, sell them at the Indian shop half a kilometer away from the house. The tricky part came when the husband had to buy brown sugar for the tea he'd be served when he got home. He bought frikadellers—or something resembling them at least—that were made from the mushy offcuts left by the butcher's electric blade. They called them "frikadellers" just to be fancy, instead of the derogatory term "isitatsatatsa," mix of everything. He bought umomotyeni, brown sugar that had been melted in butter and left to harden, from the Chinese shop a few blocks away.

The kids, including the boy at that stage, believed that Chinese people ate children, sacrificing them to Moloch or some nefarious god like that—depending on which fables, prejudice, and superstition you chose to believe from the variety going around. But a husband had to support his family. The solution came when the boy saw an adult approaching the shop. The boy walked close, very close to the adult, pretending to be his son. The shop smelled strange, too, which just added fire to the rumors about the Chinese making umuthi out of black children's pilfering fingers. The crucial thing was to not look the old Chinese lady in the eye, which, according to rumor, had hypnotic power that could put you to sleep immediately.

On the days that he couldn't muster enough courage to go inside the shop, the boy asked any adult to buy the sugar for him while he waited outside. Trouble was, the shop had several doors, and not all adults were honest folks. It was not unheard of for him to be standing outside one door for hours, waiting, while the adult had slipped out another exit. Boy, did that get him into trouble back home in their house play.

"Phew! Honey, I'm home."

"Was your day a success?"

"So-so."

"Do you have something for the house?"

"Just a few things: amretstese, umomotyeni, nemixang-xatho." The relatives, the mother, and the father.

These, ginger biscuits, brown sugar, and malt candy, were the staple food of their house.

"Sit down then, my dear husband. Let me pour you a cup of tea after your hard work."

Proud as a peacock, and content as the mule, the boy sat himself down on a makeshift chair of bricks under the windowsill while his dear busied herself on his behalf. The wind blew softly while a fingernail moon hung visible in the daylight blue sky. He liked it when the moon, having grown fatter, dragged itself up from the horizon line, warming the evening skies to hatch the stars as night fell. His brother would say the pale light of the moon doesn't warm, it chills. But what did his brother know? His brother's nose was always in books about mechanics and his mind was always looking at things from a scientific angle. After reading a book about the Romantic English, most of which, granted, was too advanced for him, the boy emerged with an understanding on some level of why he felt oppressed by the things around him. *Because I am a poet*, he concluded, rather pretentiously.

"Your head is screwed on the wrong way," his brother liked saying. The boy knew himself to be constant as the Northern Star. Besides, there were worse things than having your head screwed on the wrong way. His mother told him that, when he was young and had just started walking, the boy, noticing for the first time his own shadow, became petrified. He came screaming inside the house, craning his neck to see if the shadow had followed him. Another time, it was told by his mother, he refused to go out because he was afraid of the moon watching him. His mother was the one who put ideas in his brother's head by saying things like, "I've never seen anything like this, being afraid of your own shadow like a lunatic dog. Your head is screwed on the wrong way."

The boy hummed under that windowsill as he watched Nozi mixing sugar into their cups. He was besotted with her and scared she was going to think his head was screwed on the wrong way if he mentioned anything about the majesty of the mountain Lukhanji, or the blossoming moon above its crest. He had once dreamed that the mountains limbered and moved like people, which almost convinced even himself that his head was screwed on the wrong way. But he loved the silent grandness of those mountains, as if it were okay to tell them everything, especially fears and dreams about falling stars, without worrying that they'd think his head was screwed on the wrong way. Shakespeare, always with a language for every emotion, must have felt the same way about forests—that's why he put that stuff in Macbeth's head, the boy used to think.

While sitting like that under the windowsill, watching Nozi and the world float by, the boy would sometimes be startled by his mother's voice calling: "Phakamile! Phakamile!" He bided his time, not answering. When his mother used his full name, not the diminutive Phaks, it always meant trouble. He sat there, stunned that out of all possible meanings in the world, this name was assigned to him for his attention. This fascinated him no end. He deliberately kept quiet to see if this living thing called his life would answer without him willing it to. It never did. So this thing could not act without him driving it. This blew his mind, the power he had over this living thing. Where did he get this power? Better still, why did he get this power?

"Phakamile, I know you can hear me. If I have to come out there to get you myself then uzakuyibona into endibhinqe ngayo; there'll be hell to pay." He would eventually give in by going inside.

"Where are my swim trunks, Ma?" This time it was his brother's voice breaking his reverie. The boy's heart jerked with panic when he heard what his brother was looking for. The boy hated swimming, it gave him headaches. A moment later his brother came storming out the house, having found his swim trunks. He made his way straight to where he knew he'd find the boy, under the windowsill at the back of the house. "Get up, we're going to the public pool," he commanded with manic intensity. "You have to master the breaststroke," he continued firmly. "Everyone masters it now, even children younger than you. I'll not have you embarrassing me with your clumsy swimming strokes." There were daggers in his eyes to intimidate the boy out of any thoughts of refusing.

Can't an honest workingman have a quiet cup of tea with his beloved without people spoiling their peace with their own agendas, the boy thought to himself. His dear gave him an accusing stare but knew it was pointless to argue because he'd eventually succumb to his brother out of fear of being called a sissy. The boy wished he were man enough to answer: "So what do stupid breaststrokes have to do with me? I'm staying with my wife today." Or that he could be man enough by saying: "Woman, I'm going swimming, and shall see you when I come back." Caught between a rock and a hard place, he stood up and followed his brother with his tail between his legs. He turned his face toward his beloved before disappearing around the corner.

The look of disappointment etched on her visage haunts him still.

EVEN ON SUNDAYS

You leave Dar on Sunday in the late afternoon. The mountain air drowns everything with blue vastness as the bus drives out of the city. You lean your head against the window as you stare out at the widening plains of non-concreted space. With Sandi's head on your shoulder, her breath against your neck, you listen beyond the throbbing of the bus engine.

When you grow tired of open vistas you take out an old foreign journal you had bought at the second-hand bookshop at the market square. You had been attracted by Theodore Dalrymple's review of a book titled *A Time for Machetes* by Jean Hatzfeld. You stop reading it upon reaching the testimony of Francine, a Tutsi farm woman and shopkeeper. It makes you too emotional as it reminds you of Maman.

Francine admits that she would not be able to forgive the person who killed her family, even if he were to come begging for it. She says she often imagines a scenario where the killer(s) of her family would approach her and say: "Bonjour, Francine, I have come to speak to you. So, I am the one who cut your mama and your little sisters. I want to ask your forgiveness."

"Well," she says, "to that person, I cannot reply anything good. A man may ask for forgiveness if he has one Primus (beer) too many and then beats his wife. But if he has worked at killing for a whole month, *even on Sundays*, whatever can he hope to be forgiven for?"

You muse that it's easy to talk of forgiveness from a theoretical point of view, especially when it is not ourselves who must forgive. The Christian upbringing teaches that forgiveness is a virtue, the noble sentiment epitomized by renowned men like Mandela. So if people fail to live up to this noble ideal they're labeled bad, vengeful, full of grudges. Meanwhile nobody judges those who failed to live up to the common decency of not hurting and murdering others, their neighbors. All of a sudden the perpetrators are turned into victims. Supposedly it wasn't their fault, they were misled, abused by the system. Or even worse, it is implied that the victims had it coming to them; they're to blame for not anticipating it. So, basically, the responsibility is always on the victims: first to suffer the injustices, murder, and pain, then the consequent burden and responsibility of redeeming the toxic situation.

Suddenly there are formulas like the Gacaca trials and the Truth and Reconciliation Commission for perpetrators to lie with impunity, making themselves feel like victims through convenient lies, so they may get away with murder. All they need to do is turn up at these bush courts at appointed times and pretend remorse while lying by concealing further details beyond what's commonly known. Then they are free to enjoy the fruits of their chicanery, and most of the time are still financially well off enough to indirectly oppress the victims, hire them for menial jobs that still render them at their mercy.

And then people wonder about the collective anger in places like South Africa, why the majority of its people feel so angry. They feel robbed of justice, that's why.

You recall your tentative discussions with Maman on the subject. It is clear her sentiments are like those of Francine in the journal article. They can be summed up by a line from the poem "Snow for Wallace Stevens" by Terrance Hayes: *I have a capacity for love without/forgiveness.*

Could this be the real meaning of Yehoshua's command to love our enemies? That we must love our enemies even if we have no ability to forgive them? Phaks wrote, in one of his note-books, that the act of remembering is an attempt to engage with the present through the idiom of the past. That the past goes nowhere, especially not for the defeated, because often memory is their only weapon.

Your thoughts travel to your home country where the so-called victors are still the defeated in the South African situation. The end of apartheid brought little to the victors besides a right to vote and other half measures of freedom. The majority still live their defeated lives, daily provoked into anger by the rising affluence of those who perpetuated the apartheid system. As if that's not enough, their disappointed hopes are stoked by the Animal Farm story the country is fast turning into, by the faces of the pigs now resembling those of humans. Liberators have taken the seats of the oppressors while failing to change the system. Your Mandelas were co-opted into the system they were sup-posed to have overthrown.

From Phaks's Pillow Books, you can see that his inability to re-turn to South Africa had much to do with the fact that he felt the ideals of the struggle had been betrayed. He felt that justice had not been done. Why did so few Hutus and apartheid perpetra-tors ask for forgiveness, you wonder. To you their refusal to ask for forgiveness when they've *worked at killing for a whole month, even on Sundays* is a sign of consistency on their part. If a person forgives you in that situation, they do so without your asking, not for your sake, but for their own—to limit the rise of the bile. Why should people stand in endless queues at the Truth and Reconciliation Commission, or the Gacaca trials, bloating their ankles? So they may dignify murderous liars who'll do anything to avoid prison? Say the murderers get convicted, so what? The truth sets who free?

Some things are beyond human retribution. Even if you were to hang these murderers in the cruellest manner possible, what would this accomplish?

Sandi wakes and stirs you from your darkening thoughts.

"What you doing staring into space like that, maan?" She stretches as much as the limited space of her seat allows.

"Oh, sleeping with my eyes open."

"It's much better with your eyes closed."

You smile and take out your phone, plug in earphones and give one end to Sandi to share. "Here, now we can dream together." You scroll to Sona Jobarteh while telling Sandi that she comes from a long West African tradition of troubadours, griots, and kora players from Mali and Gambia.

"These are the quintessential founders of the blues, maan," Sandi agrees.

This prompts you to add Ali Farka Touré to the playlist, who keeps the tradition in your era.

You get lost in the music as the bus makes its juddering way to Morogoro.

THE DROWNING OF MICE

Walking to the public pool with his brother's gang, some of whom were ugly as sin, the boy felt nauseated. They walked in bravado, making stupid boasts about challenging the colored kids. This was the first the boy heard of it, that they were on their way to one of those stupid street wars. So, he was fetched to boost the numbers of amabutho in the darkie warfare ranks.

To while away time until two in the afternoon when the pool opened, the group made a detour to the small bush beyond the rivulet where it was rumored the tikoloshe lived. They spent a few minutes trapping striped mice by pouring water from milk bottles into rat holes. The holes were blocked with the mouths of the bottles so that water-drenched mice climbed up straight into the bottles.

Somebody passed a cigarette to the boy. He dragged to appear macho while wondering what kind of a pastime it was that necessitated the drowning of mice. The drag kicked him like a horse's hoof. For a second he couldn't breathe. In those few seconds he reckoned he was dying of cancer like his grandfather, who died of it because he smoked a pipe. This was the gospel according to his mother who was a nurse and so knew these things. He immediately developed a splitting headache.

The trapped mice were killed, skinned and dismembered, and everyone had to share in eating their tiny livers doused with bile to strengthen the impi against the colored kids. The rest of the meat was fed to those who still wet their beds. The boy had no reason to be concerned about that, though one night when their parents were at the hospital the boy had been too scared to go out to the dark, dirty public toilets to pee in the middle of the night. Thoughts of the eerie silence of the toilets, ever fetid and disgustingly foul, had discouraged him. His brother, despite his macho pretenses, had concealed his own fear by ridiculing the boy's unmanly inability to control his bladder.

"Ma said not to open that door unless during an emergency. You'll just have to hold your bladder until morning or our parents come home, whichever comes first," his brother instructed. The boy went back to sleep with a burning bladder and a determination to man up. Their parents did not come home that night, because it was the night the boy's maternal grandmother died. His grandmother had been taken to the hospital in Lady Frere, about seventy kilometers outside town, because the local hospital where their mother worked didn't admit black people.

That night the boy dreamed he was playing soccer with friends on a green field. In the dream he excused himself. "Stymie, gents. I need to pee." He went to the fringe of the field, took out his penis and tried to push the piss but the pee was coming painfully slow as if something was blocking the urine outlet. Then there was a bursting. Suddenly he awoke to discover he had just wet his bed.

The next morning, when their mother asked what happened, he told her the whole story, how he'd wanted to go for a pee but his brother had told him to man up. Then his brother was in trouble with their mother, and the boy was in serious trouble with his brother.

On their way to school that morning his brother cussed and said, "I must suffer because you were not man enough to hold your bladder." He threatened to tell the boy's peers that he wet his bed. If that secret got out, the boy knew, he'd be done for. He was going to be the talk of the school, and chicks, even Nozi, he imagined, would have nothing to do with him, since he was a wetter. The boy could already imagine undergoing the humili-ating ritual of eating raw rat meat, drowned, skinned, and un-seasoned. He imagined the school kids' taunting laughter.

Luckily, his brother did not tell, not ever. He worshipped him for this for a day or two, but then his brother went back to being his old irritating, blackmailing self: making him wash and dry the dishes alone, make up his bed also, until the boy reached the end of his tether.

"Hayi suka! You can tell, I don't care. I'm tired of being your slave!"

But his brother never told, ever. The thing about his brother was that he could not stand seeing other people ridiculed too much, even if he taunted the boy now and then, "to make a man out of you." He liked pulling pranks, but did not like it when pranks went too far.

Around two in the afternoon, the boys made their way to the entrance to the public pool. There, colored kids had created a roadblock against the darkies. To the boy's brother and his stu-pid friends, this meant the colored kids had to be removed. The colored kids were not backing off; the darkies were determined. The boy knew in his heart of hearts that nothing good would come of this. He would have rather left for home but had to hang around for fear of being called a sissy.

"We're going inside the pool, even if it kills us," said his broth-er with a fanatical intensity that alarmed the boy. He looked around to see if anybody wished to overrule his brother's com-mand and be done with this madness. No such luck. His brother was the alpha wolf. Their faces were all wearing the same ex-pression of brave stupidity. All of them were willing to take on the colored kids, although they were outnumbered at least by half. They trusted in mice-liver fortification, the Nxele syndrome of bullets turning into water. The boy had no choice but to en-ter the spirit of things, assuming a mean look, so as to be seen as macho. Somehow he knew he couldn't pull it off. There was fakery in his efforts. He didn't fool anyone.

The darkies gathered their strength outside the pool yard by sending word to other darkies at home for reinforcement. Tipsy with fear, the boy wondered if perhaps he could be the one to carry the word around. But his brother disallowed it, probably realizing the boy would delay his return. Somebody else was sent instead. The boy longed for the peace of his home, the smell of baking bread, bacon, or pickled fish when he remembered it was Easter. He was even willing to wash the dishes, whether it was his turn or not.

He saw two police vans, the vantyis, approach. He never thought he would feel such relief at seeing a vantyi. But to his dismay the vantyis parked at a distance. The bastard police climbed onto the canopies of the vantyis—to have a better view of the ensuing fight. They started betting on the outcome. The bastards!

The boy diverted his mind by recalling the nice white man who sold his family fish and chips at Hexagon Fisheries, although he was not supposed to sell to black people. The man got in trouble with other white people, who threatened to report him to the police. The boy had wished to leave, but his mother and the white man had stood their ground. The family had sat down to eat their food, with white people gawking and the black staff cheering them on.

"It's because he's from Europe," his mother had explained later, which hadn't actually explained anything to the boy. He was just grateful they'd left the place in one piece. But from there on, in his mind, Europe became a place where white people didn't mind selling fish and chips to black people. Where they even let them sit at their clean tables, passing vinegar and tomato sauce to them without asking questions or sneering and lifting their noses. The boy hated vinegar on his fish and chips, but that day, because that kind white man had passed it on to him, he'd drenched his chips in it, still making sure it at least didn't touch his fried battered fish, because, kind white people or not, putting vinegar on your fried fish was just blasphemy.

As the scramble with the colored kids heated up, the boy wondered what would happen were he to turn around and leave in front of everyone. Would his brother tell everyone he pees his bed to embarrass him? Would his mother protect him against his brother later on if he told her upon arriving home that he didn't want to fight itshaba with colored kids? The boy knew their mother did not approve of such fights, and so thought it would be the best tactic to defend himself against his brother. Different questions spun in his mind. He felt trapped, like a drowning, bottled rat that would soon be skinned alive for a colored kid who wet his bed.

When it was finally deemed that the darkies had enough strength for the attack, his brother issued the command. Now would be a good time for his mother to come calling, sending him on some errand to the ends of the earth, the boy thought, as he pushed within the center of the attack as instructed by his brother. Now would be an even better time for those useless policemen watching from the vantyis in the distance to disperse the crowds, instead of shouting: "Slaan hulle hard! Gaan slaan hulle! Moer hom! Hit them! Fuck them up!" Now would be the best time for the sun to lose its shine.

Everyone was gathering around the party led by his brother. How did their group end up right in the middle of this battle, the boy thought to himself. Did getting to the battlefield first qualify you to be a commander? The boy distrusted the sudden fame of their group but to the battle they had to go. A Tennyson poem recitation from class was the last thing he remembered as they charged:

> Theirs not to make reply,
> Theirs not to reason why,

Theirs but to do and die.
Into the valley of Death
Rode the six hundred.

The actual battle took place at the sides of the pool, with stones and expletives as major weapons—things had still not degenerated to the advanced stage of knives and guns then. The worst one got was a split lip, a swollen head, from fists and stones, and bruises from falling. This was not the first time they'd fought with the colored kids, neither would it be the last. Apparently, the boy later learned, this was a revenge attack for two darkies who had been pounced on by colored boys because one of them had hooked up with a colored chick. And the darkies were sending a stern message by taking them on on their territory, since they disallowed darkies swimming in the municipal pool because it was in the colored area of the township. The darkies repaid them in kind with the bioscope, since the municipal hall was on the darkie side.

The battle his brother led became something of a legend in their township—since it was the only time the darkies had won on foreign ground. It became exaggerated in the telling of how the coloreds outnumbered the darkies by ten to one. Everybody kept referring to the initial numbers and conveniently forgot that they had sent for reinforcements.

The boy's brother became untouchable after that, feared and respected by almost everyone. The only thing that trumped this bravery was becoming a hawk, going into exile, not fighting coloreds but the boers. The boy would, a year later, when his brother was in boarding school, be expected to be the ringleader—okay, not really the ringleader, but that's what he made his brother believe in the letters they wrote each other when he asked.

The boy didn't feel much like celebrating the victory that day. So he stole out when everyone was busy patting one another on the back. He heard people say that he, the boy, was brave as

a lion too, and describe things he didn't really remember doing. And not wishing to tempt fate, lest the colored kids were
regrouping somewhere for a rematch, he made himself scarce.
At least everyone had seen he was in the thick of things, that was
enough. No one could ever accuse him of being a sissy. But he
had had enough of the testosterone stuff for the day and wanted to lick his wounds with his amica. He found she had already
gone inside the house, and immediately he knew there would
be a storm in their "marriage" the following day. The boy then
went inside his home in a cranky mood to find his mother in an
even nastier mood, anxious to send someone to the shops for
kerosene before it got dark.

"Where have you been?" she demanded.

The boy took the money and the empty two-liter container
and got on his bicycle with an annoyed now-you-send-me-to-the-
shops-where-were-you-earlier-on face. He pedaled vehemently
under the darkening skies where ucel'izapholo, the milk beg-
gar, was hitching a ride on the fattening fingernail moon. He
tried to remember the name they'd been taught at school for
ucel'izapholo. Venus, the goddess of lovers. Everywhere this
thing of wanting to smooch was getting out of hand, the boy
was beginning to notice—goddess of love, my foot.

The wind increased its biting force against his face the faster
he went. He had about seven minutes to get to the shop before
it closed. If he came back without the kerosene he wouldn't
hear the end of it from his mother. It'd also mean no warm supper. The smell of the blighted canal, voyizana, with its banks of
solid rubbish, gripped him by the tonsils. He pedaled more and
more until he was obstructed by a small crowd gathered around
something. He nearly ran them over because the brake-pedal
nonsense made the back wheel of his bike skid when he braked
too hard. On the ground lay a man, struggling with death in
his chest. Whoever had stabbed him didn't have enough time
to retrieve the knife; it bobbed with every difficult breath the

man took. When the struggle finally stopped it irritated the boy that the most feared thing, death, was so ordinary. He was expecting a supernatural drama, angels and demons fighting over the man's soul or something. He continued spying around for the hidden signs as to which direction the dead man's soul was going, heaven or hell. Nothing! Nada! A seed of suspicion was planted in his soul against the stuff they say at church but he had no time to philosophize. He had to leave before the shop closed.

Johnson General Dealer was luckily still open, although surely he was at least four minutes late. He bought the kerosene, and a can of Pepsi-Cola with the change. The Bible says the working-man is entitled to his pay, so he didn't feel like he was pilfering his mother's money. Soon after, his bravado deflated and he was dreading facing his mom and explaining what had happened to the change, so he took the longer route home that passed over the hill, to buy himself time to finish his Pepsi. This was where he always went when things were not comfortable, or some indefinable weight pressed on his shoulders. The hill was not that steep, but gave an excellent view of the town. From up there the town, lit up, looked bright and marvelous. When at church they preached about the devil taking Christ to a lofty place to tempt him with earthly glory, the boy always imagined him on this hill, drinking Pepsi, eating sweets and ginger biscuits, and chilling.

IN LOVE

The boy was now thirteen years old. Things were happening in his body he was not entirely certain about. His beloved was nine months older but not yet fourteen. Now her breasts scooped beneath her clothes, making the boy fumble over what he wanted to say when speaking to her. Her thighs were becoming nubile as a nymphet's, inducing ideas in the boy's dreams that gave him unruly hard-ons in the morning which embarrassed and delighted him at the same time.

One early evening, the boy and his beloved were coming from the shops. Their love gave them courage to take the tikoloshe ditch because they wanted the concealment of the bush there to steal a kiss. An intense urge came over the boy to give free rein to the warm surge within him. Encouraged by the pale darkness of dusk, he gave her a tender kiss. The contact was so minimal; her lips quivered to the touch. Her breath smelled of cooked pumpkin. She giggled from the realization of what he had just done, but he didn't know what the next step should be, so they walked in veiled excitement and obscure awareness of things coming to a head between them. At one stage their hands brushed as they walked. This charged and convinced the boy that, as the poets insinuate, their love was writ in the skies. After that, thoughts of her became amorous in his every dream, but he didn't yet possess the conceptual language to define and express his feelings. All he knew was that the pressure on his senses doubled with every encounter they had.

So, one evening, encouraged by a strong compulsion to materialize his dreams, he kissed her. This time the kiss was long, calm, and deep, following the dictates of overheard talk between his brother and his friends, as well as the prophetic images in the boy's own dreams. This time he was determined to experience even the wonder and ecstasy of what his brother and his friends called the "French kiss." He was still inexperienced and his maneuvering clumsy. Accidentally having trapped her saliva in his mouth, he drew back a little, not knowing what to do with it, or how to proceed. By instinct he knew it would be rude to spit it out. For a moment he remained stuck, until he braved it and swallowed her saliva. That cooled his interest in French kissing somewhat. He suspected himself of being in love. To be sure, he thought about what it actually entailed to be in love. All the disgusting stuff his brother and friends described as being in love did not correspond at all with what he felt: light-headed, rushing blood, racing heart and all, as if he had just run the race of his life. His brother and friends talked about touching wet panties and romping against walls. The boy just didn't see where all that fitted in with how he felt. And he definitely didn't want to make his beloved scream, since it sounded painful, and he wasn't touching nobody's undies: *No, sir, not me!* he thought to himself. As they reached Nozi's home, he watched her flip-flops, clap-clopping, flip-flopping as she disappeared through the front door into the lit passage.

Soon he reached his own home and went straight to his mother's bedroom to think things through before the full-length mirror. He concluded that the kiss did happen and was not just a figment of his imagination, since he still smelled of her. He needed to put to rest the issue of his swallowing her saliva—was it disgusting or not? He watched himself in the mirror, studying the glowing features of his face before shaking his head in satisfaction and admitting that it actually wasn't that bad. He winked in self-congratulation. *You're in love. You're a sly thing, aren't you?* He came closer to the mirror so that he could see the pupils of his eyes because he'd read in a magazine that they dilate when one is in love. He smiled at the universe. Determining this being-in-love thing was very important to him because he wanted to know for sure where they stood with each other. But before he was able to figure out the imperatives of someone who is in love, the sand had run out in the hourglass.

The boy and his beloved usually walked home from school together, but one Tuesday she was not at her school gate, their usual rendezvous point. He thought nothing of it beyond that she must be on detention or finishing her homework or something. He looked and waited for her with growing impatience until he noticed a small crowd at the far end of the street. He went to investigate out of curiosity and for something to do while he waited. The thought struck him that she must have also been curious about the commotion and had gone to investigate. When he came closer, he noticed the crowd was chanting freedom songs. It was South Africa in the Seventies, everyone had a political grievance of one kind or another, it spread like a rash around every street corner. Then he saw something that would never leave his mind, ever. He shoved his way through the crowd to take a closer look. By then he could hear her name being mentioned against the sound of the freedom song. Most definitely those legs and shoes were hers.

She was in the midst of it all. His heart jerked and missed a beat. A cold shower ran down his spine. They'd tied and gagged her. His mind locked. He couldn't breathe. She was kicking and screaming, intrepid as she was, trying to force her way out of their circle; but it was no use. The racket of the freedom song was already proclaiming her fate. The usual jumble ensued. There were some who questioned why she had to die for the sins of her father, but the voice that wanted to teach her father an unforgettable lesson for "undermining the liberation movement" prevailed. Her father had availed himself for the position of councilor in the apartheid regime, thus committing a cardinal sin, thus playing Russian roulette with the lives of his loved ones. They'd bound her with barbed wire. Some threw bricks at her face, bruising the delicate forehead he had kissed just the other day. Some kicked her as she fell. They made her imbibe gasoline and threw some more over her body. It overwhelmed and intoxicated her. She fell again, this time on her lip, which immediately swelled. She struggled against their kicks. A Molotov cocktail spread its fire over her back. She grimaced and winced against the lust of death. Her face deformed and performed the rites of death. Her body became a flaming torch that charged the howling crowds. Staggering, she ran. Shouting, she called. Raging, she screamed that she'd be their last victim. Shuddering, she fell. She fell and surrendered her guard against the chants of the crowd. Some kicked her while she was down. Others cursed her as his soul drowned.

A terrible silence reigned for a moment, the ghastly ring silence makes when it is brooding disaster. Her sizzling body jerked its last protest against the futility of things before ceasing to struggle. The crowds stopped chanting and waited for the sickening thud of the skull's explosion from the exothermic reaction. Someone laughed.

"She's brave for a girl. She died like a young lioness."

Satisfied expressions of pompous perversity were painted on their faces. He thought it must have been like this on Golgotha, when the Roman soldiers pierced the side of the Savior of the world. Still the realization didn't console him—if anything, it made him angrier. Gratified, they hummed again to the tutelary gods of the liberation.

The Mellow Yellows, police armored vehicles, came, late as usual, yelping sounds of alarm. Vantyis trundled along the street, their headlights, protected behind steel wire, lit. Like hunting dogs they probed the shadows cast by the late-afternoon sun. Everyone dispersed in running haste.

She lay there, a derelict in the wild, and the victim that wasn't mild.

The boy stood dazed next to her body, against the cruel nature of things. Tears ran down his face, but he uttered not a word. He felt pinned to a shaft of light disappearing with the descending darkness. He tried to think of a way to trick the light into staying but he was out of ideas. All of a sudden he became acutely aware of the weight of his schoolbag on his back, and realized that the gutters of his gray socks were pinching him. Something hit him on the head from behind as he was about to bend and scratch that itch. Darkness fell.

He woke hours later in his bed, damaged, with an open vein at the back of his skull. He could identify his mother's voice sounding as if from a cellar down below.

"He was lucky the police came when they did." Thinking through his biblical filter, he wondered how lucky Peter felt for fleeing from the Roman soldiers and denying his Lord. Through his window he could see a solitary bird, maybe a swallow. Immediately he understood its significance. He resigned himself by accepting the verdict of fate. Since then all solitary birds have haunted him. In them he saw Isis looking for Osiris' fourteenth piece, swallowed by the fish in the Nile. And he has now lived long enough to know that locusts are symbols of perennial wanderers. He understands clearly now the verdict of fate that creates, in every age, lost Dantes and Wordsworths to be guided by their Beatrices and Lucys as inspirations of conversion and grief. He shed a tear, more for the nature of human things and the suffusedness of the living by the dead than for himself.

SPINNING THE LOOM

After another busy week at the hospital, you take Maman the presents you bought for her in Dar. She is delighted about the fabric and the two of you immediately start planning the clothes she will make.

Maman tells you of the latest garments she's fashioned for clients. The wedding industry is growing in the region and everyone wants a special dress for the occasion. Her excitement diminishes somewhat when she says, "You won't believe what happened at the market last week."

"No, what happened?" you ask.

"I go to this woman who owes me 100,000 shillings for the wedding dress I made for her daughter who got married six months ago. I ask for some yams from her vegetable stand. She go refuse me since I don't have enough money with me. Can you believe it?"

"That's terrible!" You cannot bear that Maman is being taken advantage of.

"The daring of it! Mahaba! That's what it is, a scandal. Lord of my jabali!"

"Did you ask her for your money?"

"I didn't have the heart for it. Our ombi is for amani, when the evil tests us."

"Perhaps you are being too charitable," you suggest hesitantly. You don't want to overstep your boundaries.

"Her daughter is still out of work. I don't know why she wanted to be married in such expensive clothes. What a jamil she is."

And that makes it all right for her to rob you clean? you think to yourself, but keep quiet.

"You know," Maman continues, "Beast...your father, he blamed the pastor and his wife for encouraging the rise of the expensive wedding industry and accused them from profiting from it. But it's not our church. It's how things are done in this region."

You nod, but think she might be protesting a bit too much. Phaks might have been right. You know that many churches in this country have made a point of accumulating power—both financial and political. This is why charismatic pastors are now sometimes elected as presidents here, or why only those with affiliation to these churches are politically successful. In fact, this adoption of desperate superstition is resurgent in African and global politics all over. Politics are getting suffused with the naive sophistication of dangerous little knowledge. Uniformed conservatism feels justified to challenge even genuine scientific knowledge with bold ignorance. The world in general has fallen under the cloud of willful, triumphant ignorance.

Maman changes the subject to dinner and you move to the kitchen to help her cook. You are spending the night and after dinner you sit down at Phaks's desk with one of his Pillow Books while Maman starts working on patterns for the dresses she wants to make.

You wish you had the courage of Francine and Maman, the courage to believe, to scrape for the spark of goodness in all human hearts.

To see things clearly now you find yourself thinking through Phaks's metaphoric classical imagery. You've crossed over your familiar frontiers, left Ur, your home, and those who are familiar to you behind. But the God of Abraham frightens you—He demands too much sacrifice, too much blood. You cut your teeth on the God that is incarnate, whose cross has a clear purpose of redemption: hope. Things are a little foggy with the God of

Abraham. For instance, Ishmael (God Hears), though older born, must leave home to live by the sword in the desert; become a menace to his brothers, *like thorns in their sides.* Palestine still burns today. Why, according to this Bible story? Because Ishmael was not the chosen one. The chosen one? God! What does that even mean?

You think you can like this God, but even his disruptive interference is bound by hierarchy. It disturbs you also that the Jewish God tiptoes too much around patriarchy, especially in the household of his chosen ones. Look at Hagar, the African slave. Though she's able to invoke the God of Abraham—*You are the God who sees me...I have now seen the One who sees me*—she's in patriarchal and racial clutches. So she must go wander the desert, risking her and her baby's lives when the woman of the house is threatened by her.

What of Isaac—thrown into permanent silence after seeing the hand of the father he loved put a sharp blade to his throat? The chosen ones and their God frighten you. Their hypocrisy infuriates you. They can, for instance, pinpoint any strip of land they desire and call it their Promised Land. To acquire it they murder and spill the blood of all who stand in their way, looking to God to justify their crimes. After all, "goy" blood is a small price to pay, and the fate of the unbelievers is in the edge of the sword, or burning fire. The chosen ones are conveniently justified by faith to murder in the name of their God.

You're scared of the battle sounds of this God and their settler myths.

The myth Virgil enacts mercurially in the *Aeneid* is also present in the Jewish religious and Afrikaner foundations where the settlers work with the greed of colonialism and nationalist ideology of Ethnology by the ethnologists. The golden heroes of the *Iliad*, favorites of the gods though they may be, are nothing short of sexual predators at best, rapists and pillagers at worst, who scorn the downtrodden with the glorious delusions of honor derived from rapine and plunder. They justify violent conquests, implicating their gods and God as the driver of blood-drenched victories. Whenever the chosen ones conquer and multiply, the natives reduce.

Then they raise memorial statues and plaques to placate their moribund consciences and call the lands of settlement their Promised Land: Troy, Rome, Jerusalem, or Pretoria.

From the angle of the conquerors these are heroic expeditions, but such things challenge the humanist in you. You've become your father in your head. You think this is what Virgil meant when he made Aeneas carry his father on his back before taking to the hills, leaving the burning city behind to be razed to the ground. You're wary of all nationalist dreams, because they often lead to the extermination of the non-chosen.

Why did your mother never marry, or even have a lover, you ask yourself. Did her memories of Phaks usurp all things and condemn her to Penelope-like devotion? Make her into umfazi womlindo, according to Ndebele. What was behind it? A hope for restoration? What does your mother's life teach you, if anything? That the art of survival is in finding strength in what you're left with, even if it is just spinning the loom? That the secret to contentment is letting every situation be what it is? Who was Homer's Penelope by the time Odysseus came back from his wanderings? What had she seen, resigned to?

Phaks says the God of Abraham is not accommodative of poetic lies. Had Phaks come back he would have found a graying woman, perhaps a little embittered by the wasted years of her womanhood; the years she would always toast his health on his birthday. She might also have wanted nothing to do with a weathered old man coming back too late. In that state, perhaps, he could act only to erase the dearest memories of the handsome, young lover who, in his disruptive spontaneity, got off the taxi to change her life forever before going off to war.

Your mother preferred the crestfallen anger of dancing

around the kitchen table with her only child to the glories of being a freedom fighter's wife.

We only have this world and its miseries that bring the fear of Isaac who, baffled by a knife to his neck from the hand of a father he adored, chose permanent silence rather than to challenge or contradict that faith, his fate. Nothing much is said of Isaac in scripture, except when he has to find wives for his sons. Could it be, for Isaac, that the memory of a brandished knife and the cold metal on his throat is what he associates with the God of Abraham? Was he afraid his voice of complaint about the knife might bring shadows on the light of Mt. Sinai, and collaborate with the strength of darkness at Calvary? Did Isaac even know that? Did he have his father's unquestioning faith? Was there really any choice for Isaac but to assume his father's faith? If not, would he damn himself by wandering a Bedouin desert, like Ishmael? Would he have a lifelong grudge sapping vitality from his heart? In fact, there was never a choice.

We do not choose our parents' fate or faith, we're born into it. Either that or the desert. The wandering in the desert has its price of nursing a grudge, becoming *a thorn in the side of your brethren*, the curse of Cain, of all the wanderers: *My punishment is too great for me to bear...*Hence the ancient Romans feared exile even above the punishment of death.

AGAINST THE PEACE
OF ITHACA
16/10/99

Today, in this month of the lilypad, eyeDwarha, I mark the fortieth time I've circled the sun on this earth. I feel old as the hills. What had years of war and wandering done to Odysseus when he woke on the shores of Ithaca to be informed, by his patron goddess Athena, that she would disguise him as an old man, *that thou mayest appear mean in the sight of all the wooers, and of thy wife?*

Cruel fate this wondering of wanderers.

I'm tired of craning my neck out the window. I feel exhaustion laden on my shoulders. I pray this cup passes from my lips. Death is a frightful mirror that quivers even the soul of the God-man. But when you've lived too long at death's threshold you grow numb to the fear to such an extent that death loses its power to scare. It becomes meaningless. I'm now not afraid of death. Yet I'm not not afraid.

When you think the world through, seeing is an aspect of perception, and perception that of knowledge. Then, if the end, after the accumulation of knowledge through experience that makes for our consciousness, is permanent, one can only say that the farce of life is senseless, nonsense, absurdity.

Take to the deep.

Look at what other mortals have done and been. What does it mean to be a man of faith if not one with indomitable hope against the liquidating seduction of absurdity. For hope means standing your ground even when the language of logic fails.

Others' processes of perception are evidence based; they require intelligence to understand, not hope. The understanding of hope is linked to faith, that is blind trust where there's no evidence, or the evidence is contrary. That's the real meaning of Pascal's leap of faith.

Hannah Arendt says the ancients understood greatness as being received into the bosoms of history. That in their era they gained immortality through history, being talked about across generations, mythicized. Those mortals who, through their deeds and words, proved themselves worthy, became historicized, received an everlasting fame, gained immortality despite their mortality, or because of it. They entered the company of things that last forever.

I'm not interested in that.

Homer's Achilles is probably the quintessence of this type. We still talk about his mythical, heroic life, the manner in which obsession with revenge stoked his anger to the point where it consumed him, only because he trusted in his own strength too much. Worst still, think of Euripides' Hecuba, that anomalous version of the Trojan war story with a shocking moral ugliness, perhaps still the most insightful drama of the poison in the seed of revenge. This prompted Dante to put her in the Inferno where, deranged, she barked like a dog: so far had anguish twisted her mind.

Their passion for revenge doesn't interest me. I am drawn to those who achieved immortality not by the brute force of the Greeks and Romans, but by the bare knuckles of their faith, that indomitable strength against the annihilating effects of absurdity. Hence I seek my elucidation from the life of Abraham, the quintessential wanderer and the equinox of this phenomenon —himself mythical perhaps; but it is the spirit we seek, not the proof of his historical existence.

Abraham's life was always unlikely to end happily, for the consequences of a man trying to kill his own son are too great for poetic lies. You'd have to have gone beyond common humanity to reach that stage of crisis in your life. Imagine, praying for a son all those years, and when he arrives you place a blade to his neck, because of the whispers of faith? My God! Such fate, such faith! In retrospect, we may see the interconnectedness of things brought about by this faith: because a knife was laid on Isaac's throat on Mt. Moriah, Moses, for Israel and people of good faith all over the world, received the Torah at Mt. Sinai.

What has history done to my people? What have I done to my wife, my child? Mandela is free! Is that enough? Those who fought against us are now his protectors and guardians. They acquired him the way others acquire a myth—as a manipulative symbol for reconciliation and keeping the status quo of their own privilege. They made him into a justification for their immoral gains against the demands of justice by the majority. They used him as an instrument against our hopes for justice. Mandela is now a symbol of their reconciliation and a burden of betrayal to those whom he purportedly freed. And where do the majority of South Africans feature in all this? Dying in remote corners within and beyond our borders. Dying of hunger, curable and incurable diseases; of neglect and poverty. As things change, they stay the same. They still rely on dirt under their fingernails while flying flags of political freedom. I do not say this because I'm bitter—angry, perhaps, but not bitter—but please don't ask me to celebrate reconciliation that is based on injustice. What has become of Mandela is not the final judgment of our history, at least not my history.

Odysseus reconciled his enemies to the sharpness of his sword before there was peace in his household, and Ithaca. But those who live by the sword die by the sword, says the Prince of Peace. I abhor peace founded on blood—the haunting silence of graves which is interpreted as peace. *Making a desert and calling it peace*, according to the ancient Greek historian Tacitus. There the wounds of those who died for justice fester. Justice does not have to be vindictive, but it must be just. Things cannot simply go back to what they were as if we were not fighting for justice, else we're inviting the *fire next time*.

TEARS IN MORTAL THINGS

Sandi arranges for you to meet her new love interest, Djimon. The three of you spend the evening drinking beer and chatting in her staff cottage, until Sandi hints that perhaps it is getting late and Djimon should take his leave. You can see that he is not very pleased to depart, especially since you are still lingering. Sandi will be eager to discuss Djimon when he is gone, you know, so you do not budge.

When Djimon finally kisses Sandi goodnight and drives off in his double-cab pickup, Sandi asks, "Well?"

You're not sure how to respond. You find Djimon slightly obnoxious and a contrarian personality. He seems to feel superior to anyone who does not have an interest in preening his ego. What does Sandi, with her radar for patriarchal bullshit, see in him, you think to yourself.

"He's attractive," you offer, since anyone has to admit that it is true. That he's a metrosexual type is very hard to miss; tight-fitting T-shirt accentuating muscular arms, six pack and all.

"That he is," Sandi says with a sly smile.

You can't help but laugh.

Sandi starts to set out her plans for the three of you to travel to her home village of Moshi using his pickup truck. So at least, you think, he will have another chance to prove his worth.

As you say goodnight to Sandi and return to your own cottage, you curb your judgment of Djimon.

Who are you to criticize anyone else's choice of romantic

partner? After all, you've made some of the worst choices in the past.

As you get into bed, you remember the day Litha took you to the train station to depart for Wits University.

Shimmering hot was the day you left for medical school in Johannesburg for the first time. The arrangement was that Litha would meet you at the Public Gardens in town after you'd finished buying your provisions, and then go with you to collect your bags at home before taking you to the train station.

The forty minutes or so you spent waiting in the gardens felt like a private valedictory moment between you and your hometown. You'd hardly ever been out of the town, let alone out of the province going to the city of gold. The excitement came muffled somewhat by anxiety about whether you would be able to cope, given your small-town, Johnny-comes-late-to-Joburg mannerisms.

Litha felt guilty that he was not able to accompany you all the way to Joburg, but you were confident you'd be okay. As you sat under the eucalyptus tree, watching the lazy afternoon traffic and clouds throwing shadows on the ground, you kept trying to identify the shapes the clouds made, remembering when your mommy played Joni Mitchell's song "Both Sides Now." What amazed you was the exactness by which Mitchell described what was on your mind about flowing angel hair and ice-cream castles. Okay, they looked more like candy-floss castles to you, and sometimes like white forested cliffs. Sometimes you saw galloping white horses or bulls, once squadrons invading a town in the style Don Quixote would tell it.

You didn't notice the man with glaucoma eyes approaching until he threw himself down next to you on the bench. Disheveled with a hollowed and haunted look, he scared you a little the minute the whiff of his stale body odor hit your nose. He had what your mother called a smell of poverty. His unkempt beard, crinkled and bushy, looked like that of a prophet who had been living in the wilderness for far too long. The visible skin around his ankles was scaly as a lizard's and dark as tar.

"Could you tell me, my daughter, if this road goes to Johannesburg?" he inquired after making himself comfortable, pointing to the road before you that led to the suburbs. Johannesburg was more than nine hundred kilometers from where you were seated, in the other direction. It felt a strange coincidence to be asked directions to Johannesburg on the day you were leaving for it.

"No, my old father, this road goes kwizindlu zabelungu, the white suburbs. The road to Johannesburg is the other way," you replied, more from cultural etiquette than a desire to be helpful, fighting the urge to brush the gunky remnants of whatever he had been eating from his beard with a handkerchief. You noticed huge gaps between his black teeth as he spoke again.

"When I was down there, near the shops, they said I'd have to climb the bridge," he said with a rasp of what sounded like suppressed anger.

"They must have meant the other bridge." You pointed to the other direction, where, eventually, there is a bridge you need to climb outside of town toward Aliwal North, which is the right way to Johannesburg.

"It doesn't matter. I don't trust you anyway. I trust abantu bomlambo who direct me." He then stood to leave as he said that, hunching his shoulders before turning his back on you. "I shall continue on this way until I reach Aliwal North, where I'll be spending the night." He also mumbled, in a truculent tone, something about planting tomatoes on cornfields you couldn't properly make out, as he walked away. "Tomorrow morning I shall be hot on the heels of the sun, pushing for Bloemfontein. You don't understand the things I have to do." The heels of his shoes, slanting toward the outer sides, gave him a crab-like gait that was somehow palsied and slow-bobbing.

Since, obviously, he was a man easily offended, you decided

not to point out that his journey would be two hundred kilometers to Aliwal North. What you didn't understand was his mention of abantu bomlambo, the river people, as his directors. Did this mean he was of the clan of Gaba, who associate themselves with the river people and everything that lived or came out of it? Your mother was of the clan amCirha amahlophe, which she loved to mention, reminding you that she came from the lineage of prophets like Ntsikana. Their clan was not supposed to come close to river mouths, lest their ancestors lured them in. If they were lured into the water deeps by the ancestors, they'd spend the rest of their days caught in between worlds as abantu bomlambo, which one could translate as "mermaids," though they are not the same thing. For one, abantu bomlambo are not only females, but guides caught up in the numinous divide between this world and that of the ancestors. They're closer to the Catholic saints.

It occurred to you then that the last holiday your mother and you took had been spent at the Kei River Mouth Lodge. She'd spent the first day being scared to cross the waters, even at low tide. Then you'd woken up around 2am one morning and she had been gone from your cabin. You'd gone out looking for her everywhere, including at the river mouth, although you'd known it was the last place she'd be caught dead in. But that was where you'd found her, sitting on a rock with a blanket around her shoulders. At first you'd thought you were seeing umamlambo, a mermaid, then an otter. Then you'd realized it was her. You'd been unsure whether you should disturb her or walk away. About to make light of the moment, you'd realized she was in some kind of a trance. You dared not disturb her and so kept your distance. You'd never seen her do that sort of thing before, so you were a little confused. Sitting down on the ground, watching her, you'd fallen asleep. She'd roused you at about 5am, telling you that the two of you needed to get back. She'd acted as if nothing had happened as she tucked you into bed when you got back to the cabin. You'd spent the rest of the morning looking at the ceiling with foreboding feelings.

As the old man talked, you recalled that it was from that day she'd started being solicitous about teaching you things, living skills and all, telling you that you must be able to stand on your own feet, even if she should be gone.

You'd never thought much about that day before, nor understood its significance, until your path crossed with that of the old man who told you he had been given directions to Johannesburg by the river people. At that moment you knew, somehow, that you were receiving a message from your mom. That she had found a way to filter it through the old man. In your culture, the mentally challenged, especially the seeming schizophrenics, are respected because of their ability to cross over the divide between the living and the dead. They're taken care of by everyone in the community in the same manner that other cultures protect their totem animals, like the Hindus do with cows or monkeys. At that moment you also understood that your mother must have received the notice of her summons from her river people at the Kei River Mouth. She'd gone there to keep a vigil with her ancestors, or to beg them for a little more time to get you ready for her permanent absence.

Apparently Litha had been watching the old man and you from a distance all along. When you raised your eyes, you saw his car parked not far off and you walked toward it.

"You're not even out of town yet and you're already being unfaithful to me?" he teased as you got in. You kissed, habitually, before he drove to go collect your bag at the house. Because you still had time you made love with a demanding urgency that startled him. You had a need to feel him, to feel everything, real and tangible. Sex, as usual, unbuttoned his mood. At the station where he couldn't proceed any further without a ticket he hugged you with the tenderness of a father rather than that of a lover, mussing your hair and all. You returned the hug with an unrestrained clinging to his body, breathing in his scent. You boarded the train with an aching heart but also an eager curiosity to discover your new life.

You took what felt like one last look at the bold mountains of your hometown, especially the quiet dignity that is Mt. Lukhanji. You couldn't help but wonder how your mother would have felt, seeing you off. Still lost within these thoughts, you heard a tap on your window. The old man from the Public Garden bench was before you, outside the window, disregarding the regulation about non-passengers not going beyond the ticket-checking counter. This time he was asking for R2. You gave him a R2 coin and more. He became silent and dour for a moment. When eventually he spoke it was to give you a message for his brother who supposedly lived in Joburg. You didn't know him, or his brother, but such trifles were minor technicalities to him. You're not even sure he remembered you from the Public Garden.

"Tell my brother," he said, speaking strenuously fast, "to stop sending money through his wife, because she became too familiar with road workers from East London and absconded with one of them. She now cooks at their tents in the slums of Ziphunzana, we are told. We're told also that she's expecting their bastard. The devil be on her back. Tell him our father did not survive last year's frost. We didn't have money for his burial so we told the police he was a vagrant who staggered into our yard to die. This is what everyone does now when they want the state to bury their loved one. The police buried him, without grief, above the stadium, attaching a name of 'Anoni' (anonymous) on his grave. I was so affected I told the daft police bastards at the graveside that his name was Filimoni (Philip), not Anoni. But they disregarded my tirade and threatened to lock me up.

"Tell my brother the cat is sleeping at the hearth for us here. Last week I had a good mind to walk to Joburg to inform him that my sister is blowing our blind mother's pension money with a married man that loves her only when she has money for the drink. She becomes angry when we ask her about groceries for the house. I'm tired of being hungry all the time, and my blood being a feast for the fleas. Sleep goes away in my eyes at night because my stomach is always grumbling. Tell him things are not looking good here. Nomasomi, his firstborn, has yielded to a boy whose prepuce has not even been cut yet. Our women are cursed with lust here. The borders of wickedness have reached even the churchyard. Our reverend was caught with a married woman only last week. He is now living boldly in sin with her. Nothing will persuade him otherwise, not even the talk of the God he no longer believes in. No one sees any use in hoping in God anymore; everyone drinks according to their wallets and appetites. Last week our nephew was so drunk he spent the whole night galloping around the house like a mad horse. We were concerned. They say it's the weed he's been smoking since he was eleven. He set his face to the desert, like a wild ass, and we have not heard from him ever since. I think he's no longer right upstairs.

"Even our dogs have fled by the ways of the fields and the paths of the hills. We couldn't afford to feed them anymore. It's quiet now at night, no barking, which brings eerie forebodings if you are home alone. The dogs had lost their fawning joy and tail-wagging bliss in any case.

"As for myself, tell him my heart is still following the ways of our forefathers. Nothing will take my hope away from God. My heart will not swell against God. Ask my brother why he no longer comes home to visit. If he thinks he has reasons to be angry, let him wait till I tell him news. We're about to lose our house to our older stepbrother. He claims he has papers for it. No use going to the courts because he has greased the hands of the clerks. The rich people want to build a shopping mall where our houses stand. We're told compensation was paid to us but we have not seen a cent of it, because they only have our stepbrother's details at the deeds office as the owner of the house.

These are the repercussions of the things our mother did, hoping that our stepbrother would be able to pay the rates because he had gone to school and we had not. What has his schooling gained us now if we're going to be thrown on the street while he lives comfortably in his own house with the money of the house our father worked for? I told my stepbrother that he's shaming our father's name who raised him in the same manner as he did us, even though esisizananina, born of another man. We're the only legitimate children of our father, yet we must now live in the wild like foxes and jackals.

"Our stepbrother has taught his mouth to speak lies. He frequents and inhabits the houses of iniquity. I suspect he's been sharing his blanket with Nomasomi, though she's practically his daughter because she's our brother's daughter. I suspect the bastard Nomasomi is carrying is his, and that stripling she's going out with is just a scapegoat. Poor, foolish boy, he'll learn to count the cunts he puts his cork on. Nomasomi still wears the garments of gladness, though she's pushing a wheelbarrow, pregnant as a carrying kangaroo. She fishes for truck drivers at the truck stop. People are talking. My brother must send money so I may come and stay with him in Jabavu. Things are getting worse here..."

The message went on until the train began to pull away. By then the old man was sweating, occasionally rubbing his face with a dirty handkerchief that had bloodstains on it. As the train pulled away you gave him another R10 note with misty eyes. He gave you an enthusiastic wave before starting to sing a folk song you knew very well that was popularized by your hometown boy, Stompie Mavi. With his deep baritone voice it acquired a woefulness and deep poignancy:

Lomlungu uTebha	This white man Tebha
ngokwenene ndiyamzonda	in truth I grudge
Ngoku thatha isithandwa sam	For taking my lover away from me

Andisoze ndiy' eGoli	I'll never go to Johannesburg
Uzu bathuthe loliwe	Take them away train
bathuthe loliwe	take them train
Andisoze ndiye eGoli	I'll never go to Johannesburg
Ubathuthe loliwe	Take them away train, take them away

The old man ran along the platform with the departing train, and just before he reached the end of it, he shouted: "I trust you now! Your mother told me you're a good child. I believe her now."

You were flabbergasted. You lamely threw your hand out of the window as a last gesture to touch his blood. Did he grow up with your mother? Is that how he remembered you somehow? Had you met him when you were younger? Or was he communicating with your dead mother's spirit? All these questions jolted through you as you journeyed to the big city.

The old man was the last thing you saw at the station, his head dangling unbearably as he faded into the distance. You felt warm tears tiptoe onto your cheeks but gained confidence that your mother's spirit, somehow, was guiding you.

THE HANGING TREE
14/06/99

In his essay "A Hanging" George Orwell recalls how he watched a condemned Burmese man walk toward the gallows, swerving to avoid a puddle on the way. What does it matter if you are hanged with dirty feet or not? An atheist mind cannot fathom the need to depart this dirty world with clean feet.

As iMfengu I belong to the group of people, who described by Primo Levi in his book of grief, *If This Is a Man*, takes courage in seeing what a person does when they're about to die: preparing food for today's journey when they know tomorrow they'll take their last breath. Who take leave of life in the manner that most suits their personality: some pray, some drink to excess, others even become intoxicated by the final lust for carnality and life. Some avoid muddying their feet on their way to the gallows. And when all is ready, like elephants, they ring out their grief, bagxwale emswaneni, wailing and ring-fencing their pain with a song and a dance, a moving circle, the cure most preferred by African people, as seen in Rwandans also. Levi calls this the ancient grief of those who have no land to protect them, no exodus to make: AbaMfenguzi, The Wanderers.

You'll recall the ancient Jews on the banks of Babylon, and not so ancient ones in the factories of death in Auschwitz and the camps of Monowitz-Buna and Birkenau, as they "sat on the bare soil in a circle for the lamentations, praying and weeping through the night," to experience "within ourselves a grief that was new to us, the ancient grief of a people that has no land, the grief without hope of the exodus, renewed in every century."

I believe myself to be an existentialist communitarian. I trust in intuition and strive for the attitude of collective living that allows one to try and come to grips with one's own reality. I guess that's philosophical, even if not strictly epistemological. I've a bleak attitude toward life. Bleakness is not fatalism. It is mostly an accurate portrayal of life. This is why I'm attracted to the ancient Greeks and Romans. I share their sentiment that there's always a peculiar poignancy and tragic turn of events in the nature of things. I try not to become somber even when I don't really delight in this life and live by merely enduring it.

As a young boy I was attracted to the priesthood, because I saw it as a calling of holiness. That died with the years and the exposure of contrary evidence in some of our men of the cloth. I thought perhaps I'd be a revolutionary, a liberator of political entities, was even lured by the likes of Che Guevara. That died, too, when I realized revolutions always eat their young. I saw in existentialism a way of authenticity but was subsequently appalled by the posturing of its practitioners, and some of its consumerist mentality masquerading as faux enlightenment.

From experience I know it is more dangerous to fall into the hands of your own revolutionary comrades than that of the enemy. The enemy you can handle, especially if you have spent all your revolutionary years preparing to fight them. But you are never prepared to see the enemy in the eye of your own comrade; nothing prepares you for that kind of betrayal. It turns your world upside down.

The desire to be authentic and real stayed with me all my life. I wanted to be good, to be a man of goodwill, so in the end I thought it wise to just try being me. With time, due to mostly my own failures, I was more interested in the liberation of my own conscience. I discovered that the truest liberation begins with the self.

Now I know, if God exists, His glory is inseparable from our peace on this earth; or rather, to put it more crudely, there's no peace on earth without the glory of God. If God exists, it makes sense that what He created will establish its peace only by honoring His will, since He is the reality upon which it exists. Only when God is glorified will justice flourish.

Does this mean I espouse fundamental religious tendencies? God forbid, no! I see clearly the mess religious people have done in history in the name of God. Yet I understand clearly also that it is humans, not God, who should be in the dock.

I now follow what Augustine (my paper wife introduced me to him) meant by the history of the world being the struggle between two kinds of love: love of self, whose conclusion is in despising God for self-autonomy; and the love of God that must necessarily reach the distrust of the selfish self if it is sincere.

I used to regard humanism as the consequent conflict of true human authenticity with organized religion. I believed myself to be agnostic—that thorough evasiveness of non-confrontational characters. When I went through the history of thought, I discovered believing thinkers I had neglected because of my suspicion of organized religion, the likes of St. Augustine and St. Thomas. I found their thinking to be more humanistic than most humanists of the so-called Enlightenment. Once, I even thought I saw the spark of faith kindle in my heart. But priests happened, with all their disgusting abusive tendencies we're only now starting to be aware of. I came to the understanding that humanism is not a religious nor secular cult of man, but an open-ended perspective that seeks to grasp the truth of existence through human experience.

I've always had this distinctive desire, even obsession, to grasp human things in human terms, without converting them to something else, even if that something is transcendental. My error, I see it clearly now, was in limiting human nature to the materialistic, to physical laws, mechanical systems, biological drives, and psychological orders, without stopping to think about the roots of them all. Then I was given Efuoa to be my life teacher. I'm tired! What time is it in heaven? Is that a valid question to a timeless place, or to one like myself for that matter who has fallen away from the flow of time, who has entered into the real meaning of living with death by being severed clean from the habits of time; who lives with the silent, heavy crush that comes with the realization that soon he must die; who now lives in a sharp sensation of profound alteration, being changed essentially by the focused clarity and poetic intensity of the effervescent light of the Reaper's halo. Changed by the experience of living with fear and trembling from the awakened death within his blood that, with every pump, brings closer the end; of living in the burning whiteness at the edge of the dead; of the pausing of time in disassociation to the heart's urgent needs; of psychotic efforts to rent a temporal space—an interval—in which to write, a desperate attempt to emerge from the fog of death that is at the center of these diaries; an attempt and a foolish wish to leave a clean slate.

You say I must prove the existence of God. I tell you there's Truth. You say you do not believe in Truth but in truths, what you call the condition of truthfulness. I say, conditions need a realm to exist.

Nothing is certain, you say. Well, amen to that, but remember, that is true of your statement also. So there may be one certain thing it helps to find an all-consuming name for—"God" is just as good as any for me.

I'm not religious, you say. I believe in the Socratic method; the application of reason to any and all ideas.

Pardon me. I just recalled something. Death is definitely certain! Does that establish certainty?

You say you are still not convinced about the existence of God. Fine, argue your facts. But do not say: "I do not believe in God so God does not exist." That's solipsistic narcissism and decadent atheism. What if it's just your psychological prejudices that are keeping you away from God? Surely the perfection of Truth raises it above the conditions of knowledge, especially your flawed creaturely knowledge.

CITY OF GOLD

You notice an email from Ami when you fire up your computer. The line in the news-filled letter that grabs your attention most reads: *Write to me again soon. I often daydream about you, especially after reading your emails. You seem to have found yourself, and with it your peace. Whereas I'm still haunted by doubts and plagued by restlessness.*

Have you really found yourself? You're not sure, but you seem to be getting closer. At least you are much closer than you were as a student when you first met Ami.

You don't know why you should think of Jozi as being misty, but you conjure a memory of it being misty the day you arrived for the first time at 2 Jan Smuts Avenue as an adolescent and greenhorn. The columned stone façade of the university buildings exiled you the minute you set eyes on them. Entering the campus, next to South African Breweries' headquarters, you climbed the concrete steps toward the Natural Sciences building and became conscious of your own intellectual inadequacies just by looking at the imposing structures. A group of tattooed white students were studiously squatting on the stairs, elbows on their knees. They were dressed in black, sporting tacky septum and belly rings, high leather boots, and weird pink and orange spiked haircuts. When you inquired about the location of the Medical School, they gave you blank looks. You now know, with their glazed and redrimmed eyes, that they were probably stoned. Then you interpreted it as hostility.

When you eventually found your way to the Med School in Parktown you registered and provided the check that Litha had given you as a deposit on your tuition fees. You were directed back to the main campus to the residence of your choice, Jubilee Hall. There you registered and paid another deposit check. Momentarily, you discovered your roommate to be a sensational Indian-looking girl of your age from Pretoria, thin as a bootlace. She welcomed you with the enthusiasm of a long-lost friend, introducing herself as "Amiwajera, but everyone calls me Ami."

After your introductions she accompanied you, on foot, to Park Station to collect your luggage. On the way you talked as though you'd known each other forever. You returned in a metered taxi, on account of your heavy suitcase and bag. After dropping the bags you immediately went to the dining hall for supper. Ami talked through the varsity schedules for Orientation Week with you as you ate. Back in your room, with darkness drawing the curtain of the day, she asked many questions about your family, your hometown and your culture while offering details of her own.

"Salaam-alaikum!" was the greeting she taught you—your first lesson about her culture. As well as the reply, "Wa-alaikum-assalam" or "Allahu Akbar!" God is great. You had your own issues with God but didn't feel comfortable voicing them to Ami.

Soon you also learned to say thank you: "Shukran."

And you're welcome: "Afwan."

Ami told you that, strictly speaking, she was Pakistani and Muslim, but her family were not fundamentalist or anything. With time you learned she wasn't a hijab-wearing, Allah-spreadeth-forth-the-heavens-as-a-curtain-and-pulleth-on-the-light-as-a-garment kind of Muslim.

Although you had always liked spicy food, the dishes Ami introduced you to were on a whole new level. This is why Maman's hot food is child's play to you. At university you got used to eating chappati and bhunjiya; a thali covered with a pattal; hot curried vegetable and lamb curry stews. Your favorite dessert became chhuara, made of dry dates cooked in syrup and served with caramel custard. To date you know how to properly sip cups and cups of chai, to eat nimkis thereafter.

Ami was engaged to be married, but there was a mounting complication: the fiancé was Hindu. She liked pretending it didn't matter, although it clearly bothered her because she was constantly telling you about the difficulties the arrangements would entail. Her fiancé thought she lived too much like a giaour, because she refused to wear traditional dresses.

"Do I look like a heathen to you?" she once asked, pretending to be furious. "In any case, I live according to the demands of my situation and era. Imagine turning up for a lecture in a sari?" She tried to convince herself that being married to a Hindu would not bother her, even though the anticipation clearly already did. Although her father didn't really-really approve-approve, he seemed to be delegating the whole matter to Ami's mother, who secretly thought there was still enough time for Ami to find a good Muslim boy to please her father.

"Engagements are not cast in stone, you know?" was her leitmotif to appease both Ami and her father. The real complication was not in the fact that Ami didn't care to wear manjas, or show her religious devotion through her garb. Yes, she wore jeans and T-shirts, but the real problem was that she was most attracted to militant African guys, the Biko or Malcolm X type, with dreads. Brusque and daring, sincere in communicating her opinions, she was always dragging you to Black Consciousness-related meetings around campus, screaming her head off when she saw a guy of the type she liked, not necessarily for his political astuteness. You told her she stereotyped things but you liked her too much not to indulge her. At night, when you'd switched off the light and both of you were lying supine in your beds trying to summon sleep, she would all of a sudden start up.

"Paresh is mad. It's his parents he fears most. They're conservative, and have a stronghold on his life. If he thinks I'm going to live a closet life, he has another thing coming. He wants us to marry in a traditional Hindu wedding under the panthal and all. That won't do, girlfriend. Not for this Muslim."

It was the first time you learned there existed untold tensions and complications between Indian-Indians and Pakistanis. In fact, it was the first time you realized that not all "Indians" are Indians, from India. Somehow, the finer details of differentiating between Muslims, Hindus, Indonesians or Malays had escaped you growing up in the township. One needed to have grown up in Durban or Cape Town to appreciate that sort of thing.

Despite all his education—he was about to qualify as an architect—and specious freedom of thought, Paresh was a traditionalist at heart. "This girlie won't stand for that," Ami continued in exaggerated frustration. "Fancy me getting married hooded with a sari's pallu, a kurtle and a pujari, mumbling strange prayers? What next? Attending kirtans and religious darshans? No one is making a dahaati out of me."

By then she'd be pacing up and down the room, priming herself up while depriving you of much-needed sleep for school the following day. When she calmed down she'd ask to get into your bed, which was how both of you managed to go to sleep most of the time.

"In any case, there are many strands that go into the making of tilkut," she would softly say as she dropped into sleep.

"That's the spirit, girl..." would be your dreamy response. "There has to be some twisting and grunting, turning and wrenching; the merging of separate ingredients."

She raised her torso up, taking a closer look at your face, before bursting out laughing, amazed at how fast you were catching on.

You both spent that year waiting for her to admit to herself that she would not be marrying Paresh. In the end she didn't, as expected. And when the resolve finally came, it was something like: "I'm not getting myself into a nullah of murky Hindi waters, with my eyes wide open, making myself a slave of fly-sucking skinflint benaami landlords." You knew then things had reached a point of no return, her eyes becoming large and wide, the way they usually did when she was in bewilderment and animated about something.

"If Asura is not just a demon, then where's my ghar?" This she said a little sadly. That was when you realized she had made a decision.

Then one day, after the fated phone call, she came back to your room dejected. You took her out for a mango-and-passion-fruit frozen yoghurt. After a few spoonfuls she deflated.

"He'd have required me to speak Tamil, cook rotis and have a kumkum on my forehead and all. Who wants that?"

"You could have made the compromise if you really loved him," you ventured.

She looked at you for a moment before answering. "What do you know? For all you know, when you get home some guy will claim you as his wife because he has already paid lobola for you to your family without even notifying you." She waved a hand to dismiss your point as you both laughed it off. "I just had this nagging feeling that the boy was gonna jumble up my life like a bhoolbhoolaiya."

Your talks went deep into the night. Although she tried to pretend otherwise, you could feel your friend was hurting from her decision, or was at least shaken to the core. It was not only about her rejection of Paresh, but her way of interrogating all assumed identities about herself. And so, when you woke up with her sobbing on your shoulder you were not too surprised.

Before you boarded the plane to Tanzania, the last person you saw, both of you sobbing, was Ami. You left everything you thought was of importance from your South African life with her, certificates and all, also giving her power of attorney over your affairs.

LITHA

Dear Mother

Since I arrived here at varsity I've been too busy to write. Also, I suppose, trying to avoid having to talk to you at length about Litha. The funny thing is I never even thought I was using him as a step-ladder for my dreams, because part of me genuinely liked him. I even thought I loved him at some stage. In retrospect, I see things differently. I liked the attention he gave me; I was extremely lonely and confused. I liked the distraction from my depressive brooding. He gave me the freedom to pursue my academic dreams, introduced me to the life of restaurants and expensive wines, bought me stuff, like music, movies, cell phones, and clothes I fancied. I guess you can say I fell for Veli's error, trying to associate myself with people I admire, thinking it would rub off on me.

I didn't necessarily want popularity but I wanted respect, which I guess are different sides of the same coin. I wanted people to stop feeling embarrassed for me because I was an orphan, to instead admire my success. I wasn't aware how fake it all appeared from the outside.

I won't say I didn't realize he was married. Even from the beginning, the signs were there. I just convinced myself of my right to be with him also. Worse still, later on I naively believed him when he said his marriage was on the rocks and he was trying to find the best way to end it amicably. I know now that this is the usual bullshit all married men say when they cheat.

But I take full responsibility for my actions. The question is, had I known what I know now, about his shenanigans and all, would I have behaved differently? The sad answer is no. I would have done the same thing. As I said, I did what I had to do to get myself out the ditch that life conspired to bury me in. Did I fall for a shortcut? Most probably! I could have worked at a bank, saved money for four years or so, before going to med school. But realistically though, would I have done that? I probably would have ended up being a bank teller for the rest of my life, doing a correspondence course for a commerce degree or something. If lucky, I could have climbed the sexist and racist job ladder, perhaps ended up a manager in my middle age, because the bank would be in need of a black woman's face for window-dressing. I would have ended up angry and resentful, giving birth, back to back, to Irish twins and driving my husband, say Hlumelo, to drink, because we would not be able to keep up with our mortgage, car, and school-fees payments. Not that there's anything wrong with living that sort of life. I just don't see it for myself. Things would never end well with me on that sort of path; I probably would have ended up hanging with a noose around my neck. I know myself too well to have tempted that fate. And I would have left Hlumelo with a deep depression, poor bastard, wondering what he did wrong when it was all me and not him, because I do not know how to be resigned to things I am not satisfied with. Worst of all, I'd scar my children for life. Dear Lord! No! I took the road that led me where I needed to go, to misquote Robert Frost. It might not have made much difference in the end, but at least I'm able to live with my life.

Litha gave me hope when I needed it most; when my life looked forlorn. He also gave me a way out of the dead end my life had threatened to become after you died. Being a doctor was always your dream for me as far back as I can remember. I understood it as a way of you living your life vicariously through me. So, in a way, you are also complicit in this, Mother. I wanted to please you. I always want to please you.

You're the best thing that has ever happened to me. I don't just mean you giving birth to me, but you as a person, your personality and mannerisms. You're the best and the kindest person I've had the bountiful privilege of knowing. Although I still feel chained— I wanna use the word cuffed—to your death, my soul is slowly becoming free. Your thoughts and care were what gave me joy. I was lost as to where to start living without you. At least my appetite for life is returning. Although my intellectual energies are often employed in literature, I shall see through my medical studies.

I'm in desperate need of coffee now...

LIBRARIES

Dear Mother

I came back to the university early last week to be re-examined on Medical Ethics because I was given a supplementary on it. I hardly attended the course after I had a serious issue with the lecturer last year. We were writing a term test and some of us were delaying handing over our papers because we had not finished. He went on and on about our lazy tendencies and how we were just here to waste taxpayers' money because we were on government scholarships. I was not even aware it was only us, the black students in class, who were left behind. I stood up, without finishing, and threw the paper in his face on my way out. I expected to be called to the office for some sort of warning, but he never reported the incident, and it is now as if it never happened. He decided to act out his revenge during the marking of the paper, I suppose. Needless to say, he failed me on that paper. In anger I just stopped going to his class. I suppose he was proud of himself for that because he knew I would not be coming back the following year since there's no way one can proceed to the next level without passing the course. In the end the faculty gave me another chance because I had maintained a B+ in all my other courses. Eight of us wrote the sup this January, all of us black students. Two failed, I subsequently learned. I don't know what will happen to them. Perhaps they will be asked to change to another major, study Dentistry or something. The rest of us will be allowed to proceed to the fourth year.

We had a small party at res, celebrating the occasion before resuming classes on Monday. There was noise, drinking, talking about boys, and all the rest. Well, as you know, I'm not one for glee clubs, singing circles, and all that, but I'm conscious these days about trying to avoid being seen as glum. Ami is still at home because the main campus is only opening in two weeks' time. I regretted my decision to go to that party, though, the minute I got there. After two drinks, when I was sure everyone had seen me, I retreated to my room. I always feel like I'm getting sick with something. I think I'm becoming a hypochondriac.

When I have to study at the library I prefer the city library at the Johannesburg Gardens to the Med School one. For some reason I can't stand our main library, which is where I need to go when in res. I like the studious rustle of public libraries, the smell of old wood–modern libraries have aluminum shelves. I first discovered public libraries after you had died. They're mostly daytime shelter for homeless people, especially against the cold and the rain. I think they're also places where they can sit to rest when it's too cold in the park or they don't feel like being outside. It must be their way of keeping in touch with the world by reading newspapers and all. I always let them have first pick of the newspapers and magazines. I like their company, watching them walk in wonder in between row after row of books, desiring to consume all that knowledge. There's one white guy with a bushy beard and sandy hair who's always deep in reading the Classics World Series. I'm impressed by the strength of his mind over matter, to be able to read with such attentive concentration on an empty stomach and with the gnawing anxiety of an unstable abode.

When I first entered a library with so many books, I had this burning sensation I can't explain. I looked at the books and became greedy for the information they might provide. At first, I thought I would read them alphabetically. Then I realized I would still be on A by the time I die. Then I decided perhaps by genre, but that didn't work either, so I just went to the library and took whatever I fancied, or what was on display. Libraries are a great shelter against the oppressive weight of life, and probably the last refuge against the inequalities of modern life. We're all equal within libraries, or rather our masters there are those who can consume books with astonishing powers of concentration. Of course, with the homeless frequenting them, the smell of poverty dominates most public libraries now, and their chairs and couches are jumping with fleas. If I was a city official in charge of libraries, I would provide showers and lunch for the homeless, or some sort of a shelter nearby. I know they're a challenge to look after and some are difficult characters, but I feel a strange kinship with the homeless as my general clan of the defeated. I wish they could find a way to wash, to restore their dignity somehow. I like spending time around them, regardless of their rudeness and their selfishness sometimes. You can sit in prolonged peace, disappear in the anonymity of the crowd in public libraries. You can even take the occasional snooze when the librarian staff are not looking, smelling the smell of oak wood on the desks, and waking up with your drool all over the table.

I checked out The City of God at the library last week because of a series on Catholicism I had watched on TV. It reminded me to continue my reading of St. Augustine. I'm proud to say that I am probably the only person I know who actually read and finished Confessions. Did you, Mommy? After all, it is your book, which I trust some priest had given you as a gift. So, when I was looking for The City of God I came across Rousseau's Confessions, which caught my interest also. I wanted to read and compare it with St. Augustine's. I discovered, unlike St. Augustine, Rousseau has a deep-seated belief in the natural goodness of people, whereas St. Augustine thinks that we're fundamentally damaged by what he calls the original sin, and it is impossible for humans to recover without God's grace. Differentiating between them becomes a little easier once you understand this. They both exaggerate their feelings for show.

What I like in St. Augustine is that he respects historical facts even when they don't support his project. Rousseau manipulates them to compel them into contributing to his thesis about the understanding of himself, or what he portrays as his self and society. To me this explains the enduring power of St. Augustine, whose subjective ideal was never crushed by the fall of the Roman Empire. (In fact, Mother, I strongly believe the fall of the Roman Empire makes for the foundation of the modern world through the occidental history. I'll tell you more about this at length one day when I've studied it enough.) In contrast, the bankruptcy of the Enlightenment age left Rousseau exposed and led to Hobbes' dog-eat-dog world becoming triumphant. I become impatient with people who think nothing has meaning except what they give to it, which is my major beef with Rousseau.

One thing I appreciate about Rousseau is that he sides with the poor and the oppressed, whereas St. Augustine thinks they only have dignity if they're fodder for salvation. This pompous cruelty irritates me in St. Augustine. One is seething (St. Augustine), the other is seditious (Rousseau), and they're both looking for opportunities for petty victories and petty amazements in the name of religion and culture.

St. Augustine's obsessing with numinous things is more attractive to me than replacing the God-shaped hole in my conscience with culture or education, as Rousseau suggests, so I am a little biased toward St. Augustine. I'm a living example to myself that trying to replace that hole with culture, art, and education doesn't work—if anything, it deepens the hunger for that which is numinous.

MOSHI

If happiness matters, the Easter holiday you spend at Sandi's rural home is significant.

She's still going out with Djimon, who is acting as your designated driver in his double-cab pickup truck. You start early, with the liquid sun of dawn. One of Phaks's favorite quotes by the ancient Greek poet Hesiod comes to mind: *...dawn brings the traveler on his way, the laborer forward with his task.*

"You so full of pretentious shit, sister Ruru," Sandi laughs when you excitedly quote that as you pack your bags in the double-cab. Your itinerary involves traveling to Dodoma before continuing to Arusha, where you plan to spend some time sightseeing, perhaps even visiting the Serengeti National Park, Ngorongoro Crater, and Olduvai, the cradle of mankind. It will be your first time seeing these places up close. You planned to proceed from there to the southern slopes of Kilimanjaro, and spend three days at Moshi where Sandi grew up, before traveling back.

Sandi is wearing a *Black Labor White Guilt* T-shirt you gave her as a present, looking busty on top of her baggy army trousers. Djimon sits behind the steering wheel in a plain white T-shirt and safari trousers with a seen-it-all look. Occasionally he inquires non-committally—"You girls okay?"—as you pack your bags in the canopied back of his double-cab.

Scenes similar to those going to Dar replay outside the window as you drive along—hills shrouded in mist hiding the jumble of lowroofed houses, vast fields, and clear, snaking waters—until you reach Arusha, where the mountains come close to meet you. Sandi tells you that Arusha was built to be the business capital of Tanzania, but most businesses chose to remain in Dar, the same way it defied following political power to the legislative capital of Dodoma.

"It's best we buy what we need at the shopping complex near the International Conference Center," she says as you enter the town. You pass the bus-and-taxi-terminal-cum-town-market, which reeks of compost, because Djimon needs to buy weed. There isn't much else to look at except people disembarking or boarding decrepit buses with goats, bicycles, bed frames and mattresses, oil drums, corrugated-iron sheets, timber poles, doors, window frames, and cement loaded on the roof-racks. Building materials are for sale everywhere, as if everyone in the country is constructing something. You mingle with fish-mongers auctioning their catches on open market. You stop at a newspaper vendor where you're offered wilting flowers with your newspaper. "Cheap, cheap!" the Indian vendor informs you. "Or you want a best deal in town for money changing?" he persists when you show no interest in the flowers. He has noticed your foreign accent, so is aiming at swindling a tourist. He shows you cloths lying on the rough ground with transparent plastic coverings. "Best material at a cheap price," he says. When you still show no interest, he gives you a dismissive smile, saying, "You don't know what you want, my friend."

Variations of hooters honk all the time, everywhere, as though Tanzania has just won a Soccer World Cup. "Hooters are a mode of communication between drivers here," Sandi tells you when you mention this. She tells you they do that also to disperse invisible spirits that are known to congregate at junctions. You're not sure if she's pulling your leg or if she is in earnest. The vivid charm of everything makes you feel as though you're at the Proustian moment where smell becomes associated with pleasure and relaxation. You all leave for the supermarket at the International Conference Center when Djimon finally returns. At the mall you buy provisions, mostly for Sandi's home.

"My mjomba, my uncle, is the only one living at home. Highly probable we not gonna find no food there, so we better go prepared," Sandi tells you in a relaxed, jovial mood, which seems to encourage Djimon's dour mood.

"Can we bring him something? A present?" you ask, excited to meet him.

"Mjomba decided to simplify his life by being interested only in few things: alcohol and tobacco."

You add brandy and whisky for him, gin and wine for yourselves. As you come out of the supermarket, bloated clouds threaten rain, but there's still trembling ringlets of sunlight stranded here and there, giving a yellow streak against the visible mountain summits. It looks like something Yeats had in mind when he wrote of clouds as *cloths of heaven*. You sit in the open car park eating rotisserie chicken with chipati bread. Following that, you drive with the background of *Bosavi: Rainforest Music from Papua New Guinea*. "E-Yo, E-Yo!"

Telephone poles pass by on their perpetual pilgrimage. Mountains float in the soft orange mass of dying light. Lighted windows flow by in a continuous stripe as darkness slowly settles. Slow-moving trucks create problems, belching out black smoke while your car is too close behind, sometimes speckling the windscreen with oily droplets that splinter and splay and blind you in the glare of the oncoming traffic.

"We're now driving among herds of buffalo, antelope, zebra, wildebeest and such heavy-horned folk," Sandi cautions. The moment she says that you start picking out red and blue glassy protuberant eyes not too far from the road.

"What happens if I want to pee?" you ask, looking at the fence that doesn't look very secure or high enough.

"You hold it in, or you find other means. But whatever you

do, you do not get out of the car, unless you want to risk becoming somebody's supper. You could disappear without even your bones ever being found out here." As with Sandi, you're not sure if Djimon is joking or in earnest when he says that, but you decide not to test the truth of his claim.

The snow-capped mountains, accompanied by the chanting voices of children in the rainforest music, painfully young and sweet, brings unexplainable tears to your eyes.

"I'd recognize that cold and smell anywhere. We're approaching my hometown," says Sandi. You notice a broad smile across her face even in the dark. The more you drive into the white silence the more you feel giddy from the thin air and excitement. You also feel you're getting closer to whatever it is you're looking for.

You reach Moshi, at the foot of Kili's slopes, at about 9pm. Sandi's mjomba is already asleep. You feel guilty for waking him. When he realizes who has arrived, his favorite niece, and that you come bearing gifts, he opens the door with uplifted spirits. In the photos Sandi had shown you, he had a bepop look: beret and four eyes and dark brown crimplene suits and beige cotton shirts. But he's in navy blue woollen pajamas this evening. The minute you're settled he begins with the drink, pouring a little of the brandy on the threshold for the ancestors, before taking several swigs for himself. Then he passes the bottle to Djimon, who takes a direct swig before passing it to you, and you do as the Romans before passing to Sandi. Soon you're all on high glee. Mjomba's caprine eyes bulge, their whites slightly streaked with blood. His weather-beaten face has leathery pleats.

You and Sandi get busy in the kitchen spicing meat, and chopping cucumbers, onions, and tomatoes for a salad. You hand the spiced meat to Djimon as you sit around the fire drinking wine. Your eyes smart from the smoke, prompting you to take any and all opportunity to go outside to give them respite. The night watches you watching the night. You can't believe such silence is still possible. You see your life roll before you like a carpet of prayer, dirty stains and all. Perhaps those who say to pray is to let the silence of God invade us are onto something, you think.

When you re-enter the house, Sandi's mjomba looks at you with slightly drunk eyes and says, "Not expecting a prince to be living in a hovel? Well, welcome to the real Africa, where harsh necessity oppresses like a tyrant. Not your Africa for beginners in the southern tip."

You don't really follow his meaning so you smile without responding. Sandi had warned you that he gets cryptic and philosophical when he gets drunk. The smell of the meat on the fire is appetizing. Sandi is whisking a vegetable omelette for herself.

"When are we eating?" you say to change the topic, having been forewarned not to entertain too much of Mjomba's love of arguing. You remember it is not polite for a visitor to ask such questions about food, so you try to change the topic again before anyone answers.

"I heard distinctive sounds of elephants nearby. I hope we will not be getting visits from the big guys or cats tonight."

This is met with startling laughter from Sandi's mjomba.

"Mjomba and his cabals scared big game away long time ago in the area by hunting them to extinction," Sandi says. "The big cats were a nuisance to domestic stock, especially during times of drought. It is very rare to get them around here anymore."

"That's comforting to know. Elephants I've no problem with, my clan name is maNdlovu," you declare.

"Is that so? What do you know about elephants? Do you think they'll say, 'Sorry, cousin, we didn't know it was you, we were just annoyed at the other lot?'" asks the amused and slightly tipsy Mjomba.

"I know very little about elephants, except what I read from books and watch on National Geographic," you admit while uncorking another bottle of wine. "I was expecting to see plowed fields all over Tanzania. I'm surprised to see almost all fields lie fallow except for a few shambas and commercial farmers. What happened to the programs of Ujamaa?" This social and economic development policy is something you read about and seems like a good topic of conversation. As you understand it, villages and communities were supposed to work together to provide the essentials of living, especially farm produce.

"It failed dismally," Sandi interjects as she stands to go to the kitchen.

"Ujamaa did not fail," her mjomba is quick to disagree.

"Perhaps in the eyes of its adherents, just like communism has not failed to its die-hards. But to the rest of us ordinary folks they both failed," she calls from the kitchen. Tension immediately crackles between them. You feel they've had this argument before and it was left unresolved. You wonder if it was wise to raise the subject.

When your stomach starts to cramp, you try to block out the pain by listening to the conversation intently.

"Ujamaa did not fail. Its implementation, or rather lack of proper implementation, is what failed. It was a well-thought-out program, but when the politicians took it over they spoiled everything as usual."

"By politicians you mean yourselves."

Sandi pops her head out of the kitchen door again and looks at you before continuing. "You see, Mjomba was a director of the government Social Services that decided to collectivize agricultural production. They wanted Tanzanian people, scattered as they are all over the country, to live in compact villages for collective agricultural production. That on its own was not bad, but when people didn't want to go to the compact villages the government started forcing them."

"It's not as simple as that," Djimon feels the need to have his opinion heard here, or to defend the male honor.

"Tell us the complex version then," Sandi interjects. For some reason this topic is vexing Sandi, who is now directing her irritation at Djimon. Her mjomba comes in again. "The government was supposed to establish a few pilot villages all over the country with willing workers who had farming expertise. These pilot villages were supposed to attract others gradually to establish more villages according to demand. But the politicians were impatient. They started coercing people into these compact villages by force. That made the concept very unpopular. Worse, the government was supposed to supply people with things like seed, fertilizer and top-range domestic stock that would be able to withstand the country's conditions. They put people in these villages without farming equipment, waiting on the government. Planting seasons were missed, so there was nothing for people to harvest. Famine became a common thing, and so the people became angry."

"Rightfully so," Sandi interjects again.

"The villages were to be run according to communal values, but the communist wave that was sweeping the country took advantage of people's grievances, eventually replacing our government. The program was then abandoned before it was even properly implemented."

"It failed with a poverty boom, setting the country back about two generations," Sandi insists. "Ordinary people suffered and had to pay with their lives for the politicians' fantasies."

Djimon, whose eyes follow Sandi as she moves, adds, "Moving people forcefully is always a recipe for disaster, but the ultimate failure when it came to Ujamaa was an economic one. The government didn't have enough funds to meet its obligations for the program. That failure cannot be laid on the vision. In the end a lot of things contributed to its failure—drought, national economic collapse, corruption, government inefficiency, and so on."

"Me I blamo visions wit no properly means of implementation," insists Sandi sharply. "To me that's not a vision but a fantasy. A vision which copies other people's failures, for it was already clear from Russia and China that such things not worko. To be proud and unyielding about utopianism is foolish. Look at you now, Mjomba, after giving the best years of your life to the government, you sit here day and night, wasting your life away on drink and false memories."

"I do not feel I'm wasting my life here!" Mjomba deliberately speaks slower now, as if trying to bring his thoughts down to our intellectual level. "The greatest lesson of my life has been to live with the masses. Not everything needs to be given a social and political use. I'm happy to sit here, forgotten by the world I do not respect. I'm happy to have been released from the turbulence of politics. Perhaps in my old age I shall yield some fruit after all; fruit that'll last this time."

There is a tense silence before Mjomba continues. "I do not see proper vision in the present systems either. Just a copying of political programs from other countries, be it West instead of East. This, too, will never bring us anything. What is needed are Africans of some deep thought to come up with solutions that are native to our situation. Unfortunately, African springs of thought are drying up, and it won't help diverting other fountains to our wells if we do not have something original of our own. Perhaps you'll only discover my value when my ghost is blessing you one day."

Another silence ensues. You rub your abdomen as inconspicuously as possible and move closer to the fire.

"Perhaps," Mjomba continues, "Ujamaa could only have worked in a much more integrated society than ours then. It needed widespread shared beliefs. Bludgeoning people into belief, or your own values, achieves nothing." He pauses to take a swig from the brandy bottle before adding, "I regard, for that matter, the swaggering bullies in your present government as worse than what we had back then. They combine the instincts of old tyrants with ideals of democracy and the superficial talk of development. From Rwanda to Zimbabwe the African tyrants now rely on the constitutive muteness of their citizen victims."

You feel the pain momentarily ebbing away and feel strong enough to contribute to the conversation. "Yes, they stave off oxygen from all forums not explicitly aligned to their failing visions. They make it look like you're anti-African, anti-liberation, and a colonial stooge when you dissent against their now oppressive regimes. They want to create automated citizens that worship only their propaganda through direct censorship, or over time by systematically degrading institutions of democratic strength through corruption and political favoritism. That is how they effectively gaslight people and make the act of discernment almost impossible."

"At least we have an independent thinker here," Mjomba compliments you.

You smile at him before going to the kitchen to drink a pain tablet with water. You eat soon after and Sandi's mjomba keeps on speaking as the night crosses over into the morning. He now speaks with a delicacy and perception you did not associate with him when you first met him. There's a certain weary gentleness about him, a profound injury and innate austerity that makes you regard him with awe.

Close to four in the morning the leaden fatigue in your temples and the dull pain in your abdomen can no longer be ignored so you bid your companions goodnight. Sandi shows you where you'll be sleeping. Slipping out of your clothes, you feel a spasmodic warmth flowing onto your legs. These flows, minor side effects of your operation, used to scare you because, unlike normal menstruation, they happen in six to nine month periods. In the months between, you have relief but you know they spell a growing need for surgery in five year intervals or so, to remove the newly grown fibroids. Quickly you call Sandi when you notice you're left with only one sanitary pad in your purse. She gives you some of hers for the night. You struggle with sleep for a long time until it eventually descends like a soft fog. Still you sleep in uncomfortable bouts, dreaming that you, Maman, and Phaks are living in the same house, with a green manicured lawn. You occasionally wake up with a hollow pain and sweat pricking on your skin.

NGORONGORO

You wake in the morning to rain showers curtaining everything, including the much-anticipated cordillera of mountains that form a guard around the permanently ice-capped prince, Kilimanjaro. Sandi, jaunty and capricious, as if to insult your mood from a pounding headache, is already up and washed. She greets you with a flourishing smile, offering a cup of coffee.

"Have you been out already?" you ask.

"Yes. Mjomba and I had to go get more wood for the fire."

You browse yesterday's newspaper while sipping your coffee. The headlines shout out news about the novel Coronavirus found in the Chinese city of Wuhan. As an aspirant virologist, this pricks your interest and provokes a mild panic because the virus is reported to have a high mobility rate. You think back to how the Ebola virus inspired you and others to go work in the DRC to learn more about it. In a way, the succession of those events are what made you choose to come to Tanzania also.

"Scary, isn't it?" Sandi says, reading over you shoulder. "Do you think the Chinese are giving us all the information? It could be more serious than it seems."

"I don't know," you say. "Could be." You hope not, but you have a bad feeling about this. Next in the news is the refugee problem from Ethiopia's civil war, which their government keeps calling the flushing out of the criminal element in the northern regions. There's something about a need for a new economic vision for Tanzania but your stomach cramps are back and are making it difficult to concentrate. Then comes the building material and cellular phone adverts, followed by sport and obituaries.

Your group was meant to have been hiking the mountains, but the rain keeps you inside. Sandi's mjomba feels the mountains will be too treacherous in wet weather for your novice selves. Instead you spend the day around the fire getting to know each other better, which doesn't feel like such a waste of time. You all try to stay off politics after last night, preferring instead to talk about romantic adventures and all. Secretly you are glad, because at their height the cramps incapacitate you. You would not have been able to climb any mountains.

The following day progresses almost in exactly the same manner. You wake to the smell of brewing coffee next to Sandi's mjomba, who is sitting by the fire. You greet him, still yawning. You've already taken a pain pill with bottled water and now you feel in need of coffee.

"It is still drizzling outside," he says. "It seems the gods of the hearth are calling us to the fire ringside again. There won't be too much shame in it. We still have history and literature to iron through." He pauses for a moment before asking, "May I pour you a cup of coffee?"

"Please." You realize that something about Sandi's mjomba reminds you of Phaks, or how you imagine Phaks to have been from reading his journals: his eagerness for debate, his knowledge of a wide variety of topics.

Looking at the distant garden trees, he says, "The pomegranates are splitting because we've seen extremely dry weather before these rains." The two of you sit in companionable silence for a few moments as you try to clear your head. Thoughts of Phaks have sparked a question in your mind.

"How did the arrival of the South African freedom fighters affect your society in this town?"

"Well, Sandi warned me you might be interested in that," says Mjomba with a chuckle. "Look, the coming of South Africans was more of a government thing. The Organization was given a budget by our government, allocated land to place their own people. Those who didn't live on its reserves stayed in our townships and assimilated well, marrying and all. There were occasional incidents, of course, of people trying to settle personal squabbles with xenophobia, but it was not a widespread thing. It was the children of the cadres who later had some grievances. Most of them felt abandoned by their cadre fathers when those men had moved back to South Africa. But we generally took the cadres as our brethren who were fighting for their country. We were prepared to help wherever we could, to the extent that our government even deployed its own military force, secretly of course, to train the Organization soldiers. We couldn't afford an open conflict with apartheid forces for various reasons, like the UN, IMF, and all." He pauses, preparing to light his pipe. You have noticed that Mjomba spends copious amounts of time cleaning his pipe with wire cleaners. "When we were young, our folks fought the German occupying force. Many of them died, before Germany became our colonial master and made us speak and swear in Deutsch. Then came the English, who kicked out the Germans and took over from them. They made us fight for them also. We were not able to plant our fields. So on top of everything else came the famine in our villages. Of course, nobody cared for us, we were just askaris."

You remember the statue you saw in Dar, gifted by the English to commemorate the Tanzanians who fought in the war. Sandi said that you should ask her mjomba about it.

"In fact, a great confusion happened during that war," Mjomba says. "As Tanzanians we found ourselves siding with one colonial master or the other. When the country got its independence, all was forgiven and forgotten. We were supposed to be English natives but we already had a German colonial soul, so, as I am sure you've noticed, our national psyche is more Swahili-Deutsch than Swahili-English. And we're bitter about all the wars they made us fight here, including those for freedom because, by the time we achieved freedom, we were no longer sure what in particular we were being freed from and by whom."

"I thought Nyerere was your national hero?"

"We were unlucky enough to have come to know too much about our liberators by the time we gained freedom. In South Africa you were lucky because you didn't know much about your Mandelas, so you idealized them. By keeping him a mystery in prison, the boers endeared him even more to you. A mere man was raised to mythical levels. And your liberators were in exile, mythologized heroes also. Hence you at least had a naive liberation honeymoon. We were not that lucky. By the time our freedom came, we were already weary of our liberators. After the liberation honeymoon is gone, people are almost always left dangling, feeling growing resentment from its inadequacies. Then you'll find that the democratic dispensation and its demands for the rule of law are no longer suited to serve the consumerist greed of your liberators. They quickly ditch all pretense about being a liberation movement and start to fight each other for turns to loot the country. That is why we had political turmoil every three years or so, when we were due for elections. The talk for liberation quickly got replaced by the self-aggrandizing tendencies of those who managed to hold onto power for longer. When they left the country with very little else to loot, a void was created. The void is now being filled by the religious politics of self-appointed prophets and their talk about the gospel of prosperity. Sadly, if history has taught us anything, it is that such things can end in organized national suicides, otherwise referred to as the spirit of millennialism within amaXhosa nation."

Mjomba's left foot convulsively taps the floor as he talks, which you take to be a sign of nervousness.

As Xhosas you have your fair share of that, from Nxele to the present-day charlatans who are making your people eat grass and drink gasoline. The spirit of desperation rakes the fires of millennialism on your people.

"But I fear more the Putin wannabes like Kagame and Museveni," you say.

"Exactly. In the beginning all were self-sacrificing heroes for the liberation of their people before power happened to them. The power-mongering consumed them to the bone. The under-rated thing that makes Mandela greater than all of them was his wisdom in not allowing himself to be consumed by the power-mongering demon that befalls almost all great African leaders."

Sandi enters, limp as a dishrag and smelling like a wet chicken. "I went to the neighborhood to greet some old friends," she explains when you ask. Sandi puts her foot down when she notices you two are again discussing politics. "I'll lose my mind if you two talk about politics again the whole day. Why don't we all drive to the Ngorongoro Crater? Mjomba, you can come too; the two of you can catch up on your talks."

"Yes, it'll give us more chance to talk," you say, urging Mjomba, who shrugs his shoulders in agreement.

The morning is still overcast, although the rain has temporarily halted when you leave. The gaunt summit of Mt. Meru is partially obscured by gray-white mist.

"It's the proudest mountain among the sentinels of Kili-manjaro," Mjomba says when he notices you taking a cellphone pic of it. You tell him about Virgil, who made Aeneas put his father on his back as he took to the mountains. When he asks where your interest in classical literature and mythology comes from, you tell him about your father and how he left his books with your mother before going into exile.

"It's almost like the myth of Proserpine," you say. "The books are the pips of the pomegranate Pluto had her eat to keep her with him in the underworld." By the end of the day he starts referring to you as "Proserpine who reigns over ghosts."

The moment the car climbs out of the valley you're on the rolling high country. No more millet fields with barbed-wire fences surrounding homesteads of ramshackle huts with roofs held by stones and pumpkins. No more children shouting and racing the bouncing car, or fascinating women carrying firewood on their backs rather than their heads as they do at home. Then the rain falls in a sudden frenzy, with rattling thunder and lashing winds.

"This weather has been sent for someone," Sandi says. And she tells you how sometimes the forces of darkness, like demons, use thunder to abduct strangers in the village in order to use them as zombies. Her expression is serious as she narrates different cases of this happening. You wonder why this belief is dominant in many African countries, and why the fear of evil seems to form the foundation of African myths more than the love of goodness.

Potholes, large as canyons, control your speed, causing Djimon to swerve and crawl along. The closer you get to the crater the more the land becomes a panorama of jagged rocks and twisted forest growth, looking hard as steel. You reach another summit and Sandi points down to a flat landscape clothed in green.

"That is the Ngorongoro Crater, stretching about twenty-five kilometers in diameter," she tells you. You drive down precariously on a stony track, next to the steep side, until you reach the gate to the park, where you pay a conservation fee. Driving into the park, you immediately find herds upon herds of animals grazing in bovine sturdiness: an obstinacy of buffaloes, a zeal of zebras, a tribe of antelopes, a conspiracy of wildebeests and such. You step out of the car when you reach a designated place where it is safe to do so. The soft rain drizzles in the struggling sunshine. Angular men with thin, sinewy calves protruding from their blood-red cloaks, their faces chiseled by the elements, carrying sticks and spears, look askance at you.

"These are the Maasai shepherds, herding their cattle,"

Mjomba tells you. "They move with seasons between Kenya and Tanzania."

Without the use of binoculars, two young cheetahs capture your attention. Behind the cheetahs is what looks like a brown rock mass but you soon see it's a pack of hyenas who are following the pair of big cats to bully them out of their kills. Majomba's eyesight just doesn't travel that far so he says he doesn't really see the cackle. You point out more Maasai shepherds beyond the hill belt and a drift of calves and lambs lying dreamily in the meadow warmth. You drive past this biblical picture to a picnic spot next to the salt lake where a cloud of pink flamingos is fishing in the shallows. Sandi takes out and passes around your lunch. You eat with the manners of a dog, since you're famished. Then you gulp down some of Djimon's beer with the ease of an open drain.

It grows hotter as your group drives to the Olduvai. Inside the buildings you see a replica of the skull Zinjanthropus, which you're told is one and three-quarter million years old, discovered by Mary Leakey. You wish you can say it moved you to some form of reverence, but the truth is you're preoccupied with finding a toilet for a change of pads, not to mention to relieve yourself after all that beer.

The thing that moves you the most on the drive back is the harmony of coincidences that brought all of you here on this particular day. You don't mean to belittle the significance of the place, which you're sure has merit to the claim of calling itself the spiritual center of humanity. You're just more fascinated by smaller things, and the ocean of time, that managed to bring you this far.

And, you admit, there's something unseen and emotionally poignant about the place, as if you are standing where history, with all its trickery, evaporates before the eyes, leaving only the nakedness of nature. And a lament for the passing age walks across your soul each time you glimpse the sad, puckered face of Sandi's mjomba.

MAN IS A GIDDY THING

The morning I woke from my paper wife's rural home she walked me to the taxi stop when her father left for the fields. Not much was said between us on that walk; in fact she kept ignoring me whenever I tried to start a conversation with her, as if she was embarrassed by what we had done—I later learned it was the religious thing creeping in.

"Will I ever see you again?" she asked as we waited for the taxi.

"My life depends on it. I'll come and visit you whenever I get the opportunity, if you tell me where."

She gave a slight grunt, followed by a hesitant, faint laugh. Her young girl's smile aroused a sense of the marvelous in my heart. True to my word, I visited her two weeks later in her East London nursing residence, ending up staying with her for some months when the Special Branch came after me.

That Saturday evening I got off a taxi to be in her arms for the first time saved my life, most probably. Nine of our comrades, the political leadership I was part of, were rounded up by the security police at our university hostels in Fort Hare at the same moment I was lying in her arms. Her love literally saved my life because two of our guys that were rounded up were never seen or heard from again. After that I had to go underground because the police were hot on my heels also. The only sensible thing was to go to stay with her. No one knew of our connection. The streets of our townships were aflame from the political uprising then.

Uneasy about the situation, she brought me food, washed and ironed my clothes, nursed me like a bird with a broken wing. All I did then was read and read while being fattened like a capon. In the evening we got a chance for walks, taking care not to wander too deep into white areas like Amalinda, Selborne, and Vincent Heights. Southernwood was the only place we felt comfortable since it was slightly cosmopolitan. I felt guilty for making her life complicated. For one, she stopped visiting her father for fear of implicating him in case the secret police were onto me and watching me, which turned out to be the case.

I knew our arrangement could not last. Word was getting around even at the college that she was harboring a guy in her quarters—matrons called her twice but she denied it. Other nurses were jealous, not knowing it was a matter of life and death for me—Aesop frogs again.

On one of our walks she said, all of a sudden, "I found out today that I'm one and a half months pregnant."

I didn't know what to say.

"Are you not going to say anything?" she asked, irritated when enough time had passed without my answering.

"I don't know what to say."

"How about: Are you feeling okay? Or something?" I could see she was angry, which confounded me even more, so I kept quiet.

"I'm sorry," she continued after some time. "It's just that this will ruin my chances of graduating. I'll have to drop out of college."

It felt as though I was the one who was ruining her life. "Look, it's April now, and you're one and a half months pregnant. That means you'll deliver somewhere between December and January, after the college closes in November. You've a slim figure, so buy bigger clothes from now on, and I guarantee you no one will notice your pregnancy until the end of the year. Then you can deliver and come back next January." I was disappointed to see she didn't share my enthusiasm.

"You have answers for everything, don't you?" she said in a cold tone that cut through me. "And what am I supposed to tell my father, that ndimithiswe yicofi?" Her sarcasm cut through my heart.

"We'll go to your home and explain our situation. Your father is a religious man. He'll have compassion, even if he does not approve of me. I'll tell him we want to get married when I finish my degree." That somehow put her more at ease.

I went with her to her home the following week. The reception I got from her father was not good, but I had expected that. I told him I was planning ukunyuka ngengalo, to marry her, and would be sending a delegation yonozakuzaku soon to start negotiating ilobola. None of that materialized of course. Actually, I knew at the back of my mind it was just a doomed wish. The moment my name was regarded as a threat by the apartheid Special Branch I knew I was living on borrowed time. It was the end of any semblance of normalcy in my life.

In the following weeks it became impossible for me to hang around in the country anymore, definitely not in East London, since I didn't want to get Nozi mixed up in the dangers of politics. Each time I came from political meetings I took different routes and taxis to confuse the Special Branch guys who followed us around.

The time we spent together was the happiest I'd ever been in the country of my birth. She doted on me, propped up my ego, which in those days was always sliding like a drunk into a puddle of self-pity. I read books and wrote stories, which I read back to her. She'd listen with a look of solemn concentration, occasionally paddling me on and raising her little hand through my verbal gossamer.

"Whoa! Whoa! Phakamile Maseti!" she'd say. "Back up a little. Whoa! Who speaks like that around here? You're making people speak like they do in white people's books." True, the books I read then, beyond the political ones, were mostly Greek or

Roman literature. When I didn't pay attention to what she said she'd accuse me of not caring about anything but philhellene literature. "You think Greeks were the acme of Hesperian civilisation? Why don't you ever talk about your own people, Jolobe, Jordan, Plaatje, Rubusane, Soga, Knox and all? You act as if we don't have literary giants here."

"You misjudge me," I protested. "Besides, our literary giants were themselves influenced by the classics. Soga loved Bunyan, Plaatje was obsessed with Shakespeare, the influence of Homer and Aesop is obvious on Mqhayi. Sure, the Greeks and the Romans had their faults, lusty liars and treacherous egomaniacs as they were; often they were childish, cruel, heartless people who almost worshipped violence as a supreme measure of gaining honor and virtue; but the truth is that we can't dispute the brilliant delicacy of their literature, raw as the stuff of life itself."

She'd look at me in her way that communicated mysterious tenderness. She understood exactly what classical literature meant to me. I loved those moments. They helped dispel the curious atmosphere of strain and foreboding in my life, for we knew the security forces were closing in.

She'd give me a warm smile and say, "I judge people not by the smoothness of their tongues, but by the grace and sobriety of their living."

"The Greeks considered none above them in grace of living," I'd retort.

"I mean true grace, not aesthetic self-aggrandizement. They had no moral shame. The Romans might have been crude and rugged, but they had a real sense of moral honor that came from an external standard everybody revered. I think that was their strength."

"It's because you're Roman Catholic that you favor the Romans."

"It has very little to do with that. I just find their universality appealing."

And so our debates would go on and in such ways we spent our evenings, arguing about literature or religion. I soon learned to be less critical about religion because it meant a lot to her, and lived with it as my way of respecting her.

Why did I leave her like that? Did I have any choice?

I had gone to a political meeting in Mdantsane. On my way back I discovered a security-police car parked outside the building. I was certain they had recognized me as I went into the yard and were just waiting for me to settle down before they would raid the building in search of me and my protectors. I went through the yard, jumped the fence on the other side, and looked up at her window before disappearing on the streets forever. When I took that last look, her window was lit, her silhouette moving about. She must've been preparing supper, humming softly to herself as usual. That's the last image I have of her, a shadow behind some puppet show. I moved to a safe house in Mdantsane and was advised, for both our protection, not to make contact with her until I was safely outside the country. We all agreed that my cover was blown.

In a week I was in Mbabane, Swaziland, eating pap and chilli stews of pig's head, thinking about her all the time, taking comfort and strength in the hope that the security officers couldn't have known which of the two hundred rooms I was visiting. I thought about the humiliation she would have to bear for being impregnated by a guy who abandoned her and absconded. I wondered how she'd explain my disappearance, even to herself. I wrote to tell her when I was safely outside the country, promising lies of returning soon for her and the baby. Those broken promises are the shame of my life.

I felt a slight relief in leaving South Africa, as I was no longer waking up startled with a constant fear of every door knock or banging, or the rush of feet in passages and on stairs at night. But mostly I felt regret for the things left undone, unsaid. Regret is a useless emotion. It saps you of vitality.

The memory of the peace of our last days was the greatest force of strength for me. For a while, it was what lifted my mood when the spirit of Mephistopheles clutched on to me. To me, for whom very few things generate enough power to occupy the mind, it meant a lot. But the truth is that within six months in Lusaka, she started to grow faint in my mind. I left her with a promise in my heart that *Aut Inveniam Viam Aut Faciam*: I will either find a way or make one, for us to be together. But soon I met others, who gradually dissolved that steely resolution for, as Shakespeare saw, *man is a giddy thing.*

The script kept on rewriting itself. Odysseus, away for too many years, desperate to get home, worries that when he gets there he will find his wife remarried, or no longer in love with him, and his child a stranger. Or worse still, his wife loving another. How then will he appear to them? A deserter? How will they appear to him? Betrayers? After lost years of painful adventures have taken their toll on him, what is left for him to come back to? What has Penelope done in those years? Did she spend them in her chamber, weaving at her loom, listening to the carousing of the suitors in the great hall of the palace? What can she still feel for the man who has been away for so long? What can they still have in common?

Most often, time vanquishes and changes everything without improving anything. The past comes to assist or accuse us. There's no journeying home for the wanderers of Abraham's God; they must change their names to transform. There's no marriage bed, carved from the trunk of a living olive tree, waiting to be shared for them. They must love slave women, the Hagars they meet along the way, and lie to kings by disowning their wives as sisters to survive. They must disown those they love to be faithful to those with whom they want to spend the rest of their lives, whom they'll also leave in the desert, along dried water wells, to make way for the chosen sons to assume their heritage, making firstborns into warriors that live by the sword to be a menace to their brethren. That is the nature of things; the tears in mortal things of Abraham's God, who is a harsh master that saves only by severe mercy. Homer had no strength to give life to such tragedy. In the ancient era the Greeks liked dramas where a hero's epic journey ends by righting the wrong done. Only the Jews understood tragedies properly, where two rights compete on equal footing with tragic consequences, because no one is necessarily in the wrong—it is just the tragic nature of things.

The God of wanderers, wamaMfengu, is ruthless in his mercies; will drive you to a desert where you watch a vulture snatch a baby from a mother's back when she becomes too weak to defend it. But no one can blame the vulture or other buzzards as they circle; they too must feed their young and clean the earth. In this script, of Abraham, there's nothing without consequences, no returning to what was. In this script we shame those who love us, and love those who shame us: *I was not in safety, neither had I rest, neither was I quiet; yet trouble came*, complains Job, whose voice cascades through the years.

MT. KILIMANJARO

You and Sandi, with guides Mjomba organized for you, hike up Mt. Kilimanjaro a month later on another holiday. Mjomba, un-characteristically, has not been feeling well, bodily pains and all, which is rare in a sixty-seven-year-old who still jumps fences. The guides, wishing to earn their keep, talk incessantly about Kili fast losing its ice-cap, with frequent fires damaging the forests. They say you're approaching it from the southern side of the mountain. The climb begins through the coffee plantation hills. You're disappointed that there's no coffee smell. You didn't know coffee smells only after the beans are roasted. The north-eastern side is more arid and dry and retains the original natural look of the mountain, and is less developed.

With panting breath you reach the tropical montane forest zone, what is called the Shining Mountain. Here the vegetation pronounces more the uniform lush garb of greenery. You see a greater variety of butterflies and birds, a duiker here and there. As you prepare for camping at dusk the butterflies disappear and the birds hush. Out come the nocturnal animals, civets and bush babies. Monkeys with white capes swing through the overhead canopy of trees, while baboons patrol the camphor tree paths with occasional *baagoom-baagoom* noises. You're told the bigger game, like elephants, buffaloes, and lions, are still present on the northern side.

The next morning, as you proceed, breathing starts becoming an issue, as if you have Sisyphus' boulder sitting on your chest.

Sandi starts to be concerned for you.

"Don't compare with me, sister. I'm born to this altitude. My lungs evolved through ages to cope with it. So you tell us when you've had enough and we call it quits."

Daytime mists become common and the mountain above girds herself with a white apron of clouds. Giant protea plants become abundant. When you reach what is referred to as the moorland, the animals become scarce, because it is too high for most of them, the grass and vegetation here too acid for their liking. So say the guides. Though you don't see any, they tell you this is the habitat of the mountain lion, where they raise their young, going down only to hunt. "You must be careful because they're protective of the area," the guides caution. Civets, who feed on rats and mice, are still plentiful. Buzzards and white-necked ravens patrol the skies. You reach your limit at the Alpine Desert zone. Never have you seen a space so vast and toweringly high. It makes you vertiginous. The guides say you're between four thousand and five thousand meters above sea level. The winds are scouring. You camp for the night again.

The following morning you're shown the ground-hugging craters, from this height, like the famous Mawenzi, and the snow-crowned Kibo. But feeling sickly, your vision doubles and they undulate before your eyes. The guides are aggrieved, complaining about turning around at the penultimate stage. Sandi puts her foot down by informing them you're all going back down. Feeling a little embarrassed, you try to appease them by promising to better prepare next time. They like the talk about next time because it means more business for them.

You can identify the shaved scalp of Mt. Meru when Sandi points it out to you as you go down, which from the town of Arusha you mistakenly thought was the real summit of Mt. Kilimanjaro. Bald with a bright snow cap it stands, still defiant though now it's almost at your feet.

You muse on what one is supposed to do after conquering a

mountain like Kili. The sad thing is that once you've reached the summit you've nowhere else to go but down. Your vision gets shrouded by the clouds, the anxieties that clutter mountain tops where others have left their litter. And you must collect it on your way down as you negotiate the mist. You're exposed to the scouring winds where you lose the mystery.

THE MIST

Back from the Kili climb, at Sandi's home, you encounter a tragedy. Mjomba is engulfed within a halo of silence. He's sitting like a column in a wheelchair next to the window in the lounge. He looks dark against the reflection of firelight. His eyes peer for recognition through his grime-rimmed spectacles when he hears your voices. You take out your medical bag and examine with a flashlight the dilation of his pupils. His corneas have the cloudiness of advancing cataracts, which is not something to be too concerned about on a man of his age. The worry is the pigmentation and muscle collapse around the sclerae. It's clear he has suffered some form of thrombosis. After testing all his joints also your worst fears are almost confirmed that it is not just a minor stroke but some form of sclerosis. You berate yourself for delaying this check-up since you had been noticing that his laughter, almost always, morphed into a cough before slopping into a hack.

You go to the kitchen to share your diagnosis with Sandi in the most non-alarming way you can muster without hiding the truth. You get caught up in the grimy condensation on the window through which you can faintly see the snow-capped Mt. Meru in towering majesty against other mountains. Your soul is suffocating.

When you try to feed him soup later, Mjomba, who has not spoken in hours, speaks in English, almost out of breath.

"Proserpine, who reigns over ghosts." Selfishly, you're more excited that he recognizes you than that he can speak—not only that, but by the fact that he's keeping his humor and wisdom to the grave. Sandi turns to ask what he had just said. You shrug your shoulders, although you had heard it. He falls into a stupor again and loses track of things.

Outside the flurrying snow follows the wind without falling. Sandi tells you Mjomba used to sit for hours at the window when it snowed, always commenting that his wife departed with the snow to the grave. It occurs to you that Phaks hardly ever mentions the weather in his journals. He talks about the sun and the moon, not the weather. You guess this means the only weather that ever mattered to him was that inside his head. The mist he is forever referring to. When that clouded over he got lost inside the labyrinth of his mind.

Looking into his eyes, you can see Mjomba is struggling to find a way out of the labyrinth of his mind. Perhaps his wife is the Ariadne of his Theseus against the legendary tricks of Daedalus, the only thing keeping him from despairing, as was Efuoa to Phaks. You can swear Mjomba laughed with that thought.

At a short distance the trees are shaking the snow halos off their crowns. The land is as quiet as the lake. The sky has grown claustrophobic with fog, hiding the details of the day as the mist filters everything. And Mjomba quietly expires that early evening, to join his ancestors on the cycle of the Eleusinian Mysteries.

FILL ME A BRIMMING BOWL
29/10/99

I woke this morning with the ache of a broken sleep still in my bones. It's days like these my life accuses me with a stabbing pain. When we joined the Organization, it was not a matter of sacrificing everything, but of finding a home, a front, from which we could be who we believed we could be, and fight against the forces that sought to put us down. Imagine our surprise when we discovered we had not escaped those forces even inside the Organization.

What difference has the part of my life spent in the Organization made? Or, let me put it this way: if I knew what I now know, would I have joined?

Yes.

Many things have happened to us. We were treated badly, horribly sometimes, by the Organization, but I would have joined anyway. The cause I believed in was not taught to me by the Organization. The Organization provided me with a platform to express it, and then they betrayed it in the end. The irony is too tragic—escaping apartheid forces to be put in arrest by your own comrades. One minute you're fighting the apartheid enemy, another, in a blinding flash, you are accused of collaborating with them. It's a brutal dislocating force that leaves you silent and confused. And, of course, a submissive sheep is a find for a wolf. *A person who is not inwardly prepared for use of violence against him is always weaker than the person committing the violence*, says the Russian political novelist and historian

Aleksandr Isayevich Solzhenitsyn. That was our first error. We could not imagine any circumstances that could compel us to use force against our own comrades. Most people who joined the Organization were genuine, believed in fighting for the freedom of our people. Sadly, there were those opportunists who went into exile to flee from their chaotic criminal lives in South Africa, not because they were really inspired to fight apartheid. Others were just fleeing their failed lives, looking for opportunities, even new mischief, and so on and so on. The saddest part is that the non-genuine ones were often very motivated and passionate about making their new situation work for them, and were thus more organized. It was common knowledge, spoken of in hushed tones, that some of our commanders were known criminal lords who used the Organization corridors to traffic drugs and stolen cars from South Africa. Those who profited from such things formed themselves into cliques that were ready to undermine the real values of our movement with impunity. Added to them were moles planted by the enemy to cause confusion inside the Organization.

Perhaps some of us stayed too long in occidental hives, where we inhaled the hot air of corporate hustlers and made ourselves vulnerable to the opportune suspicions of comrades who were less sophisticated, especially those slumming it in the bush, or those who saw in the Organization a perfect vehicle to smuggle contraband. Too many wide divides like that developed between us underground. Suspicion was endemic among comrades at the time, and our Western lifestyle didn't help. But some of us, despite appearances, were no renegades from the aspirations of the Freedom Charter. We were not consumerist cosmopolitans, despite the bourgeois trappings.

All water under the bridge now.

Working in the Lusaka propaganda division of the Organization, responsible for writing radio pieces for *RF* and other propaganda publications, was supposed to be the highlight of my career within the Organization. But it didn't take long for me to become embroiled in the scandals created by certain personnel who didn't shy away from employing false confessions to implicate people suspected of being impimpis. Some of us were adamant not to see the Organization fall for tactics similar to those of apartheid security personnel. We wanted to maintain discipline, to be a true liberating army. We didn't want to see a scenario where our people become more afraid of us as their liberators than the oppressors. This is a scenario seen too often in other African liberation armies. But the personnel we accused of underhandedness had powerful connections they used against us, and so it was us who ended up in detention camps. Very soon the cases became more personal than political, mining already existing grievances in the Organization. The whole thing deteriorated into a confrontation between the African Socialists and the African Nationalists; those who were trained in the USSR and the Republic of China against those who were in Western Europe. Comrades sometimes locked comrades behind bars to settle political scores. As a form of lenience some of us were clandestinely transferred to SOMAFCO—a benign way of keeping us out of the way, of sending us to the second exile.

The initial frustration was tamed by the realization that we were still alive, which was not to be taken lightly, since some didn't make it. At least the Organization paid a teacher's salary, not much but enough for a living. I had my books. I thought I could still maintain my influence by writing pieces for the Organization publications or other international journals. But the Organization editors were instructed not to consider any of our contributions. Cicero's late writings suddenly took on more relevance to me. I told myself it was not the end of the world, although I was overwhelmed by a cynical world-weariness. Reading became my only companion. I lived for, in, and with books till I met Efuoa, who slowly pulled me back into life. I found myself little by little giving up drinking and smoking. In a way they gave me up because I just lost the taste and craving for them. Just to discover a few years later that I was dying. Efuoa keeps reminding me, while trying to keep me alive, that I am going to be an important man of books, because I had told her I would write books that would make us important and famous. She believed me. Because she believes everything I say. How was I to know I had run out of time?

Still, I took up the pen from the ashes of my life, and wrote this journal, using my own blood as ink.

I found it more difficult with each passing day to teach students who mostly saw themselves as soldiers, soon to be fodder for the cause, and thus found learning a waste of their limited time since they'd probably soon die in some godforsaken forest or desert anyway. In the end I, too, gave up trying to convince them otherwise. I gave up my pretensions of teaching and allowed them to do as they pleased, which meant raiding villages for alcohol and girls. *Whatever tears one may shed,* so says Heine, *in the end one always blows one's nose.*

Of course there are things that haunt me still, I may never forget, ever! Some I record in these Pillow Books, just to pluck out the thorn and lance the boil.

THE GRADUATION

Momza

Aunt Zenzile and I came back from my graduation in Johannesburg with a bus this morning. We're exhausted and sleepy. I can't believe she is preparing to go eDekini this afternoon. I didn't miss you, Mommy. I know you were there. I just know!

LIVING IN MEMORY
11/11/99

My memory, the trusted friend of my years that gives my life some form of continuity, is slipping away from me, sometimes misfiring. What do we have, if not our memories, the last battlefield of our experience? Grief? Proust was of the opinion that memory is stereoscopic consciousness, basically recreated experience.

Grief is the overwhelming feeling of my soul now. I grieve for my own life. Our thoughts are supposed to be the sediments of our experiences that make our lives into memory. I wish I could say memory clarifies the mess we make of our lives, but that would be a lie. I reach for these diaries as an attempt to give sense, some form of continuity, to my life. Perhaps to acquire understanding also. Writing, sometimes, takes away the weariness of the heart, even feels like a process of purgatory, of eliminating one's life weeds, of letting go of cheap consolations. The best thing about dying is that it unmasks all pretense and sham.

The Polish poet Milosz says the nearness of death destroys shame. I'm not sure about that, because my experience has been toward the opposite. Unless he means by exposing our inner shame death takes out the sting that grieves us. Then I agree. There has been something about this urgent process of dying that has robbed death of its power over my life: *Death, where is thy sting*, in the words of St. Paul.

I know we're supposed to be fearful or awed by death. For me the whole thing feels more ludicrous than awe-inspiring at this stage. I mean, what is the point of it all, of life, if we must in the end permanently die? You acquire experience, but for what, if you must be eternally extinguished in the end? Only if my consciousness survives my experience of death would I be fine with that, for it means death is just a transformation into another state.

More than tired, my body is sad. It feels the urgency of pending separation from its own life. It knows the soul, the seat of its thoughts, experiences and memories, is going somewhere it cannot follow. I don't know how to console it, to thank my body for the service it provided me when it had its strength in the last forty years, except perhaps, again, to reach out to the Christian belief, the consolation of the resurrection that implies the ultimate indestructibility of our formed matter. In the resurrected Christ, the Christians claim, we shall have new bodies whose energy travels faster than the speed of light. Hence Christ could be seen in different places at the same time. How marvelous and stupendous. Christianity, indeed, has the most radical claims of all beliefs in the world. Beliefs that are tailor-made for our deepest natural yearnings, I hasten to add. Its brilliance lies exactly in that. That it elevates absurdity to the heights of mystery. It requires patience, though, to see through its powerful mythical speculations which have, through the years, been skillfully infused into history of experiences, invention, and otherwise. Especially when that rubbish is used for what Kierkegaard called Christendom, the use of religion for the promotion of imperial and white supremacy notions. But I do not think most people understand the radicalness of Christianity, like the claims that our weakness or haplessness destines us, through grace, into divinity. The psalmist puts it well: *I have said, Ye are gods; and all of you are children of the most High. But ye shall die like men, and fall like one of the princes...*

I wonder if my soul, the unbounded cosmic force and living spirit that livens the arrangement of my atomic structure, felt sad or excited when it was ordered to temporarily limit itself by the Source of Life who confined it within my weak and limited body when I was conceived in my mother's womb: *Before I formed thee in the belly I knew thee; and before thou camest forth out of the womb I sanctified thee, and I ordained thee a prophet unto the nations...*I think Jeremiah had a similar question as to whether this incarnation is a prison sentence or an opportunity for a microcosmic adventure of a glorious order—the thing we call human life.

These Pillow Books are my way of flinging abroad my life amid the planetary music. Of telling whoever wishes to listen that I am haunted by men who lived their lives permanently aware of their own mortality. I presume this is what is meant by living poetically. What is poetry if not just another means of questioning being, of recognizing that in birth we're mortally wounded by the gift of life? Poetry helps consolidate and sustain our strength against the fear of death in our collision with reality.

I'm tired.

What do I remember about Swaziland, Mbabane? Sun-drenched, slow days. Creeping boredom and unengaged exercises. Dumbfounding orders and senseless dithering about. The never-ending wait for non-existent orders. Sweat-seeping boredom. Scarce food. Stomach-wrenching hunger. Dating in a fish-bowl; fucking like rabbits in open fields; dark shapes coalescing in the gloom; rain on the muddy red-clay streets; stuffed knapsacks, moving from village to village...More fucking as the gift of slow death enters your system.

What do I remember about Lesotho? Endless exercise. Boredom. Brain-draining boredom and the slowness of time. Weed smoking, dagga puffing, cheap alcohol quaffing. Energy-sapping boredom, and maddening, meaningless orders. Lank, skinny girls ambling with pointed elbows and a raunchy gaiety. Permissive sexual manners; satisfaction colliding with anticipation in a stew of depraved morals. Krantzes, whitesnowed mountains. Soldiers in heat feeding the fire of death and puffing it to a blaze; bloody panties from ruptured hymens, dirty underwear and the scorpion-sting pain of venereal diseases. Dislocation attenuating the sense of self...

What of Mozambique? Steamy, misting forest, the smell of damp, verdant earth, dappled fallen leaves with blood spots and silky dots of the sun. Lying next to a slapping river, being nauseated by the fertility at the banks. Eating inkobe and Jabula soup day in and day out. Hunting for meat and meeting giggling girls collecting wood; fucking with ass exposed to the blue sky and racing clouds, women whose husbands/boyfriends were away in South African mines; giving free pass to the rut. Guilt seeping in small doses during ungodly early hours of the morning. More fucking! Toddlers with wheezy chests and streaming noses whining and tugging at the skirts of their orgiastic mothers. Feasting wild as bacchanal from the idiosyncratic hospitality of different villages. Fucking until you have a burning sensation in your cock...

What of Angola? Insomniac positions; lying flat with hands buckled across the stomach under the ectoplasmic darkness of forest nights. Furtive, chronic masturbations, ecstatic stridulating crickets, a flailing leg, ritual aggression, submission, and revolt. Whine and gripe and picking of scabs. Psychological pabulum; rowdy arguments and lack of intellectual intimacy. A sense of solitude taking physical form. Insipid mornings and vapid evenings. The boredom, the urgent, burning boredom of it all against the setting sun. Clucking and frenetic calls of birds followed by rumbling gunfire. Death approaching by degrees. Resignation to death? Not yet, when you survive the morning. The never-ending marches through forests. The poisonous snakes and burning fear of mambas and pythons that are attracted by your heat while you sleep under the dripping leaf. The ache and pain of joints; the dizziness and attendant nausea; exhaustion from being too exhausted by exhaustion. Rolling thunder when the weather broke; barking baboons; the trees that looked like marching people at night, giving a foretaste of death; and the delirium of your comrades dying from strange diseases. Again life as a sexual epidemic when you reach the villages. Then six months in Lusaka awaiting orders and fermenting the virus. Nature fueling into delirium the snares that catch you by your weaknesses. Confusion feeding on moral and political chaos and disorder...

What of the Soviet Union? Two years of snow; blue rivers, stranded birch trees, factories smoking languid sulphur and sewer gases and heavy air from kilns. Fields and fields of potatoes, and drinking its fermented juice: Vashe zdorovie! To your health! And lots and lots of spitting on the floor. More months in Lusaka, Zambia. The loneliness of having nothing to come home to. Another stint in the USSR, St. Petersburg. A lot of pale skins from the inadequate light of Russia. Byzantine architecture and Gothic church buildings swimming in lusterless air. Undigested political theories and awakening to your true self through the discovery of Russian literature: Pushkin, Gogol, Turgenev, Chekhov, Tolstoy, Dostoevsky, Pasternak. Beautiful written things that read like a greeting from the future through the past. Being blown to thought by the aphoristic Nietzsche, and prophetic signs of instability aligned with the great communist system. Russia becoming Welt-Frühling, a world of your awakening...

What do you really remember about Russia? Standing in front of a window watching frozen streets, longing to see at least one fly, just one fly, and getting used to an empty room. Visiting a whore whose idea of kindness is to fuck the brains out of you while shouting: "Moor! My black moor. Mine Pushkin!" Her urine hissing like a horse's on frosted grass as the flashing eye of her pink clitoris salutes you. The pleasure of discovering she's naked as a knee under her vixen coat. Her simian face; her sleek forehead. Her habit of applauding her own orgasms with an air of ceremony. Her fake sophistication, beautiful mind. Mein Gott!

What do you remember about your life? Getting invaluable exposure to living foreign languages; reading voraciously everything and anything you could get your hands on. The fascinating medieval rusticity of Russians. Holidays in Germany; blood sausage and sauerkraut. The austerity of Deutschland despite all her modern techniques. The symmetry and artistic throb of Berlin. The German anger against apartheid and heightened awareness of their own deplorable past. The indictment of the apartheid system by German chicks who showed up to fuck your brains out. The generosity of Scandinavian people.

And the horror of fighting apartheid soldiers with SWAPO in a dream, only realizing those who were shot really died. A knife going through a boer's neck; the wind gushing out of his windpipe. The turning away of your eyes. My God! So much wind! So much pressure! So much wind from one man! It stays with you: his green eyes; his refusal to die. Why wouldn't he die? Why? Why the serenity in his eyes; the lack of rancor; the shocking incongruity of the nature of things? God! What have we done with our lives? The terrible, ageless watchfulness, and the generosity, of the sun; the indifference of the meadows and their lion-mane color in autumn. The trembling nearness of death and the far distance of the sea. The crawling into a blunder; the pealing noise of an exploding grenade and the deafness it caused in your left ear; lilies in the field flying with the shrapnel? Dark smoke. Living by sheer effort, with death jammed in your stomach and breath constipated in your lungs. The vicious tendencies of hyenas on fallen comrades; the assertive, penetrating intelligence of monkeys, mocking your sadistic frenzy; the howling doom of baboons! Heaven and hell shaking in the soul; and the wound which must die to heal. The comradely song:

Sabashiya abazal' ekhaya,
Saphuma sangena kwamanye amazwe,
Lapho singaboni ubaba nomama,

Silwelwa inkululeko
Sithi salan', salan', salan' ekhaya
Sophuma singena kwamanye amazwe…

We left our parents behind,
We went out and entered different countries,
Where we don't see Father and Mother,
Where we prepared to fight for our freedom,
We say stay well, stay well at home,
We're going to other countries,
We'll soon be back with freedom…

SAUDADE

You're glad you could be there for Sandi during the mourning and burial of her mjomba. Djimon was not much of a help and you think Sandi's fascination with him has fizzled out. In a way saying goodbye to Mjomba also felt like saying goodbye to Phaks. You feel like, in the end, you did meet your father after all. From the Pillow Books you learned more than you would have ever been able to learn in real life. The only thing missing is that you would have loved to hear his voice. You now know the betrayal he felt from his fellow comrades while in exile, when his voice was effectively silenced. You know the trauma he experienced fighting, the killings that still haunted him, the times he sought solace in the simulation of love, and the shock of his sickness. You are thankful that he found Efuoa, who has become like a mother to you.

On your return to Morogoro, you take out your laptop and write the email to Hlumelo that you've been putting off for a while.

The last time you saw Hlumelo was when both of you were about to leave SA. He had invited you to his book launch in Johannesburg. You were still living in Cape Town then. Ami had picked you up from OR Tambo Airport. The drive on the freeway felt like a lucid dream during the early evening.

The hug and the smells from Ami's car's leather seats were pleasing, comforting, and reassuring, making the car into some form of anechoic cabin against the city. The city held a jumble of joyful and painful associations for you. You felt the return of the sexual charge of your youth in it.

You felt happy for Ami for realizing that dream of staying in Sandton as you approached through the roller-coasting roads, entering avenues of espaliered trees and synthetic lawns. You wondered at how Sandton, at night in particular, exposes itself as a stream of artifice and invention, cascading glass walls, artificial rocks, cement cliffs of magnificent glamor, pedicured lawns and all.

On reaching her townhouse in Morningside you discovered that her hubby was on some study trip in Singapore. They have no children—"too busy at the moment building our careers." You followed Ami to the kitchen after dropping your bags in the guest room you were shown to. Although the lounge was spacious, the flat had a small Frankfurt fitted kitchen. Nothing suggesting any love for cooking, giving the impression that food was mostly delivered from outlets and restaurants.

"When I got your email that you were coming I couldn't help wondering..." Ami cocked her head. "If perhaps there was something else? I mean, more than your childhood sweetheart's book launch? I know you better than that. Don't get me wrong, I love having you here, but what made you need to come?"

"Saudade, the Portuguese call it, I think."

A slightly tense silence hung between you before Ami stood up to open a bottle of wine.

"I also needed to see you, babes, before I leave," you admitted.

"Leave? Leave Cape Town, you mean? To where? When?"

"Tanzania for a while. I got a position through Doctors Without Borders. But I also need to go to deal with this issue of my father that's strangling my life."

"Well, I guess it's better than the DRC. I was worried sick while you were working with those Ebola patients. I can't go through that again."

Ami has never forgiven you for leaving Joburg in the first

place, never understood your urge to serve in the Eastern Cape, where you felt more needed since its educated get drained by bigger cities. And she certainly didn't understand your stint in the DRC. Not even your most recent life in Cape Town. To her, Joburg is everything.

You noticed for the first time the fake fire ruminating artificial warmth from a pretend grate. It was warm but not cozy, and instead of woodsmoke it had a gas smell. You stood to play music on her home theater system. After some deliberation you chose *The Best of Sarah Vaughan*. Her fusion of operatic jazz and melancholy longings defined, dissected, and lulled the saudade feeling in you. The two of you danced, deliberately slow, to the rhythm, swayed actually. Of course, the two of you had danced that dance many times before, bending close into each other to the melancholic melody.

"Bend with me, hold me close..." you whispered in her ear. She understood your need all too well.

"You've no idea how I sometimes long for this," she whispered back on your shoulder.

"You think I don't know how deep loneliness can burrow, babes? It reaches to the marrow of the soul."

You both moved to the kitchen after the song, to toss a green salad and warm a pesto pasta in the microwave, dishing it all to eat with a free-range rotisserie chicken. After knocking back the first bottle of wine you were feeling woozy. You sat on opposite chairs at the dining room table as you bled another red, discussing, for reasons now lost to you, the light fixtures of their lounge, while you squelched the urge to ask Ami if she was happy. You were both inching toward your thirty-eighth year of circling the sun, but there were cross-hatched wrinkles in her face that seemed premature, perhaps caused by a hidden strain in her life you knew nothing about. This worried you.

DAYS LIKE THESE

When you awoke in the luxurious double bed in Ami's guest room, you lay still, remembering your time as a student in this city. You remembered the day you sent Litha your last email, composed with the helping lies of the poets. It took you the greater part of the afternoon to write that one-pager you still keep in your Google Drive:

Dear Litha

I shouldn't have waited for your troubles before writing you this email, for we've been unhappy with each other for a while. Now that you're drowning in your problems it's gonna appear as though I'm part of the rats jumping ship. After reading all the things they write about you in the newspapers it kind of confirmed everything I suspected and was never brave enough to confront you about. In a way your taking advantage of me put me on the path for my career. But that doesn't make what you did right. If you were the good person you like to brag about, you could have done everything you did for me without establishing a sexual relationship with a minor. I know in your mind you like to justify your sickness by claiming it normative in our culture, where young girls are sometimes made to marry people old enough to be their grandfather to rescue their families from poverty by inheriting the old man's wealth when he dies. Just because something has acquired the cruel dignity of tradition and custom doesn't make it right.

I've been reading Dostoevsky's Letters from the Underground, *which made me realize I've spikes digging into my flanks also. I feel there's an ineluctable cloud shift that is gonna bring darkness toward both our lives, and I thought, in case we never emerge from this, I'd better not leave things uncleared between us. Things are a little foggy in my mind. I know you probably think my ordeal is nothing compared to what you're faced with, and you're probably right. The difference is you brought that to your own life by your inability to control your perversions. To tell the truth, I would rather have the tangibility of your prison time than this amorphous oppression that grasps me with an anaconda's grip to suffocate my mind sometimes. This depression might be more dangerous and insidious than prison time, because I'm beginning to suspect that the grave is my only way out of this. That's the scalding truth you won't believe because you think your current humiliation is the end of the world. Anyway, I'm not here to cough up the seeds of my own misery, or trace and implicate you in the source and evolution of my depression. That field you furrowed, you didn't dig. Knowing you as I do, you probably have no clue what I'm talking about since it doesn't directly impact on your own situation and pain. Suffice to say then I'll never be what you want me to be, so I have decided to seize this opportunity to wish you well as I break up with you. I know I could have said that in one passage, but I wanted to make you understand that I have problems too, and I didn't want to take the coward's way out by just keeping quiet...*

You remember well that email because you felt you were drowning without any straws to clutch to.

THE DAY AFTER TOMORROW

You and Ami pretended to know something about art when you reached Maboneng, lingering mostly at the David Krut Art Studio and bookshop where you bought several books in the Taxi Art and Stories series. You also found numerous paintings by emerging South African artists at reasonable prices. They told you how their gallery workshop provides sanctuary for creative artists, giving them rentfree space and equipment to work with during office hours, a meal a day, and bottomless coffee.

You reached the book launch venue at Bridge Books just as the event was starting. The event was hyped with pop-up vertical signboards and a big, horizontal banner displaying the book's artwork.

"How did you say you know this guy again?" Ami asked as you collected your complimentary champagne glass and headed for the hors d'oeuvres table.

"I told you. I grew up with him."

"Oh! He's a dish!" exclaimed Ami as the two of you sat down on your reserved seats in the front row. "Did you fuck him?"

"No! Keep quiet, it's starting."

You threw a smile at Hlumelo. His salt-and-pepper beard made him almost unrecognizable to you. He gave you a quick nod while the sound guy was busy pinning a microphone to his jacket and to that of the radio presenter who was his discussant.

The owner of the bookshop moved to the podium and introduced himself, Hlumelo, and the radio presenter, and welcomed everyone to the event. As Hlumelo answered the radio present-er's first question, you noticed that his beard was a little scruffy, giving him the look of someone who doesn't really care about appearances, the bored-contemptuous-cat look of intellectuals. He was wearing a striped beret and carried himself with a non-plussed air. There was no mistaking the eyes, though, the only feature of the boy you grew up with that had not been altered by the years.

You picked up one of the books from the stacked pile close to you. The cover read: *The Day After Tomorrow by Hlumelo Mashibhini.* You quickly read the blurb on the back cover: "…*the book traces the betrayals of the ANC, from the Morogoro Conference to the compromises of Mandela and Mbeki which let in neoliberal economics by the back door, starting with their clandestine meet-ings with White Monopoly Capital that controled the economy of South Africa…*" There's also an endorsement written by the con-stitutional law expert Tembeka Ngcukaitobi, who is the author of the bestselling book *Land Matters.* You were impressed by how Hlumelo had followed his vision, because the book sound-ed like something the Biko-obsessed, Black Conscious mind of Hlumelo would surely have conjured up. You made a note to ask him about the title association with the Tom Waits song regard-ing the young, war-weary soldier who writes his family telling them he will be coming home on the "Day After Tomorrow," for his birthday.

You realized your leg was shaking as he stood to talk about the book. He spoke in practiced zippy one-liners that were un-characteristic, though still intelligent and witty as ever. The talk, somehow, didn't feel authentic, more like something he had practiced, or something his publisher wrote for him as a market-ing strategy.

He was wearing black jeans, a white shirt, and a suede mustard jacket. It slightly irritated you that he seemed to be playing the role of a writer rather than being himself. His body was slim, as if in keeping with the stereotype of writers being underweight and overboozed.

After his talk you waited for others to finish with their compliments and autograph requests before you gingerly approached him. He thanked you for coming.

"Frankly, I didn't think you'd come," he whispered in your ear.

"Why?" you asked surprised.

"Because it's been years. And I know you."

"Perhaps you used to know me."

Ami took over control of the conversation by inviting him to join you for drinks, which he gladly accepted. Eventually, you all left for Newtown in a wine-induced, vibrant mood. You discovered, to your delight, that The African Jazz Club was featuring the Afro-jazz maestros Zonke Dikana and Judith Sephuma at the Market Theater. You sat in the outside section, close to the sidewalk, drinking cheap, foaming beer from polystyrene cups as you waited for the 10pm show to begin.

"I always knew you'd become a great writer," you said to Hlumelo when Ami went inside to get drinks.

"Well, I've always liked language."

"So, tell me about your life. How did you become a celebrated writer?"

"It is the only thing I really ever wanted to do. While working for the newspaper I discovered I was tired of being a reporter. It seemed as if the only thing we were doing was providing authentic information in a world of doxing, cyberbullying, fake news, and deepfake programming."

"And you don't regard that as a worthy journalistic cause?"

"I wasn't satisfied with that. Don't get me wrong—providing accurate information is important. But I wanted to do more, go deeper. When I tried giving a historical or philosophical angle to stories, I got a slap on the wrist from the editors, who prefer trauma trafficking and poverty pornography to introspection. I got tired of hearing 'No one is gonna read that.' 'That's not what pushes sales...' and so forth. Then I got depressed."

He looked down. For the first time he did not look confident and in complete control. "I started drinking, harder and harder with every passing year. Then people around me, colleagues and friends, started dying from what were clearly diseases emanating from lifestyle choices. I realized that I needed a way to slow down on the drinking, and I have, but now there's nothing to drown out the hyperactive voice in my mind. I've not yet figured out a way to deal with it. Geez! I can't believe I'm ranting to you like this, as if ndibotshwe umnwe."

"Eliot said as we grow old we measure out our lives with coffee spoons. Some of us measure it by the ice-cubes and smaller and smaller quantities of water added to our whisky. Others with Xanax."

"Geez, Ruru! When did you become a depressive?"

A buzz of silence ensued. You wondered how you had missed it, this mystery of his personality; that he was also born of the ancient strife that tries to pluck the borer out of the corn. You didn't have the acumen nor the understanding, nor the vocabulary for it, you tell yourself.

Attracted as you were becoming to him that evening, you started fearing the turmoil he'd bring into your life. You had your own issues to deal with and you were going all the way to Tanzania to try and remedy this. You took one more look at his face, a little glad that the queue at the bar was delaying Ami. You tried to calculate, anticipate the cost of letting him back into your life, against the guilt you felt for abandoning him. Did his depression perhaps already start at that young age when you chose Litha over him? You were both too young then, given to breaking each other's hearts one way or the other. And perhaps your presence in his life would've made his depression worse— it could still make it worse, even now.

"So, ja, that's how this cookie crumbled," Hlumelo continued. "Writing, I mean beyond journalism, is something that anchors me, helps me focus. I found myself spending more and more time in archives, researching and living in my mind in past epochs. And this makes me happy, so I don't see why I should stop."

You smile. "I'm glad that you found me on Facebook."

"Yeah." He smiles too. "I saw one of our classmates had posted a scan of that old group photograph of us, the one we took at the matric dance when we showed up wearing jeans and T-shirts. It occurred to me that it was probably the day or time I was happiest in my life, when I was around you. I think I understood, for the first time really, how difficult those years must have been for you. I had always hoped to bump into you when I left East London for Johannesburg. I later heard you were in Port Elizabeth, so I forgot about running into you, until that day I rose up from the gutter, so to speak, and looked at the photograph. You were tagged in it and that's when I immediately clicked to add you. If I hadn't, you would not have known about the launch. You would not be sitting here."

Ami returned and realized something serious was going on.

"What are you guys talking about?"

"Nothing much. Hlumza"—you felt the need to use his pet name—"was just telling me about his life journey since last we saw each other."

"No one has called me that in years. My mother was probably the last person who did. She's dead now. Probably the most naive soul I've ever met," Hlumelo said.

"Why do reverends and pastors like to marry naive women?" you muse.

"Their inferiority complex—what they call religious calling —cannot deal with strong women," said Hlumelo.

"Fuck this reminiscing and nostalgia, guys, it can wait for later. We're having fun now." Ami pushed the vodka shots into your hands and raised a toast to old friends.

"Those destined to hang will not drown!" you exclaimed, and to your satisfaction Hlumelo understood this Russian proverb and its reference to the situation. You realized you would not be able to resist him if he asked you into his life. You had already checked his relationship status on Facebook and found out he was single. His naked ring finger on the table before you confirmed it and you felt relief.

Poor Ami, who must have been feeling like a third wheel, pursed her lips as she went to the dance floor just as Sephuma began your old favorite, "A Cry, a Smile, a Dance." Almost the entire house stood up. Hlumelo looked at you, a little worried, thinking Ami might be annoyed. You explained to him how her moods were like autumnal weather, coming in alternating warm and chilly fronts. He smiled and relaxed.

"I'm sorry to hear that your mother passed away," you said.

"Thank you. My father is also no longer with us. I went back to Queenstown to bury him without ever reconciling our differences. He kind of disowned me when I refused to study theology for ministry and went into journalism instead. NSFAS came to the rescue by paying for my studies at Rhodes."

Thunder rolled, threatening rain, so you went inside just as Sephuma was switching to "You Had Your Hand on Me." In the middle of the song she was joined by Zonke. The two of them transitioned beautifully to Zonke's song: "Jik'izinto." You had little choice but to slow-dance. You were surprised at how emotional you became when you listened to the song's lyrics: *Through the mountains and valleys, You had your hand on me...* And Zonke's "Jik'izinto" (things are turning) seemed apposite.

You left the Market Theater in Hlumelo's car in the early morning after numerous cups of black coffee when the show ended. Ami went in her own car. Clouds were thinning in the sky, leaving sporadic banks that surfed the pale pumice moon. On the drive, Hlumelo dropped his left hand on your skirted thigh and you allowed him with pleasure. His driving was patient and right as rain.

Ami called your cell when she got home, not happy that

you disallowed her from following Hlumelo's car to his flat in Randburg, because "I need to know where to trace the mischief when the news of my friend's death reaches me tomorrow." You normally don't get jealous with each other's boyfriends or husbands, but you detected something of that nature in her tone.

Instead of turning the lights on when you reached his flat, Hlumelo lit rosemary-scented candles. As you kissed you felt like you were giving way to your fate. Your lovemaking, like his driving, felt properly directed, unrushed, and as right as rain. Afterwards, you watched the angled shadows of cars passing in the street race across the walls and the ceiling.

It had been a long time since you'd thought about your life, how it looked from the outside. This was something that was clearly important to Ami, with her luxurious living and a smart phone as an extension of her limb, so that she can constantly present a sanitized version of herself for attention from her social media feeds, concealing resentment and silent desperation beneath it all. When you saw this in her, it triggered thoughts about how your life appeared. It made you self-conscious. At first you couldn't help feeling left behind, jealous even. But as you lay there with Hlumelo's breath tickling your ear, you knew that life, Ami's life, was not for you, and you realized what you had been missing, what you'd always wanted. You thought about how long you had waited to find beauty in another human's touch and body warmth. To feel his body blanket you with the flattery of his urgent need for your own. You tried to rationalize the notion of love as you slowly drifted into sleep. To love is to be drawn into the meaning of the other so profoundly it shatters your self-illusions and becomes some kind of personal-logic cruciform, the Golgotha of the heart, another form of transmission of the consciousness.

You woke up, startled by the hadedas' crackling howls. You discovered you were still in the reality of your dream. You felt a sense of eminence with his skin against yours. You watched his sleeping face with affecting joy. It seemed like a return to your childhood perception of things. You felt yourself spoiling the moment by mourning that childhood, the fact that you damaged each other by your unavailability when you needed each other most. What could have been done differently?

You were still thinking how your lovemaking felt like an extension of your personalities when he stirred beside you. You closed your eyes and pretended to sleep, because you still wished to be alone with your thoughts. He got up to walk to the kitchen. Muffled sounds followed, then a loud cough from what you guessed to be a champagne bottle. You opened your eyes. He came bouncing with excitement and a bottle of MMC in one hand, two glasses and orange juice in the other for the mimosas he proceeded to mix for both of you.

"Good morning, sleepyhead."

"Morning. Do you have a T-shirt I can borrow?" You pointed to the precarious situation of sheets wrapped around your upper body.

"Indeed I have." He disappeared to the second bedroom and came back holding a saffron-colored T-shirt. Upon investigation you noticed the writing on it: *By All Man's Necessary!* You wondered at the intended meaning.

"I was hoping to be woken up by the smell of frying bacon and brewing coffee."

You immediately felt bad when you noticed his eyes turning toward the floor. Your stomach dropped. You had forgotten he had this tendency of missing jokes and taking everything to heart.

"Never mind. I'm treating you to breakfast once we're done showering," you added to lighten the mood. A new light was introduced in his eyes when he realized you were planning to spend more time with him. You called Ami and she made plans to have brunch with the two of you at the Impala Market, Northcliff.

"Listen, I want to see you, spend time with you," Hlumelo said. "When do you need to go back to Cape Town?"

"I was planning on leaving in two days, but I want to spend time with you too." You realized that you had to tell him you were leaving for Tanzania in a month's time and it brought back memories of you parting ways after high school.

As it turned out, he was also leaving, a week before you, for a two-year writer's retreat in Berlin. He had been awarded a grant to write the biography of Bloke Modisane, who died in Dortmund in 1986.

So you extended your stay in Johannesburg by a few days—Ami was more than happy to accommodate you—and you and Hlumelo made the most of the time you had left.

DEUTSCHLAND

Hi Ruru

I hope Tanzania is treating you well? Berlin is good, we've slipped into winter with the air getting icy in the evening. Everyone is spooked about this novel Coronavirus thing happening in China. I hear talk about suspending flights to and from China. I don't know what to make of it. Though still like a rumor, the virus seems to be infiltrating the streets of Wuhan. I hope it is not just another excuse for Sinophobia because the Chinese markets are fast overtaking occidental ones. I almost wish that it is all just an exaggeration by our biased media, otherwise the world might soon wake up to another death spike like when the Spanish Flu hit.

I think about the few days we spent together before I left. I hear the ring of your voice in my ear all the time. I'm realizing that it's the sound I wanna wake up to every day of my life. Whether you like it or not, fate made us for each other. When you last wrote to me, you said that it would be better if I forgot about you since you would not be able to give me children. But did you know that I've always preferred not to have children? My worry about the world's future probably has a role to play in that. It is not something I easily admit as it is usually not a popular opinion and, to be honest, I had been worried that you would want kids. But now I believe even more strongly that it is fate that bound us together from the start. I thank whatever gods linked our fates and made our paths cross and cross again until we learned the purpose.

< 341 >

To say I'm thinking about you is an understatement. I obsess about you. It is the only thing that gives me courage to face my days, knowing that I'll soon have you in my arms again. Everything I look at here I see through your eyes, imagining what you would think about it. I was extremely happy to learn that Berlin University has accepted your PhD proposal. You didn't have to emphasize the fact of your coming to Germany because it is free. I wasn't going to accuse you of following me, although I would've been flattered and happy if you were. After all, if it was only about free education you could have gone to Glasgow or Edinburgh; Scotland also has free tertiary education. Anyway, I look forward to having you in the same city next year. I propose you think about living with me for both our sakes; accommodation is very expensive here.

Meanwhile, I spend most of my time thinking of ways to impress you. Last weekend I took a train to Dresden and Dortmund for my research on Bloke Modisane. Then I spent the weekend in Cologne and saw a little of the life on the banks of the Rhine River. As lady luck would have it, Sona Jobarteh was in concert. I got the tickets through my university lecturer host who managed to pull some magic for us to attend. I want to see the rest of this beautiful city with you next to me.

All my love
Hlumelo

KELEWELE

Hey Hlumza

Glad you're enjoying your stay in Deutschland. I'll admit I'm looking forward to seeing you wherever—as long as we see each other.

The Chinese say the virus causes pneumonia-like symptoms, and is not transmittable from human to human. Yet they have arrested the doctor who raised the alarm of the disease being highly transmittable between humans. They're also refusing to release the genome sequences of the virus for the global scientists the world over to make up their own minds. This is bad news, and almost a sure sign that they're misleading us. We are hearing from social media that Wuhan hospitals are filling up. I think there's a wild panic in that city. Looks like the virus has deadly momentum and is definitely human-to-human transmittable. Look after yourself and normalize wearing a mask when you're out in public until we know what's going on here.

You're eating into my lunch time...I'm dying to dig into some kelewele Maman has packed for me—it's spicy fried plantains I'll make for you one day because she has taught me how to cook it.

XX
Ruru

GEMÜTLICH, HYGGE, AND QUIZANNICKUMUT

You have moved in with Maman in the house of your late father in Kihonda township. The two of you decided to extend the house, add an extra bedroom, bathroom, and study with proper shelves for Phaks's books. In the little space between the bathroom and the main bedroom you added a long window, from the ceiling to the skirting-board. It is where Phaks's original desk used to be. "The long window will give him a grand view of the world—the dead are always with us," Maman said. It is where you also spend time talking to him, trying to see through his eyes before working on his memoirs. You've also made into wallpaper some of your favorite lines from his writings, another way of having him around to provoke and prompt your thinking.

In my mind I'm better than my life.
Some pain is beyond the attention of grief.

You're adding quotations from his favorite authors, especially those he depended on in the end—Camus, Nietzsche, the Book of Job, the Greek and Roman classics—and a few of your own from your mother's isiXhosa literature and Sol Plaatje's *Mhudi*. Though your father never mentioned *Mhudi*, you think he would appreciate being in discussion with the first historical novel written from a black person's point of view in southern Africa. Especially since it tells the story of the Mfecane also and how Mzilikazi and his people caused so much turmoil in creating the wandering hordes that became known as amaMfengu, which your people were part of. You choose lines from all kinds of books you think would comfort his restless spirit and soothe the deep sense of loss that every exile feels in foreign lands, like Modisane's *Blame Me on History*, which Hlumelo gave you. You think Hlumelo and Phaks would have gotten along—probably like a house on fire.

In the bookshelves you have put up, the poetry of Keats and Neruda are close to your heart. Phaks adored Keats and you love Neruda. Keats's poetry collection is the most worn-out book he owned. You're amused by a note he wrote and used as a book-mark in the poetry of Derek Walcott, which says: *Too much dreaming about the sea.* You wonder if the reason he doesn't talk about Walcott is because he was put off by too much talk about the sea, the waters. Well, the Ghaba side from your mother's blood loves the water, is part of the river people, so you put a little Walcott on the shelves also. The interesting part is that amaHlubi were dispersed from the foothills of Ukhahlamba (Drakensberg) and the banks of Thukela (Tugela) River. So you would have expected more affinity with the waters from Phaks. The note about Walcott's book is undated, but the bookshop re-ceipt says it was bought in London on 8 August 1991, at Foyles in Charing Cross Road. There is also a train ticket from Leicester Square to Trafalgar between the pages. You sometimes hold and smell the ticket and the receipt, to see if you can detect his natural scent from them. They have a fishy smell. So you imagine he sat somewhere, perhaps St. James's Park, to eat fish and chips, wrapped in a newspaper, as he started to read the book. You like his habit of leaving receipts and price tags on things because it gives a clue about his life. For instance, the album of Johnny Mbizo Dyani with Mongezi Feza and Okay Temiz, featuring Dudu Pukwana, which you play when doing chores around the house, has an undated Stockholm price tag.

Both you and Maman are bad business managers, the builders

take advantage of this by taking you for a ride sometimes. You made the mistake of paying them by the hour, until you realized that when you weren't looking they hardly did anything so as to prolong the job as much as possible. Fair enough for them, but, to paraphrase the frog from Aesop's Fables, their play is death to your wallets. You told them you'd decided to pay them according to the work they've finished. Lo and behold, the work is going much faster now. You're fast learning quantity-surveying skills, because they deliberately order more building material so as to siphon some for their other jobs. It's a constant headache for you, but it has to be done, or at least that is how you and Maman justify the effort when sitting on the soon-to-be-finished veranda with late-afternoon tea, reading, writing, tailoring and seamstressing in comfortable silence, things that dull the saw-tooth realities of both your past histories.

When you imagine your father's life here, wearing the woollen trousers and suede jacket you saw in Maman's wardrobe, walking that bush, intoxicated with scholarly learning and auto-poetic propensities, you feel proud you had a father after your own heart.

You look at the streets around the house with your father's eyes, the eyes of someone who wants to live everywhere while existing nowhere in particular. You begin to understand better your mother as someone who wished for roots, to exist somewhere and be nowhere else. She wished for Gemütlichkeit, hygge, quizannickumut, and all the ways to be content and deeply happy at home. Hence her Penelope-like devotion. She was the type that became charged with sacrifices. What you respect most about her is her strength of humility, her refusal to perform her pain, her self-effacing kindness. While Phaks, a spiritual Semite, felt displaced within himself and disorientated everywhere, your mother was comfortable within her own skin, as if she existed fully formed. You remember her saying something, which still baffles you, about Phaks paying too much attention to his ideals while neglecting his dreams. You felt sad hearing what you thought to be her defeatist tone in that sentence. But now, with the lengthening shadows in your own life, you think, like Mary, she chose the better path. To be at the Lord's feet rather than burdening herself with the business of the world, like the Martha that was Phaks. Ironically, she loved that scripture.

UNDER THE JUNIPER TREE
22/12/99

Today is the first time I'm able to muster enough strength to write after a long time. Last night, after a lifetime of seeing the torched eyes of wolves in my sleep, one zoomed its eyes on my soul and came down the mountain.

The day is far spent, bats have already taken to air. Soon full evening shall arrive, but for now we watch the invitation from the shepherd star, ucel' izapholo, visible mostly in the east where the sky has already paled to a hazy gauze. The ewes are rutted and lambs weaned. I must go home to milk my father's cows.

This earthly blanket soon shall be carrion for vultures and a hatching bed for maggots: Ndidleni maxhalanga ndidumbile! During the hours of our great need we all go back to the language of our dreams, the one our subconscious is controlled by: *Thina nto zaziyo asothukanga nto...Itsho into kaMqhayi kwedini. Godukani zizwe liphelil' ityala. Akuhlanga lungehlanga! (To those who've experience there's no surprise here...So says the great poet Mqhayi...Turn back nations the case has been decided...It didn't happen what doesn't happen always!)*

It brings some consolation that what is happening to me has always happened to human beings. We're lucky that with every age, throughout the ages, from the tortured laments of Job to Sappho's poems of tutored love, to the choruses of Aeschylus, Sophocles, Virgil and Euripides, there were people who chronicled the haplessness of man against death in an affecting vocabulary that wrestled with despair. The melancholic voices of Dido,

Hecuba, and others to come after, will also resonate through the ages: *Why so high a fire must burn*, be necessary to purify the failing hearts of man?

The ravens are here, yammering strange things as they beg to pull my chariot of dust. They always have something to say. VW (Virginia Woolf) quotes Dostoevsky, who talks of cattle *galloping like mad*, flocking like *homing brooks back to the tops of our trees*. Pity—I always wanted to interrogate further VW's meaning of that, but am now even too tired to verify the quote. I've run out of time. It's the ravens, not cattle, who are coming for me. The cattle rest with the ancestors in my Xhosa psyche, so they can never be a menacing symbol.

Efuoa told me this morning that it hurts her a lot when I don't recognize who she is. I tell her to blame the mist and its terrible tidings. She has been the mainstay holding me in this life, but even she now is slowly starting to fade from my mind. With that I'm gaining power over my own life and death. The grave is flung open. I'll not tip over by my own volition, but will not resist the homing rooks when they pull or push.

Since the rabbit never screams but with its last breath, let me summarize my thinking on the story of life and death as I understand it through the parable of Job. Most people think they know how the story of Job ends: rewarded by God for his loyalty, Job is paid back with even more children and sheep and property. But I'm comforted by the fact that a growing number of biblical scholars are becoming suspicious of this ending. The Job we hear in the final chapter, the one who accepts and resigns himself to God's power play, is not the same Job we hear in the preceding forty chapters. We suspect some pious mischief there. Someone, down the ages of history, grafted onto the otherwise perplexing account of Job, the one my life agrees with, a pleasing ending because, well, people can't stand too much reality. The real Job is not even Camus' Meursault, with his scornful, silent punches against the heavens. Or the paltry dent on the pent-up silence of the heavens by Nietzsche, who philosophized against it with a hammer. Or that Schopenhauer's intellectual justification of unhappiness as the beginning of wisdom. The real Job recognizes his inability to judge God's deafening silence, and so surrenders in acceptance of the situation, but not before he registers his protest to the heavens against the unjustness in the nature of things. The real Job understands the role he played in the comedy that brought him to that situation, takes responsibility for it, even of the fact that his pride of possession made him susceptible to the devil's wishes. He accepts all of that and the punishment that comes with his culpability. But he is also prepared to spit in the devil's face. And in his haplessness declares to the devil master: "You probably deserve the price of my life because you have won it by the manner I've lived it. But I shall not sin further by supposing the mercy of God is not sufficient for me. So as you drag me to hell I spit on your face: I shall not serve thee also!" He knows that the real torture, that is hell, is living without goodness. The monk Thomas à Kempis wrote, and then frighteningly erased in his manuscript, the statement that...*it would be better to be with Christ in hell than without Him in heaven*. Such faith in the power of another's goodness?

There was a moment when I, like younger Camus, thought that a man who expects no tomorrow feels no emotion, no hope. Dostoevsky mentions that the most terrible part about death by execution is not the bodily pain, but the certainty in knowing that in *an hour, then in ten minutes, then in half a minute, your soul must quit your body and that you will no longer be a man, and that this is certain–certain!* He says this certainty is terrible because it robs you of all hope. My slow dying provided me with ways of escape to sustain my hope. Hell, as the absence of hope Camus described so well, seems a precise definition to me. He lived with the fierce anguish of his life's thirsts that annihilated his spirituality in the later years. I'm seduced by the eternal Galilean, all that talk about dying in order to find your life. The body carries us to the physical limits where it must swell up into active invisibility of our minds, where we exist in soulful grandeur. I've had a taste of that in my last days. I've also lived with an active, if vague, presence of my ancestors. In fact, truth be told, I'm no longer certain that death completely dissolves the bond that unites us even in this world. I am beginning to believe the ancients who thought the earth is the deserted temple of the gods we were supposed to coexist with.

All in all, I have a haunting feeling that I'm perhaps still going to be around here in a different form. So remember me in the vague rustling of autumn leaves, those soon-to-be *dead bodies*, in Homer's words, making way for new life, for, as the wanderer, *I've felt truly rooted only in the absence of root...*

Even if I had the energy, I doubt that I have anything more to say now. Like Elijah under the juniper tree, I've lost all my efficacy. And like an elephant after its wilderness journey, I'm worn out. Enough. As they say in isiXhosa: Amade ngawetyala mawethu, there's no need to prolong this any longer. I must, in the words of the French poet François Rabelais, go and *seek the Great Perhaps*. I even have a soundtrack for my journey, a Xhosa traditional song, sung best by the soft, jazzy tones of Zim Ngqawane: Qula Kwedini, qula kwedini kabawo...(Shield yourself, gird and shield yourself for the fight, my father's young boy...) This has been the greatest fight of my life I've lost.

To the next adventure then...

The End

ACKNOWLEDGMENTS

I finalized this manuscript during my JIAS (Johannesburg Institute for Advanced Studies) Writing Fellowship in 2021. I would also like to thank my publisher and editor, Carolyn Meads, for her insightful mind and subtle ways in making this book more pleasurable for the reader. And my now partner in the writing crime Alison Lowry, for her sharp and careful eye in copy-editing this book. The rest are my faults where they exist. Though based on recognizable historical facts, this is a work of fiction.

ABOUT THE AUTHOR

MPHUTHUMI NTABENI contributes to various national and international publications. He's trained in the built environment; reads literature, history, and philosophy. He lives in Cape Town. His debut novel, *The Broken River Tent*, won the University of Johannesburg Debut Prize in 2019.